Parallelograph

by

Richard Veit

WingSpan Press
Livermore, California

Published in the United States and the United Kingdom by WingSpan Press, Livermore, CA

The WingSpan name, logo and colophon are the trademarks of WingSpan Publishing.

First edition 2017

Printed in the United States of America

Publisher's Cataloging-in-Publication Data

Name: Veit, Richard.
Title: Parallelograph/ Veit, Richard.
Description: Livermore, CA : Wingspan Press, 2017.
Identifiers: ISBN 978-1-59594-552-5 (pbk.)
ISBN 978-1-59594-693-5 (hardcover)
ISBN 978-1-59594-927-1 (ebook)
Subjects: LCSH: World War, 1939-1945—Fiction. | Fiction— Time travel.| Texas—Fiction. | BISAC: Fiction / Science Fiction / Time Travel
Classification: PS3552.A431 P66 2017 (print) | PS3552.A431 P66 (ebook) | DDC 813—dc23.

1 2 3 4 5 6 7 8 9 10

ACKNOWLEDGMENTS

Richard Veit wishes to express his gratitude to the men and women of the Allied forces, who placed their lives on the line against the enemy during World War II. Among this heroic generation were Mr. Veit's father, Richard Earl Veit, his uncle, Wesley Arthur Veit, and his wife Patti's uncles, James Philip Haston and Robert Weldon Haston. The author would also like to thank two friends and literary mentors: British television writer and producer John Finch and American playwright and screenwriter Horton Foote, for their invaluable counsel and personal encouragement.

We must welcome the future, remembering that soon it will be the past. And we must respect the past, remembering that it was once all that was humanly possible.

George Santayana

Parallelograph

The airman was staring at every move she made. Bonnie was sure of it. His gaze was not vulgar, but she could tell that he found her shyness to be attractive—maybe even exciting. She adjusted the top of her dress by pulling it up a bit, exposing as little flesh as the neckline would allow. To her shame, the airman seemed to interpret this innocent gesture as a "come on." He laid down his deck of cards and wandered over to the refreshment table.

"How's about something to drink, missy?" he said.

As Bonnie ladled some strawberry-banana punch into a ceramic cup, the airman's eyes followed her cleavage with more interest than the beverage.

"So, what do I owe you?" He jingled his pocket change for effect.

"Your money's no good here, private," Bonnie told him. Her response mimicked how some of the more experienced girls talked. This was only Bonnie's fourth day as a USO volunteer, so she did not sound very authoritative.

"Say, what time do you get off work?" the airman asked.

She bristled at the suggestion. "Oh, not for hours yet. And then there's the dance."

"Tonight?"

Bonnie nodded her head.

"So that's why you're all dolled up."

"Yes."

Again his eyes strayed downward. "That's a swell dress—must have set you back plenty."

"I'm afraid it's not mine. I borrowed it from a friend."

The airman grinned his approval. "You could've fooled me," he said. "Fits you like a glove."

Bonnie gave that some serious thought. "Do you think my boyfriend will like it?"

"Beg pardon?"

"Do you think my boyfriend will like the dress?"

"Well, sure ... I ..."

"He's a snowdrop—you know, in the military police."

"Is that so?" The airman stood up straight. "He's a very lucky guy."

"Thank you, but I think I'm the lucky one," she said. "Donald is a dreamboat. Maybe you know him. Are you from Waco Army Air Field?"

"Nope, Blackland." The airman stepped back, tightening his necktie. "Listen, I hope you don't think I was out of line ..."

"No, not at all. Don't be silly."

He swigged his punch as if it were a shot of whiskey, handed her the empty cup, and walked away to deal himself another game of solitaire.

Bonnie sighed with relief. This was proof positive that what Mrs. Boggs told her at the first training session was right. "Mark my words," the old woman said. "Perhaps the most valuable skill that any USO girl can master is how to gently rebuff a man in uniform—the fine art of deflecting advances while leaving the male ego intact." One white lie notwithstanding, Bonnie was proud of how well she had performed under duress. And anyway, what real harm was there in conjuring up a fanciful sweetheart, particularly if it managed to throw a predator off the trail without dashing his pride? Much to her surprise, she began to look forward to the dance, a social burden that she had been dreading just moments before. If only the dress were not cut so low.

Bonnie Ploughwright was a student at Baylor University, a junior English major who was determined to "do her bit" by devoting a few hours each week to the war effort. This was not too much to ask of a young lady, she figured, making certain that lonely servicemen enjoyed the comforting illusion of a home away from home. Her older brother was a mechanic in the AAF, and she hoped that Keith would be shown the same hospitality wherever he might be.

A native of Corsicana, Texas, Bonnie had come to Baylor's Waco campus from the oh-so-sophisticated environs of Dallas, where her father continued to enjoy a thriving dental practice. Her mother, the former Doreen Webb, had been a housewife for as far back as the girl could remember—that is, until quite recently when she secured a war job at the sprawling North American Aviation plant in east Grand Prairie. Bonnie remained close to her parents. During the school year, she made it a point to telephone them once a week (long distance, collect) on Sunday afternoons at two o'clock. Dr. Hugh Ploughwright listened religiously to the New York Philharmonic broadcasts, but he was a casual enough aficionado to converse with his daughter at the same time.

While at Baylor, Bonnie lived with a roommate, Julia Johnston, in a three-year-old dormitory called Catherine Alexander Hall. It was an uneasy alliance, for Julia was reputed to be rather wild, whereas Bonnie was, if anything, a bit too proper for her own good. This is why it seemed so incongruous to see Miss Ploughwright wearing Miss Johnston's full-length gown at the USO dance. One of their dormitory friends later said as much, in private, though even she had to admit that Bonnie's comely figure did the dress full justice.

There was an extended curfew on Friday nights, so it was after eleven by the time Bonnie returned from the dance. Sensing that Julia would already be in bed by then, she crept silently into their shared room.

"Did it do the trick?" came a voice from the dark.

Indignant, Bonnie removed the dress over her head and tossed it onto the foot of her roommate's bed. "The trick?"

"Did you smooch with any good-looking Army boys?"

"None that I recall. Was I supposed to?" Bonnie snatched her nightgown from the dresser drawer and walked toward the bathroom to change.

"Of course you were, Bon. Why else would you borrow my most revealing outfit?"

Bonnie stopped, hands on hips. "Because I don't happen to believe church attire is appropriate for a dance. I had no other choice. All of my evening dresses are at home."

"I'm sorry to be so frank about this," Julia said, "but I think you should spread your wings more."

"Oh, please. Don't get started."

"Believe me, if I had what you do on top, I'd have the men buzzing around me like a swarm of bees."

"You really shouldn't talk like that."

"It's a fact of life. And that's why I'm thrilled to pieces that you were wearing my dress at the dance." Julia giggled. "Who knows? Maybe you boosted morale enough to help us win the war."

"That's a very crass thing to say. And unpatriotic, too."

"To think that my own dress entertained the troops tonight— and I wasn't even inside!"

Bonnie gave a loud sigh. "Actually, it isn't all that revealing, you know."

"Don't kid yourself. Did you ever look in the mirror?"

"Sure, I did. I wasn't shocked by what I saw."

"You're not a man, either."

Bonnie closed the bathroom door behind her. She was in no mood to bicker, not after investing nine hours of her leisure time to support the cause of freedom.

◆   ◆   ◆

English 206 was a junior-level course called "Writing the Short Story." It was only offered in the winter quarter, so Bonnie Ploughwright made sure to be near the front of the line for the opening of registration on the first Monday morning in December. The temperature when she arrived at Waco Hall, a few minutes before eight o'clock, was a chilly thirty-seven degrees, with light rain falling. This was the first anniversary of the Japanese attack on Pearl Harbor, a commemorative occasion that did not go unacknowledged in the print and broadcast media.

Classes began the very next day, and Bonnie's professor for English 206 was the venerable Charles G. Smith, a member of the Baylor University faculty since 1922. One of the first items on Dr. Smith's agenda was to declare that he expected active engagement when it came to the written word. Concise essays would become due in rapid succession until the end of the second week—right before the Christmas recess—at which time students would receive official notification of their major assignment for the term: creation of a completed short story, worthy of publication, by quarter's end.

Bonnie made no secret of the fact that her literary idol—after whom she planned to model her own writing style—was Margaret Mitchell, originator of Scarlett O'Hara and Rhett Butler. She hoped one day to travel to Atlanta and meet with the famous author in person. Needless to say, this pilgrimage would be even more meaningful if she were to bring along a sample of her work for Miss Mitchell to evaluate, and a marketable short story might be just the thing. Bonnie resolved to settle upon a provisional concept over the sixteen-day Christmas recess, thereupon returning to campus with outline and character sketches in hand. She had the best of intentions.

As Christmas approached, the passenger depot in Waco became inordinately populated by men in uniform, whether going home for long-overdue furloughs or being dispatched to their next duty stations. Public transportation accorded civilians a distinctly secondary status after the military, which was how it should be, of course, and few customers complained too strenuously about the inconvenience such favoritism brought to their wartime lives. In these difficult circumstances, Bonnie considered herself fortunate indeed to secure a ticket for the northbound Interurban on a Saturday morning—and just six days prior to Christmas.

"Aren't you in my English class?" someone behind her asked.

Bonnie turned to see an unfamiliar face. "I don't know. Could be," she said. "Short Story?"

"That's right. I think you sit a couple of seats in front of me." The stranger was a plain-looking, bespectacled girl who spoke with an accent that sounded anything but southern. "I guess we'll be traveling companions. Where do you transfer to, after Dallas?"

"Nowhere else—that's where I live," Bonnie said. She tried again to place the face, but to no avail. "How about you?"

"A one-horse town west of Saint Louis," the girl told her. "Have you ever heard of Weldon Spring?"

"No."

"Not many people have. I'm really from Michigan, but my folks moved to Missouri for the war work."

That sounded strange to Bonnie. "I'd have thought there'd be lots of war work in Michigan."

"Well, there is, but Daddy is an old friend of Jim McDonnell, who had a managerial position for him in his aircraft plant. They were physics classmates at Princeton."

The two coeds boarded the Interurban and found adjacent seats.

"What's your name?" Bonnie asked.

"I'm Evelyn Branch, but most people just call me Ev. You?"

"Bonnie Ploughwright." They shook hands, more formally than the situation demanded.

The passenger car was a red-colored conveyance with "Texas Electric Railway" painted in black letters within a pale yellow oval on each side. As their train departed from the station, Bonnie and Evelyn gave no more than a passing upward glance at the Amicable Life Insurance Building, McLennan County's sole true skyscraper. Both of the young women were a bit jaded, perhaps, having come from metropolitan centers where majestic skylines would dwarf the unremarkable "witch's tooth" that represented Waco.

Once the Interurban rattled across the Brazos River bridge and then snaked its way to the north, Evelyn reached inside her coat, producing a small paper sack. "Want a piece of candy?"

Bonnie looked at her and smiled. "Sure!" The yellow confection turned out to be a lemon drop, and it tasted wonderfully tart. "Mmm, thanks."

"My Sunday school teacher gave some to each of us for Christmas."

"Where do you go to church?" Bonnie asked.

"Seventh and James. My roommate and I both go there. How about you?"

"Columbus Avenue. I go with some other Baylor girls, or sometimes I hitch a ride from a friend who works with me."

Evelyn was impressed. "You have a job? How can you find enough time for studying?"

"Oh, I'm just a volunteer—at the USO. I work about twelve hours a week."

"I know a lady who's employed full-time at the Bluebonnet Ordnance Plant in McGregor. That's what I'd like to do."

Bonnie grinned at her. "Aren't you afraid you'd blow yourself up?"

But Evelyn remained serious, detecting no humor in the remark. "From what I hear, they have a perfect safety record." She did not appear to be one who kidded around very much.

The Interurban's ride was surprisingly quiet, being powered by electricity rather than diesel or steam, and it was capable of attaining speeds in excess of sixty miles per hour. It did, however, have a tendency to vibrate considerably, so the trip was not as pleasantly lulling as it otherwise might have been. Most of the seats were occupied, apportioned about equally between servicemen and civilians.

"Is your roommate an English major, too?" Bonnie asked.

Evelyn shook her head. "Music. She's a violinist in the University Symphony Orchestra."

"Then she must be very good."

"I guess so. She also plays with the Waco Symphony."

"Gosh."

"I hardly ever see her because she spends half of her life in the practice rooms."

"Lucky you," Bonnie said. "My roommate is always in the dorm—a psychology major, for what that's worth."

"I don't think I'd like to live with a psychology major."

As the trolley rolled beyond the settlement of Hillsboro, Evelyn opened her purse and began searching inside it for something. Bonnie was shocked when the girl proceeded to pull out a pack of Luckies and offer her one.

"No, thanks. Not this early in the day," Bonnie said. In truth, the time had nothing whatever to do with it, but she did wish to act nonchalant about such a fashionable vice.

Bonnie studied her companion's face. Smoking cigarettes was uncommon among Baylor coeds, at least in public, so maybe there was more to this young woman than met the eye. Evelyn was not attractive, as conventional beauty goes, but she did have a brash maturity that belied her tender years.

Curiosity having gotten the best of her, Bonnie came right out and asked. "Are you a junior?"

"Yes, I am. Why?" Evelyn struck a match and, with the practiced skill of a seasoned smoker, lit her cigarette.

"No reason. Short Story is a junior-level class, that's all."

"You probably think I look awfully old to be an undergrad. Well, you're right. This is my second time at Baylor. I dropped out in 1940 to get married." Squinting, she blew a stream of smoke straight upward.

"Gee, no kidding? Do you have any children?"

"Nope. And no husband, either, for that matter. It didn't take."

"Oh, I'm sorry." Embarrassed, Bonnie hastily changed the subject. "Do you have any ideas for your story?"

"I really haven't had time to give it much thought," Evelyn told her. "I hope to come up with something over the holidays."

"Same here," Bonnie said. Suddenly, she became doubtful of her own gifts as a novelist. Evelyn probably had a wealth of experience to call upon, whereas she herself had next to none. "Have you done much writing before this class?" she asked.

"No, not really."

Bonnie was relieved, but the feeling did not last for long.

"Oh, I've written six or seven short stories," Evelyn added, "and a collection of my poems was published by a specialty imprint in San Francisco. Nothing besides that."

Bonnie nodded her head and smiled, but she grew sullen for the remainder of the trip, until the railcar drew to a stop at the Dallas Interurban Terminal. That was when, out of courtesy, she finally spoke up again. "Say, maybe we can ride back together after New Year's."

"I'll be taking the Texas Special south," Evelyn told her. "It's a lot faster, and I don't have to change trains."

Bonnie stared at the traffic on Houston Street. "Where do you go from here?"

"I'll take a bus over to Union Station. It's just a short distance."

"Well, merry Christmas. See you next year."

"Merry Christmas." Without expression, Evelyn did an about-face and walked away.

Bonnie consulted her wristwatch and found that the Interurban had pulled into the station more than ten minutes ahead of schedule, a fact that probably explained why her father was not yet there to greet her. Secretly, she was pleased that her mother had to work today. Sometimes the well-meaning woman became overly sentimental at reunions like this, even though it had been scarcely three weeks since she saw her daughter at Thanksgiving.

Suitcase in hand, Bonnie began heading to the parking lot, only to notice that three GIs were coming toward her. There was no graceful escape route, so she gazed down at the pavement and continued on her way. A wolf whistle caused her to look up and blush.

"Hi, honey pie. We'd ask you to join us, except that you appear to be going in the opposite direction," one of them said. The others laughed at their outspoken pal.

"Thanks just the same," Bonnie told them, not unkindly. Her time as a volunteer had taught her how to reject fresh servicemen without seeming haughty. But neither did she slow her gait, sensing that this, too, would be a mistake. The three soldiers allowed the girl to pass unimpeded, studying her form with obvious appreciation but in no way becoming a physical threat.

When she was about thirty feet past them, one of the GIs shouted, "Hey, you're the USO girl from Waco."

He said it in such a cheerful, friendly manner that she saw no harm in stopping for a moment. "That's right. Which air base are you from?"

"Waco Field—all three of us," the tallest of them said. He could not have been older than eighteen or nineteen. "We've been on leave."

"Embarkation leave," the outspoken one added, "only we can't say where to."

The last to talk was a short, wiry airman with red hair. "*Blimey*, no," he said in a stage whisper. "We *bloody* well can't even give you a hint."

Bonnie smiled and waved. "Best of luck, *Yanks!*" she called back to them. And with that, they parted ways, probably never to meet again. She said a silent prayer for their safety. They were so young, no more than high school kids really.

Dr. Ploughwright must have just arrived, for he was standing beside the car, about to slam his door, when he spotted her from a distance. "Hello, sweetie," he called. They hurried to give each other a hug. "How's Baylor treating you?"

"Fine, Daddy. No complaints."

When Bonnie opened the passenger door and sat down, she noticed—backwards, through the windshield—the coveted red sticker, outlined in white, with a large, white "C" in the middle. Her father's profession as a dentist was deemed essential to the war effort, so he qualified for as many gallons of gasoline as he could rightfully use. In contrast, a typical citizen had to be content with a black "A" sticker, which granted the bearer only three gallons per week. It made Bonnie proud to know that the OPA considered her father to be an indispensable cog in the wheel of democracy.

They drove home, chatting away, never at a loss for words. The pair had always been kindred spirits, and separation during a war was not about to change that. Neither of them paid much attention to the dashboard radio, which was tuned to 570 kilocycles for "Man of Good Will," a presentation of "Little Blue Playhouse" on KGKO. Rarely, even on the briefest of jaunts, did they travel without the radio keeping them company.

"Have you heard from Keith lately?" Bonnie asked.

"Not for a couple of weeks now. We think he's still at Hickam, but of course he's not authorized to come right out and say."

"Anyway, I'm glad he's on the ground—not like the fly-boys I see at the club."

"Have you made some friends?"

Bonnie chuckled. "Well, not in the way you mean it, Daddy. Most of them are wolves, so I've learned to keep my distance."

"See that you do!" Dr. Ploughwright gave his daughter a stern glance, but she could tell that he was only half serious.

♦   ♦   ♦

Bonnie returned to Waco from Dallas on the third day of the new year, and the winter quarter resumed the following morning. Unfortunately, she was no closer to commencing her short story than she had been prior to the Christmas recess. Despite her lofty goals, she undertook precious little academic work over the holidays, so now she was in the unenviable position of grappling with a blank composition notebook. It was chilling to think that on Friday morning, barely ninety-six hours away, her professor would expect to see a viable story outline from each member of the class, and she would turn up empty-handed. Time was her enemy ... or so it seemed.

She secluded herself in Carroll Library on Monday evening, determined to make a start. With Dr. Smith's central precept in mind ("Write about what you know"), Bonnie managed to assemble a list of primary interests: Texas, family, church, wartime, Yorkies, college, cooking, clarinet, USO club, trains. Of these, the topic that attracted her the most was music—not her own clarinet, on which she was a mere dilettante, but the backstage intrigues of a modern symphony orchestra. The possibilities were endless. There could be friendship, jealousy, illicit love, revenge, and even murder. It might prove rather enlivening to shine the light of day upon such a sacrosanct organization's hidden underbelly.

When Friday arrived, Dr. Smith ushered the students into his office on an individual basis. Bonnie was none too confident that her improvised, ill-defined synopsis would pass muster, but the professor appeared to be satisfied with it.

"And are you yourself a member of an orchestra?" he asked.

Bonnie blushed. "No, sir. I was never anywhere near that good."

"But you do play an instrument?"

"Oh, yes. I was in my high school's marching band."

"Then I'd call you a musician." He smiled and handed the outline back to her. "I'm looking forward to reading your story."

"Thank you, sir."

"Remember—don't be too hesitant about putting your own experience to work for you. Your knowledge of music can lend the story some credibility."

Bonnie thanked the teacher and left. Other than listening with her father to an occasional broadcast of the New York Philharmonic or NBC Symphony, she actually knew very little about orchestras. Why did she ever select this, of all things, as the topic for her short story? It had struck her as a wonderful idea in the detached confines of a library, but now, with forty percent of her grade at stake, all vestiges of self-assurance ebbed away.

Rather than submitting to defeat, she resolved to confront the predicament with a positive approach. First she fortified herself with a word of encouragement, and then she took an honest inventory of what had to be done. Assuming that the necessary writing skills were there, the only thing missing was an absorbing story, which might very well come with a deeper understanding of the subject matter. Bonnie required a stiff dose of empirical research, and she knew right where to find it—that new friend she made on the Interurban train ride.

"You say your roommate's in the Waco Symphony?" she asked her.

"Violin," Evelyn Branch said. They were hurrying to English class, and Evelyn could not afford to be late for the second time in two weeks.

Bonnie struggled to keep up. "What's her name? I need to ask her a question."

They entered Pat Neff Hall from the front and jogged toward the stairway at the rear of the building.

"Priscilla Downing. Why? What gives?"

"I've got to attend a couple of rehearsals and a concert," Bonnie said. She trailed closely after Evelyn as they dashed up the stairs.

Upon reaching the third floor, they rushed into the classroom and seated themselves as unobtrusively as possible. Both were relieved to see that their professor was yet to arrive. Still out of breath from running, Bonnie swiveled from her chair and went to her friend's desk, two rows behind her own. "How can I get a schedule of Priscilla's rehearsals?"

"You're being very mysterious about this."

"It's just that I need to learn something about an orchestra— so I can use one in my short story."

Dr. Smith entered the room, so Evelyn had to whisper. "Where do you eat lunch?"

"Alexander."

"I'll have Priscilla meet you there at noon."

"Make it 12:30."

The ensuing rendezvous was productive. Bonnie soon discovered that Priscilla Downing was as affable as Evelyn Branch was aloof. "Call me Prissy," she said.

Bonnie smiled and invited the pretty violinist to step in front of her in the cafeteria's line. "Where are you from?"

"Houston."

"Do most of the high schools down there have orchestras?"

"Just the larger ones."

Sitting at a cherry-wood dining table, shared by six other coeds, they chatted over spaghetti topped with a meatless tomato sauce—not very filling but nicely seasoned.

Bonnie got right to the point. "Did Ev tell you what I wanted to ask?"

"Yes. What are you writing, a murder mystery?"

"Probably not, but I can't say for sure. I won't be able to devise my story until I find out what life in an orchestra is like."

Priscilla laughed. "Well, it's not as exciting as you might think. Most of the players are old enough to be my parents. If you're looking for scandals, I'm afraid you'll be disappointed."

"Do you think your conductor would allow me to sit in on a rehearsal or two?"

"Maybe so, but not right at first." Bonnie seemed confused, so the violinist elaborated. "We have a reading session on Thursday night, and that's usually pretty scruffy. I'm sure Mr. Reiter would not want an audience for that."

"Is he an ogre?"

Priscilla shook her head and had to chuckle. "Oh, no, he's extremely polite. I'll ask him whether you can come to some of the later rehearsals. I'm sure he won't mind, if I tell him what it's for. He's very much in favor of education."

She was as good as her word, obtaining Max Reiter's permission for Bonnie to sit in the wings during two future rehearsals, while the conductor prepared his orchestra for a public performance in late January.

Bonnie was most appreciative, wholly unaware of the mystifying phenomena that were soon to change her life forever.

♦   ♦   ♦

As fate would have it, Bonnie Ploughwright was scheduled to work a four-hour afternoon stint at the USO immediately prior to her first chance to observe an orchestra from backstage. This inopportune concurrence threatened to leave her with scarcely any time at all to take care of school assignments. But two factors worked in her favor: the servicemen's club was seldom crowded on Mondays, and the recent blast of freezing weather was sure to diminish the turnout even further. A blue norther had hammered central Texas overnight, plunging the temperature from a balmy eighty-three degrees at five o'clock on Sunday to a bone-chilling twenty-seven degrees only twenty-four hours later.

Just after five—strictly as a function of her voluntary duties—Bonnie struck up a conversation with a young man named Horace Midge, who sat alone at a table, holding an opened magazine. He was one of the V-5 naval reserve candidates, a detachment of aviation students that was stationed at Baylor University for training. Horace was quiet and almost painfully bashful, and Bonnie considered it a personal challenge to bring the cadet out of himself. She had seen him there before on a number of occasions, but never once did she hear Horace utter a single syllable to anyone except his buddies from Burleson Hall.

"Do you mind if I take my break here?" she asked. "I'm beat." She flashed him a glimpse of her USO armband.

"No, I guess not," he said.

Bonnie sat down and craned her neck to see what he was reading. It was the current issue of *Science*, with a cover illustration of Thomas Edison. "What's so fascinating in there?"

He turned red with embarrassment. "You'd only laugh."

"Try me."

"Page 115." He pointed to the table of contents: EFFECTS OF THE EARTH'S ROTATION ON THE RANGE AND DRIFT OF A PROJECTILE.

She did laugh—and then quickly apologized. "Sorry, but I didn't think anyone could get a kick out of something like that."

"It's very interesting, actually."

"If you say so." Bonnie took a deep breath and rubbed her supposedly aching back. Her crisp, white blouse was a little tight to begin with, so the buttons were straining to remain fastened. "Where are you from?"

"Omaha, Nebraska." Horace averted his eyes.

"Are you a college boy?"

"Yes, ma'am. I got my degree at Lincoln."

"Ma'am!" she said. "I'll have you know that I'm young enough to be your baby sister."

"Sorry, miss."

Bonnie shook her head with mock anger and then smiled at him. "So, what are the effects?"

Horace became flustered. "The what?"

"Of the earth's rotation." She nodded toward the magazine.

"Oh!" He grinned. "Quite a lot. You'd be surprised."

The girl stood up, pleased with herself for inducing him to relax a bit—even if for only a minute or two. Making the men feel comfortable was her job, and she was becoming more adept at it with every passing day.

Bonnie clocked out at six, hopped a streetcar to Baylor, and grabbed a bite to eat in the Alexander dining room. At twenty minutes to seven, with notepad in hand, she set out on foot across the wintry campus for the looming presence of Waco Hall.

Through the darkness, she could see that several musicians, carrying their instrument cases, were entering the auditorium on the east side. She was reluctant to obtrude upon their normal routine, so she walked around the closer façade of the building and went inside through one of those doors. On a whim, instead of going backstage, she decided to alter her plans somewhat and observe the first portion of the rehearsal from the balcony, which was likely to provide her with a better overview of what was involved. Then, during a break, she would return downstairs and talk with Priscilla Downing, who might offer introductions to some of her colleagues in the orchestra.

Satisfied with this revised course of action, Bonnie proceeded along the corridor and up the balcony steps. She was familiar with the main floor of Waco Hall, having attended mandatory chapel services on a daily basis, but the auditorium's balcony was new to her. She chose to sit in the second row—not as conspicuous as the first and high enough to assure visual clearance above the brass railing that extended from wall to wall.

Most of the chairs on stage were already occupied by orchestral players, but a few stragglers continued to rush in and join the others. When all were present, they tuned to the oboist's concert "A" and awaited their conductor. At one minute past seven, according to Bonnie's watch, Max Reiter finally strode into view, mounted the podium, and nodded toward his musicians. "Good evening, ladies and gentleman," he said in halting English with a thick Italian accent. "Let us please get right to work, shall we?"

Signor Reiter was only thirty-seven years of age, but his portly build and receding hairline made him appear to be much older than that. He had arrived in the United States in November of 1938, after abandoning a successful career in his native land when Mussolini's anti-Semitic policies turned violent. Now, in his adopted country, he found himself at the helm of two orchestras, one of which he founded (the Waco Symphony) and another that he brought back to life (the San Antonio Symphony).

"We begin with the Mozart," Maestro Reiter said, and he tapped his baton on the wooden stand before him. With a smile toward concertmaster Phillip Williams, the conductor added, "It is a young work, so we play energetic. *Allegro spiritoso*, please." He eyed the full assemblage for a moment, then raised his stick and gave a downbeat, and the orchestra started to play. Undetected in the balcony, Bonnie Ploughwright listened and jotted down a few comments in the dim light.

Symphony No. 24 (K. 182) dated from the great Austrian composer's fifteenth year, and its three movements tallied a mere nine minutes. Although imbued with nascent genius, the work's musical language was hardly problematic for a professional ensemble. Indeed, within a span of twenty minutes, Max Reiter was content with the rehearsal's progress, and he granted a recess. "Our singers are with us next," he told the players. "We return in ten minutes, no?"

At once, the orchestra's members began to depart from the hall—many for a hurried smoke—and this gave stage hands an opportunity to adapt the seating arrangement for operatic excerpts by Bizet, Mozart, and Verdi. High above the commotion, Bonnie scurried up the aisle and then, when she reached the balcony's lobby, turned right. She would have to be quick to locate her personal contact, Miss Downing, and follow the young violinist back into the auditorium.

Bonnie was still on the upstairs landing, perhaps twenty feet shy of reaching the down staircase, when—in the blink of an eye—peculiar transformations occurred all around her. The stage noise ceased, the carpet acquired a forest green color, and a conical ceiling fixture came into view where none had been before. Dazed for a moment, she slowed her pace, cautiously advancing down one flight until, going left, she was able to see the main-floor lobby. It looked normal enough from her vantage point, so she descended the remaining steps and then went in an easterly direction, halting just short of the exit doors.

The corridor was totally deserted. Where she expected to encounter almost a hundred musicians milling about on their break, instead there was a vacant floor supporting two glossy, colorfully decorated cabinets that stood against the interior wall. Each was as tall as a man, embellished with the stylized name of "Dr Pepper," a soda pop company that was well known in this part of the country. The machines made a faint humming noise, much like a refrigerator, leading the girl to assume that they were some sort of electronic automats. Bonnie walked the length of the corridor, tugging upon the handles of two side entrances to the auditorium, but both were secure and would not budge. She even put her ear against their wooden surfaces, hoping to detect the telltale sound of a reconvened orchestra rehearsal. All she heard was silence.

Baffled, she decided to explore further. At the end of the corridor, she pushed her way through a double door on the left.

Beyond it, she entered a vestibule that dog-legged sharply to the right and led her past a long series of offices, with nameplates affixed to their doors. Apparently emanating from around the corner to her right, there came an abrasive, squeaking noise. She stepped forward to see a cleaning lady guiding her utility cart along the hallway.

"Excuse me," Bonnie said. The woman turned around. "Can you tell me where the Waco Symphony Orchestra is?"

"They play in Waco Hall, next door."

"Isn't there a rehearsal going on?"

"Not that I know of. I didn't see any of them coming in." The cleaning woman seemed to be a kindly soul. "Are you in the orchestra?" she asked.

"No, ma'am. I'm just here to meet one of the violinists. How do you get backstage?"

The woman pointed. "Around there, but they always keep it locked."

"Can you let me in?"

"No. I'm not allowed to do that."

"Do you mind if I knock on the door?"

"Nobody will be there on a Sunday to let you in," the lady told her. "I wouldn't be here myself except to make up for the day I missed."

"But this is Monday."

The woman shook her head and chuckled. "That's the problem. You're here on the wrong night."

"This is January twenty-fifth, isn't it?"

"Yes, it is. Tomorrow is my nephew's birthday."

Bonnie took a deep breath, trying to grasp what was happening. "Can you usually hear the orchestra playing from here?"

"You sure can," the cleaning woman said, "and pretty loud, too. But they never start until seven."

Bonnie checked her wristwatch. "It's already after 7:40."

"Is it that late?" The woman glanced down at her own watch. "No, it's not even a quarter to seven."

By now, Bonnie was thoroughly confused and even a little scared. She began to suspect that some cold air might help to clear her mind. "Is that James Avenue outside?" she asked.

"Uh-huh, right through that exit." The woman gave the girl a strange look. "You're not a Baylor student, are you?"

Bonnie forced a smile. "Yes, I am. But I don't know much about this part of Waco Hall."

"This is called Waco Hall East," the woman told her. "Don't feel bad. Lots of people get mixed up in here, thinking it's Roxy Grove."

"Roxy Grove ..."

"Roxy Grove Hall. It's way over there on the opposite side of Waco Hall. People are always getting them switched."

Bonnie thanked the cleaning lady and started walking toward James Avenue. As she drew close to the glass doors, occasional moving lights could be seen passing by in both directions along the street. At least the traffic was normal. On the other hand, it did seem that the cars were traveling quite speedily for such slick road conditions.

After pulling her winter coat tightly around herself, Bonnie thrust the door open and stepped outside, taking care not to slip on the frozen landing. But the temperature had moderated considerably—and in an amazingly brief period of time. The steps leading down to street level were not the slightest bit slippery, and a cold wind no longer caused her facial skin to become numb, as it had done only an hour or so before.

The cleaning lady may have been correct. Across the street stood Seventh and James Baptist Church, and, from a distance, the east parking lot looked crowded enough to suggest that a Sunday evening service was in progress. Still, Bonnie knew beyond any doubt that this could not possibly be so. She had been to classes that very day. She had worked a Monday afternoon shift at the USO. She had attended the first part of a Monday night rehearsal.

On the sidewalk, a pair of coeds strolled by, chatting amiably with one another and paying no particular attention to Bonnie.

They wore men's trousers, and each had what looked to be a knapsack strapped to her back.

Bonnie called after them, "Pardon me, but can you tell me the time?"

Both stopped and turned their heads toward her. One of the girls pulled from her jacket what Bonnie presumed to be a pocket watch. When opened, the object emitted a faint, blue-green light, similar to that of a radio dial. "It's 6:49," the coed said.

"War Time?" Bonnie asked, but the students were already on their way again. She peered down, just to make certain. Her wristwatch was indeed running an hour fast.

She decided to wander back to the dormitory and try to make some sense of it all. That was when she first saw the silver-colored automobile, parked directly under a street lamp. The vehicle's contour was unusually oblong, short and squatty, with rounded edges that made it seem rather bullet-shaped. Tom Swift would have approved, no doubt, but it gave Bonnie the heebie-jeebies.

As she backtracked, approaching the east entrance of Waco Hall, Bonnie was obliged to circle far to her right. The massive structure now extended well beyond how she remembered it, engulfing a spacious plot of land where the women's hospital was supposed to stand.

Inside Waco Hall she went, opting for a shortcut across the corner of the auditorium's lobby. About fifteen feet from the marble foyer, the bizarre transformation happened again. She witnessed distinct changes in the carpet color and the overhead lighting. Instantly, familiar details reasserted themselves, and she perceived that her world had returned to sanity. The foyer was just as she recalled, and so were the three double doors at the front. Upon setting foot outside, she felt a blast of frigid air and very nearly slipped on the icy steps. A late-model Hudson Commodore crept along Speight Avenue.

♦   ♦   ♦

When Bonnie awakened the next morning, she wondered how much of what she had seen and heard was true and how much was sheer coincidence or the product of an overactive imagination. It was not a dream—of that she was positive—but Bonnie had no grasp of whether the strange feelings might overtake her again. This called for some detective work.

At breakfast, a girl seated at her table was reading a copy of that day's Baylor *Lariat*, the campus newspaper. It was dated Tuesday, January 26, 1943, which verified that the previous night was Monday, not Sunday. So the cleaning lady was wrong. In lieu of her normal route to chapel, Bonnie went out of her way to view the east side of Waco Hall, and there stood the women's hospital building, just where she always knew it to be. Inside the auditorium's lobby, she paused for a few minutes and watched a steady stream of students pass over the very spot where that odd sensation finally released its grip on her the night before. The young men and women suffered no discernible effects, leading Bonnie to wonder if perhaps the location had nothing to do with what she experienced. After all, the alpha and omega of her bizarre excursion transpired in separate areas—and not even on the same floor. That at least was reassuring, in a perverse sort of way.

But when she took a wider look, from across the foyer, what she discovered made her shudder with dread. Allowing her eye to follow along a vertical line, it became apparent that the two points in question formed a perfect axis, with one directly above the other. She beat a hasty retreat to chapel, trying to convince herself how childish she was behaving. No aberration of nature existed in the real world. No unseen chasm waited to devour her. By the time she reached her seat in the auditorium, she was able to giggle at her silliness.

On Wednesday evening, Bonnie met Priscilla for dinner at 6:15, and then she and her violinist friend walked together from Alexander Hall to the orchestra's dress rehearsal. Their circuitous passage through Waco Hall steered well clear of the east vestibule, which was fine with Bonnie. Although curious to learn what had happened, she also remained just the slightest bit apprehensive.

When the girls arrived backstage, sixty or more musicians were already there, taking off their coats, scarves, gloves, and hats, removing instruments from their cases, and engaging in the usual small talk. This time, Maestro Reiter was a few minutes early. He entered the room in buoyant spirits, tossing aside the remnant of his cigarette and immediately lighting another. "Today is Signor Mozart's birthday," he said, "but certainly all of you know that." Many in the group chuckled at the undeserved credit he was giving them.

From her spot in the wings, Bonnie watched and listened conscientiously to the ensuing rehearsal session, scribbling some observations in her notebook for later reference. Once the Mozart symphony was prepared to the conductor's satisfaction, the orchestra accompanied four winners of the Waco Symphony Society's Auditions for Young Singers in "L'amour est un oiseau rebelle" from Bizet's *Carmen*, "Non so più cosa son, cosa faccio" and "Non più andrai" from Mozart's *Le nozze di Figaro*, and "Ah, fors'è lui" from Verdi's *La traviata*. Then came run-throughs of Arcady Dubensky's newly popular *Stephen Foster: Theme, Variations, and Finale* and Tchaikovsky's *1812 Overture*. After a lengthy break—during which a concert grand was wheeled onto the stage and a piano technician touched up his prior tuning—soloist Adele Marcus joined the orchestra for her second rehearsal with them of Gershwin's *Rhapsody in Blue*. The thirty-six-year-old American pianist exhibited splendid musicianship, and no wonder. She was a former pupil of Josef Lhévinne and Artur Schnabel.

The following night's concert began at 8:15, and Bonnie was privileged to hear it from the tenth row of the center section, thanks to a complimentary ticket from Priscilla. The violinist's parents were unable to accept the pair that she set aside for them, due to the constraints of gasoline rationing and the fact that Waco, in accordance with the wartime speed limit, was now a good six-hour drive from Houston.

Naturally, this meant that the seat to Bonnie's left would be unoccupied, and, in the circumstances, she felt entitled to lay her winter coat there. Not until the closing segment of the concert, just before the *1812 Overture* began, was the vacancy appropriated by an Army officer. He excused himself politely, and Bonnie was more than happy to place the coat upon her lap. She noticed that he was quite nice looking and wore two silver bars on his collar.

"Is this your seat?" he whispered. "I can move if you're expecting someone."

"No, sir. There won't be anybody coming."

He leaned toward her and extended his hand. "How do you do? I'm John Decker, but my friends call me Jack."

"Bonnie Ploughwright," she said when they shook hands. "Pleased to meet you." Even through her glove, she could feel that he had just come in from the cold.

"Are you a local girl or a college student?" the officer asked.

She felt herself blush. "Baylor."

He pointed toward what she was holding. "Is that the scorecard?" She gave him her program, and he flipped to the repertoire list. "So it's Tchai-KOW-sky next, huh?"

"Yes, sir." She grinned at him. "Are you a music lover?"

"Golly, no. Far from it. For me, this is only a social obligation." He handed the program back to her.

By now, Enid Eastland Markham had returned to the onstage microphone, providing another bit of commentary between the pieces. She quipped that Pyotr Ilyich Tchaikovsky composed his famous overture to commemorate the occasion when "another undersized, overambitious ex-corporal was repulsed from the brave city of Moscow." Jack laughed heartily and joined in the thunderous applause.

Then the music resumed, low strings intoning the chorale-like introduction. The *1812 Overture* was a piece unconducive to conversation, so Bonnie and the officer exchanged not another word for fifteen minutes. Stealing a glance at him, she wondered what Captain Decker meant by "social obligation." He was wearing no wedding ring, for whatever that was worth.

"How did you like the Tchai-KOW-sky, sir?" Bonnie asked when the final ovation died down. For fun, she pronounced the Russian composer's name just like the officer had, but he failed to notice.

"Oh, fine. I kept awake all the way through it." He smiled at her. "Sorry to sit on your coat rack."

"That's all right. It kept my legs warm this way."

"I'd give you a ride home, but I guess you're home already."

"Yes. Thanks just the same."

"Say, how about getting a bite to eat with me? I've got an hour to kill."

Bonnie shook her head. "The curfew, you know." She began putting on her coat, and he reached over to help.

Jack gestured toward her program. "Do you mind if I have that? I need to prove to someone that I was really here."

"Your social obligation?"

"So to speak."

"Sorry, but it has to be turned in with my research."

"Research? What are you, a psychiatrist or something?"

She laughed. "It wasn't all that bad, was it, captain?"

"No. As a matter of fact, I rather enjoyed it. And the name is Jack."

Bonnie saw a discarded program lying on the floor nearby, and she stooped forward to retrieve it for him. "Here," she said. "This one's not too bent up."

"Swell. It looks like I gave it some serious study." The officer flattened its crumpled cover.

Bonnie offered him a bashful smile. "Good night ... Jack. I'm glad a serviceman could use my other ticket."

He looked startled. "That really was your seat!"

"Yes, sir."

"And you're a subscriber?"

"They were complimentary—from a friend."

"So, you're not a music lover either, huh?"

"No, sir. Well, not yet anyway. But I'm trying."

Captain Decker grinned at her. "You're a sweet girl, Bonnie. Maybe we'll see each other again sometime."

"That's possible, I guess. It's a long war."

♦　　♦　　♦

If nothing else, Bonnie's chance acquaintance with the handsome military officer served to dislodge from her mind much of the worrisome concern she once had over the peculiar happenings of Monday night. Those anomalies, so nightmarish in their surrealism at the time, had dissipated like mist to become a secondary, barely remembered episode in her life. Still further did they recede when she answered a call to the front desk of Alexander Hall on Friday morning and was greeted by a florist who presented her with twelve red, long-stemmed roses from Captain John Tynes Decker. Tucked inside the box was a gift card, upon which was scribbled, in pencil, "I must see you again. — Jack."

All she could think about that day, in her three classes and chapel, was the mysterious Army officer, about whom she knew virtually nothing. Having been reared within a traditional family, by parents who nurtured their two children in a protective manner and instilled in them a reverence for propriety, Bonnie was predisposed to stay clear of such temptation. This ostensible gentleman could, in fact, be a masher—in it for selfish pleasure—a moral weakness that was common enough even in the best of settings and, she suspected, more likely than not when your nation was at war. And yet, something in the captain's mien argued that he was to be trusted. Whether it was the casual, friendly way in which he approached her or the unforced charm of his self-deprecating sarcasm, she felt an attraction to Jack Decker that she had never encountered before. Well, maybe a half-dozen times when she was in high school.

Bonnie read the tiny gift card over and over again, trying to unlock its deeper meaning, if indeed there was one. It would not do for her to chase after the officer, so she interpreted his statement to say that he planned to contact her again whenever he had the opportunity, perhaps during an hour or two of respite from ... from what? She did not even know what he did for the Army Air Forces. She knew nothing about him but his name.

A whole week went by, the fragrant roses wilted, and Captain Decker made no effort to communicate with her, either by letter or telephone. Why would he go to the trouble and expense of sending her such a thoughtful remembrance if he was not interested in establishing a relationship? And if he sought a relationship, why would he then abandon the idea so quickly, without according it a fair trial? As the following Friday came and went, dragging on interminably through the customary "date night," Bonnie became so embittered that she made the mistake of confessing these frustrations to her roommate, Julia Johnston, who seemed more cynical than sympathetic.

"Typical," Julia said with a sneer.

"How do you mean?"

"Believe me, these Army men aren't satisfied with stopping at first base. He's trying to get a double or triple with one swing— maybe even score, if you catch my drift." She laughed, amused by her own cleverness.

Bonnie glared at her roommate. "That's a repulsive thing to say," she told her.

"Don't you see, Bon? The roses were just a down payment, a romantic charade." Julia pronounced that last word "shah-RAHD," like the French.

"You don't even know him, so how can you suggest such a thing?"

"No, but I do know men, and it stands to reason that Army types are even worse than the garden variety."

"Listen. Just because you've had a bad experience or two, I don't think that gives you the right to condemn all men everywhere as beasts. I'm sure there are many who are decent and worthy of—"

"Love?"

"I was going to say 'respect'."

Julia shook her head and sighed. "Just be careful. I don't want to see you get hurt. This officer may be all he's cracked up to be, sure, but I'd say the odds are very much against it."

"There's a word for someone like you, but for the life of me, I can't remember it."

"My goodness. Go on."

Bonnie thought for a moment. "Well, you seem to have a hatred for men, if you don't mind my saying so."

Julia chuckled. "Is that how I come across? I don't mean to. I'm just trying to be realistic."

"Sorry to be so blunt, but since you asked ..."

"Actually, I have a great fondness for men. It's just that they don't seem to feel the same about me—I mean, when it comes to the long haul."

Bonnie effected a smile. "You haven't found the right one yet, that's all."

"Obviously not." Julia looked away. "I'm too physical, I suppose, and not cerebral enough. Isn't that ridiculous for a psychology major to admit?"

"I don't think it's ridiculous. At least you're being honest."

"Thanks for the vote of confidence. One of my friends called me a nymphomaniac."

"Oh, dear!" Bonnie said. Instantly, her face was red with embarrassment.

"Donna's a psychology major, too, it goes without saying. Who else would come out with such a thing?"

Bonnie was aghast. "Do you learn terms like that in class, here at Baylor?"

"No, but we do stumble upon them in our outside reading—journals and such. Very clinical, you know."

"Gosh."

"By the way, you were probably thinking of 'misandrist.' It's analogous to 'misogynist,' except on the opposite side of the ledger. 'Misandrists' are individuals—predominantly females—who have a hatred for the male of the species."

"Maybe that was it."

Julia grinned. "We prefer to call them 'nutcrackers'."

The next morning dawned rather cold, but not unseasonably so. This was the first Saturday in February, when a temperature in the upper thirties is nothing out of the ordinary. Bonnie had slept fitfully, recalling those eerie visions on the night of the rehearsal, and she awakened with a renewed desire to put her fears to rest by confronting them. She downed a bowl of hot oatmeal in the dormitory cafeteria and, with a determined gaze, set out on foot across campus. Sunrise would not occur until 8:19 Central War Time—still fourteen minutes away—so it appeared to be much earlier than it really was. No one else was around at such an hour on a weekend, which was precisely why she thought this might be an ideal time to undertake her exploratory mission.

Bonnie walked the long city block that extended south on Seventh Street, between Baylor Avenue and Speight, and then turned left, stopping directly in front of Waco Hall. She took a deep breath and watched her exhalation float away like a miniature cloud. Just seconds later, the peaceful quiet was disturbed by a flight of four twin-engine trainers from Blackland Army Air Field. They soared low overhead, scaring hundreds of grackles from their treetop perches into a frenzy of evasive action. She watched the black birds fly away, sweeping well past Tenth Street before finally returning to the grassy area in front of Pat Neff Hall and settling in the tall oaks.

With considerable trepidation, Bonnie again set her sights on the auditorium. She ascended the outdoor steps and went inside the building through its main entrance, her shoes causing a pleasant, echoey sound in the marble foyer. She paused for a moment before entering the vestibule that stood between her and the intimate, hundred-seat recital hall. This spot, she recalled, had been the terminus of her strange incident less than two weeks before, so she treated it with all due caution. Bonnie swallowed hard, said a quick prayer, and took a tentative step forward. Nothing happened. She probed further, but still nothing.

She was four and a half paces into the vestibule when she passed beyond, and the transformation was unmistakable. Instantly, both the lighting above and the carpet below altered their forms, and yet she herself felt no physical sensation whatsoever. In fact, had she kept her eyes closed, she never would have noticed.

Bonnie knew how she could confirm her suspicions, and there indeed stood the odd structural addition that was called Waco Hall East. She was on the other side of what she perceived as reality, wherever that may have been.

◆   ◆   ◆

The first thing Bonnie sensed when she ventured from the building was that the air temperature was distinctly warmer than before. She hardly needed the winter coat, though a woolen sweater might have been appropriate. Her best guess was that it was around fifty-five degrees, whereas the radio announcer at eight o'clock had reported thirty-eight. A few more people were visible now than there had been just ten minutes earlier, and most of them were adults—either faculty or staff—rather than students. Judging from what the men and women carried with them, they seemed to be going to work, which Bonnie thought was rather strange for a Saturday in academia. Another peculiarity was the absence of vehicular traffic on Speight Avenue. Even at half past eight in the morning, she would have expected to observe at least an occasional car traveling down this main artery on campus.

As always, Carroll Library was there on the northwest corner of the intersection with Fifth Street, but when she approached the library, Bonnie halted in her tracks, unable to fully grasp what she was viewing around it. For instance, directly across Speight Avenue, where the Publications Building should be, she saw something called the Bobo Baptist Student Ministries Building. Nor was the Studio Theater anywhere to be found, having been supplanted by a much more imposing edifice called the Tidwell Bible Building. She pressed on, careful to remain within a prudent distance of Waco Hall, which represented to her the only means of evacuation, a sanctuary from this madness.

Diagonally across from where the Publications Building was supposed to stand was yet another unrecognized structure. A granite sign proclaimed this to be Hankamer School of Business, and she decided to go inside. Bonnie's wristwatch told her that the time was 8:39, but a clock hanging on one of the interior walls indicated that it was actually 7:39. She went to her right and then followed a long corridor to the left, which guided her to the entryway of a rectangular suite, filled with twenty large tables and perhaps six times that many chairs. Tall, dignified letters, anchored into a façade just below the ceiling, identified this as the John Graham Jones Student Center.

A girl was sitting on a sofa near the room's entrance. She held in her hands a small box, the lid of which she flipped open. What the girl found inside seemed to spellbind her, and she began to press intently with each of her thumbs. This was a music box of some sort, for from it came the sporadic sound of gentle chimes.

When Bonnie slowly inched forward, the girl glanced up at her and smiled. "You have an eight o'clock?"

Bonnie did not know what to say, but that did not matter. The girl's rapt concentration was already back on the music box.

"Aren't you in Professor Read's management class?" the girl asked a moment later. Her eyes were still transfixed by the box.

By now, Bonnie felt herself gaining a measure of confidence. "No," she said. "No, I'm not. Actually, I'm an English major." The girl's only response was a slight nod of the head.

Bonnie walked about ten paces away and sat in a chair at one of the circular tables, lounging there as inconspicuously as possible. She studied the girl and, from her attire, concluded that she was a maintenance worker, probably waiting for her shift to begin. The girl wore denim slacks with holes in the knees, and her sandals were badly tattered. Her pullover sweater was navy blue in color, with a silver star and the numeral "9" stitched upon it. On the floor next to her lay a red tote bag with a gray check mark and a single word in gray script, partially obscured by one of the bag's straps. This lettering may have spelled the name "Mike." Bonnie was tempted to give the impoverished young lady a quarter for breakfast but thought better of it.

Eventually, the worker closed her music box and opened a slim newspaper instead. "Is that yesterday's *Lariat*?" Bonnie asked.

"No, it's today's." The girl gave her a puzzled look. "Why? Did you want yesterday's? There may still be some in that stack over there."

"Thanks," Bonnie said. Trying her utmost not to arouse undue suspicion, she ambled over to a green, wooden rack that had the block letters LARIAT painted in white upon its hind panel. She had been a student at Baylor long enough to know that the *Lariat* was not published on Saturdays, so the worker must have been confused. Maybe she was employed six days a week, and Saturday was just like any other day to her.

Bonnie picked up a *Lariat* and scanned the front page. It was indeed a leftover copy of yesterday's Friday edition. But she also noticed that it had the wrong date, February 6, which was today. As she was about to toss the newspaper aside, her peripheral vision happened to catch the year. She gasped, quite loudly, and closed her eyes. In danger of falling, she leaned against the wall to regain her balance.

Startled, the female worker stood up and took a couple of steps toward her. "Are you okay?"

Bonnie managed to laugh about it. "Oh, sure, thanks. I just felt a little dizzy for a second. I'll be fine."

The worker sat back down, but her worried expression persisted—that is, until the music box chimed again and seized her attention for keeps.

Bonnie retraced her path along the perpendicular corridors, departed from the building, and crossed Fifth Street. She went up an inclined walkway and rested for a few minutes on a cement bench that was positioned outside the unfamiliar north entrance to Carroll Library. Taking a deep breath, she attempted to gather her wits. Unless this was all one gigantic hoax—with everyone in on the joke but her—it seemed incontrovertible that the current date was distorted by exactly sixty-six years. "Now" was 7:55 Central Standard Time on the morning of Friday, February 6, 2009. She was living nearly a decade into the twenty-first century.

On her way back to Waco Hall, the campus was teeming with so many students that it was difficult to walk without continually sidestepping young people who were just as determined to head in the opposite direction. She observed a good many Negroes among them—and Orientals, too—mixing freely within the student body, but there was nary a military uniform. Students of both genders were sloppily dressed. A majority of them, or so it seemed, had music boxes held up to their ears, for whatever reason. All the while, they talked to themselves, perhaps reciting lessons as they strolled along to their classes. And then there were those who chose to occupy their ears by inserting tiny plugs into them, with white strings extending down to coat or pants pockets.

Waco Hall's lobby was too crowded at this hour for Bonnie to seriously consider any attempt to return home to 1943. She could hardly traipse through the vestibule and risk vanishing into nothingness as a dozen or more witnesses stared in disbelief. That being the case, she proceeded to take the west stairway up to the balcony and attain her point of departure from the rear. It worked like a charm, despite the reversal of approach. Before she descended to the main floor, she paused long enough to experiment with her remarkable gift. Safely secluded upstairs, she stepped back and forth through her "time gate" and came to the conclusion that it was a circle—or, more accurately, a vertical cylinder—about four feet in diameter. She also discovered that the angle of passage made no difference whatsoever. It was like a toggle switch, very simple, just on and off.

After avoiding the downstairs portal, soon Bonnie was out the door, huddled in her winter coat, and crossing Speight Avenue amidst the relatively sparse Saturday morning traffic. Life around her went on as if nothing had happened. She detected the pungent smell of cigarette smoke and glimpsed a group of four or five soldiers, who sat idly chatting at the base of a university monument, the statue of Judge R. E. B. Baylor. Hurriedly, she adjusted her path to slant toward Seventh Street, but from behind her came the sound of a wolf whistle and some male laughter. She did not turn to acknowledge the men, as that would only encourage them, and there were much weightier issues on her mind than engaging in aimless flirtation.

♦   ♦   ♦

While nothing of an overtly threatening nature had occurred, being projected into an alien tomorrow was a terrifying ordeal, and Bonnie wanted no further part of it. She resolved to stay clear of the cylinder, at least for now, though she did leave open the possibility of another excursion someday, provided the portals remained accessible to her, and there was ample cause. Meanwhile, she consciously allowed her daily existence to revert to its regular routine—attempting, with variable success, to forget all about her implausible preview of things to come.

She used her neglected studies to fill the void. English was her main concern, naturally, and there was plenty of room for improvement. Evelyn Branch was head and shoulders above the rest of the students in Dr. Charles G. Smith's upper-level course, "Writing the Short Story." The winter quarter's major project was not due until February 24, and yet Evelyn had hers ready for evaluation by the first of the month. This entrancing story told of a Michigan jeweler who repaired a cameo locket but, through clerical mishap, was unable to locate the address of its owner. All he had to go by was the likeness from a miniature photo that was hidden inside. The narrative was touching, even heartbreaking, and Professor Smith had Evelyn read her entire manuscript aloud to the class for purposes of instruction.

Bonnie felt like throwing in the towel when she heard it. Her own literary effort was not going well, decidedly amateurish in contrast to Miss Branch's honest depiction of selfless giving. A complete rewrite was in order, starting with the basic premise of an orchestral musician who falls in love with an escaped convict on the lam. She had tried her best to tell "about what you know," but still the story line careened out of control like an inferior "B" movie script. Bonnie was envious of her friend's writing ability, her knack for capturing the truth on paper without so much as a nod to contrivance. But Evelyn, of course, had an unfair advantage. She was the beneficiary of bitter experience.

After class, Bonnie found sufficient boldness to approach this woman of the world. "Would you read over my story and give me your honest opinion?" she asked.

Although flattered by the novice writer's confidence in her, Evelyn frowned as she responded with a query of her own: "Do you really think that's a good idea?"

"You're the only person I know who'd be objective about it."

"Well, you're right," Evelyn said. "I can be brutally candid when it comes to literature." She smiled, privately amused. "If Tolstoy were alive today, I would insist he drop that damned epilogue to *War and Peace*." Coming from anyone else, this would have sounded awfully arrogant, but Evelyn's unblinking certitude somehow legitimized the statement. They parted company, with Bonnie fearing the worst.

Two days later, just before their Wednesday class began, a dour Evelyn returned the manuscript. "How long did it take you to write that?" was all she said.

"It's only a first draft."

"How long?"

"A week and a half. Why?"

"I'm afraid you'll have to rewrite the whole thing."

Bonnie could not disguise her hurt. "Really? It's that bad?"

"I'm sorry to be the one to tell you."

"That's all right. Better you than Dr. Smith." She tried to maintain a positive face, but it was not easy. "Exactly what about the story didn't you—"

"Everything."

"I see," Bonnie told her. She glanced down at the offending papers. "I trust your judgment."

"There's no reason why you should. Maybe the prof will like it more than I did."

"No, you're absolutely right. It's garbage."

"I didn't say that."

"Not in so many words." Bonnie tossed the manuscript onto her desk, facedown. "I thought your story was wonderful, by the way. Everyone did."

"Thank you. I enjoy writing."

"That's obvious," Bonnie said. "As for me, I struggle with every word."

"That'll change, once you find a story that really grabs your interest. Then it will write itself. You'll see."

Bonnie sighed. "Well, it had better grab me pretty soon."

But worthy material can prove maddeningly elusive for a young writer, particularly when the sense of urgency becomes dire. In Bonnie's case, she had boxed herself into the untenable position of needing to submit a completed draft in a mere fourteen days, and the suggested length was five thousand words or, roughly, twenty pages.

That night, in Carroll Library, she found a quiet table and appraised her dwindling options. Could she salvage anything from her futile first attempt? Unquestionably, the opening sequence would have to go. It set the scene for a gangster melodrama, which was the underlying source of her present troubles. Moreover, her protagonist was two-dimensional, a cardboard figure who was not dynamic enough to effectively advance the plot. And surely the oboist—who fancied himself an amateur gumshoe—was too omniscient, devoid of human failings that might make him more believable to the reader.

"May I?" someone behind her asked. Bonnie turned around to see Captain Jack Decker, visor hat in hand. He was unsmiling but courteous, motioning to an empty chair next to hers.

"Yes, sir, please do." She was rattled by the suddenness of his appearance. "The roses were lovely," she told him. "Thank you."

"You're entirely welcome, and I want to apologize for taking so long to track you down. I must not be a very good detective."

Bonnie grinned. "Well, you found me."

The officer was in his dress greens. There were wings pinned to both lapels, beneath the US insignias, and service ribbons and flight wings were displayed above his left pocket. "Actually, I haven't been looking for you all this time. I was assigned to a base in Childress for ten days, and I've just come back. Your roommate told me you might be in the library."

Bonnie looked shocked. "You met Julia?"

"Yes, I did," he said. "She came down to the waiting room, and we had a nice talk."

"She didn't ... uh ... try to pick you up, did she?"

"No, no. Nothing like that." Jack studied her eyes and decided to be frank. "Well, yes, I think she did, as a matter of fact. Something she said might be construed that way."

"Oh?"

"When I told her that I was going to ask you to the pictures tonight, she volunteered to go if you couldn't. Maybe she was only kidding."

"I doubt it."

"*Seven Sweethearts*," he said.

"Seven ...?"

A chubby coed with pigtails looked up from her studies, as if annoyed by their discussion. Jack did not seem to notice.

"*Seven Sweethearts*," he said again. "That's the name of the picture. Van Heflin's in it—and Kathryn Grayson. What do you say?" When Bonnie hesitated, the officer added, "Please come. Your roommate is really not my type."

As much as Bonnie yearned to accept the captain's invitation, she could not, in good conscience, justify doing so. "Gee, I like Van Heflin, but I just can't," she told him. "I need to write a whole story, from beginning to end."

"Point well taken," he said. "Not much advance warning on my part."

The chubby student cleared her throat and glared at the perpetrators.

Jack leaned closer to Bonnie. "Why is it that we always seem to be whispering to each other? First the concert ... and then a library. I suppose a movie house would be no better, so maybe it's just as well you can't come."

"Thank you very much," she said with a chuckle.

"I wonder if your roommate is still available."

"What? You're not serious!"

He suppressed a smile. "She did offer, you know."

"Don't you dare."

"And why not?"

"Julia is definitely not your type. You said so yourself."

"But I'm all dressed up, with no place to go."

"Go back to the base, and read a good book."

Jack laughed loudly and winked at the chubby student. "Anyway, Miss Ploughwright, it was a pleasure speaking with you again. Maybe some other time, huh?" He stood up and put his hat back on, ready to leave.

"Maybe so. I'm sorry about this."

He smiled at her and touched his black visor.

"Wait!" Bonnie whispered. "There's a Valentine party at the USO on Friday. I'm a volunteer worker, but they don't mind if we have boys in uniform with us."

"Swell. What time?"

"I have to be there at six, to help set up, but it doesn't really start for another hour or so after that."

"Seven it is, then."

"'Bye!" She started to wave but instead returned to her abortive paper, all twenty-three useless pages of it. Above everything else, she did not wish to seem too anxious.

◆　　◆　　◆

Local radio station WACO carried a quarter-hour of Bob Wills and His Texas Playboys at 7:15, and music from that program could be heard as Bonnie Ploughwright and Julia Johnston stood in the breakfast serving line on Friday morning. Clearly, someone in the kitchen was a Wills fan, which was not all that unusual in central Texas.

Bonnie and Julia giggled at the twangy lyrics, "Take me back to Tulsa. / I'm too young to marry," but the coed in front of them was offended by their dismissive attitude. They knew her to be a farm girl from Limestone County.

"He's in the Army now, so I would think you'd be willing to keep your opinions to yourselves," she said.

Julia, never one to accept criticism graciously, sneered at their accuser. "I just don't care much for caterwauling cowpokes, which is how he sounds to me."

Recoiling from the affray was Bonnie, whose embarrassment led her to scan the dining room for an available table.

"Well, lots of people around here do like him," the farm girl said, "so please don't make fun."

Julia scowled. "Who are you supposed to be—Goebbels?"

"Mr. Wills is in uniform."

"I can't see that over the radio," Julia told her. "Besides, this song isn't exactly 'The Star-Spangled Banner.' Pardon me for not snapping to attention."

Carrying their respective trays, the farm girl went one way in a huff, and the two roommates went another.

Julia and Bonnie were joined at their table by Carla Hamilton, who provided an explanation for the coed's outburst. "Her name is Nancy Werth. She's from south of Groesbeck, and her home is only about fifteen miles from Kosse, where Bob Wills was born. I guess she feels possessive of him, for some reason."

Julia stared across the room at her adversary. "That's creepy," she said.

"And Nancy's boyfriend is in the Army, just like the singer," Carla added, "so maybe that's it."

Julia stirred some milk into her coffee. "Well, lots of boyfriends are in the service. Most of mine are, too." She laughed to herself. "I hope she doesn't expect me to shed any tears over that."

It was thirty-seven degrees when the roommates exited the dormitory together for their eight o'clock classes. Bonnie's destination was Pat Neff Hall, whereas Julia continued all the way to the brick Psychology Building beyond the tennis courts, almost to where the unfinished Student Union Building—long delayed by the war—stood with its steel girders riveted in a skeleton frame near Fifth Street.

As it turned out, Bonnie may just as well have stayed in bed. She learned little or nothing that morning, owing to the fact that her mind was preoccupied by two more compelling concerns: a fruitless literary endeavor that refused to coalesce and a USO party that she anticipated with some excitement but also a frightful case of the jitters.

Later in the day, after her short-story class was over, she conferred again with the teacher, confiding to him that she had run into trouble with character development and narrative realism, leaving her with no possibility of rewriting in time to meet the deadline. Dr. Smith gave her a sympathetic ear but could not go so far as to grant an extension. "We simply have no leeway, Miss Ploughwright, as you can see from the calendar. Perhaps the completed story is better than you fear."

But she knew in her heart that it was every bit as weak as Evelyn Branch had pronounced it to be. Out of sheer desperation, Bonnie decided then and there—even before she left the professor's office—to take drastic measures. In the interest of her literary career, she convinced herself to make yet another tentative probe into the twenty-first century, perhaps as soon as daybreak. Strictly speaking, there was nothing dishonorable or plagiaristic about setting her short story many years in the future. However unconventional the method of research, she would be composing every last word of it.

Despite Julia's insistence, Bonnie dressed quite modestly for that night's Valentine party. She was, after all, on duty for the occasion, and there were plenty of USO girls in classy attire to entertain the troops. A baker's dozen of them were delighted to pose for the Waco Army Air Field cameraman in a pre-soirée shot that was slated to be published, so he assured them, two days later in the February 14 edition of the *Waco Sunday Tribune-Herald*. The girls were grouped around a decorative heart, and they smiled becomingly when the khaki-clad photographer counted to three.

A typically diverse aggregation of servicemen had been coming and going throughout the daytime hours, but then a sizable influx began making an appearance around 6:45. While a few sailors were interspersed among them, most of the new arrivals were enlisted men and officers from either Waco Army Air Field or Blackland Army Air Field. Several soldiers from the Tank Destroyer School made the forty-mile trip north, all the way from Camp Hood. The evening's jazz band, crack musicians from WAAF, had yet to finish setting up, but the bespectacled leader promised to have his men ready by the top of the hour.

Bonnie stationed herself at the refreshment table and served finger sandwiches, cookies, and punch to those who wanted them, all the while keeping an eye out for Jack Decker. Circumstances were not ideal, inasmuch as USO workers were permitted to leave their posts for just one ten-minute break for every two hours on the job. She hoped that her guest would understand the dilemma and make allowances for her responsibilities as a volunteer.

She spotted him at 7:35, the moment he entered the doorway from Washington Avenue, and her gaze followed his every step as he walked through the noisy room toward the refreshments. He was at least six people deep in line when Bonnie caught his eye. "Go find a couple of seats," she mouthed to him. "I'll come over on my break."

Jack nodded a greeting and edged forward to within hearing distance. "How long do you have?"

"Ten minutes."

"When?"

"As soon as I can."

Locating a pair of vacant chairs was easier said than done. This was at the height of the party, and the entire first floor of the USO building was brimming with GIs and their prospective dance partners—in a ratio of roughly three to one, or so it seemed to the boys in uniform. When Jack finally glimpsed two available places to sit, he hurried over and staked his claim to one of them, only to have a lovely young woman—perhaps sixteen years of age, if that—take it upon herself to commandeer the other.

"Do you mind if I sit here for a minute?" she asked. "My feet are about to fall off from all the jitterbugging." Her voice sounded slurred.

"Actually, I am expecting somebody, but you're welcome to it until she gets here."

"Cynthia Rummage is my name. And yours?"

"Jack."

She flashed him a seductive smile. "Just Jack?"

"That's right. Just Jack." He frowned, a little peeved at her impudence.

"And I suppose 'just Jill' will be coming along shortly?"

"You catch on fast."

The girl put her hand upon his arm, and he pulled away.

"Forgive me," she said, "but there's a war on, you know."

"So I heard."

"No time to waste on formalities." Her visage had become rather drowsy, and an unmistakable smell of alcohol permeated the air. The girl wavered in her seat, eyelids heavy, as if on the verge of nodding off to sleep.

Jack studied her face. "How old are you, if you don't mind my asking?"

"The same age as if I do mind."

"And what would that be?"

She thought for a moment, then opened her eyes and spoke with defiance. "Twenty-one, sir."

By now, Bonnie was right there in front of them, looking a bit confused. The tipsy girl gave her a hateful glower and asked, "Who's this, then?"

Jack motioned for her to stand. "I told you my friend was on her way over here."

With dilated pupils, the teenager scrutinized her rival. "So this must be Jill," she told the Army officer. "You go for the really stacked ones, huh?"

"I think you've said enough, miss."

"Well, you don't need to get snotty about it." She stood up on unsteady legs.

Captain Decker gestured for a noncom to come closer. "Sergeant, send that snowdrop over here, will you? Tell him he needs to drive this child home to her mother. No charges. Just let her sleep it off."

"Yes, sir." The sergeant did as instructed, and soon an MP came to escort the girl away. She was nearly dead on her feet and offered no resistance.

And so, Bonnie and the captain were finally seated next to each other. "What was that all about?" she asked him.

"Just an underage girl trying to act grown up beyond her years. I'd like to find out who gave her the hooch. Probably some fly-boy with a flask."

Bonnie was appalled. "They bring that right into the USO?"

"Sure they do. No one frisks them at the door." Jack smiled at her and changed the subject. "You only get this one break?"

"No, sir. We earn ten minutes off for every two hours of volunteer work."

He rolled his eyes. "Do me a favor and drop the 'sir' business. I get enough of that during the day."

"All right," she said. "What'll I call you?"

"My best friends call me Jack."

She grinned. "Do I qualify?"

"You do. At least I hope you'll feel comfortable with the idea."

Bonnie was tempted to say something clever, but instead she played it safe by simply nodding her head.

"Ready for a drink?" he asked her.

"Gosh, no. I've had enough punch to float a battleship."

"Well, do you mind if I get one for myself?" He started to stand, but she grasped his arm.

"If you can hold out until I'm back at work, you won't have to wait in line."

"Preferential treatment."

"Actually, I'm being greedy. I wouldn't want to spend my whole break by watching you queue up at the refreshment table. I should have brought something over to you. Still can, I guess."

"No, don't bother with that."

A first lieutenant passed by, saw Captain Decker, and muttered a one-word greeting: "Jack." He smiled at Bonnie but kept walking, not wishing to intrude.

"Hey, Scotty," the captain shouted. "What's your hurry?"

The lower-ranking officer turned around. "Hot date, Jack. I need to get some iced punch to cool her down."

"Oh, sure!" Jack turned to Bonnie. "Don't listen to him. Scotty here's a confirmed bachelor who's never dated the same girl twice."

"That's not true. I date *every* girl twice—the first time and the last time."

All three of them laughed, especially Colton Scott himself, who was proud of his witty repartee.

"And who might this be?" the lieutenant asked. He eyed his superior's companion with tacit approval.

Jack cleared his throat. "Miss Bonnie Ploughwright, please say hello to Lieutenant Scott of the North. He's our squadron mascot."

"Not so, miss. I was recently promoted to class clown," Scotty said. "Somebody's got to do it, and it sure as hell ain't going to be J. T." He leaned over to the girl and whispered, "He's rather a stuffed shirt, once you get to know him—strictly by the book. Me? I've got my own book."

Bonnie giggled, without quite knowing why. "J. T.?"

"John Tynes Decker, the man you're sitting next to at the present moment. You really should be more careful about the company you keep."

"Say, I think your date is beginning to smolder," Jack said.

"Ah, yes, the punch." Scotty winked at Bonnie and headed toward the refreshments.

"He's one of my instructors," Jack told her. "Great pilot—the best—but sort of a gadabout in his private life. I don't think he'll ever settle down."

"Where's he from?"

"Why do you ask—his accent?"

"You called him 'Scott of the North,' so I was just curious."

"Harbor Springs, Michigan—way up near Mackinac Island—and he'll never let you forget it. I think his parents used to work at the Grand Hotel, a very exclusive establishment."

She stared at Captain Decker for a moment. "Why did he say you're a stuffed shirt? You don't seem that way to me."

"Thanks. I suppose Scotty's just jealous because I'm with the prettiest gal in the place, and it irks him."

Bonnie's face flushed warm, a surefire sign that she was turning red. Looking around, she deflected the flattery with a modest smile. "Lots of the girls here are prettier than I am—just within a stone's throw."

"Not from where I'm sitting."

"Thank you. That's a very sweet thing to say."

"Do you realize that we hardly know anything about each other?" Jack said.

"I know you love Tchai-KOW-sky, right?"

"Who?" He laughed. "Like I told you, that concert was nothing more than a social obligation—which may have suckered you into thinking I was cultured. If you can handle the bitter truth, I don't know Beethoven from Bert Lahr."

"Did you go to college?"

"Oh, yes, I paid my dues."

"Baylor?"

Jack shook his head. "No. I'm a DePauw University alum. Want to see my striped tail?"

"That's not necessary. I believe you."

"I graduated in the spring of '41, and two months later I joined up. They were searching for officers at the time, and I must have fit the bill."

She glanced at the metal insignia on his breast pocket. "Do you fly?"

"Yes, I do," he said. "Well, actually, I teach flying. I'm an instructor at Blackland."

"But you yourself fly, too, don't you?"

He grinned. "Sure. I'd be a worthless instructor if I couldn't get my own crate off the ground."

"If you graduated in 1941, you should be about ... twenty-four now?"

"Twenty-five. You?"

"I'm twenty-one."

"From?"

"Dallas."

"Seems to me I've heard of it. Almost as big as Veedersburg, so they say."

"Is that where you're from?"

"Yep. It's about sixty miles to the northwest of Indianapolis. Haven't been home for two years, though."

Bonnie looked concerned. "Why not? Don't they give you any leaves?"

"That's a long story. My parents split up when I was a freshman in high school."

"Are they still living?"

"My father is—in Fort Wayne. Mom died not too long after the divorce."

"How sad."

Jack had a faraway look in his eyes. "Yes, it was. Still is," he said. "They never did find out what happened to her. A car crash—that's all they know. They say she probably had a heart attack while she was driving, but I'm not so sure about that. She didn't have heart trouble, and there was no history of it on the Borman side of the family."

"Are all of your relatives in Indiana?"

"No, we're pretty scattered. Some in Wisconsin, some in Maryland, some in Illinois. My uncle lives right here in Texas—down in Houston. His younger daughter's an Army nurse, so God only knows where she is now."

All of a sudden, a beaming smile came across Bonnie's face. "Oh, I love that song, don't you?"

Jack paid close attention to the jazz band for a quarter-minute or so, but there was no hint of recognition. "Sorry, but I don't know anything about music. Never listen to it."

"Haven't you ever heard of 'We'll Meet Again'?"

He shrugged his shoulders. "I've heard the title, sure, but I don't know what it sounds like."

"Benny Goodman's was the big hit over here, with Peggy Lee, but Vera Lynn had already made it famous in England."

"I'll take your word for it."

Bonnie was swaying to the melody. "Do you care to dance, Captain Decker?"

"I thought Baylor girls weren't allowed to dance."

"That only applies to dancing on campus," she told him. "And, of course, at church."

"What church do you attend?"

"Columbus Avenue Baptist Church. How about you?"

"Oh, just on base—in those rare instances when I choose to go."

"Are you a Baptist, Jack?"

"Nope. Lutheran."

"Well, Lutherans dance, don't they?"

"I imagine so."

"Come on, then. It's perfectly legal for me to dance at a sinful place like the USO, and it won't count as part of my break."

"Sorry, Bonnie, but no dice. I'm about as far as you can get from a romantic." He looked down at the floor, pulling uncomfortably at the front of his shirt collar. "There—now you know my dark secret. I'm an uncouth lout."

"Please don't say that about yourself. I happen to think you're very romantic. Nobody gives a dozen roses who isn't."

"Hah! It's easy to buy flowers. Who can't do that?" he said. "But you'll catch me dancing on the same day as your first bombing run in an AT-11. I'm just not the dancing type—and never will be."

Bonnie reached over and, with an index finger to the captain's chin, gently turned his head toward her. "Someday, Jack Decker, I'll make you eat those words."

"Five dollars says you're wrong."

"Deal." They shook hands.

Jack smiled in amusement, but Bonnie was serious, her eyes glimmering with moisture.

"Oh, well, I need to be getting back anyway," she told him. "My break's nearly over, and they'll wonder where I've gone."

He sighed. "I've enjoyed our time together. Sure does beat a symphony concert, huh?"

"I'll have another break at 9:50, but you probably can't wait that long."

"No, I've got to go." He put his hat on and straightened it. "May I see you tomorrow—just to make up for our abbreviated date tonight?"

"Jack, I can't. Tomorrow is my only time for research, and I won't be around for most of the day. What about Sunday instead?"

"Sorry. Flying to some God-forsaken place called Pyote, out in west Texas."

"For how long?"

"Six days, at least—maybe up to ten."

Bonnie shook her head and frowned. "It seems like we're destined to be apart."

"When is your paper due?"

"The short story?"

"I guess. Whatever you've been working on so hard."

"Not until the twenty-fourth. Then I should have more free time."

They stood up, and Jack took both of her hands in his own. "It's been swell."

"I think so, too. I've had a wonderful time—brief though it was."

He leaned toward her, and they shared a first kiss. In so doing, her forehead bumped his visor slightly, and he smiled at her as he straightened the hat again.

"I'll look you up when I'm back in town," Jack said. "Good luck on the research."

"Yes, sir." She pretended to salute. "Fly safely."

◆   ◆   ◆

Bonnie needed to plan the excursion very carefully, for this was to be her most extended visit yet. Judging from previous experiences, she reckoned that her arrival, unless something went terribly awry, would be in the year 2009 and on a Friday morning, around 7:30 Central Standard Time. She did not tell her roommate any more than she had to—only that she would be digging through musty records and manuscripts in a warehouse, accumulating bibliographical information for a term paper in her "Research for the Writer" course. She hoped that Julia would not ask too many questions about this hypothetical class, and fortunately that turned out to be the case. "I may not be back until after dark," Bonnie told her. She laid out her shabbiest clothes the night before, in anticipation of mixing freely with Baylor students of the early twenty-first century.

Julia was still in bed on Saturday morning when Bonnie tiptoed from the dormitory room at 7:45 Central War Time. She shut the door as quietly as she could, so as not to disturb her roommate's sleep—and, more than that, to make a clean getaway with no last-minute interrogation. Julia could be quite nosy when even the faintest intrigue piqued her curiosity, particularly if someone with whom she was acquainted happened to be involved. That, Bonnie figured, was a derivative of the psychologist in her, always trying to determine what made people tick.

After breakfast, during which there were only five other coeds scattered about the dormitory's dining room, Bonnie put on her winter coat and departed into the thirty-four-degree dawn. Sunrise had occurred a few minutes earlier, at 8:13, and the frosty grass across Seventh Street reflected a whiteness that resembled snowfall. She had no way of foretelling what sort of weather awaited her, so she dressed for the present and would make do when the situation arose.

She entered the doorway to Waco Hall and stopped for a few minutes in the foyer. It was essential to bear in mind that there could very well be more activity than she now saw around her. The time in which she expected to find herself would be a weekday, not a weekend, and her assumption that school was unlikely to begin prior to eight o'clock was little more than an educated guess. She double-checked to make certain that the notepad and pencil were in her jeans pocket, and she glanced again at her folded ten-dollar bill. In the event that Alexander Hamilton's likeness was not retained for the better part of the next few generations, payment in such vintage currency might arouse suspicion. That was a chance she would have to take. If all else failed, she might be compelled to go hungry for most of the day—not a life-threatening prospect. Then again, maybe she could learn to use one of those electronic automats, but a unit that dispensed food instead of beverages. Her coins, presumably, were still admissible as legal tender, so she carried with her a small pouch of assorted denominations that totaled $2.39. Surely that would be more than enough for a couple of nice meals.

Bonnie tried to consider every contingency, beginning with the least perilous. What if the twin portals (which she had come to picture as a single "cylinder" because of the common axis of the upper and lower components) had ceased to perform their miraculous function? That would impose upon her nothing graver than restriction to the present day, a tolerable disappointment at worst. Much more problematic—in fact, quite horrifying—were those other potential breakdowns that plagued her thoughts. What if the cylinder transmitted her into a distant future or, almost as bad, into a distant past? For that matter, arriving at any juncture prior to 1931, when Waco Hall was inaugurated, could leave her marooned and unable to return home, for there would be no host structure for the passageway. And if she waited for the building to materialize, she would be consigned to living out her life twelve or more years ahead of the appointed time, all the while holding no assurance that the portals would ever appear.

Without question, she was playing with fire, and it took all the courage Bonnie could summon to approach the invisible cylinder. She did so very timidly, pausing just short of the abstract line where she estimated the perimeter to be. Then she took a deep breath and continued forward. One step. Two steps. She said a prayer and closed her eyes. Three steps. Another breath and slow exhalation. Four steps. Standing absolutely still, she forced herself to open her eyes, ready to respond if the unimaginable happened. She stepped again, and the carpet and lighting fixtures, as before, changed their characteristics in a flash.

She proceeded forth with conscious effort, steadfastly ignoring the survival instinct, which meant fleeing back to her own world. A dozen more paces, and Bonnie was able to see the mysterious annex called Waco Hall East. From there, she forged ahead into the unknown, ragged slacks and sweater partially concealed beneath her heavy coat. This trip, she knew, would be far different than its precursors. Now she would be an active rather than passive visitor. She had a sense of mission—gathering data for writing, much like a newspaper reporter.

Something, perhaps its quaint familiarity, drew Bonnie initially toward Carroll Library. This structure was already forty years old when she enrolled as a freshman at Baylor University. It represented a faithful friend, a tangible link that tied her to what she regarded as the present. And yet, all around the building were unsettling reminders that she was inhabiting a strange world, to which she had no right to belong. Among the most freakish, perhaps, was the utter nonexistence of streetcar tracks. The intersection of Fifth and Speight, where she had hopped aboard many an electric-powered transport for the trip downtown, was paved over and closed at three sides, in effect forming a traffic circle with only northbound Fifth Street vehicles admitted to its rotary flow and then—for some reason—directing their drivers to return from whence they came. This was a most peculiar design, and she made a crude sketch of it in the notebook. By now, her winter coat was starting to feel a little stifling, with the temperature hovering at an unseasonably balmy fifty-seven degrees.

Bonnie's fact-finding objective at the moment was the Student Union Building, where she was sure to encounter some currently enrolled young people who might supply her with beneficial information. This stately, three-story edifice, under construction for as long as she could recall, now seemed to be complete and fully functional. During the intervening decades, it had also been renamed: the Bill Daniel Student Center.

She entered, removed her coat, and almost at once came upon an enticing doughnut stand. A few budding scholars sat at small tables close-by, textbooks lying open before them, but most of the students appeared to be relaxing in the adjacent dining room, a much larger space that was arranged in cafeteria fashion. That is where Bonnie chose to go, for there she was able to position herself strategically, in a booth that permitted her to view and listen in two different directions at once.

"I went, like, at six o'clock, and his roommate—Brad, you know—was, like, sitting on the sofa, eating a bowl of cereal," a blonde said to her brunette friend. "Jeremy was nowhere in the apartment—at least that I could see—and I was, like, totally, you know, blown away that he would leave me, like, totally alone with Brad. Do you know Brad? I think he's a Sigma Chi." Her plump cohort was sipping a drink from what appeared to be a paper cup. There was a name printed vertically upon it, but Bonnie could not decipher the red script because of the girl's hand, which obscured all but a few letters: "Ch..." and "...-A."

"Kevin did that to me once," the brunette said, "and he didn't come back for, like, an hour. I don't remember his roommate's name, but we didn't have, like, ten words to say to each other the whole time. He was on the football team, I think, but he never did play—just, like, stood on the sidelines. Seems like a waste of time to me—especially since he was just, like, a walk-on, and Coach Briles is landing some good recruits these days."

In the other direction, Bonnie listened to a boy conversing with his girlfriend, but they were not nearly so boisterous and thus more difficult to hear. That was just as well, for none of it made much sense anyway. He told her, "The pictures are only two megs apiece—something like that—so my USB stick will hold all of them, easy. It's got a sixteen-gig capacity." The girl said something unintelligible, to which he replied, "No. I'll upload ten or twelve of the best ones to the website tonight and then flow some text around them with links to the syllabus. It'll make a good presentation if I can figure out how to get the MP3s to play without clipping off the last few seconds. And, you know, Ashley's doing a PowerPoint that's awesome—animation and everything. We'll be good to go."

At first, Bonnie felt self-conscious about her old clothes, but the uneasiness vanished when she realized that she was better dressed than most everyone else. As she wandered back to the Bill Daniel Student Center's entrance, she paused for a moment at the doughnut stand and discovered that there was not just one coffee for sale but several distinct exotic styles—bearing names like "café mocha," "café latté," and "au lait"—many of them listing for upwards of three dollars. Surely that was for a whole pound of roasted beans and not for a single serving. In any case, she was pleased to observe that the prices were stated in American dollars instead of German marks or Japanese yen, so presumably the war ended on terms that were favorable to the Allies.

This brought up a vexing issue, a fundamental one that she would have to resolve posthaste, even before she arrived at the library. Just how deeply did she dare to investigate the future? For example, was it safe to learn precisely when the global conflict would end? Might she not inadvertently divulge sensitive information upon her return to the present? Could she thereby influence the course of history? On a more personal scale, was there intrinsic danger in researching her own years to come? Would her brother, Keith, survive the war? When would her parents die? It was sobering to comprehend that she herself would be eighty-eight in 2009, so her parents would have departed the earth long ago.

"Is that still the library?" she asked a shaggy-haired boy next to the water fountain. He did not hear a word she said. "At Fifth and Speight?" she added. Again, no reply. There were plugs in his ears, and their white strings or electronic wires were connected to a music box that he held in his left hand. The poor lad's face appeared to be comatose. Tattoos covered both of his arms.

When she posed the same question to a pretty Negro who passed her in the doorway, the girl stopped walking and looked perplexed. She nodded toward the street. "No, the library's way down there. You can't see it from here, but it's a big brick building with glass all around." Bonnie thanked her, and then off she went, with a plan of action gradually formulating in her mind.

En route, she was almost run over by a four-wheeled cart that emitted virtually no noise and drove along the sidewalk in a hazardous coexistence with pedestrians. Far behind her, bells within the dome of Pat Neff Hall chimed the customary Westminster sequence and proceeded to peal eight full-voiced bongs.

♦   ♦   ♦

Moody Memorial Library stood three stories tall—or four, counting its basement. Bonnie ascertained this by going down to the lowest level and then resolutely climbing the entire staircase, each step of the way, from bottom to top. She was afraid to use the elevators because no operators were there to assist, and she was not sure whether she would be able to manage the controls. Oddly, no one else seemed at all troubled by the self-service character of these contraptions. Students went aboard drowsily, as if it were second nature, something that even a five-year-old could master.

Upon reaching the library's upper floor, Bonnie judged that everything looked quite normal from a distance, with shelves of books aligned laterally across the entire room. But when she approached through the glass doors, she was startled to come upon seven or eight movie screens atop a large table. Bonnie presumed that these were specimens of that vaunted invention called television, which she had heard so much about for most of her her life but whose proliferation was stunted by the outbreak of war. If that indeed was what now sat listlessly before her, the apparatus was ballyhooed far beyond its worth. The depicted images, while brilliantly lifelike in color, changed from one to another at random, and there was no further movement except for the occasional floating of various words across the screens.

The stack areas were of greater interest. Straight ahead, and both to the left and right, loomed the religion section, though inexplicably now designated as "BX" instead of the more common "200." Very likely, a few of these books were the same ones that she had consulted when they were housed across campus in Carroll Library. With that in mind, she flipped open some of them, bracing herself for the shock of spotting her own name written on a yellowed circulation card. She need not have bothered, for no cards were to be found. Nor were there any glued-in pockets, upon which the due dates would be stamped. Were students unable to check out any of these books? How were they to study?

Farther to the right, where "BX" gave way to "C" and then "D," she happened upon a gold mine of sources for research—much of it, unfortunately, falling outside the parameters of her self-imposed guidelines. These innumerable holdings constituted what she had come to know as the first part of Dewey's "900" section, with books on world history stretching along shelf after shelf, row after row, range after range. Reading the lettering on their spines was tantalizing beyond belief, almost overpowering her determination to resist, but she could not, as a responsible American citizen, permit herself to probe more deeply than an indiscriminate perusal of the titles. There were publications galore on such topics as "The Second World War," "The Big Three at Teheran," "The Desert Fox," "The Battle of the Bulge," and "The Death of Hitler." But why so much material on "Harry S. Truman," the Senator from Missouri? And what was this "D-Day" that received so much coverage? Most incomprehensible of all was a vast category with title upon title alluding to "The Atomic Bomb."

What Bonnie would have given to learn of the mysteries that these books held hidden between their covers! But, once known, how could she justify withholding from her contemporaries the life-giving properties they were sure to provide? She had no choice but to steer clear of factual information that could conceivably alter the prosecution of this war. Unless she was able to devise a foolproof way of circumventing the quandary, she felt morally obligated to refrain from anachronistic sleuthing to unlock secrets that postdated her biological present—which meant no books copyrighted later than the end of 1942.

Reluctantly, she tore herself away from the history section and wandered back, as if in a daze, toward the stairway. Again she passed by the televisions, but now there were three people seated in front of them. So hypnotized were they by the invention's marvels that these students, two young ladies and a young man, remained totally oblivious to her presence. Bonnie saw, upon closer inspection, that each of the color movie screens had a typewriter keyboard resting before it. Whenever a student typed an occasional word or sentence, the television would respond by changing its visual content, sometimes dramatically. This prompted the student to move an eraser-looking object across a tiny breadboard for further entertainment to emerge. All of the critical instruments—the television, the typewriter, and the eraser—were connected, by means of thin, electronic wires, to a vertical box that resembled (in its general shape but not function) a radiator for heating your bedroom.

The young man reached into his knapsack for a candy bar and, upon seeing Bonnie out of the corner of his eye, turned to her and smiled. She stepped away, embarrassed and a little frightened. What would she say to this twenty-first-century inhabitant, were he to engage her in conversation? Speaking to a cleaning lady was one thing, but trying to bluff a technician about her grasp of modern science was quite another.

She hurried through the glass doors and went down the stairway to the library's second story, which, at this early hour, seemed to be even more deserted than the third. Found here were magazines of every description, and Bonnie began at once to roam the aisles without rhyme or reason, suddenly feeling the need to reestablish contact with the present. But everything looked unearthly to her. She gave a wide berth to one grotesquely menacing piece of machinery, as large as a radio-phonograph console. It possessed a metallic flap, slanted at a forty-five-degree angle over a horizontal window that framed nothing but darkness. She longed for something familiar, any artifact whatsoever from her own world.

Bonnie viewed the titles of bound periodicals, which stood like bricks in a wall, enclosing her on all sides to well above eye level. Enigmatic names jumped out at her—*Group Decision and Negotiation, General Linguistics, Gifted Child Quarterly, Gerontology News*—and she experienced a swell of vertigo. So foreign was she in these surroundings that her place of origin may just as well have been some planet in a distant galaxy. Coming to her aid was the library's exhaustive collection of *Good Housekeeping*, spanning all the way back to 1903. Bonnie took two wartime volumes from the shelf, carried them over to a wooden carrel, and, for nearly forty minutes, reacquainted herself with everyday life on the home front. She felt much stronger now, invigorated, ready to resume her exploratory visit with notepad and pencil in hand. Such were her revived spirits that she even indulged in allowing her fingers to turn the magazines' pages past 1943 and into 1944. It boggled her mind to think that she was holding a product of the days to come, an issue that did not yet exist in her realm of cognition. She studied the cover of the April 1944 edition and vowed to "remember" the charming illustration when it appeared on the local newsstands: a little girl in her Sunday finery, sitting in a church pew and singing from a hymnal, which she naïvely held upside-down.

Thus refreshed, Bonnie became intent upon talking at length with a Baylor student from this future day, something she had promised herself would happen. She was curious to know what a young person's most pressing concerns might be on this typical morning of February 13, 2009. On her way to the down staircase, in search of a likely interviewee, she happened upon a couple of electronic automats, both fully six feet tall and standing with their backs abutting against the west wall. The machines were cheery and inviting, not intimidating in the least, but their manner of operation was too arcane for her to attempt without watching someone else manipulate them first. Each had a coin slot and, beneath that, a grooved aperture labeled INSERT BILL HERE. Asking prices for individual candy bars and sacks of salted treats varied from eighty-five cents all the way up to one dollar. Among the colorfully packaged foodstuffs were snacks with previously unknown monikers like "Skittles," "Twix," and "Chips Ahoy." What truly astounded her—after the passage of two thirds of a century—was to discover, alongside these novelty items, a group of such old favorites as "Fritos," "Mr. Goodbar," "Snickers,"

"PayDay," "Cheez-It," and "Kit-Kat." She entered these names in her notebook and went down the stairs.

Bonnie noticed that there were eight young people seated at long tables in the main entry hall, a spacious room distinguished by ceiling-to-floor windows that let indirect sunlight flow in from three sides, even on mostly cloudy days like this one. She seated herself among the others and considered her prospects, just as a journalist might do. The students were scattered about, rather than congregated into cliques, so she had a variety of informants from which to choose. Upon further assessment, she saw that two of them had music boxes pressed to their ears, and three others were viewing portable televisions, handily plugged into outlets along the walls. When she removed these five from contention, that left only a pouting female with eyeglasses, a stout, bearded male whose head was entirely bald on top, and a boy whom she could not see very well because he had turned his chair around to face Third Street.

By default, she approached this last young man from the rear and was about to address him when two ebullient girls came inside the library through its south entrance. One of them smiled at her, so Bonnie's natural inclination was to gravitate toward the pair.

"I wonder if I might ask you some questions about Baylor," she said to them.

The girl who had smiled kept walking and seemed unwilling to linger. "I'm going to Jones," she told her friend, "See you at lunch. Jason might drop by after he's finished at the Slick. Would you tell him where I am?"

"Okay."

The girl who remained behind plopped her knapsack onto a table and sat down. Bonnie pulled out her pencil and scribbled something in the notebook.

"Do you work for the *Lariat* or something?" the coed asked.

"No, nothing as official as that," Bonnie said with a chuckle. She seated herself next to the girl and tried not to act too suspicious. "I'm thinking of enrolling at Baylor in the fall. Do you like it here?"

"I love it. This is my second year."

"Where are you from?"

"The Woodlands."

Bonnie looked confused. "Where's that?"

"North of Houston, between Spring and Conroe. What about you?"

"Los Angeles." Bonnie disliked telling untruths, but feigning a distant hometown promised to be the best way of eliciting information without requiring very much in the way of current knowledge.

"LA is so awesome!" the coed said. "I was there with my family three years ago, and we went to 'The Price Is Right'—back when Bob Barker was still the host. It must be nice to live near Hollywood and go to tapings whenever you feel like it, huh?"

"Sure. I guess so," Bonnie said. Not having the faintest idea what the girl meant, a change of subject was in order. "What's the Slick?"

"The Student Life Center—SLC. We call it the Slick, for short. Madison, the girl I was just talking to, has a boyfriend who works out over there in the weight room. It's included with the student activities fee."

Bonnie wrote that in the notebook, too.

"So, what would you major in at Baylor?" the coed asked her.

"Maybe English," Bonnie said. "I'm a writer—or at least that's what I hope to be someday. What's your course of instruction?"

"I'm majoring in Museum Studies."

"You want to work in a museum?"

"That's the general idea. But as an administrator, eventually."

Bonnie drew a dollar sign in her notebook and waited to fill in the blank. "How much does it cost to go to Baylor?"

"I'm not exactly sure. My parents pay the bills, you know. I think the annual tuition is somewhere around twenty-four thousand."

Bonnie nearly choked. "Twenty-four thousand dollars—a year?" She jotted down that startling figure. The last time she checked,

Baylor was six hundred dollars per year—and that included room and board, plus all of her miscellaneous fees.

"Well, like I say, my parents handle the money," the girl told her, "so don't quote me on that."

A few minutes later, Bonnie was about to leave when a pair of boys came toward the coed and wondered where "Maddy" was.

"She's at Jones Library," the girl said. The taller of the two young men, presumably Jason, thanked her and walked away. His friend, though, remained at the table. Indeed, he went around to the opposite side and seated himself directly across from the Museum Studies major. He glanced at Bonnie, too, and then proceeded to lay his head down on his knapsack.

"Sleepy, Ryan?" The coed's sarcasm was unmistakable.

"Beat. We did double reps on all of the leg stations." Ryan's voice was partially muffled by the cloth bag, which was Baylor green and gold in color. "Who's your friend?" he asked without raising his head for an answer.

The coed giggled. "Well, I don't know." She turned to the stranger. "What's your name?"

"Bonnie Ploughwright."

"Her name's Bonnie Ploughwright, and she's from Los Angeles."

"That's nice," the boy said. "Tell her I'm sorry to be such bad company."

"Ryan wants me to tell you that he's a total loser."

"I heard that!" Ryan looked up and smiled. "Hi, Bonnie Ploughwright. Sorry I'm so pooped."

"That's all right."

"How are you classified?" he asked with a yawn.

"Huh?"

"Are you a freshman, sophomore ... graduate assistant ... full professor?"

"Bonnie's nothing right now," the coed said. "She's thinking of coming to Baylor in the fall."

"Wow, you sure don't look like a high school kid to me."

He was smirking at her, but in a playful way, and Bonnie blushed. "No. I'll be a transfer student."

"Where from?"

She thought quickly and hoped for the best. "UCLA."

Ryan nodded his head. "Neuheisel's got that program headed on an upward curve," he said. "Just like he did at Colorado and Washington."

Bonnie could only shrug her shoulders and agree. "I suppose."

Suddenly, the boy was alert and on his feet. "Hey! How would you like for me to show you around the campus? I'm done with classes until 1:25." He was only about five foot ten, but that was a good four inches taller than Bonnie.

"Gosh, I don't know. Maybe. That's very nice of you to offer."

"Glad to do it." He grinned at the Museum Studies major, who just rolled her eyes and sighed.

Bonnie turned to her and apologized. "I never asked your name."

"Heather Whaley. I used to be his roommate's girlfriend."

"Michael still proclaims his undying love for you, by the way," Ryan said.

"Yeah, sure. Same here."

◆　　◆　　◆

Ryan Andriessen gave Bonnie an all-inclusive tour, guiding her to every point of interest east of Fifth Street. He even took her to the Baylor Ballpark, where they sat in the grandstands for a few minutes and shared a package of roasted corn nuts. Bonnie was very hungry by now and hoped that her stomach was not growling audibly. She could find something more substantial to eat whenever Ryan was through escorting her around the campus.

That was not to be. At five minutes before noon, the boy shocked her with a question that she considered to be rather fresh, particularly inasmuch as they had known each other for only about an hour and a half. "Would you like to come over to my apartment?" he asked. "I'll fix you some of my famous microwave pizza."

"Gee, I don't think that would be proper, do you?"

"Sure, why not?" he said. "Listen, I'll leave the door ajar if that will make you feel better. I've got to eat anyhow, and I'd be happy to nuke two boxes instead of one."

"Nuke?"

"Microwave. You know, zap it with radiation. Don't they have microwaves in California?"

"Oh, yes," she told him, "but I had never heard that verb before: 'nuke'."

"You've led a very sheltered life."

The rooms in Ryan's apartment were smallish, but there certainly were plenty of them—a kitchen, bathroom, and living room downstairs, plus two bedrooms and another bathroom upstairs. The first thing he did, upon unlocking the front door, was walk over to the coffee table, pick up a Hershey-sized device, and press one of its electronic buttons. When he did so, a movie screen came to life, with a man and a woman taking turns discussing the latest news about basketball and ice hockey.

"You don't mind if I obsess on 'SportsCenter,' do you? I like to keep up with what's happening." He strolled out of the room.

"No, that's fine." Bonnie sat on the threadbare sofa and wondered what was next. Surely Ryan would not become aggressive with her, for he appeared to be very polite, the perfect gentleman.

"Want to keep me company in here?" he shouted from the kitchen. "You don't seem to be much of a sports fan, so it's kind of selfish for me to push that on you."

"I'm not, but I don't mind if you watch it." Actually, Bonnie was finding it difficult to keep her eyes off the color images that flickered not fifteen feet away. Never had she seen anything quite like this machine. "How long have you had your ... screen?" she asked.

"The TV? Almost a year. Sorry it's not high-def." He had returned to the living room, carrying a package in each hand. "Do you want the supreme or the sausage and pepperoni?"

Bonnie looked at the pictures on them. "I'll just take the one you don't want."

He grinned at her. "You sure are easy to please." Something in the way he said it made the remark seem more like a compliment than a complaint.

She followed Ryan into the kitchen and then observed, with fascination, as he tore into the packages and placed their contents inside a breadbox. The instant he pressed a sequence of numbers, the breadbox's interior light came on, and the sound of a fan motor could be heard. "You want a Coke or DP to drink?" he asked.

"What's a DP?"

"Dr Pepper."

"Ah, of course." She gave it some thought. "Either one is fine with me."

Ryan shook his head. "Why am I not surprised?"

Bonnie seated herself in one of four chairs around the square table. Only about two minutes later—or so it seemed to her uneducated senses—Ryan opened the breadbox and rotated both products a half turn. After a couple minutes more, a bell dinged, signaling that the meal was ready to eat. Ryan placed a steaming-hot pizza pie in front of her on a paper-thin, cardboard plate and laid an opened tin can of Coca-Cola beside it. Leaning over, he sliced the pie into quarters for her. "Well, dig in."

Bonnie gingerly pawed at the noontime cuisine.

"You don't like it?" he asked.

"I ... I'm not sure. I haven't ever eaten this before."

"You've never had frozen pizza?"

"My family is very old-fashioned—traditional, you might say."

"What are you, a Quaker or something?"

"No. Nothing like that. It's just that my mother makes all of our meals from scratch."

Ryan laughed. "Well, sorry to disappoint you. I'm not very good at twirling pizza dough over my head."

Bonnie blew on the hot slice and took a bite. It was surprisingly delicious. "Say, this is wonderful," she said. "Really wonderful. What do you call it?"

"I don't know—DiGiorno, I think, or maybe it's Red Baron. I threw the packages away."

There were no dishes to wash when they finished eating, so that left Ryan with a half-hour before he had to depart for his next class. "Watch whatever program you want," he told her. "I'm going to check my email."

"This is fine," Bonnie said. She pretended to be captivated by a story about some athlete named Al Thornton.

"Are you a Clippers fan?"

"No. Not really."

"Baron Davis is one of their guards. He was a UCLA Bruin, so maybe you've heard of him."

"Probably so."

"And Brian Skinner went to Baylor. He's a power forward, but he doesn't get very many minutes."

Bonnie tried to appear interested in what Ryan was saying, but she must not have been very convincing because he walked over and offered her the electronic device. "Go ahead and turn on a soap opera if you'd rather. I'm not forcing you to be a sports fanatic like me."

She gazed at the marvelous instrument. "How does it work?" she asked. This was an awkward confession, but part of her mission was to learn about the future.

He was dumbstruck. "You don't know how to use a remote?"

"No. I'm sorry."

"Jeez, you really do come from an old-fashioned family."

"I told you so. I've had a very traditional upbringing."

Ryan sighed, amused but frustrated too. "I need to give you a crash course in modern technology." He sat down next to her on the sofa, so close that his left leg was pressed tightly against her right. He was holding the device in plain view, with one end pointed directly toward the movie screen. "Now, look. This arrow makes the channel number go higher, and this one makes it go lower. Simple. And these other arrows control the volume—louder and softer."

"I see."

"Want to try?" He gave her the device, and she cradled it with utmost care. When she touched the up button, the picture magically changed from basketball newsreels to a story about pre-season baseball. She recognized the national pastime with no trouble, but the players' uniforms certainly were strange— snugly fitting and more colorful than she remembered. Pants legs stretched all the way down to the shoe tops, so precious few stirrup stockings were in sight.

"You can also punch in a channel number and go straight to it."

She froze, paralyzed with fear.

"Go ahead. You won't hurt it."

"What do I do?"

"Just type in a number. Push sixty-nine if you want to see the news."

She pressed six, but before she could locate the nine, the channel had already changed.

"You need to be faster. Push six-nine, fast."

Bonnie pressed six, then nine, and the movie screen displayed a light-skinned Negro man walking in a nicely tailored suit.

"See? There's the President. That's the Fox News Channel."

"He's the President of the United States?"

Ryan smiled at her, suspecting some sort of a joke. "You don't know what the President of the United States looks like?"

"No. All we have is radios. We don't have any of ... these."

"Your family doesn't own a television set?"

"No."

"What do you do for entertainment?"

"We read a lot, and we go to the pictures. And, of course, we listen to the radio ... and gramophone records."

Ryan simply could not get over it. Life without television was almost unthinkable. "What's your favorite radio program?" he asked.

Bonnie was hesitant to reply, leery of the harm that a careless answer might bring. She decided to play it safe. "The 'Lux Radio Theatre,' I guess." That, she figured, was surely still on the air.

He snickered at the name. "Hmm, sounds like something you'd hear on NPR."

She grinned along with him, though unsure why. "What's NPR?" she asked.

"National Public Radio. It's a network."

Bonnie recollected many a Monday night at home, dialing the radio console to KRLD at eight o'clock. It was practically a family ritual. "No, 'Lux' is on the Columbia Broadcasting System," she told him.

When Ryan reached over to retrieve the electronic device, his left elbow happened to bump against her breast. It was accidental contact, of course, but Bonnie felt uncomfortable about the incident nonetheless. She leaned away, as casually as she could, in order not to embarrass him for something so inadvertent. Besides, she rather liked this Ryan Andriessen and did not wish to discourage him from becoming her friend.

"Here's a channel you might like," Ryan said. He called out the numbers as he pressed them. "Five. Eight." With that, the picture screen became a movie—one that Bonnie actually recalled having seen. It was an odd sensation. There in front of her, nine years into another century, were Constance Bennett and Roland Young. They looked youthful and fresh, oblivious to the passage of seven decades.

"This is Turner Classic Movies," he told her. "My roommate watches it all the time, so I should know. In fact, Michael and I have a running battle around here—TCM versus ESPN. I usually win because it's my TV." Ryan gathered up a pamphlet that lay atop the coffee table. "He even subscribes to a monthly guide." He handed the booklet to her, and she saw that its title was *Now Playing*. The cover photograph showed a woman and a man, each wearing sunglasses and posing in a convertible automobile. Bonnie turned the pages until she came to Friday, February 13.

"Be sure to subtract an hour," Ryan said. "All the listings are in Eastern Time."

Bonnie did so and felt her eyes becoming a little misty when they settled upon the current entry.

1:15 PM *Topper Takes a Trip* (1939) A glamorous ghost helps a henpecked husband save his wife from gold-digging friends. Cast: Constance Bennett, Roland Young, Billie Burke. Dir: Norman Z. McLeod. BW-80 mins, TV-G, CC

She had seen this very movie during her junior year of high school, on a date with Brantley Higgins. Remembering that particular Saturday night, now so appallingly distant from her, she suffered a pang of homesickness that threatened to bring her to tears. Worst of all, she could sense that Ryan was staring at her, as if concerned by the wave of emotion that invested her face. She looked away, swallowing hard.

"Are you all right?" he asked.

Bonnie bit her lip to keep from crying. "Oh, yes. I'm fine. Something just came over me. I'm being silly, that's all." She turned toward him with watering eyes. "You must think I'm a ninny."

He chuckled. "That depends. What's a ninny?"

"I don't know. Someone who acts foolishly, I suppose."

"You don't seem so foolish to me. A little eccentric, maybe, but there's nothing wrong with that. I think you're sort of nice, actually."

With the backs of both hands, she brushed the moisture from her eyes. "Thank you. That's swell of you to say." Bonnie glanced at her wristwatch—furtively, she thought.

But Ryan must have seen her do it. "How long will you be in Waco?" he asked.

"Just for a few more hours."

"Are your parents here with you?"

"No. They're in Dallas for the day, visiting relatives."

"Really? What part of town?"

"Uh ... Grand Prairie."

"I'm from Euless, out near DFW airport."

Bonnie smiled at her host and stood up. "Well, I'm sorry to take over your whole afternoon. You probably have more important things to do than be my nursemaid."

Ryan scribbled something on a slip of paper. "Here. Take this," he said.

"What is it?"

"My number, in case you want to get in touch with me."

"Oh. Thanks." She folded the paper and tucked it into her pants pocket.

"Where'd you park?" he asked. "I can give you a lift to your car on my way to class."

"I rode the train." This seemed to her a logical statement, but Ryan's reaction made it clear that she had let her guard down. Quickly, she tried to repair the damage. "I mean the Interurban."

"Is that Amtrak?"

She had a blank look. "I guess so."

"Well, you'll have to go to McGregor to catch it. Amtrak doesn't come through Waco."

That complicated matters. "Yes, I know," she told him. "A friend of mine brought me to Waco from there, and he's going to take me back to the passenger depot."

Ryan pressed a button on the channel-changing device, and the movie screen went dark. "Is he a boyfriend of yours?"

"A friend of the family. I hardly know him."

They went outside together, and Ryan turned around to lock the front door. "Any chance that I'll be seeing you again?" he asked.

"Probably not. I'll be far away from here, you know—at least until the fall."

He shook her hand. "Anyway, it was great meeting you, Bonnie. I hope you decide to come to Baylor."

"You've been very kind," she said. "And tell that girl thanks, too."

"Heather Whaley?"

"The one in the library."

"Will do," Ryan told her, "but I don't think she cares for me very much. My roommate dumped her a few months ago, and I think Heather blames me for it."

"Why?"

"Beats me. You know how girls are."

◆   ◆   ◆

Bonnie was determined to get a wider view of her new world than a collegiate campus could yield, but she had no practical way to expand those horizons without promptly running out of daylight hours. The municipal streetcars had long since been retired from service in Waco, and, as she was soon to learn, the local shuttle service barely reached beyond the protective domain of Baylor University.

An obliging student, with whom she spoke on the sidewalk beside Fourth Street, advised her to board what he described as the "Gold Route" bus, a transport that would carry her as far north as Robinson Tower. This she proceeded to do, but the culmination of her circuitous, fifteen-minute junket turned out to be a stop that stranded Bonnie well short of downtown. She could view the Amicable Life Insurance Building from there—and she even used it as her guidepost—but the skyscraper appeared to be much closer than it actually was. The more she walked, the farther away it seemed to recede.

Her ultimate destination was the corner of Fifth and Austin, which she knew to be the heart and soul of Waco. Department stores were in the vicinity, and movie houses, and restaurants, and centers of commerce such as banks and cotton brokers. She planned to parallel the Brazos River until she reached Bridge Avenue and the public square. Then, upon turning left at city hall and the police station, she was sure to be inundated by frenzied activity, a teeming citizenry energized by the promise of plentiful goods and services.

The problem was, Bonnie had only made it as far north as Webster, and that left seven or eight long blocks yet to go. She seriously considered hitchhiking, but the visionary automobiles—like something out of a Flash Gordon comic book—whizzed by so fast that she dared not hold out her thumb for fear of having it fractured by the onslaught of steel. A green and white street sign told her this broad thoroughfare, six lanes across, was named University Parks Drive. She kept that in mind, for it would be the key to finding her way back to campus, to Waco Hall, and home.

As she pressed onward, a suspicious figure loomed into her field of vision. Far down the roadway, scarcely discernible, was a shoddily dressed man who appeared to be coming toward her, trudging along in a southerly direction. While she felt reasonably secure from physical assault with so many vehicles passing by in the middle of the afternoon, still this solitary presence was sufficient cause for concern. The instant she spotted an opening in the traffic flow, Bonnie hastened across the boulevard, only to discover that the mysterious pedestrian had done likewise.

Now she was genuinely fearful. At her first opportunity, Jackson Street, she went west near the train tracks, hoping to avoid direct contact with the ominous stranger. This was a warehouse district—none too inviting—so she was anxious to hurry through as swiftly as possible. From behind her came the sound of an automobile, and it seemed to be approaching with every elapsed second. Bonnie glanced around and noticed that the vehicle had something affixed to its roof, but evidently it was neither a police car nor a taxicab, for the exterior paint was white in color instead of the customary black or yellow.

When the slowly moving vehicle finally overtook her, it angled toward the curb about twenty feet ahead and stopped. Only then did Bonnie see for certain what was emblazoned on the door. The word "POLICE" was printed in large, red letters, and just above that, in much smaller, black lettering, were the words "CITY OF WACO." Two men, attired in dark blue uniforms, sat inside, and one of them rolled down his window to speak to her.

"Can we give you a ride somewhere? This isn't the safest part of town." He was staid in bearing but accommodating, too. "You really shouldn't be walking here, all by yourself like this."

"Thank you, sir."

"Where are you headed?"

"Downtown."

"Whereabouts downtown?"

Bonnie thought for a moment, unsure how to answer. But then a familiar address came to mind. "Maybe 701 Washington. Is that all right?"

"Hop in. We'll be happy to drop you off," the man said. "We're going to the courthouse anyway, and that's just down the street from there."

She opened the back door of the car and sat down inside. Law-enforcement gadgetry was everywhere, and she could hear the constant murmur of wireless transmissions from a female dispatcher. After Bonnie slammed the door shut, the policeman who had greeted her earlier spoke again. "I'm Officer Quintero, and this is Officer Brody."

"Hello, miss," the driver said. He was a Negro, large of stature and powerfully built, but his eyes were gentle and reassuring. So bald was his head that it gleamed as if freshly waxed and polished.

"Buckle up, please," Officer Quintero told her. "We can't be riding around with an unrestrained passenger."

Bonnie seemed befuddled, so the driver added, "Click it or ticket." When the girl still failed to respond, Officer Brody gave his partner a questioning look, wondering whether their young acquaintance might be mentally impaired.

Patiently, Officer Quintero said, "Reach back and pull that metal part of the harness across yourself to the seat-belt buckle on your left. Insert it until it clicks." By trial and error, Bonnie did as she was told and eventually accomplished the task.

Once Officer Brody shifted into gear, his massive hands made maneuvering the patrol car a matter of child's play. Bonnie was impressed by the smooth ride of the vehicle and also by its stunning visibility. Never had she been in an automobile with such large windows surrounding her. The driver steered north onto Sixth Street, and the McLennan County Courthouse came into view. Despite the passage of so many decades, it looked more beautiful than ever.

Officer Quintero glanced at her over the seat back. "Are you a Baylor student?" he asked.

"Yes, sir."

"What brings you so far from campus on foot?"

"Historical research, mainly. I'm working on a project." Officer Quintero nodded his head and turned to face forward.

"What's so important at Seventh and Washington?" the driver asked. He sipped coffee from a paper cup.

"That's where the USO is ... or was. I think a relative of mine used to work there during the war."

Officer Quintero began searching for something in the glove compartment. He asked the passenger, "Are you studying history at Baylor?"

"No, sir—English." Bonnie saw little reason to shirk the truth entirely. "I'm writing a short story," she said, "but I need some historical background to fill in a few gaps."

Officer Brody put the coffee cup down while keeping his eyes on the road. "Getting information on the past, huh? Well, Waco's got a lot of history—that's for sure."

Bonnie flashed a knowing smile. "Yes, sir, it certainly does."

The patrol car pulled up to the curb at 701 Washington, and Officer Quintero said, "This is your stop, miss."

After pushing a button to release the safety harness, she tried to open the door but failed. "Is there a trick to getting out?" she asked.

"Just pull that silver lever towards you," Officer Brody told her. Bonnie did so, and, as promised, the door latch relinquished its hold. She stepped out and gazed at a pale reminder of what used to be. The three-story brick building was marginally recognizable, having retained some of its superficial properties, but all the life was gone.

"Do you have a way back to Baylor?" she heard the driver ask.

"I appreciate your concern—both of you," she said, "but I'll be all right on my own."

Officer Quintero was having none of that. "Miss, it's our job to protect the public. We can't just drive off and leave you here all alone. Do you have a mobile with you?"

"A what?"

"Is there anybody you could call—to come pick you up?"

She remembered the slip of paper. "Well, there is one person."

"I'll tell you what," Officer Quintero said. "We'll take you to the courthouse with us, and you can telephone from there."

"That's awfully kind of you, sir, but there are still some other things I need to see."

"Sorry, but we insist. It's just not very safe, hiking all the way to Baylor from here."

Bonnie shrugged her shoulders and climbed back into the car, buckling her seat belt. Officer Brody drove three blocks and parked in the sheriff's lot at Fifth and Columbus. When they entered the building, Bonnie had to walk through what the policemen described as a "metal detector." It was painless and uneventful, and the uniformed attendants were courteous.

Now inside the so-called "secure area," Officer Quintero departed upstairs for deposition of case testimony, so it became Officer Brody's sole responsibility to shepherd the Baylor girl. He led her to a drab room with eight mismatched desks, each of which had a female civilian repetitively typing information onto a movie screen. "Jennifer," he said to one of them, "this young lady needs to borrow your phone for a minute."

"Be my guest." The woman clerk smiled at Bonnie and turned the telephone toward her. It had buttons instead of a dial.

Bonnie unfolded her paper for the woman to see. "Do I push all of these numbers?" she asked.

"Yes, and you'll need to hit nine first, to get an outside line."

"Is there an operator to assist?"

The female clerk glanced at Officer Brody, who suggested a way to save further embarrassment for the girl. "Why don't you go ahead and punch in the telephone number for her?"

The clerk leaned forward and began pressing digits on the numeric pad. "Six-eight-two ... Is this a local call?"

"Must be a mobile phone," the officer said. Yawning, he flipped idly through a *Texas Monthly* that lay on the desk.

The woman keyed in a protracted sequence of numerals and then waited for a few seconds. "It's ringing," she said.

When the clerk gave her the telephone's handset, Bonnie held it up to the side of her head, just as she had seen the woman do. A moment later, she spoke into the mouthpiece. "Ryan?"

"Yes?"

"This is Bonnie Ploughwright. Do you remember me?"

"Bonnie? Sure, I do. I figured you'd be long gone by now."

"No. I'm at the McLennan County Courthouse."

"Are you in some kind of trouble?"

"I'm not in jail or anything, if that's what you mean." She grinned at the officer, who chuckled quietly. "I've been sightseeing around Waco, and this happened to be one of my stops."

"You must be pretty hard up for entertainment."

She brushed aside the comment. "Say, Ryan, I have a favor to ask. Would you be able to bring me back to campus? The police don't think it's very safe for me to be walking around this part of town."

There was a pause on the line, and she could hear noise that sounded to her like traffic. Finally, Ryan spoke up again. "Sorry, Bonnie, but no can do. I'm headed home for the weekend."

"What time do you leave?"

"I already did. I'm almost to Waxahachie."

Bonnie eyed the slip of paper again. "I thought I dialed your apartment."

"Nope, my cell phone," he told her. "I've been on the road for nearly an hour."

That was a staggering revelation. "You have a telephone in your car?" she asked.

"It goes wherever I do."

Bonnie said nothing. Although she had no concept of what a cell phone was, neither did she deem it wise to further demonstrate her ignorance of modern amenities. People might start to wonder about her, and that was the last thing she needed—especially with police and lawyers all around.

"I'll give Michael a call," Ryan said. "Maybe he can pick you up. Baylor will be a safer place to wait than downtown."

"Who's Michael?"

"Michael Tinsley—my roommate."

"Would you mind? I have no other way to get to campus."

Two brief telephone conversations later, Ryan arranged for Michael to meet Bonnie at the front entrance of the courthouse. They had never seen each other before, so descriptions were exchanged. He would be the one driving the red Nissan GT-R, and she would be the one wearing the pink cashmere sweater—with a winter coat draped over her arm.

◆　　◆　　◆

Michael Tinsley arrived twenty-five minutes after that, but he was not alone. Seated next to him in the futuristic automobile was a young lady whom Michael identified as his fiancée. Her name was Nicole Hulen, and she had blonde hair and enchanting brown eyes, though with a trifle more mascara than was necessary. So devoted to one another did the couple appear to be that a casual observer, failing to look closely enough at the ring finger of her left hand, might have been excused for assuming that they were already newlyweds. Nicole cooed whenever she said, "Mickey," which, as time would tell, was rather often.

The jaunt to Baylor was exhilarating, for this modern machine was well designed to take hairpin turns in stride, with its proud operator seldom pausing to acknowledge anything as irrelevant as a stop sign or traffic light. "A prototype was clocked at 193 on the test track," Michael told his captive audience, and Bonnie could see no reason to doubt it. For someone accustomed to a wartime speed limit of thirty-five, this dash from courthouse to campus was as breathtaking as a time-trial heat on the proving grounds. By now, Nicole was used to his driving skills, so she smiled lethargically but refrained from articulating her thoughts.

When the three of them entered the apartment, a silence set in that became awkward. Bonnie felt distinctly out of place, and Nicole was uncommunicative to the point of rudeness. Finally, just as an icebreaker, Michael said to the newcomer, "Ryan tells me you're planning to enroll at Baylor in the fall."

"Maybe. I'm down here to have a look at the campus."

"Are you from Dallas?"

Bonnie tried to keep her story straight. "No. My parents are there to see Dad's family. We live in California."

"You sound like a Texan to me," Nicole said. These were the first words she had spoken to Bonnie in the apartment, and they were not delivered with conspicuous warmth.

"Well, my parents are from Texas—both of them—so I guess that's where my accent came from."

"Hmm. Could be."

Michael stepped between them. "Ryan says you're taking the Amtrak to Dallas."

"Yes, I am. It leaves from McGregor."

A thought seemed to strike Michael from afar. "Hey, why don't you let me drive you to the depot? We can all go together. Nicole won't mind, and it'll give me a chance to put some highway miles on the car." He turned to his girlfriend, who responded eloquently with a chilly stare.

"That's very considerate of you," Bonnie told him, "but a friend is planning to take me there."

"When?"

"I'm not sure. Soon." Bonnie glanced from boy to girl, unsure that they believed her. He appeared to, but she did not.

"I'll check the website," Michael said. He walked over to a small table, on which sat a dormant movie screen that was only a couple of inches deep. He reached behind it and activated a button of some sort, bringing the screen to life.

"May I watch?" Bonnie asked. Michael was agreeable, so he pulled up another chair beside his own.

But that left Nicole to stand by herself on the other side of the living room, which was not agreeable to her. With a scowl, she picked up the channel-changing device and switched on the television. A black-and-white movie called *Here Comes Mr. Jordan* began airing. It was the 1941 film of a reincarnated pugilist, starring Robert Montgomery, Claude Rains, and Evelyn Keyes. Finding this to be of scant interest, Nicole tuned instead to an arbitrary commercial that advertised the most effective variety of bathroom tile cleaner. She pouted under the guise of making herself comfortable on the sofa.

Meanwhile, only twenty feet away, her fiancé was busy conducting an investigation for the visitor. He typed in the words "amtrak schedule" and clicked, and there appeared before him a blue screen, onto which he proceeded to type "mcgregor" and "dallas" inside little rectangles. The instant he chose the date, February 13, 2009, this remarkable machine provided an answer for them: #22 Texas Eagle = $13.00 / Departs McGregor, TX 11:51 AM / Arrives Dallas, TX 3:20 PM / Duration: 3 hr, 29 min.

"Good thing we checked," he told his observer. "Today's only northbound train was supposed to leave at 11:51 this morning—and not even Amtrak would be late enough for you to catch that."

Bonnie had to fabricate an alternate plan. "Then ... he can drive me up there in his car," she said. "He'll take me all the way to Dallas if I pay for the gasoline."

Michael smirked. "Sounds like your boyfriend owes you a mighty big favor for something."

The way he said it made her feel cheap. "What are you insinuating?" she asked.

"You know, 'services rendered'."

Bonnie stood up, offended by the bawdy innuendo. "First of all, I'm not that kind of girl. And secondly, he's not my boyfriend. He's just a friend of the family."

Michael's face flushed with embarrassment. "Okay, okay," he said. "I was only teasing. Really, I didn't mean anything by it."

He seemed sincere, so Bonnie accepted his apology at face value and sat back down. Ironically, the affront had more of an effect on Michael himself. Impressed by Bonnie's assertive spirit, he gazed upon her with new respect. He realized, as if for the first time, what an adorable girl she was, with lovely eyes, sparse make-up, and an appealing shapeliness that heaved with anger beneath the sweater.

Anxious to change the subject, Bonnie pointed toward the magical screen. "What do you call that thing?" she asked.

"My PC? Oh, it's an HP ... a Hewlett-Packard."

"That's a brand name?"

"Sure. Like Dell or Macintosh. You know, a computer."

"How does it work? I mean, what's it hooked up to?"

"Nothing. My computer's receiving a wireless signal from that router." He pointed to a small, flat box with two vertical posts.

"But where's the information coming from—McGregor?"

Michael laughed out loud. "The internet, of course, through a modem. You really don't know anything about this, do you?" He looked in wonder at the girl. How insulated from the world could one person possibly be?

Bonnie grinned sheepishly. "I'm afraid all of this science is beyond me."

"Didn't your California schools have computers?"

"I believe so, sure. Don't blame my ignorance on them."

Michael stared at her, and his expression was both affectionate and protective. "You remind me of something," he said.

"Oh, dear!"

"No, nothing bad. Actually, it's something very sweet and innocent." He paused, as if considering whether to proceed. "You remind me of a movie I saw called *Blast from the Past*. It was about a thirty-five-year-old guy who'd spent his entire life in a bomb shelter. Then he came up to the surface, and—*voilà!*—it was modern-day Los Angeles. To him, it was a brave new world."

She beamed with recognition. "Huxley!"

"Huh?"

"Aldous Huxley. He wrote the novel, *Brave New World*."

"I've heard of it."

"You need to read it sometime—it's really very good. That title comes from Shakespeare's *The Tempest*: 'How many goodly creatures are there here! How beauteous mankind is! O brave new world!'"

Michael was stunned. "Jeez, you sound like an English major."

"I want to become a writer, like Margaret Mitchell."

"Who?"

"*Gone With the Wind.*"

"I've watched it on TCM."

"Have you ever read the book?"

"No," he said.

"You should. The book has much more in it than the movie."

"Maybe so, but it takes a lot longer than three and a half hours to read the book."

Unbeknownst to the pair of them, Nicole had been eavesdropping on their verbal exchange for several minutes. There was something about this Bonnie Whatshername that she did not like. Glowering, Nicole gripped the sofa cushion so hard that she heard its frayed edge start to rip. Friday the thirteenth was becoming a miserable day after all, and it had begun so romantically, too—in her own apartment, in her own shower, in her own bed. Cold determination crept into Nicole's beautiful eyes, and she fumed in silence.

Adding insult to injury, the guest exhibited no sign of being ready to leave. In fact, she informed Michael that she did not have to meet her family friend until around dusk. They would drive up to Dallas after dark, probably stopping along the way for dinner. But for now, she seemed quite inquisitive about the technological marvels on display in this scientifically advanced apartment.

And Bonnie's interest was genuine. She was especially enthralled by a small gramophone, which was able to play eighty minutes of audio content from a shiny disk measuring only four and three quarters inches in diameter. Michael had a collection of music dating back to the Jazz Age of the 1920s, and all of it was stored inside these miniature records, rather than on the normal ten-inch 78s. He even had releases by some of Bonnie's favorite artists—people like Bing Crosby, Tommy Dorsey, the Andrews Sisters, Vera Lynn, and Harry James. They sounded better than ever on this particular gramophone, with not a single snap, pop, or swish to be heard. It was eerily authentic, almost like being in the front row of a nightclub.

Nicole suffered her boyfriend's gushing show-and-tell session with far more charity than might have been expected, given her proprietary nature. But that is not to say that Michael was committing his breach of trust with impunity. Nicole, as a future wife, was busy stockpiling mental pictures of her bridegroom's wayward attentiveness, for such times as she might wish to press them into service. Finally—between a Frank Sinatra song and one by Jo Stafford—she spoke right up, but in a deceptively cordial tone that placed her alleged betrayer squarely on the defensive.

"Mickey, don't forget that we still need to go to Walmart," she said.

"How come?"

Nicole let him fret for a few seconds before adding, "What is tomorrow, sweetheart?" She was all smiles.

"Saturday, the ..." Michael floundered momentarily but made a nice recovery. "Oh, Valentine's Day. Sorry, dear. I got caught up in the music." Then, sensing that the slightest hesitation could and would be used against him, he turned to Bonnie. "Listen. We're going to have to cut this short. I sort of promised Nicole that I'd take her on a shopping spree for Valen—"

"Because you forgot to buy me a gift ahead of time," Nicole said.

Michael shrugged his shoulders. "Guilty as charged."

Taking the hint, Bonnie stood up and reached for her winter coat, which she had laid on a chair. "That's perfectly fine. Anyway, I feel like a terrible intruder. You've been swell—both of you." She was looking directly at Michael when she said it. "Tell Ryan thanks, too, when you see him. I had nowhere else to go, and I appreciate the hospitality."

"Our pleasure," Michael told her. "We've enjoyed meeting you." He rose to his feet and smiled. "And we hope to see you again sometime. Don't we, honey?"

"Oh, sure," Nicole said.

Michael found himself gazing at Bonnie with something more than a passing regard. "Do you think you'll be enrolling at Baylor?" He asked this so quietly that it was just above a whisper.

"I wouldn't be surprised."

◆　　◆　　◆

Bonnie acquired her typewriter skills as an elective in the tenth grade, but never until now, her junior year of college, did she subject them to such a rigorous test. The time limit for her English assignment was already running dangerously close when she consented to work an afternoon shift at the USO for a war wife who was taken ill—a benevolent gesture that, however commendable, nonetheless placed completion of her short story in jeopardy.

Baylor University's winter quarter was scheduled to end on March 1, 1943, with the writing project coming due five days prior to that—on Wednesday, February 24. In the tight circumstances, the best Dr. Charles G. Smith was able to offer Bonnie was a special dispensation to submit the paper to his home that same night. No further extension could be granted, but Professor Smith was willing to accommodate her, insofar as bending the rules did not violate the stated deadline.

The clock showed 8:25 as Bonnie typed "THE END" at the bottom of page twenty-two. Donning her winter coat, she ran down the stairs to Eighth Street with manila folder in hand. Fortunately, her English teacher's house was near the campus. Dr. Smith and his wife, Cornelia, lived on the corner of Tenth and James, which was only about six short blocks away from Catherine Alexander Hall. The couple were listening to "Mr. District

Attorney" on the radio when Bonnie rang the doorbell, and she apologized profusely for disturbing their evening's enjoyment. Her mentor's warmhearted rejoinder, "Nonsense. I'm looking forward to reading your story, Miss Ploughwright," only flustered the girl, for she did not believe very strongly in its merits.

Her revised tale was a product of great haste, imbued with all of the concomitant shortcomings that implied. After she struggled in vain to retain some of her original pages intact, Bonnie finally surrendered to the inevitable and abandoned almost every vestige of that previous attempt, beginning anew from scratch. The resultant work of fiction, "A Tomorrow for Abigail," delineated the adventures of an Ivy League girl whose twin sister had died in a train mishap when the siblings were sixth-graders—a tragedy for which Amanda felt partially responsible. Prayerful entreaties gained her a miraculous access to newspaper and railway records of the distant future, which enabled Amanda to realize that her debilitating sense of guilt was, in fact, without foundation.

"I should probably warn you," Bonnie told her professor, "that my current story is not much at all like the rough draft you saw a couple of weeks ago."

"Oh? No symphony orchestra?"

She was pleased that he recalled. "No, sir. I'm afraid not. That other piece was falling flat, so I had to go an entirely different direction."

"Well, that's a shame. I thought it had real possibilities." He stroked his chin, pondering. "Still, you're the author."

"I hope you won't think it's too far-fetched."

"Did you write about what you know?"

"Actually, yes." She smiled at the irony. "Yes, I did."

"Then I'm sure it will be splendid."

A quarter-hour later, when Bonnie arrived back in the dormitory room, Julia Johnston was sitting at her desk, reading from a voluminous textbook. That, in itself, was not unusual. Despite her rough exterior and sometimes salty language, Julia was a serious student who invested considerable effort in the pursuit of respectable grades. What shocked Bonnie was the fact that her roommate was wearing nothing but a bath towel, heedlessly wrapped around her waist. Her breasts were bare.

Hearing the door click shut, Julia hurriedly covered herself with the towel. "Sorry," she said. "I just got out of the shower and remembered I hadn't finished reading chapter eleven."

Bonnie tried to act undisturbed by what she had seen. "That's all right. I shouldn't have barged in like that. I thought you heard the key."

"I probably did—but my mind was miles away."

"Psychology exam?"

"Tomorrow at eight." Julia looked at her book and turned the page. "We have a double date on Friday, by the way."

Bonnie's jaw dropped. "I beg your pardon."

"You and I are going out with a couple of Army boys on Friday night."

"Who says?"

"Now, don't fight me on this, Bon."

"What right do you have to—"

"The only way Greg would agree to accompany me was if his buddy, Luke, came along, too."

"He needs a chaperone?"

Julia giggled. "Hardly. No, Luke wouldn't be a chaperone. He'd be more of a—"

"A bodyguard?"

Again she laughed. "Maybe so—to protect Greg from me."

Bonnie rolled her eyes. "What makes you think I'd want to go out with this Luke person?"

"For one thing, he's very good looking—a Golden Gloves boxer from Wilkes-Barre, Pennsylvania."

"Oh, swell. A tough guy."

"No. He's very sensitive, as a matter of fact. That's why Greg wants to bring him along. Luke is kind of shy."

"I'll bet."

Julia picked up something from the desk. "Here's his picture. What do you think?"

Bonnie stared at a two-by-three-inch snapshot, and she could see at once that Julia was right. In fact, the soldier's face closely resembled that of matinée idol John Garfield. "He *is* rather handsome," Bonnie said. "Have you ever met him?"

"Not in person, no. But Greg speaks very highly of him. Luke comes from a religious background—Roman Catholic, I think."

"What's his last name?"

"Bortoletti. They're Italian."

"In other words, he's a hot-headed Italian prizefighter?"

Julia studied her roommate's face and sighed. "Well, then go ahead and lock yourself in the dorm, for all I care. I was only trying to give you a chance to have some fun. It's up to you."

"Thanks just the same, but I don't care for blind dates."

"It's not blind! You saw his picture."

Bonnie frowned but said nothing.

"A lovely girl like you—with your dynamite figure—should be in circulation more often," Julia added. "Don't hide your light under a bushel."

Bonnie looked askance at her. "Oh, I see. So, you're organizing this for my benefit."

"Not entirely. Like I told you, there's something in it for me, too. Greg won't come if he can't bring his pal along. And Luke has no reason to come if he doesn't have a date. Pretty simple, really."

"That's easy for you to say."

Julia glanced at the floor, smiling to herself. "Greg has wanted to become ... shall we say ... much better acquainted with me for a long time."

Bonnie was intrigued. "How do you know that?"

"I can tell by the way he shifts his weight whenever I reach into his pants pocket for the keys."

"That's disgusting. You don't miss a trick, do you?"

Julia grinned at the catty remark, making no effort to conceal her amusement.

"By the way," Bonnie said. "Jack Decker will be back from west Texas any day now. And that complicates matters."

"Does it? Why?"

"That should be pretty obvious. I think Jack happens to like me ... quite a lot."

"Pfff! Is that all?"

Bonnie glared. "What's that supposed to mean?"

"Captain Decker may have his wings, but he's no angel. He's bucking for a roll in the hay, just like the enlisted men."

"You don't know what you're talking about."

"Listen, I'm an expert on men. Get Jack into a dark corner, when there's no one else around, and watch what happens between you two."

"Who says I'd try to stop him?"

With a chuckle, Julia began walking toward the bathroom. "That's the attitude, Bon! Maybe there's some hope for you yet." She stopped, turning to face her roommate. "Just think of Friday as a practice date for the real thing. And, to spice up the evening, you can wear one of my slinkiest dresses."

◆   ◆   ◆

Never before had Bonnie seen Greg Furmin, but she had no trouble identifying him the moment she and Julia entered the movie house's lobby. Unmistakably, Greg was the corporal standing next to John Garfield. The likeness was uncanny. So closely did Luke Bortoletti's appearance mirror the famous actor's that Bonnie might have been excused for feeling as if she were at a Hollywood premiere. But facial similarity and physique were where the kinship ended. In the company of attractive young ladies, poor Luke's confidence deserted him, and he seemed incapable of vocalizing even the most basic of sentences.

Julia's attire did not help. She was wearing a strapless dress and a supportive brassiere that drew attention to her bosom like a searchlight on a moonless night. Even the Rivoli Theatre's middle-aged janitor, though happily married, nearly put a foot into his mop bucket when the girl bent down to retrieve the nickel she had fumbled. Bonnie's outfit was not as suggestive—she had refused her roommate's offer of a sinuous gown—but what red-blooded American male could resist the charms of that nicely contoured sweater over the innocence of a high-collared, frilly blouse?

Compared to the introverted Corporal Bortoletti, his slightly older and vastly more experienced buddy was cocksure and utterly composed. It may very well have been that prior inspection of Julia's curvaceous assets obviated the need for much imagination on his part.

"Ladies, this is my pal, Luke," Greg said. "And Lukie, this here is Julia, and that's her friend, Bonnie."

Bonnie forced a smile. "How do you do?"

In reply, Luke managed but a single syllable. "Hi."

"Julia says you're a boxer," Bonnie told him.

"Yeah."

"That must be very exciting."

"Yeah."

"Are you any good?"

"Yeah." He laughed, seemingly at his own lack of communicative skills.

Witnessing their stalled exchange of words, Greg rushed into the void. "Feel his bicep, Bonnie." When she hesitated, Greg told her, "Go ahead. He won't sock you."

Obediently, Bonnie reached forward and squeezed the arm that Luke flaunted in front of her. His flexed muscle, bulging within the wrist-length khaki sleeve, felt as solid as iron. "Ooh, I would hate to get into a fistfight with you," she said.

"Yeah."

Once inside the darkened cinema, Greg went to work without much preliminary fuss. His left arm went around both of Julia's bare shoulders initially, but that was nothing more than a flanking diversion. Soon his probing hand negotiated a tactical retreat, adopting an oblique motion to descend to her neckline and find temporary repose upon the folds of her loosely fitting bodice. This frisky interlude accomplished, he turned to kiss her right cheek, a cunning stratagem that opened the way for his right hand to venture beneath the dress and enfold the left cup of her satin-smooth undergarment. By all appearances, Julia did nothing to deter his intimacy, though in the dim lighting it would have been unfair to accuse her of outright encouragement, either. He had plenty of self-motivation.

As for the other couple, they were as sedate and attentive as movie critics at a sneak preview. One vacant seat separated Luke from his fellow soldier, so he took full advantage of the wooden armrest to his left. The other armrest he granted to the college student, should she choose to make use of it. *Seven Days' Leave* was showing, and the auditorium was nearly two thirds full—a decent turnstile count for any picture's final night on the Waco circuit. The stars of this screwball comedy were Victor Mature and Lucille Ball. Harold Peary ("The Great Gildersleeve") was in it, too, as were popular musicians Freddy Martin, Les Brown, Ginny Simms, Mapy Cortés, and Buddy Clark.

At one point during the film, Bonnie happened to look at the heated activity to her left, and she felt sick to her stomach. How could an intelligent girl like Julia permit this casual acquaintance to take such liberties with her body? Allowing it to occur in public only made the salacious behavior that much more degrading. And yet, despite her avowed revulsion, Bonnie remained transfixed—fascinated by a display of sexual exhibitionism only eight feet away—and she stared far longer than normal curiosity might justify. Then, as her eyes finally shifted from the scene of Corporal Furmin's lusty indulgence to the passivity of her own date, she was struck by a bleak sense of longing. Was Luke going to try nothing at all? If she could not even tempt a GI on the prowl, what did that say about her physical attributes? Not that she wanted to be groped by a perfect stranger, but it would have been rather pleasant to feel his hand in hers or his arm resting upon her shoulders.

As imperceptibly as possible, Bonnie straightened her back and thrust her chest forward, hoping that he might take notice, but Luke seemed more interested in the on-screen whirlwind romance of Johnny Grey and Terry Havalok-Allen than in true flesh and blood. With growing impatience, Bonnie decided that their mutual armrest was the logical meeting point. They were entitled to share it, and he would suspect nothing untoward if an incidental bumping occurred. She settled her left arm there and allowed her hand to fall open, palm up, across the theoretical dividing line. No response.

A muted disturbance was heard, and Bonnie gazed to the left, three seats beyond where her well-mannered airman was sitting. She could see that Julia's eyes were closed, her head leaning back against the top of the chair. Greg's free hand had strayed at will, on both sides of the Mason-Dixon line, and Julia was yielding herself completely to his touch—with an occasional quiet moan, perhaps, but presenting no resistance whatsoever.

Bonnie was stunned by this degenerate vision, which would stay with her forever. It burned its way into her memory—and not in an altogether repellent fashion. The flickering dimness of the setting endowed it with delicate nuance, rather like a sepia-toned daguerreotype or rotogravure. Indeed, were she honest enough to admit it to herself, Bonnie was, at this compromising moment, a bit jealous of her roommate. She envied Julia's freedom of expression, her boldness, her uninhibited sensuality. Bonnie felt certain that such a transcendent rite of passage would never, in her wildest dreams, happen to her, especially in a movie house with onlookers around. Simply put, she was not that sort of girl, and there was little likelihood of radically changing her personality at this stage of life. She accepted her repressive modesty as an outward manifestation of who she was, a product of her traditional upbringing. But that did not lessen the regret.

With a sigh of disappointment, Bonnie looked around the auditorium and discovered that more than half of the customers were either soldiers or their female companions. Most members of these dating pairs sat very close to one another, his arm cuddling her or her head leaning upon his shoulder. It was all very affectionate and steamy—not to mention demoralizing.

Was she the only young person there who was being treated like a pre-adolescent Girl Scout? Time was wasting, and *Seven Days' Leave* was only eighty-seven minutes long.

She steeled herself for action, as it was quite obvious that the corporal seated to her immediate left was waiting for her to make the first move. Glancing down, she noticed that there was only an inch or so of clearance between her hand and his government-issue trouser. That would be a good place to start. Taking careful aim, she rotated her wrist slightly, just enough to allow two fingers to accidentally brush across the khaki material and alight atop his right thigh. "Excuse me," Luke whispered. Hastily, his leg shifted away in the mistaken belief that he was the predator. Bonnie, who at this moment was sorely in need of vindication as a desirable female, felt as if she had been slapped in the face, and her eyes began welling up with tears. Infuriated, she leaned heavily upon the armrest to her right. She would show him—the AAF's only uniformed altar boy—that two could play this humiliating game of rejection.

It was then, while she was maneuvering as far away from Luke as was possible, short of actually vacating her seat, that the smutty high jinks between Corporal Greg Furmin and his frolicsome collaborator came to a premature, and presumably unsatisfying, climax. When a fiftyish lady sitting behind Julia loudly proclaimed that she had heard "just about enough" of the girl's ecstatic groans, an usher arrived to shine his flashlight in the general direction of the disheveled couple. If the lad was treated to a glimpse of Julia's nether regions, he remained professional enough to keep that gratification to himself. Whatever the case, the daring tryst was at an end. As with any interrupted dalliance, superheated passions cooled even more quickly than they flared, and recovery was unthinkable.

A wearisome hour later, while the two airmen and their dates were exiting with others through the Rivoli Theatre's lobby, Greg was surly to the point of contentiousness, and Julia found this to be hugely amusing. "What's wrong?" she asked with a sportive grin. "Didn't you enjoy the picture?"

"I'd like to knock out some of his teeth."

"Whose?"

"That pimply-faced usher—nosing around, acting like a brownshirt."

"How do you know he was pimply-faced? It was awfully dark in there."

"I could tell by his voice. Yeah, he was a high school kid all right. Too cowardly to put on a *real* uniform—hiding behind that flashlight of his."

Julia laughed aloud. "I think you enjoyed yourself well enough." She swatted him on the arm, and he smiled back at her.

Luke continued to be his tight-lipped self as the four of them walked along together, so Bonnie, too, turned to Greg. "Who was your favorite character?" she asked him.

"Mine?"

"Yes. Which character did you like the best?"

"I don't know," Greg said. "That dame, I guess. Why?"

Bonnie giggled. "And what was her name?"

"How should I know her name? What is this, 'Information Please'?"

"Oh, lay off, Bon!" Julia told her. "Greg didn't care to watch much of the picture, and you can blame me for that." She added with a sneer, "Maybe you should give your quiz to Luke instead. He seemed pretty observant."

Bonnie frowned but knew she had it coming. "Well, did you like the picture?" she asked her date.

And Luke said, "Yeah."

As the two couples ran to catch the last streetcar, Bonnie stared at the swishing motion of Julia's sultry skirt and felt another rush of jealousy. Some girls possessed an innate ability to drive men crazy, and this plucky roommate of hers, without question, was one of them—which, of course, presented an intriguing possibility for the person fortunate enough to share the same living quarters. Perhaps there was a secret list of fail-safe pointers that could be passed down from savant to neophyte. After all, education was more than just Psychology and English.

♦   ♦   ♦

John Tynes Decker breezed back into Bonnie's life on the last day of February. More to the point, he returned to Waco on Thursday, the twenty-fifth, but did not bother to contact her for an additional three days. That, at least, was how Bonnie saw it.

From Jack's perspective, the delay was unavoidable. As a junior officer in the midst of worldwide hostilities, he had very little control over where and when his next assignment would be. The week-long mission in isolated Pyote stretched to eleven days before his superiors finally released him and seventeen others from their special-duty course. Situated about 160 miles west of San Angelo, Pyote Army Air Field was known—for good reason—as "Rattlesnake Bomber Base," but it was considered to be fertile training ground for instruction in B-17 flight operations. Captain Jack Decker would soon be graduating to heavy bombers, a prospect that promised a higher pay grade, eventual deployment abroad, and, in all probability, instatement to combat status.

But those contingencies were yet to develop. Until his new orders came down, Jack was again in Waco, compelled to plunge into a daunting array of neglected matters at Blackland. On Sunday morning, he was finally able to disengage himself from Army responsibilities for a long enough spell to renew acquaintances with his pretty friend from Baylor. Even then, it was destined not to be at some exotic hideaway but in the unpropitious setting of a church service.

When Bonnie spotted him, Jack was walking toward the pew where she sat among a group of fellow coeds. Her first inclination was to upbraid him for the way he persisted in taking her for granted. To the best of Bonnie's recollection, Captain Decker had notified her that he would be out west for about six days—and now here it was, more than two weeks later, without so much as a peep during the interim. Yes, she would give him "what for" all right. However, at the sight of the officer's warm smile and nattily creased uniform, her resolve melted away. She surrendered to his forthright embrace and allowed herself to be kissed on the cheek—in full view of five awestruck Baylor girls, who no doubt fantasized that they were in his arms instead of Bonnie. It was 10:50, and the worship service was due to commence in five minutes.

"Sorry to drop in at the last second," he whispered to her. "Have you ever tried to find one person in a crowd as big as this?"

"How long have you been at it?"

"Ten or fifteen minutes. I must have missed you the first time I checked this section. Now I'm glad I tried again."

"So am I." Bonnie was smiling—but blushing, too.

"I figured you had to be here, being a good Baptist and all," Jack told her.

"I don't know how good I am, but you did get the Baptist part right."

"And the right church, as it turns out."

"I'm very impressed," she said. "Did you write down 'Columbus Avenue Baptist Church' in your little black book?"

"Actually, it's a great, thick tome." He was holding his forefinger and thumb about three inches apart.

The organ prelude was followed by a pair of congregational anthems, during the singing of which Bonnie and Jack shared the same hymnal. Although his self-described "unmusical" voice was barely audible, it pleased her to see that he was quite conversant with the words. Evidently, these two pieces, so familiar to Baptists, were also sung by their brethren in the Lutheran church. While ruminating on this hymnological issue, Bonnie suddenly noticed that she was not the only one whose eyes followed Jack's slightest movement. Sheila Griffin was gazing at the handsome officer, and that came as a distinct surprise. Sheila's boyfriend was in the sanctuary choir.

Pastor Hubbard Hoyt Hargrove's sermon topic that morning was "Man's Need of Redemption," and several points in it caused

Bonnie to feel the sharp sting of her conscience. Most distressing of all, she recalled her impure thoughts at the movie house, and now they came again to mind, though thankfully in a rather sanitized version, almost suitable for church. Much to her relief, Bonnie was able to dismiss this fleeting sense of guilt in short order. Temptation, she convinced herself, was a giant step away from actual sin.

When the service concluded, and the small assemblage of Alexander Hall girls stood up to leave—retrieving the coats, hats, and gloves that were piled neatly beside them—Sheila Griffin was the first to tell the officer goodbye: "Nice to see you, sir." With a flirtatious wink, she waited for Bonnie to make proper introductions.

"Sheila, I think Eddie is waving to you," Bonnie said. As Sheila turned toward the choir loft, Bonnie whisked Jack away.

"That was sort of inconsiderate, wasn't it?" he asked her.

"No. That Sheila's a pest—very childish—and she'll talk your ear off if you give her half a chance."

Outside the building, the couple trotted down the front steps, arm in arm. At a quarter past twelve, the temperature had climbed to a comfortable fifty-nine degrees, whereas it had been forty-six when the girls reported for Sunday school at 9:45.

"My car's parked in that lot across the street," Jack said. He gestured with a nod of his head.

Bonnie gaped at him. "You have your own car?"

"What's so strange about that?"

"It's not the Army's? It's actually yours?"

"Yes, the car belongs to me." He chuckled at her dazed expression. "To me and my wealthy financial partner, the bank. I bought it on time."

"You drove the car here from Indiana?"

"That's right. And it's in great shape—except, of course, for the tires." He glanced over his shoulder. "Say, will those girls assume that you have a ride back to Baylor?"

"Oh, sure. They know I'm in good hands. Don't worry about them."

Jack's automobile was a black 1940 Ford coupe, and it appeared to be newly washed—maybe for this very occasion.

"Gee, that's a beauty," Bonnie said as she came near.

Grinning with pride, Jack opened the passenger door for her, then slammed it with a satisfying *whump* once she was safely inside. Bonnie could see that the windshield had a "C" ration sticker, like that on her father's car, only this one represented a soldier on active duty instead of a dentist.

Jack took his place behind the wheel. "Hungry?" he asked. "I'll take you wherever you want to go—my treat."

"Famished!" Bonnie said. "All I've had is a bowl of oatmeal and half a grapefruit."

"Where are your friends going?"

"To the Chicken Shack, I'm sure. That's where we always go on Sundays."

"Well, it's up to you. Pick your poison."

"Anywhere but the Chicken Shack."

"Tired of it?"

"I'm just not in the mood to watch Sheila and the others drool over you while we eat."

The new Elite Café #2 stood on Waco's traffic circle, a busy confluence of no fewer than five separate roadways that carried a multitude of vehicles traveling between Austin and Dallas. Never before had Bonnie eaten at this second location, though she was not a stranger to the Colias brothers' venerable downtown facility on Austin Avenue. As she and Jack sat inside the restaurant with menus in hand, Bonnie sensed that something important was preying upon the officer's mind, but she elected not to press him on it until he felt good and ready.

She did not have to wait for long. Even before their salads arrived, Jack drew a deep breath and abruptly changed the subject from his old neighborhood's favorite soda fountains to a matter that, more than likely, would change his life forever. "I got word yesterday that I'll be relocating away from Waco— and rather soon, too."

"Overseas?" Bonnie asked.

"Yes, I can tell you that much."

"Flying?"

"Flight instruction, at least for starters. Then ... who can say? There's a certain amount of attrition involved, if you understand what I mean."

"Oh, dear."

"You know my trip to Pyote?"

"Yes."

He lowered his voice. "That was to give me a refresher course in heavy bombers—aircraft that I was familiar with before I was transferred here."

"You've flown them?"

"Lots. And it seems there's a demand for experience in that particular area now—advanced training, so to speak."

Bonnie turned away, catching sight of an OD-green Army bus as it made its way around part of the traffic circle and continued northward on the Dallas Highway. "When will this happen? How long will you be in Waco?"

"Only seven or eight days, I'm afraid. Not long enough to suit me."

She looked into his eyes and saw that he was referring to her. Bonnie could not speak. What should have been a beautifully fulfilling moment was instead tainted with the sadness of impending loss.

"I intend to write to you," Jack said. The girl's face remained somber, though, so he felt the need to add, "That is, if you don't mind. You *don't* mind, do you?"

A single teardrop fell from each eye, and Bonnie told him, "Of course I don't mind. And I promise to write to you, too."

After Bonnie made the obligatory telephone call back home, the rest of her afternoon with Jack became nothing but a blur. However much joy their burgeoning relationship yielded was overshadowed by the grim knowledge that these precious seconds of togetherness were ticking away. For some unaccountable reason, Bonnie was dead set against going to a movie, so they indulged in mouth-watering cones from Robertson's Ice Cream Company on North Eighteenth Street and then spent an hour strolling arm-in-arm around Baylor University, stopping once to sit quietly on a wooden swing that hung from a tree limb in Burleson Quadrangle. Later, they enjoyed springlike weather conditions amidst the natural beauty of Cameron Park. After a quick bite at the Roosevelt Coffee Shop—not much else was open for business so late on a Sunday afternoon—Jack drove Bonnie back to campus, where they whiled away the evening hours in the drawing room of her dormitory, listening to the console radio with several other couples. NBC's "Jack Benny" came on at six o'clock, and that was followed by the Blue Network's "Quiz Kids." Then, at seven, it was back to NBC for "The Edgar Bergen and Charlie McCarthy Show" and "One Man's Family."

When Army officer Jack Decker and English major Bonnie Ploughwright said their goodbyes at eight o'clock, they did so with a lingering kiss on the front steps of Alexander Hall. Sunset had come at 7:27, so there was plenty of welcome darkness to cast a poetic veil upon this special moment. They would see each other again in the near future, but, beyond that, the impersonal brutality of war had contrary plans for their lives.

♦　　♦　　♦

The comprehensive examination for Baylor's English 238 course, "Development of the English Novel to 1800," was administered to the upper-level students of Miss Mettie Azalee Rodgers in their regular classroom on the third floor of Pat Neff Hall. It was Thursday morning, March 4, and, for Bonnie, this represented her penultimate final for the winter quarter. Assistant Professor Rodgers hailed from Hico, Texas, in Hamilton County. She held a bachelor's degree from Baylor University and a master's degree from the University of Chicago.

About halfway through the two-hour test, Bonnie noticed that Miss Rodgers accepted a note from her graduate assistant, who marched grandly into the room as if on a vital mission. Miss Rodgers glared at him for disturbing the exam but nevertheless laid the mysterious communication on the edge of her desk. Out of a sense of impartiality for the class, she betrayed no hint as to the sealed envelope's designated recipient. Only when Bonnie completed the last essay and placed her bluebook in the teacher's wire basket did Miss Rodgers finally whisper to her, "I believe this is yours."

"Thank you, ma'am," Bonnie said. She exited the room without displaying any visible curiosity about the envelope's contents, but it was a foregone conclusion that the sender was Jack Decker. Who else would be so audacious as to disrupt a university's final examination for the deliverance of a confidential message? And yet, she forgave him for this indiscretion, keenly aware that an officer in service to his country—especially during a period of warfare—had very little time to call his own when it came to matters of the heart.

Once out of Professor Rodgers's purview, Bonnie stopped on the stairwell landing and tore open the paper flap. Frantically, she unfolded the note inside and allowed her eyes to scan directly to the bottom: "Love, Jack."

Just then, Gale Tunney, a boy in her English class, greeted Bonnie on the landing. He, too, was fresh from the exam. "Pretty grueling, huh?" he asked.

"Some of it," she told him. This was scarcely the proper moment to start a conversation.

"Did you write on Defoe, Richardson, or Fielding?"

"Samuel Richardson." She edged away from him, as politely as she dared without prolonging their discourse.

"I could have filled a whole bluebook on Jonathan Swift," the boy said. "How about you?"

"I suppose so."

Gale seemed to be waiting for Bonnie to elaborate, but instead she looked down at her wristwatch. So much for being polite.

"Well, I need to be running along," he told her. "See you next quarter."

"Sure. See you." She genuinely wanted to be friendlier to this nice fellow, but that was all but impossible with Jack's handwritten letter burning her fingertips.

When Gale departed, Bonnie thought she heard the footsteps of another approaching student, so she scampered down to the first floor, hoping to find some privacy there. But hectic administrative offices surrounded her on every side, and the area seemed to be even more chaotic than usual on this particular day. Worse yet, here came Virginia Flood, always ready to talk. With no decorous means of evasion, Bonnie made a beeline for the ladies' rest room. There she secured a stall, took her seat (fully clothed), and proceeded to read the message from Captain Jack Decker.

My dear Bonnie,

It is painful for me to tell you this, but I will be leaving Waco on Monday, the 8th instant. I'm sure you can appreciate that I have no choice in this reassignment. Otherwise, I would elect to remain at Blackland for the foreseeable future, sensing that I am doing some good at my present post. Still, I have complete confidence in the Army's decision and am convinced that I can better serve my country in the new capacity I mentioned to you a few days ago. I trust that you are doing well on your tests at BU and that you will consider meeting with me before I leave. I have something very important to ask you—no, not that!—but I feel it can best be done in person, rather than through a note like this one. Are you free for a while tomorrow morning (Friday) after your test? I think you told me that was your last exam and you would be finished by ten o'clock. This matter cannot wait, so I hope you are able to meet me in the Alexander lobby around eleven, and we'll go out for an early lunch. If you are not there by 11:30, I'll assume that you were unable to come. That would be understandable because this is awfully short notice from me, and you may be headed back to Dallas by then. In case I don't see you again before Monday, I have your mailing address and will be sure to write soon.

Love, Jack

The next morning, Bonnie was already sitting in the drawing room when Jack arrived at ten minutes before eleven. As he entered the bustling lobby from outside, a dozen or more coeds were scurrying by—going home after finals—and yet most of them saw this as a chance to take an admiring look at the Army captain. Bonnie greeted him by squeezing his hands, but they did not kiss each other in such an obtrusive campus setting as this. Without a word, he led her out the door and toward his automobile, which was parked curbside on Seventh Street, almost all the way to Speight. His countenance was less than cheerful.

"How was your exam?" he asked when both were in the Ford.

"Not too terribly bad."

"Did you pass?"

"Well, I would hope so." She grinned at him, and he smiled in return.

Jack began to reach for the ignition but instead leaned toward Bonnie, and they kissed. "Was this your last test?" he asked.

She nodded her head. "I'm finished for the winter. Spring classes start on Tuesday."

"When's registration?"

"It's supposed to be on Monday, but maybe I can get my advisement done this afternoon."

He started the car, pulled out from the curb, and turned left onto Speight. "So, I take it you're not going home over the long weekend."

"No. There's hardly time," she said. "But of course that isn't stopping lots of the girls."

After turning left at Fifth Street, Jack switched on the radio and tuned its dial to CBS's "Kate Smith Speaks." He seemed awfully quiet, distracted by worrisome thoughts. "Is the Purple Cow all right?" he asked. "I've got to be back on base in under an hour, so it has to be something pretty quick."

"Fine with me," Bonnie said. "I'm really not very hungry." Straight ahead, towering in the distance, stood the Amicable Life Insurance Building. Upon seeing the skyscraper now, her mind drifted to a day that was yet to come on the calendar—but already filed in her personal experience. She had taken a long hike up a future road called University Parks Drive when two policemen extricated her from a dangerous part of town. The image was a ghostly specter, and she promised herself never to leave the present again. For better or worse, this was her world.

As Jack and Bonnie neared the intersection of Eighth and Austin, the radio announcer proclaimed, "Rinso presents ...'Big Sister'," and there came the sound of four loud chimes. "Yes, there's the clock in Glens Falls town hall, telling us it's time for Rinso's story of 'Big Sister'."

Jack laughed. "Do you listen to that serial?"

"Only during the summer sometimes," Bonnie said. "My mother used to sweat bullets over whatever problems Ruth Evans was having."

"Is your mother still alive?"

"Oh, yes, very much so. Why do you ask?"

"You said she *used* to listen to 'Big Sister'."

"Well, now that the war's on, she works at North American Aviation, so she almost never gets a chance to hear that program anymore."

Jack parked his Ford in the first available spot at the curb along Austin Avenue, and then the two of them had to walk several doors east, back toward the restaurant. A roving cameraman stopped them momentarily and snapped the couple's picture—very romantic, arms around one another. Jack gave the photographer four bits and, in return, received a voucher, which the man loftily termed a "claim check."

The Purple Cow occupied corner space on the bottom floor of the Raleigh Hotel. It was too early for the restaurant's lunch clientele to have gathered in force, so Jack and Bonnie were able to seat themselves close to the front window. Across the street, they could see the Stratton-Stricker Furniture Company ("Furniture for Everybody") and, immediately to the right of it, the Greyhound Union Bus Terminal coffee shop. When the waitress brought their sandwiches—sliced turkey for him, deviled chicken for her—Jack appeared to be more interested in talking than eating. "I need to ask you something," he told Bonnie, "and I hope you'll take it the right way."

"My goodness. That sounds very ominous." She tried to smile, but her nerves would not allow it.

"I'll be leaving Blackland on Monday, you know—shipping out for good," he said. "And it's almost certain that I'll never be assigned here again."

Bonnie swallowed hard but did not interrupt.

"What I'm wondering is whether you'd be willing to ride along with me when I take the car down to Houston."

"Why Houston?"

"I've arranged to leave it with my uncle for the duration. He'll drive it for me occasionally, just to keep it in running condition."

"What about your father?"

"He lives nine hundred miles away. With this speed limit, that would mean a three-day trip, and I have to be back at the base by Sunday."

"What if I split the driving with you? Could we make it then?"

"I don't think my tires would last all the way to Indiana, and it's impossible to buy new ones these days—or even find retreads. I could always sell the car, but I'd hate to do that."

"So would I. It's a swell car." Bonnie bit into her sandwich and considered for a moment. "I'd have to sign out from my dorm for the weekend," she said while chewing. "I wasn't planning to leave during the break."

"Would your parents disapprove?"

"I'm sure they would—if I told them."

"Oh."

"For one thing, they'd be upset that I didn't come to see them. And, of course, they'd wonder ..." She hesitated, so he completed her thought.

"Where we spent the night together."

"That too, yes."

"How would you explain it to them?" Jack took a bite of the pickle spear that was on his sandwich plate.

"I don't know." She grinned. "I guess that depends on what you have in mind."

He laughed, careful not to let his eyes wander suggestively downward. "At thirty-five miles an hour, we could make it to my Uncle Foyle's in six or seven hours, even allowing for a meal stop. We'd leave here in the morning and stay overnight at his house."

"Is he married?"

"Oh, yes. My aunt's name is Kathleen, and they have two daughters. The older girl is married, and the younger one, Cindy, is a nurse in the military. I suppose she's still serving abroad, but I haven't heard lately."

"Is this the Decker side of the family?"

"Uh-huh. Foyle is my dad's brother."

Other customers had entered the Purple Cow by now, leaving only a couple of tables empty. Three NCOs from the Army recruiting unit arrived together. Their permanent duty station was the second floor of the Federal Building at Eighth and Franklin. Jack recognized Sergeant Robert Hodges and gave him a genial wave.

"How would we get back to Waco—bus or train?" Bonnie asked.

Jack smiled, obviously reveling in the moment. "It just so happens that I have some friends at Ellington Field, and I'm not above pulling rank when that's what the situation demands."

"I don't understand."

"There's a cargo shipment flying into Blackland on Sunday, and we're going to be on that plane."

Bonnie looked around the room. "Is this by the regulations?" she whispered. "I mean, can't you get into trouble for doing it?"

"No, I doubt it. A troop transport would be out of the question, but this is a cargo flight."

Her eyes widened, and she cleared her throat. "Gosh, I've never been on an airplane before."

Jack was shocked. "Never? You've never flown in your whole life?"

"Nope."

"Well, it's about time we changed that. You'll love it. In fact, you'll probably want to go up again, once we land."

"Won't someone ask why a woman is aboard?"

"I've thought of that. I plan to bring along an olive-brown overcoat for you to wear. No insignias, of course, so you won't be impersonating a WAC. They'll be making the Houston-to-Waco run anyway, so no one cares. Officers hitch rides left and right. It's just part of the game."

◆　　　◆　　　◆

Only once before had Bonnie ever been to Houston, and that was back when she was much too young to retain any memory of it. So now, everything was new to her, at least from the point where they exited US Route 77 at Cameron and headed southeasterly through such towns as Milano, Caldwell, Somerville, Brenham, Hempstead, Prairie View, and Waller. Texas weather had taken a nosedive in the wake of a significant cold front. The temperature was hovering at twenty-eight degrees, which—were it not for the automobile heater—would have felt decidedly frigid after the previous day's high of seventy-five.

Radio broadcasts accompanied Jack and Bonnie throughout their journey, but mainly in the role of background noise and little more. Weekend programming on all networks fell far short of the weekday standard: children's shows in the morning and a string of public service discussions in the afternoon. An exception was "The Blue Playhouse," which carried a nicely staged production about Jane Addams from 10:30 to 11:00. It was a shame that neither traveler had a passion for grand opera, for that day's matinée presentation from the stage of the Metropolitan featured Wilfrid Pelletier conducting Verdi's *Aïda*, with Zinka Milanov, Giovanni Martinelli, Bruna Castagna, Richard Bonelli, Norman Cordon, Lansing Hatfield, and John Dudley. Bonnie's laudable cultivation of serious music did not extend quite that far.

Foyle Decker and his wife, née Kathleen Creel, lived in a pleasant section of Houston called River Oaks, a community designed in the 1920s by developers William and Michael Hogg, who were sons of former Texas Governor Jim Hogg. When a 1940 Ford came driving up, Foyle stepped outside and onto the front porch, protected from the winter chill by his coat and gloves. Identifying Jack at the wheel, he motioned for him to continue around to the rear of the house. One half of the double garage had been cleared of accumulated belongings in expectation of the supplementary vehicle.

"Golly, I can see that my car will be well cared for," were the first words that Jack spoke to his uncle. "Private parking!"

They shook hands, and Foyle looked appreciatively at the soldier's lovely companion.

"Uncle Foyle," Jack said, "this is Bonnie Ploughwright, my friend from Baylor University."

"Baylor, huh? Well, I won't hold that against you."

Bonnie smiled. "Uh-oh."

"Uncle Foyle went to the University of Texas," Jack told her. "Or was it A&M College?"

"Hey, no cussing in front of the lady," the ex-Longhorn said. He ushered his visitors up the back steps and into the house, where Jack greeted Aunt Kathleen with a hug and introduced her to Bonnie. His aunt had been busy in the kitchen, and a savory aroma filled the air. Hefty balls of yeast dough were neatly arrayed on two cookie sheets, ready to be placed in the oven.

"What's that I smell, Kate?" Foyle asked.

"Two baked chickens and cornbread dressing. Does that sound okay?" Kathleen looked at her husband and then at the guests.

Jack inhaled deeply. "Mmm, yes, ma'am. It'll be nice to have some good home cooking for a change."

"Don't they feed you well, Jackie?" she asked.

"Can't complain, but they don't put much loving care into it. The officers' mess sure doesn't smell this good."

Foyle turned to his wife. "What's the sleeping arrangement going to be, then? As you can see, we have both sexes represented, so that poses a problem."

"Yes, dear, I know all about the birds and the bees. Bonnie can have Cindy's bed, and we'll let Jackie use the living room couch." She apologized, in advance, to her nephew. "It's really very comfy, and I'll bring down all the sheets and blankets you could ever want."

Jack smiled. "Fine with me, Auntie. I can think of a lot of things worse than spending the night on a plush sofa."

"Sorry about the imposition, Jack," his uncle said, "but there's just that one extra bed now. We've got a boarder in Nanette's old room."

Kathleen nodded her head. "Her name's Christine, and she's a real nice girl. Very patriotic, too—took a train all the way from Kansas for the war work."

"Chrissy's a burner at Brown Shipbuilding," Foyle added. "Keeps odd hours—shift work—and car pools down to Green's Bayou every day. She won't get here until sometime after midnight, and then it's straight upstairs to catch a little shut-eye before morning. You'll probably meet her at breakfast."

Kathleen laughed. "We warned her that our favorite nephew might show up at the table, so she won't be totally flabbergasted to see you."

Saturday dinner was very satisfying, but its bounteous portions had the residual effect of inducing sleepiness in the travelers, who were already rather weary from their long day on the road. Bonnie and Jack retired to the living room, where they sat next to each other on the sofa. The domestic scene was complemented by Foyle when he descended into his favorite easy chair and pored over the afternoon newspaper while smoking his pipe. Kathleen stayed in the kitchen, washing the dishes, a mundane chore in which she steadfastly refused to allow the visiting coed to participate. "I'll have none of that," the woman said. "No guest of ours is going to be treated like a common servant."

For the second time in less than a week, Bonnie declined an invitation to accompany Jack to the picture show. "I just don't care to, that's all," she told him. But she balked at verbalizing a plausible reason, which naturally made Jack wonder what she had against movies. He would just have to be curious, Bonnie decided, because she was not about to describe for him the recent lewdness of her roommate, in full view of anyone bold enough to stare at her through the dim lighting. Besides, a part of Bonnie remained a bit envious of Julia's libertine attitude, and that was something she could never acknowledge to any man, much less to herself.

The home's radio console was on, carrying a pair of Saturday night favorites—"The Adventures of Ellery Queen" and then "Abie's Irish Rose"—but no one was paying much attention. Indeed, by the time Kathleen joined the other three, Foyle had laid his pipe aside in the ashtray and was fast asleep, chin upon chest. Jack, Bonnie, and Kathleen devoted the balance of the evening to browsing through photograph albums, including one that contained a few snapshots of youthful Jackie Decker on the beach at Galveston.

"Is that Cindy in the two-piece swimsuit?" he asked. His aunt assured him that it was. The girl could not have been more than eleven years old at the time.

Jack giggled at the photo. "Has she been home on leave?"

"Not since July, before she went overseas. We're beginning to think we won't see her again until after the war. She writes pretty often, though, so we almost feel like she's been here."

When the entryway's grandfather clock struck nine, the loud bongs stirred Foyle from his slumber, and Kathleen chided him for being such an ungracious host. "Poppycock," he said. "Looking at those pictures would have put me to sleep anyhow, so what's the difference?" He picked up the pipe and tobacco pouch, changed his mind, and laid them back down on the end table. "What time do you have to leave tomorrow, Jack? I'm an early riser, so whatever you say is fine with me."

"We need to report to Ellington around 8:30, so if someone could give me a nudge at 6:30, I think that should be about right."

"Okay. I'll wake you, and your aunt can make sure Bonnie's up on time." Foyle yawned and climbed stiffly to his feet. "It'll be a good excuse not to go to Sunday school."

Kathleen glowered at her husband. "Honey! Don't talk like that. Jackie and his girlfriend might think you're serious."

Foyle ignored her. "Say, Jack, my plan is to take you to the air field in your own car, rather than ours, if you don't mind. That way, I can get used to driving it."

"Fine. It's yours for the duration. Eventually you'll need to get that 'C' sticker replaced, but not until you go to the filling station next."

"Shouldn't be too hard to get an 'A,' huh?"

"Just a formality."

Bonnie had trouble falling asleep that night, but she could not blame her bout with insomnia on the unfamiliar bed. There were simply too many thoughts flashing through her consciousness, among them the heady anticipation of her first ride in an airplane. Then, too, there was the unsettling knowledge that the handsome officer lay downstairs, having cheerfully consented to surrender the bed to her, while he himself made do with a sleeping surface that was four inches shy of his six-foot-two frame. Never before had they slept under the same roof, and this awareness brought a warm wave of pleasure to her mind and body. She gazed toward the open door and, envisioning the shortest route, calculated that he was less than twenty seconds away.

As for Jack, he experienced no such wakefulness whatsoever, at least initially. His eyes were tired from driving, and it felt wonderful to close them the very moment his head touched the pillow. He fell into a deep sleep almost at once, and the insistent touch of a hand upon his shoulder did not awaken him until he began to wonder whether it was already time to get up. He forced himself to open his eyes, but it was still dark, and he could not see who was there—apparently a young woman kneeling beside the sofa. "Bonnie!" he thought. The hand gently took his own and, as if in a dream, drew it over to her bosom, even pulling up the nightgown to allow him to fondle the rounded breasts. Provocatively nestled between them was some sort of pendant or locket, suspended from a thin chain, and that added to the sensual allure. But the girl had other ideas for him, and, very deliberately, she guided his hand downward. That was when her other hand slipped beneath his white cotton boxer shorts, where it remained active until, at length, she emitted a soft moan, and her legs pressed together so tightly that he was compelled to curtail the caressing motion of his fingers. Shuddering, she arched her back and peacefully moaned once again, this time muffling the sound by covering her mouth with the wadded material of her nightgown. She leaned over, kissed him on the forehead, stood while permitting the diaphanous gown to fall to ankle length, and disappeared up the stairs, just as silently as she came.

◆ ◆ ◆

The sun had not yet risen when Bonnie made her way to the kitchen, but Jack's uncle and aunt were already sitting at the breakfast table, one across from the other, enjoying their cups of black coffee as they read the Sunday morning *Houston Post*. Foyle laughed to himself over the color funnies, and his wife enumerated aloud the wedding parties of the previous day's nuptials—no matter that she was a personal acquaintance of none of the principals involved.

Foyle was facing the doorway at the time, so it was he who first spotted Bonnie. "Good morning, Miss Ploughwright," he said. "Did you sleep well?" He removed his eyeglasses and began to clean them with a napkin.

"Oh, yes, sir. Just fine, thanks." She smiled at him and his wife.

Kathleen leaned over to pour some more coffee into Foyle's cup. "Was the bed all right, dear?" she asked their guest.

"Yes, ma'am. It was very comfortable. The only problem I had was worrying about that airplane ride."

"Kate here has never been on a plane, either," Foyle said, "so that places you in illustrious company."

"I don't know if I'm more scared or excited," Bonnie told him. "But Jack seems to think I'll do fine—once we're up in the air, that is."

Foyle put his eyeglasses back on and returned to the comics. "Sure you will. No question about it."

"I'm afraid poor Jackie will have a stiff back or crick in his neck this morning," Kathleen said. "I didn't think about him being too tall for the couch." She motioned for Bonnie to sit down and began preparing a plate for her.

Breakfast may not have been very original—eggs, bacon, and toast—but careful thought had gone into stretching these commodities for maximum nutritional and economical benefit. Two meager strips of bacon were allotted to each diner, the eggs were an amalgam of powdered and authentic, and the toast was spread with white oleomargarine, which had acquired a more appetizing color through the expedient of mixing in a capsule of yellow dye. Unlike her host family, Bonnie was not an enthusiastic coffee drinker, so she opted for a glass of refrigerated tomato juice instead.

"Well, good *afternoon*, sleepyhead," Kathleen said to Jack when the captain made his belated appearance. Actually, the time was only 7:10, and sunrise would not be for another forty minutes.

He grinned. "Good *morning*, Auntie. Good morning, Uncle Foyle."

"Hello, son," came the man's response.

Kathleen placed two slices of bread in the toaster. "I hope there was enough hot water for your shower."

"Plenty, thanks." Jack contrived a smile for Bonnie, too, though he was not sure how she would act toward him after what had transpired.

"Sorry I was a little behind schedule in shaking you awake," Foyle told him, "but I overslept by fifteen minutes. Usually I'm up like clockwork, and I never even have to set an alarm."

"That's okay, sir. I can shave later on." He sniffed the kitchen aromas and said to his aunt, "I thought I'd better get in here before everything was gone."

Kathleen walked over to the stove. "No danger of that." She spooned some scrambled eggs onto his plate and used tongs to secure two strips of bacon.

"Kate was concerned about your physical condition this morning," Foyle said.

Taken aback by the comment, Jack pretended to scan the headlines. "My condition?"

"You know. Having to sleep on a couch that was not quite long enough for you."

"Oh." Jack sighed with relief. "No, it was swell. I slept fine, for the most part." He glanced at Bonnie, who was spreading orange marmalade on her "buttered" toast.

"Have a seat, Jackie," his aunt said. "Take that chair at the end, next to Bonnie's. Are eggs and bacon all right?"

"Yes, ma'am. I'm not a big eater in the morning." Jack pulled out the chair and sat down, but he did not speak to the girl or even make eye contact. He felt terribly self-conscious—though, in all honesty, he would not have traded the experience for anything in the world. Occasionally, whenever Bonnie happened to be looking elsewhere, he stole a peek at her well-endowed bustline, marveling at the way it pressed against the confining fabric of the starched blouse. She really was a beautiful young woman, and he wished that he had met her much sooner.

A toilet flushed upstairs, and Kathleen—keenly attuned to household noises—told her husband, "That sounds like

Mrs. McCallister is up. Goodness! I guess she's scheduled to work the day shift." She hurried over to the cupboard and retrieved another clean plate.

"Who's Mrs. McCallister?" Jack asked.

"She's a war worker," Foyle said. "I thought we mentioned her to you."

"I don't think so."

"Yes, I'm sure we did, dear," Kathleen told him. "Christine McCallister—our boarder. She works at a shipyard."

"We call her Chrissy," Foyle added.

"Oh, Chrissy—yes. I didn't know what her last name was, and 'Mrs. McCallister' didn't ring a bell."

His aunt chuckled. "That does make her sound rather ancient, doesn't it? And I think she's all of twenty-two. Her husband is in the Marines." Kathleen returned to the stove, placing two more strips of bacon into the hot frying pan. They began to sizzle at once.

"Where does your older daughter live, Mr. Decker?" Bonnie asked.

"Nanette and her husband are over in Nacogdoches now. They moved there from Shreveport back in November."

Kathleen shook her head. "October twenty-eighth, honey, the day before my birthday."

"So they're not too far away, then," Bonnie said.

Foyle's face was beaming. "No, thank God. Which means we get to see our swell grandson and sweet granddaughter several times a year."

Jack, who had just taken a bite of toast, said, "And spoil them."

His uncle grinned at him. "Well, naturally we spoil them. That's what grandparents are supposed to do, aren't they?"

When the boarder, Mrs. Christine McCallister, finally strolled into the kitchen, she gave the others a friendly nod and went directly to her accustomed spot at the table. She looked a little older than Bonnie expected, and quite attractive, too. The men at Brown Shipbuilding no doubt gave her the once-over and then some.

Dispensing with social graces for the time being, Kathleen hurriedly laid the young woman's breakfast in front of her. Introductions could wait for later, but war industries were always on the clock. "If you need to be at the plant by eight, you're going to have to race."

"No, ma'am. Not due until four. This is my relaxing day." Chrissy blew a stream of breath on the scalding coffee and attempted to take a sip.

"So, it's a good weekend for you," Foyle said.

"The second half of it is—yes, sir. Two swing shifts in a row give me sixteen straight hours off. But I'll pay for it tomorrow, believe you me."

Positioned at the end of the table, Jack was just an arm's length away from either of the two girls, who were seated directly across from each other. From this unique vantage point, it seemed clear to him that these young ladies, while separated in age by scarcely a year, were nonetheless worlds apart when it came to maturity and confidence. That stood to reason, of course, because Chrissy was married, a member of the great American labor force, and a woman of independent means for the duration of the war. Bonnie, on the other hand, had only recently moved away from home, and even then she continued to be shielded from harsh reality by her dormitory mother and other appointed officials, whose unwritten mandate was to act in the capacity of surrogate parents. Now that Jack thought of it, maybe this was the very trait—her endearing quality of girlhood innocence—that attracted him to Bonnie in the first place. But how, then, was he to reconcile the accomplished prowess of her intimacy when she awakened him in the dark? Was there a more experienced side to this girl, a compulsive sexuality that she could not always restrain?

His eyes wandered to the boarder, who was not as pretty as Bonnie in the face, but whose sublime body would stir any male's imagination. She wore a stylish, light green blouse that dipped at the neckline, and wavy, brown hair cascaded halfway down her back. Chrissy's eyes were green, superficially like the blouse but of a much deeper hue. Her fingers were long and slender, with a wedding ring that shimmered as only a fine gemstone can do. If anything, her bust was even more pronounced than Bonnie's, and the blouse's décolletage offered him the tantalizing glimpse of a lacy, black brassiere. He could also see the uppermost stretches of a thin chain, the strands of which curved together at the base of her neck and then plunged from view into the cleavage below. The chain ...

Suddenly, his stare became more intent, and he turned away, stunned in disbelief. Betraying no outward emotion, Jack laid down his fork and reached for the cup of coffee. He needed time to think, but this was hardly the place. Holding the cup to his lips as a form of cover, he glanced back at the boarder, only to see that Chrissy was gazing straight at him. She did not smile, but neither did she avert her eyes in guilt or shame.

"Foyle, dear," Kathleen said, "those blackbirds are going to eat up your garden unless you do something about them." In the dawn's light, three dozen or more starlings could be seen through the window. They were pecking at a patch of furrowed soil, over which Foyle had scattered handfuls of seed earlier in the week.

"They're perfectly welcome to the gleanings, Kate. I tilled that square section, over there by the shed, and whatever happens to take root will survive. I'm a lot more concerned about the planted rows."

Kathleen turned toward Jack and Bonnie. "You really should let me show you our victory garden. It got us through the winter, and now the spring crops are in the ground."

Foyle scoffed at that notion. "Oh, come now—*crops*! You make it sound like we're operating a farm instead of a two-bit plot of bird feed."

"Well, it's a sixth of an acre, isn't it? That's a *small* farm."

"Whatever you say, dear." He winked at his nephew.

"Bonnie, do you want to see it?" Kathleen asked.

The girl gave Jack a questioning look. "Do we have time?"

"You go ahead. I haven't shaved yet." He consulted his wristwatch. "We need to leave in twenty minutes or so."

"Oh, that's too bad," his aunt said, "but I understand. The Army waits for no man, right?"

The officer smiled at her. "From general down to private."

There was a coat rack near the back door. Kathleen rushed over to it and slipped an old jacket over her housedress. Out the door she went—to a fluttering frenzy of startled birds—while her husband and the Baylor coed trailed obediently behind. "Here. Put on one of my ragtag coats," Foyle said. "It feels like Siberia out there."

"Thank you." Bonnie bundled the oversized garment around herself and waited for him to do likewise.

"Don't expect too much," Foyle told her as he opened the door. "Sometimes Kate blows things a little out of proportion."

Jack expended little time in evading the boarder. He mumbled a curt goodbye and hurried upstairs to shave. Less than ten minutes later, stripped to his undershirt, he was using a washcloth to wipe away the excess lather when someone knocked on the door. The water was still running, so he took a deep breath and shouted, "Come in, Mrs. McCallister."

She stepped inside the bathroom, looking a bit surprised. "You knew it was me."

"Well, everyone else is outside." He walked over to the window and gazed down at the back yard. "They're still doing a tour of the 'farm'."

Chrissy took a couple of steps toward him and stopped. "I want to apologize," she said. Her voice began faltering. "And also ... to thank you."

Jack stared directly at her. He nodded slightly but said nothing.

"You see, my husband, Glen, is in the Marines. We were only married for five months before he was posted overseas."

"So?"

She advanced closer to him, and tears were welling up in her eyes. "So, I miss him terribly. I'm lonesome for male companionship, and he's not around—may not be around for years to come ... maybe never again."

"I don't see what that has to do with me. Millions of war wives are in your situation, and they don't go around crawling into strangers' beds."

"But you don't seem like a stranger to me, Captain Decker. Your uncle and aunt talk about you all the time. They talk about you whenever we're eating or just sitting in the living room with the radio on. The person they describe is someone I admire and respect—someone I'd like to know ... and love."

"Until Glen comes marching home."

"Yes, that's right. Believe it or not, I am a one-man woman, though I'm sure you'd point out that I have an awfully funny way of showing it."

Jack tossed his washcloth onto the countertop. "To be perfectly honest, I can't say that I tried to fight you off last night. The blackout curtains were up, and I just assumed it was Bonnie, the girl who rode down here to Houston with me."

"She's lovely. I'm surprised you couldn't tell us apart, even in the dark."

"We've never been together like that."

"How long have you known each other?"

"A little more than five weeks."

Chrissy blushed. "Glen and I got right down to business. He was on two weeks' leave, and we spent our third date in a hotel room with a bottle of champagne on ice. We were engaged the very next day and married before he went back to Parris Island. I'd recommend that you and Bonnie climb between the sheets. There's a war on, and you never know what the future holds. Don't wait until it's too late."

"That's probably good advice, but our time has already run out. We fly back to Waco today, and I ship out tomorrow."

"Can you spend the night together?"

"She's not that kind of girl."

"Bad luck."

Jack walked over to look out the window again, studied the three of them below for a few seconds, and then returned to Chrissy. "There's one thing I don't understand. You came in here to apologize, but then you thanked me. Why did you do that?"

She thought for a moment, struggling to find the right words. "I'm twenty-two now, and I have the physical needs of a young woman. Worst of all, I'm married, so I've tasted what it's like to have sex whenever we want—you know, without having to sneak around or do it in the back seat of someone's car."

He nodded with a smile.

"Anyway, the Deckers had shown me several pictures of you, and I liked what I saw very much, so I decided to take a chance. I sure didn't know that you'd have a girlfriend with you."

"Neither did I—until two days ago."

"To sum it up, I was sort of hot to trot, I guess. And you were my victim."

"Hardly that. You could probably tell that my reaction was favorable."

She giggled. "Mmm. Yes, that was kind of obvious."

"Tell me the truth. Were you thinking of your husband when you were with me?"

Chrissy gave a sheepish grin. "I'll plead the Fifth on that."

"Fair enough," Jack said. "I was thinking of Bonnie."

Abruptly, her smile vanished, and she became rather pensive again. "Captain Decker, I want to formally ask your forgiveness for what I've done to you. I put you in an unfair position, and I'm sorry."

"You were just being human."

"But I didn't get your consent beforehand."

"All right, then. Please consider yourself forgiven." Jack put his government-issue shirt back on and started to button it. "Listen, Chrissy. Your body's a real knockout—from head to toe— and I'd be lying if I told you I didn't savor every second of our little escapade."

"Even though you thought it was your sweet, innocent girlfriend?"

"Especially so," he said. "In a way, last night just showed me what I've been missing all along."

"Too late for you and Bonnie?"

"I'm afraid so—unless, of course, I happen to make it through this war, and she and I ever cross paths again and become serious."

They heard a sound from downstairs, so Chrissy ran forward and kissed Jack on the cheek. Then, with tears in her eyes, she mouthed the words, "Thank you," and left the room.

Jack sat on the edge of the bathtub, and it was all he could do to keep from shedding a tear himself. He did not know why he felt that way. Was it something Chrissy had said? Was it the war? Or was it regret for the lost years of his youth, which he had misspent on inconsequential things that did not include nubile girls? Was it the numbing realization that he might never come to know these sensual delights, having squandered the opportunity when he was young enough to pursue them with abandon, no strings attached?

Most of all, he wished it had been Bonnie who approached him in the night.

◆   ◆   ◆

As the crow flies, Ellington Field lay about twenty miles southeast of Houston's River Oaks district, on the Galveston Road between Deer Park and Friendswood. Although Uncle Foyle had offered to chauffeur Jack Decker and his girlfriend there in the officer's car, Jack nixed the idea, explaining that they would need to check in with military police before passing through the main gate, so having a private citizen as the driver would only slow them down. The real reason was that it gave him a valid excuse to take his beloved Ford for one final spin.

The instant they pulled up to the guard booth at Ellington, two MPs snapped to attention, saluted Captain Decker, and, upon request, provided him with directions to the cargo depot. Jack also asked that they telephone ahead to Staff Sergeant

Kuykendall, and one of them did so without delay, in turn receiving confirmation that all was in readiness for the flight. The other noncom peered into the vehicle and gave a slight smile to Bonnie, who sat nervously in the back seat. She was mightily impressed by the tact and professionalism of these guards, and it made her proud of Jack to see him treated with so much deference. As the car slowly pulled away from the gate, she felt like the pampered wife of a four-star general.

They rounded a curve leading to the central cargo hangar, and Jack could see at once that a Douglas C-47B stood primed and waiting. This was to be the aircraft that would transport them to the landing strip at Blackland. To Bonnie's unschooled eyes, the Skytrain seemed positively immense, and she craned her neck to get a better view. It stood 17 feet tall, stretched almost 64 feet in length, and had a wingspan of 95½ feet. The C-47 differed from its civilian cousin, the workhorse DC-3, in being fitted with a cargo door and a structurally reinforced floor.

Sergeant Kuykendall was there to receive them when the car came to a stop. Jack climbed out, and Kuykendall stepped forward and saluted. "Good morning, sir," he said.

"Good morning, sergeant." Jack returned the salute but then relaxed. "How's life been treating you, Rudy?"

"Oh, I've got the world by its tail, Jack. You know me."

Jack laughed. "You always did land on your feet."

Bonnie had gotten out of the car, too, and she walked over to the officer.

"Saaaaay, you're not doing too badly yourself," Kuykendall said when he saw her.

"Put your eyes back in their sockets, Lothario. She's already spoken for."

Kuykendall's jaw dropped, as if in shock. "Jackie boy! You don't mean ..."

"No, no. Nothing as drastic as that."

"I just thought that maybe ..."

"Don't think, Rudy. It can only get you into trouble—as you well know."

"You have a long and cruel memory, captain." He stared admiringly at Bonnie. "Well, aren't you going to introduce us?"

Jack complied. "Rudy, I'd like for you to meet Miss Bonnie Ploughwright. And Bonnie, this is Rudolph Kuykendall, an old friend who's helped me locate some badly needed supplies—liquid and otherwise—on more than one occasion."

"I'm also his travel agent," the sergeant added.

Bonnie glanced at the airplane. "So I gather."

Kuykendall took a step back, and his eyes lingered upon the girl. "Gosh, you would make one lulu of a WAC," he said with a roguish grin. He was right. Bonnie looked fetching in the olive-brown overcoat that Jack had borrowed from a BAAF quartermaster.

All this while, Foyle Decker remained in the car, though by now he was sitting behind the steering wheel, patiently waiting. Jack shouted to him, "Hey, Uncle, come here and meet an old friend of mine." Foyle opened the car door and ambled over to the others, a little grim-faced out of reverence for the uniforms.

Jack turned to the sergeant. "Rudy," he said, "this is my dad's brother, Foyle Decker,. He lives here in Houston, and I've asked him to baby-sit while I'm gone."

Kuykendall seemed confused, so Jack added, "The Ford."

"Oh, yeah. That's what I thought." The sergeant shook Foyle's hand.

"When do we get this crate in the air?" Jack asked.

"Hurry up and wait," Kuykendall told him. "The crew decided to grab some coffee, but they'll be here in a couple of minutes."

"Who's taking us?"

"Blake, Hanson, and O'Brien. You know them?"

"Kirk Hanson?"

"That's him."

"I don't believe I know the other two, though."

Foyle extended his hand to Jack. "I'd better be saying goodbye then, son. Godspeed to you, and remember to drop a big one on Herr Schicklgruber for me."

Instead of shaking hands, Jack embraced his uncle and patted him on the back. "Will do. Thanks for your hospitality last night—and of course for keeping the car going while I'm away. Give Auntie my love again."

Foyle turned to the girl. "And goodbye to you, Miss Bonnie. It was wonderful having you with us." They hugged. "One thing about Jack here. He's got very good taste in women. I guess that sort of runs in the family."

She smiled. "Thank you, sir. That's very nice of you to say."

Moments later, Jack was saddened to watch Uncle Foyle drive away. His fondness for him and Aunt Kathleen had grown to be almost like that of a son-parents relationship. In so very many ways, Foyle reminded him of his father, whom he had not seen since shortly after Pearl Harbor and was unlikely to encounter again anytime soon. On a less personal level, he would also miss his 1940 Ford, though he felt assured that he was leaving the car in the best of hands. Foyle's kindhearted decision to donate half of his garage space as temporary shelter caused Jack a twinge of guilt, as if he were taking advantage of a blood relative. And yet, his uncle probably would be quick to acknowledge that this imposition was not without its affirmative aspect as well. If nothing else, the addition of a second automobile for the duration was certain to increase the roadworthy life of Foyle's own vehicle, and that was a wartime boon that money could not buy.

The flight crew arrived not long thereafter and immediately set to work, implementing its checklist with dispassionate authority and firing up the C-47's twin engines. Just over a quarter-hour beyond the appointed time of departure, the aircraft powered itself down the runway, into the prevailing breeze. Unremittingly, it picked up velocity and then, with a deafening flourish of thrust, severed its ties with the earth and soared upon invisible currents, instinctively banking for optimal lift, like a bird of prey aloft in the winds.

Once Bonnie grew accustomed to the novel sensation of being airborne, her initial unease evaporated and gradually distilled into a healthy curiosity. She turned to gaze through the nearest of six starboard windows, engrossed by how rapidly the familiar things of life—trees, automobiles, houses, high schools, city blocks, entire towns—shrank to negligibility, while somehow managing to blend into an orderly pattern of aerial design. She watched the green farmlands pass beneath, their irregular shapes fitting like pieces in a jigsaw puzzle, the blanket of verdant terrain interrupted by an occasional creek or pond.

Inside the noisy fuselage, there were fourteen folding metal seats attached to each side of the aircraft, enough to accommodate twenty-eight fully equipped troops. None were aboard this particular flight, however, which is why Captain Decker was able to secure impromptu conveyance not only for himself but for one "stowaway" as well—and a woman at that. The interior of the craft was strictly utilitarian, with little thought given to such petty concerns as comfort and appearance. Cargo tie-down rings dotted the floor, making it precarious to traverse about—not that there was much desire to do so amidst the nearly three tons of freight and assorted supplies that were being dispatched to airfields in Waco, Fort Worth, Mineral Wells, and Wichita Falls.

Bonnie spent some of her time in the air by watching, with mixed feelings, as Jack figuratively wore a path between passenger hold and open cockpit. He devoted so much energy to chumming with his fellow aviators that she wondered whether Jack's professed affection for her stood any chance of challenging his insatiable love of flying. Although there was a war on, at times this male quartet's coarse "shop talk" sounded more like the locker room of an athletic club than a legitimate military mission. But never for a single instant did Bonnie doubt the men's dedication to duty, nor their abiding commitment to the noble cause.

Compared to the coastal city of Houston, inland Waco loomed very cold indeed as they neared the runway at Blackland Army Air Field. The late-winter "blue norther" that hammered central Texas on Friday night had sent the mercury tumbling into the upper twenties by the following morning. Sunday was even nippier than that, with a thermometer reading of twenty-two degrees at eight in the morning and, as the plane began circling on its approach, still just a paltry twenty-seven by half past ten. Jack sat next to Bonnie, holding her hand, as the C-47 descended and then touched asphalt with a convulsive *thump-hop-thump* landing, considered quite acceptable in the unceremonious world of military cargo aviation. While skillful at the controls, this seasoned pilot was not unduly infatuated with finesse. Such niceties as pillow landings would wait for the last all-clear.

After deplaning, Bonnie and Jack could see their breath as they walked together toward the hangar, where a driver was supposed to be awaiting them. Sure enough, the moment they reached the structure, an airman came forward, saluted, and identified himself as Corporal Halloran.

Jack saluted him and said, "Take us to the rec room at HQ, if you don't mind. What's your first name, corporal?"

"David, sir."

"This is Miss Ploughwright, David. However, she'd prefer that you just call her Bonnie."

The airman nodded in agreement, but it was a moot point. He appeared far too bashful to be doing much talking to his female passenger.

Hardly a word was spoken in the staff car as it carried Captain Decker and his companion on the short trip to Headquarters Company. The heater was on, and it felt good to the skin, the first opportunity Bonnie had to be comfortably warm since exiting the car at Ellington Field. In that respect, the best that might be said for the flight itself is that she was never in imminent danger of contracting frostbite.

By the time they arrived at HQ, Jack was all spit and polish. "Thank you, Corporal Halloran. Meet us back here at 1130 hours. Is that clear? You'll need to drive Miss Ploughwright to Baylor."

"Yes, sir."

"Thank you, David," the girl said. "You've been very kind."

Halloran grinned and touched his cap. "Ma'am."

With that, the corporal hurried around to open the car door for her, and then, once she and the officer had gotten out, Halloran placed the overnight bags at their feet. He was smoothly competent, with no wasted motion, as if he had been doing this for ages. He saluted, and the captain returned it with an appreciative wink.

Sunday morning was not a very busy time in the recreation room. Most off-duty personnel were either at church or still asleep in bed. But this did not mean that training operations were discontinued—far from it. All about them, Bonnie and Jack could hear the incessant, droning sounds of aircraft taking off and landing, and a company of cadets was shouting to the rhythmic cadences of PT and rifle drills on the adjacent parade grounds.

While Jack strode over to the austere snack counter, Bonnie took a seat at one of the dozen or so identical tables. Dolefully, she looked around. So here was where it would end, she thought, and she could feel her composure withering away. She had been strong until now, but no longer was there any valid justification for anticipating what still lay in store. A gloomy realization had seized her that the instant she walked out of this nondescript room—spartanly furnished with straight-backed chairs, reading lamps, radio/phonograph console, and secondhand pool table—a beautiful interlude in her young life would be terminated forever. More chilling still, something told her that she would never see Captain John Tynes Decker again. There was no rational explanation for these doubts and fears, but neither could she shake free of them. Bonnie was not very good at whistling in the dark.

"Sorry—I know you don't care much for coffee," Jack told her. He was holding a cup in either hand. "They didn't get their shipment of juice."

"That's all right. Coffee might help me take my mind off other things."

"Want some make-believe sugar or powdered cream?" he asked.

"No, thanks. The stronger, the better."

Jack sat down beside her. "It's depressing to say goodbye. I'm not too skillful at it, so don't expect anything profound or terribly romantic."

"You keep insisting to me that you're not romantic, but I think you are—very much so."

He chuckled at the idea. "Well, maybe around you I am. You're easy to be romantic with."

She smiled, but her eyes remained sad. "When do you have to leave?"

"For good?"

"Yes. When do you leave Waco?"

"Tomorrow at sixteen hundred hours," he said. "That's four o'clock to you."

Bonnie shook her head. "You don't have to translate it for me, Jack. Surprisingly enough, I am capable of adding four and twelve."

He was puzzled by the remark. "Look, I didn't intend for that to sound condescending. All I meant was that you're a civilian, and I shouldn't be forcing my world onto yours."

"But I enjoy being in your world. Did you ever think of that?"

Jack took a deep breath and slowly exhaled, allowing his cheeks to bulge like sails. "Is your coffee okay?"

"I haven't tried it yet. Just between you and me, I could have done with something a lot stronger."

He grinned at her. "Why, Bonnie Ploughwright! Are you a drinker?"

"I had a glass of champagne once, if that counts."

"Yeah, I suppose it does—technically."

Bonnie took a sip of coffee and then watched as a solitary wisp of steam arose from the cup. "Will you write to me?"

"Of course I will," he said.

"You don't seem like much of a writer."

"Normally I'm not—but I would like to stay in touch."

Two Army nurses rushed in from the cold and sat down at a table across the room. The light of recognition came to Jack's eyes, but he disguised it well and did not call out to them.

"Do you have a girl back home?" Bonnie asked him.

"Not any more. We split up a couple of years ago."

"Before or after you went into the service?"

"*When* I went into the service. She wasn't in favor of it."

"That's not very patriotic."

"She wanted to get married."

"So, you two were pretty serious."

"She was very serious."

"Oh, I see." A slight smile crossed Bonnie's face. "Did you ever ... uh ... consummate the relationship?"

Jack gave a nervous laugh. "That's kind of personal, don't you think?"

"Uh-huh." She pursed her lips. "Well, tell me. Did you?"

"Will it make any difference between us?"

Bonnie looked down at her coffee cup. "I'll take that as a yes."

"Gee whiz, that was a long time before I ever met you."

"Have you been very close to any other girls since that one?"

"A few—two or three. Why?"

"I just want to know where I stand. It's important to me."

Then and there, Jack decided against revealing the overnight incident with Chrissy. He had wanted to bring the subject up, as a way of clearing his conscience, but now he knew that would be a grave mistake.

"What about you?" he said. "Couldn't I ask you the same things? How many boyfriends have you had?"

"I don't ..."

"Give me their names, ranks, and serial numbers."

"That's not funny, Jack. You know full well that boys are much wilder than girls."

"Who says? Whenever a boy is acting wild, so is a girl. That's a mathematical equation. It takes two to tango."

"Maybe so, but boys play the field a lot more than girls. They're more ... promiscuous."

With a frown, Jack shook his head. "Are you telling me that you've never dated at all?"

"Sure, I have. What girl hasn't?"

"Were you serious about any of them?"

"One or two. At least I thought so at the time."

"Did you ever sleep with them?" he asked, much too loudly. The nurses glanced over and started giggling.

Bonnie's face reddened, and she lowered her voice. "No! How could you even ask such a thing?"

"And so ... you're a virgin?" he whispered.

That took her breath away. "I guess you could say that, if you really wanted to get crass about it. What's gotten into you anyway?"

"I was just showing you how it feels to be interrogated, to be on your witness stand. We all have past indiscretions—skeletons in the closet, so to speak. Dredging them up serves no purpose when you're in love with someone."

Her eyes widened for an instant, but she quickly discounted his declaration, which was, after all, stated under duress. "I won't hold you to that, Jack Decker, because the situation may have pressured you into saying it when you really didn't want to."

"A 'train station' confession?"

"Exactly. It just wouldn't be fair to you."

"Why don't you let me be the judge of that?"

Bonnie was the first to detect the presence of Corporal Halloran at the entrance of the recreation room. He was standing at ease, staring straight ahead, not at them. "There's David," she whispered.

"Who?"

"Our driver."

Jack glanced over his shoulder and saw the corporal, who did not move a muscle or even blink. The wall clock read 11:28.

"Well, I guess this is it, then," the officer said. He stood up and put his visor hat back on his head. "I'm going to miss you."

Bonnie walked over and took both of his hands. There were tears in her eyes. "I'm going to miss you, too—something awful. I can't bear to even think about it." Rising to her tiptoes, she kissed him on the cheek.

Jack took Bonnie in his arms and squeezed her to him. Their lips met in a long, heated kiss, and their hands wandered feverishly across the other's back, two bodies becoming as one.

"Oh, Jack," she told him, "I've never met anyone like you. I'll think of you every minute that you're gone. I love you so much."

Jack stroked the girl's hair. "And I really meant what I said earlier. I do love you, my dear Bonnie." He could feel the wetness of her tears against his face. "I'm praying for the war to end soon, so I can come back to you. Please be there for me."

"I promise."

When they stepped apart, Jack happened to notice that the nurses were still there. But now they were quite solemn, and they avoided looking at the young couple at all costs. Students of the human condition in wartime, they gave them proper respect and silently wished them well. The corporal, too, as he escorted Bonnie back to the car, had eyes that were moist and a little bit red.

♦   ♦   ♦

Bonnie's yearning for Jack caused her to imagine that she knew just how every young war bride must feel when a husband is sent overseas to fight. She was not married to the Army captain, but his sudden departure provoked an intense loneliness that no amount of positive thinking could quell. Moreover, she was absolutely certain why this might be. Her weekend excursion with Jack had convinced Bonnie, beyond any question, that he and she were ideally suited for one another, and only the war itself could change the course of destiny.

The war could also impinge upon her attitude as a student—and not for the better. Monday, March 8, signified registration for the spring term at Baylor University, but Bonnie's heart was not in it. Although she managed to clear the requisite academic hurdles without serious mishap, the hours drifted by as if in a daydream. Her mind was numb from despair, and at times she caught herself visualizing Jack Decker instead of the critical task at hand. She devoted more than a little energy to choking back tears, regretting the myriad lost opportunities that she and Jack had for being together while he was stationed in Waco.

The next morning brought the start of lectures, invariably an exciting chance to meet new teachers, greet old friends, and explore unfamiliar topics. And yet, her distracted thoughts rendered the sessions banal and pedestrian, surely her own fault rather than that of the three professors, each of whom was an effective communicator and worthy of far stricter attention than she was prepared to give. It was all Bonnie could do to sit through these introductory meetings, even allowing for their customary truncation on the first day of class.

When she and the eleven other students were dismissed early from English 272, "American Prose," Bonnie felt driven to do something impetuous for the revival of her downcast spirits. And the remedy came to her in a flash: she would march herself directly over to Waco Hall, locate the cylindrical passage to AD 2009, and permit her sensibilities to be enlivened by the dazzling miracles that were yet to come. She would not plan beforehand. She would just go. There was no more surefire way to forget about her personal heartbreak than becoming completely surrounded by the unknown—a bizarre, parallel life in which she could behave without the confinement of inhibitions. What was to stop her from acting like an entirely different individual? It might be fun at that.

Waco Hall was virtually deserted, so Bonnie was not obliged to take the precaution of going upstairs. She went straight through the lobby to the east vestibule, and, in the blink of an eye, was projected forward by means of the same effortless method as before. She simply walked from Tuesday, March 9, 1943, to Monday, March 9, 2009. In so doing, the temperature outside the building jumped from fifty-nine degrees to seventy-six degrees, but the skies remained partly cloudy, and the day still held no promise of rainfall. She was surprised to see that very few automobiles were parked in the lot behind the Bobo Baptist

Student Ministries Building and in the one adjacent to Waco Hall East, where the women's hospital used to be. The campus was exceptionally quiet and devoid of humanity, with more squirrels than people wandering the grounds.

Bonnie encountered only one person along the walkway leading to Burleson Quadrangle. This gentleman, probably a member of the Baylor staff, pushed a two-wheeled cart, on which were stacked three heavy-looking boxes. He was in his forties and quite friendly.

"Excuse me, sir, but why is it so empty around here today?" Bonnie asked him.

"Spring break," he said. "Most of the kids are in South Padre Island or Mexico by now."

"How long does it last—this break?"

"All week," he told her. "At least it's easy to find a parking space around here." The man smiled and pushed the cart ahead.

Surveying the campus, Bonnie could see—far off in the distance, alongside the Judge Baylor statue—four boys playing golf, and she decided to venture toward them. The closer she approached, the more evident it became that the yellow-orange balls these students whacked across the manicured lawn were much larger than those used in traditional golf. They were tennis balls, and the game seemed to be an informal lark, testing who could come nearest to the designated tree or lamppost.

Although it went against her nature, she resolved to strike up a conversation with these strangers. They appeared to be Baylor boys, so how dangerous could that possibly be? As she continued forward, Bonnie observed that they were rather well built and tanned from the sun. The weather being unseasonably temperate, all four were clad in pullover shirts and shorts, with some sort of athletic shoes and white socks that stretched above the ankles. Three of them donned caps resembling those worn by baseball players, except that the bills faced backwards, like a catcher might employ beneath his protective mask.

Bonnie walked to within thirty feet of the young man whose turn it was to swing, confident that either he or one of his fellow competitors would speak to her, but they merely gave her a passing glance and nothing more. She thought herself more attractive than that and felt slighted by their disinterest. Even so, injured pride notwithstanding, it was up to her to take the initiative, and she proceeded to do precisely that.

"Can any of you tell me where the bookstore is?" she asked the foursome. "I don't know much about the campus."

One of the boys with a cap on backwards pointed his golf club to the northeast. "On the other side of Waco Creek from the bear pits. It's part of the parking garage."

"Is it open this week?"

None of them answered. They shrugged their shoulders and looked at each other. Finally, one of them spoke up. "I don't know for sure," he said, "but I would guess so."

Bonnie nodded her head and gave him her best smile. "What's this game called?"

"Quad golf. Haven't you ever played?"

She laughed. "No. I've never even seen it before."

"Want to take a hack?" another of the boys asked. "Here." He offered her his club.

"I'm afraid that I'm not dressed properly for golf," Bonnie told him. But she accepted the club and concentrated on a ball that he rolled in front of her. She swung and missed, not even close.

"I'll show you how," a boy named Justin said. He was the shortest of the golfers—about two inches taller than Bonnie, or around five foot eight. Standing behind the girl, he draped his arms over her shoulders to grasp the backs of her hands. "Now do this kind of action." Justin made a slow-motion arc, with Bonnie still holding the club. Contact was made, but they topped the ball badly, and it skipped forward only about three feet.

"As you can see, I'm not very athletic," Bonnie said. She handed the club back to its rightful owner.

"Well, you can't hope to be Tiger Woods on your very first try," Justin told her. She assumed that this was meant for encouragement.

One of the young men, Brent by name, was becoming restless. "Back to work, guys," he said. "This is the sixteenth hole, and I've got a cool one waiting." The other two, Marcus and Sean, nodded in agreement and positioned themselves for their next tee shots.

"Thanks for the lesson," Bonnie told them. She turned to go away.

"Wait. Don't you want to watch?" Brent asked. He was the bareheaded one.

"I'd better not. I need to get something at the bookstore."

"I'll drive you over there when we're done."

"No, thanks. That's nice of you, but it's just a short walk."

Brent stared at her, incredulous. "It's way over on the other side of the SUB," he said, and Bonnie consented to stay.

When the round concluded, with Sean using his pitching wedge to chip up to a lamppost for the win, Marcus hurled his tennis ball at the victor and stung him squarely between the shoulder blades. Both of them were laughing as Sean chased his attacker toward the women's dormitories.

"They can be pretty infantile," Justin said. "Not like us." He tossed his ball at Brent, who caught it just before it struck him in the face.

"How come you're not down in Mexico with everyone else?" Bonnie asked. She figured that such a line of inquiry might help her to become accepted.

"No pesos," Brent said. He reached over and knocked Justin's cap to the ground.

Justin retrieved it and told the girl, "It would cost about a thousand bucks for the week—easy."

Bonnie gasped. "A thousand dollars? How can people afford it?"

"Mom and Dad fork it over, that's how," Justin said. His comment was punctuated by a sigh, affirming that such a self-evident question required no answer.

Brent headed toward his automobile, and his friend, Justin, was right behind him, golf club and ball in hand. "Come on," Brent called out to the girl. "I said I'd take you to the bookstore."

Parked on Seventh Street, the car was a silver convertible of some sort—sleek, modernistic, and no doubt very fast. Bonnie sat in front, next to the driver, and Justin sprang into the back without even making use of the door. Brent roared the engine.

"Golly, what kind of car is this?" Bonnie asked him.

"It's a 2008 Lexus SC 430. I got it used—for a good price. I'm not sure, but I suppose it was a repo."

"Do you like it?"

"Yeah! How about you?" He grinned proudly.

"Sure," she said. "Who wouldn't?"

Brent looked at her legs. "How come you're all dressed up?"

That flustered Bonnie momentarily, so she resorted to telling him, "I had to attend a funeral this morning."

"Oh. Sorry."

"That's all right. It wasn't anybody close." Bonnie noticed that the dashboard had a panel with brightly illuminated numerals. "Is that a clock?"

"Sure, it's a clock. What did you think it was, a microwave oven?"

"No. But it's an hour later than I thought." That was true. She had presumed the current time to be sixty minutes behind her wristwatch, but now the two were synchronous.

Brent laughed. "You must have forgotten to change your clocks."

"What do you mean?"

"We're on Daylight Saving Time now. It started yesterday."

"Oh, of course. How stupid of me!"

Brent, Justin, and their new acquaintance browsed around the bookstore for a half-hour or so, during which the girl seemed to be particularly interested in the Baylor University shirts, displayed on racks at the front of the shop.

"Is this the cost?" Bonnie asked. She held up a white tag for Brent to see.

"Uh-huh. Eighteen dollars." He replied without the slightest shock or disgruntlement. "Do you want it?"

"Not at *that* price!" she said.

"I'll pay the difference, if you don't have enough. How much did you bring?"

Bonnie was embarrassed to say, but Brent insisted. "Tell me." He reached for his money. "Really, I don't mind."

"Two dollars." From her purse, she produced two one-dollar silver certificates and showed them to him.

Brent was nonplussed. "That's all you have with you?"

"Apparently so."

"You expected to buy this shirt for two dollars?"

"I thought I had more than that."

In desperation, Brent turned to his pal for assistance. "Hey, I promised to help her buy this Baylor shirt, but all I have is a ten."

"How much do you need?"

"Six dollars, plus tax. It's an eighteen-dollar shirt, but all she has is two."

Justin gave her a look that suggested either pity or compassion and pulled a twenty-dollar bill from his wallet. "Here. This'll cover it." He held out the money to her.

"No, I really couldn't. Let's just forget the whole thing."

"Take it." Justin continued to dangle the money in front of her. "Twenty dollars isn't exactly Fort Knox, you know."

But to Bonnie that seemed an outrageous amount to pay for informal wear. "Sorry, but I've changed my mind," she told him. "I don't care for the shirt as much as I thought I did."

They left the bookstore a short while later, and Brent asked the girl, "Where do you want me to drop you off?"

"I need to meet my father at the Business School."

"We never did find out your name," Justin said.

"Bonnie Ploughwright."

"I'm Justin, and that's Brent." He stared at the girl, trying to figure her out. "I guess you're not a Baylor student."

"No. I'm just here with my father."

Brent reached into his pocket for the car keys. "How long will you be in town, Bonnie?" he asked. "We're having a little get-together tomorrow afternoon, and you're invited."

"I'm here all week," she told him. "My father's on spring break, too—he's a professor at SMU—so we're staying with his sister and her family in Waco." She was getting quite inventive at fabricating the truth.

"Is that where you go—SMU?" Justin asked.

"Yes. Free tuition for me, being the daughter of a faculty member."

"Awesome!" he said.

Brent directed the conversation to something more urgent. "So, do you want to join our shindig tomorrow?"

"Sure. Why not?" She did not give it much deliberation.

"Great. I'll pick you up right where I leave you off now. Let's say ... uh ... three o'clock."

"Swell."

Suddenly, Bonnie felt apprehensive about the whole affair. She hardly knew these boys, and here she was, subjecting herself to whatever their idea of a good time might be.

♦   ♦   ♦

Immediately after her Wednesday afternoon class concluded, Bonnie went to Alexander Hall to change into the oldest clothes that she could find in her cluttered dormitory closet. Then she slipped free of 1943 again and walked to Fifth and Speight, site of the Hankamer School of Business. Brent Holley drove up at a quarter past three, and he took them straight to his apartment on Tenth Street, about five blocks from campus. It was not yet a festive atmosphere. In fact, no one else was there but Justin Sheppard and his girlfriend, Kayla Dykes. The pair of them sat at a table in the kitchen, drinking beverages from tin cans.

"The others won't get here until around five," Brent said. "You already know Justin, and that's Kayla."

Bonnie smiled at them, trying her best to be liked. This girl, Kayla, was wearing one of the lowest-cut blouses she had ever seen, and that made Bonnie feel self-conscious, wondering if perhaps her own top was too tight.

"Thirsty?" Brent asked.

"No, thanks."

"We've got Coke, Sprite, and Dr Pepper if you're not partial to beer."

"Well, maybe a Coca-Cola," Bonnie told him. She wanted to be sociable.

Brent went to the refrigerator. "Here. Bring it with you. I've got to check my email." With that, he disappeared upstairs, and, eager to please, she followed behind.

The room was larger than she expected, furnished with a desk, a chest of drawers, a dresser, a table supporting what she now knew to be a computer, a queen-sized bed, and still plenty of square footage to spare.

Uneasy to be isolated with this boy in his bedroom, Bonnie thought it might be wise to start a conversation. "What kind of computer is this?" she asked.

"A Dell. My roommate has a Macintosh—and never the twain shall meet."

He smirked when he said it, so Bonnie grinned at the perceived witticism, not quite knowing why. "Is Justin your roommate?"

"No, thank goodness. Justin lives in North Village, so you know he's got a few bucks." Brent switched on his computer, and the screen came to life. "My roommate is Nathan Brooks. He went home for spring break—to Odessa—which means I've got the run of the place all week long."

Bonnie was struggling with her Coca-Cola. "Do you have a can opener I could use?" she asked.

"Just pull up that ring and bend it toward you."

When she did as instructed, there erupted such a loud fizzing sound that she nearly dropped the beverage on his clean carpet.

"Now push the tab back to where it was, and you're ready to drink." He gave her a bemused look. "Haven't you ever seen a pop-top can before?"

"I come from a very old-fashioned family," she said.

He laughed at her, none too kindly. "I guess so!"

Bonnie looked over Brent's shoulder as he read various electronic messages that had been transmitted to his computer. But this did not intrigue her as much as did the machine's research capability, and she found herself becoming impatient for him to finish with the trivial correspondence. She recalled an afternoon in February when a boy named Michael discovered for her what time the trains ran in McGregor. If a computer could determine that, then it must be aware of just about everything.

"Knock, knock!" Justin shouted. He and Kayla were coming up the stairs. "Just wanted to make sure you two were decent."

"So far," Brent said.

"Who's bringing the food?" Kayla asked. "Or are we just going to wing it?"

"Marcus and Chad will order some pizzas whenever they get here, and those sorority girls know someone who can supply a couple of kegs for dirt cheap."

"How many people do you expect?" Justin asked his pal.

"About twenty-five, I think—not counting friends of friends. And Sean knows a bunch of MCC students. Not too bad for spring break."

"Bekka's bringing some DVDs," Kayla said with a suggestive grin.

Brent chuckled. "Is she in them?"

It was around ten minutes after five when the crowd started to arrive, and Bonnie could sense right off that she was in way over her head. Everybody else seemed to know each other, and no one expended much effort in becoming acquainted with her. Somebody put an ugly-sounding record in the gramophone slot, and it assaulted the ears for an hour or more of cacophonous instrumentals and screaming. This is what passed for music in the early twenty-first century.

More drinking occurred than eating, though the kitchen table offered never fewer than three fresh pizzas, already sliced, in cardboard boxes. Each of the pies measured a good two feet in diameter, and more were being delivered every quarter-hour or so. Disposable cups, made of some sort of innovative plastic product, held twelve ounces of beer, which flowed freely, at the flip of a valve, from two enormous kegs. The girls seemed to be at least as thirsty as the boys.

Brent saw that Bonnie was turning into a wallflower, so he went to her rescue, beverage cup in hand. "Here. Have some."

"I really don't like the taste of beer," she told him.

"Have you ever tried it?"

"No, but I don't like the smell."

Brent shook his head. "This is what we call 'light' beer." He handed her the cup. "You can quaff a lot of it and not feel bloated. I predict that you'll be a beer drinker before the night is over." He turned to walk away and, within a few seconds, was talking to somebody on what she presumed was a portable telephone—probably ordering another couple of pizza pies for the hungry masses.

Bonnie studied the liquid's bubbles for a moment and then, while none of the others were paying attention, she willed herself to take a swallow. It was harsh tasting, bitter to the palate, and she wondered how anyone could acquire a fondness for this stuff. Still, eventually she managed to consume the whole twelve ounces and was game for another cupful, should peer pressure bring her to that. Without a word—not a soul bothered to talk to her—she passed through the kitchen to sample a slice of the pizza pie and learned that it was very flavorful indeed. She placed it and a second slice on a thin napkin, apparently made of paper, and went into the living room, where some of the revelers had paired off and were unabashedly necking on the sofa or even while standing up.

What she saw on a large screen hanging upon the far wall was enough to make her eyes bulge. Never before had she witnessed anything so decadent. Two attractive young people, a woman and a prodigiously gifted man, were engaging in the sex act with nothing hidden from view. Close-ups abounded, and the only sounds, besides a monotonously repeated riff for flute and bongos, were frequent groans of pleasure and improvisations on such dialogue as "Yes! Oh, baby, yes!" The film was depraved, to be sure, and yet Bonnie found it surprisingly difficult to look away. Others around her, no doubt jaded by familiarity with this cinematic genre, seemed to wear their passive indifference as a badge of maturity.

By seven o'clock, the gathering was in full swing, and another keg was brought in to satisfy the demand. Many of the guests were intoxicated, and particularly so a trio of young ladies from the local community college, who insisted upon staging an extemporaneous competition. Before long, they had poured water over their shirts and, while sinuously dancing, reached underneath to remove their brassieres, to the encouragement of male onlookers. The brunette went so far as to fully expose one of her breasts, and she was declared the winner by acclamation.

Determined to fit in with this well-lubricated adult crowd, Bonnie carried her empty cup into the kitchen for a refill. A young man whom she vaguely recognized had beaten her to it, so she awaited her turn at the spigot. He glanced at her and pointed. "Aren't you the girl who watched us play golf yesterday?"

"Yes, that's right."

"What's your name?"

"Bonnie Ploughwright."

"I'm Sean Nixon—no relation to Richard Milhous."

Clearly, he considered that a clever thing to say, so Bonnie smiled in response. "Hello, Sean—again."

"Are you enjoying the party?" the boy asked. He stepped aside from the keg.

"Oh, sure. How about you?" She had observed Sean's operation of the spigot—curiously labeled "LITE"—and so her drawing of the beer was flawlessly executed.

Sean took a large swallow, burped under his breath, and said, "Not much. As a general rule, I don't care for binges."

"Is that what this is?"

"Didn't you see that guy drop his beer on the wood floor when he fell asleep? He was out on his feet."

"No."

"And I heard someone throwing up in the john."

"My goodness."

"Yeah. I'll be glad when it's over with, though I don't want to act like a wuss by leaving early." He took another swallow of the brew, and she did likewise.

Bonnie thought of something and laughed. "Did you see that picture in there?"

"What picture?"

"The movie on that screen."

"Oh, yeah. Pretty poor acting, I must say." Sean smiled. "Nice props, though—especially hers."

"And his."

"Yeah, his too, I suppose. Give credit where credit's due."

"Is it against the law to own movies like that?"

"Porn flicks? Nah, they're perfectly legal. Why do you ask? Are you planning to buy some?"

"Of course not," Bonnie said, "but I would think there'd be laws against companies selling such vulgarity."

"You can get plenty of it on the internet—for free."

"What's the internet?"

Sean could not believe his ears. "You don't know what the internet is?"

"I'm afraid not," she told him.

"Don't you have a computer?"

"I come from a very traditional family."

Sean stared sadly at the girl for a moment, but then his face brightened. "Hey, I've got a great idea." He scanned the crowd. "Judas Priest! Where's Brent when you need him?"

"Search me." The beer was beginning to make her just the slightest bit light-headed.

"Wait here, Bonnie. Whatever you do, don't go anywhere." And Sean disappeared into the throng of humanity.

Doing her utmost to rank as an acceptable partygoer, Bonnie filled her cup again, took a substantial gulp, and waited for Sean's return. But nature intervened, as a consequence of all the drinking, and suddenly she felt the intense need to relieve herself.

Off she went, carrying her beer, in search of the downstairs bathroom—unaware that the waiting line was five people long.

By the time Bonnie finally made it back to the kitchen, Sean was noticeably upset with her. "Where have you been? I told you to stay here."

She giggled at him. "Well, I had to pee, didn't I? And I couldn't just do it in the kitchen sink." Her speech was becoming rather slurred, but she seemed awfully happy. She saluted him in military style. "Reporting for duty, sir."

"I was going to show you how to use a computer," Sean told her, "but some of Brent's friends are on it now. It's in his room, upstairs."

"I know. I've seen it."

Sean tried to mask his surprise by perusing what remained in the four boxes of pizza pies. "You've been in Brent's bedroom? When was that?" He reached down for a slice.

"This afternoon, of course. I only met him yesterday."

Sean took a bite of pizza and spoke while chewing. "My offer still stands, by the way." The girl looked perplexed, so he added, "Teaching you how to use a computer."

Bonnie was skeptical. "Would we have to go up to Brent's bedroom?"

"Nope. I've got a newer computer than his, and it's sitting right there on the first floor of my apartment. How about it?"

"Without any hidden conditions?"

"No obligation—no salesman will call," he said.

"Well ... all right, then." An embryonic plan was developing in her mind, and a knowledge of computers was a crucial part of it. She finished the beer and laid her cup on the table.

"How about tomorrow?" Sean asked.

"What day is that?"

"Wednesday."

Bonnie closed her eyes and tried to concentrate. That would be Thursday in her time, and she had to work at the USO after class. These date discrepancies were maddening enough with a sober mind, and now, muddied by the alcohol, she was thoroughly confused. "It'll have to be the next day. What day is that?"

He smiled at her, amused. "Thursday."

"Oh, yes. Will that be okay for you?"

"No problem. I'm on spring break."

"I am, too, but my father's taking us to … somewhere … tomorrow." Her mind was becoming foggy, making it difficult to remember the litany of falsifications.

"Where did Brent say your father teaches, TCU?"

Bonnie shook her head emphatically. "No. TCU is in Fort Worth, so it must be SMU." She blinked several times, trying to clear her mind. "Sorry, but I can't even think straight. I've really had too much to …"

"You're from Dallas?"

"That's right. SMU's in Dallas. Daddy is an SMU Mustang, and so am I. And proud of it, too."

Sean put his arm around Bonnie and gave her a brotherly squeeze. "Do you want to leave this party? I'm ready whenever you are."

Suddenly, panic set in, and she gazed through him with reddened eyes. "What time is it?"

"Just 9:40. Why?"

"I've got curfew, and I need to get out of here!" She scrambled to find her purse.

"Jeez, your father must really be strict."

"Do you have some gum I could chew?" Her voice sounded frantic.

"No. Sorry."

"Drat! Okay, it doesn't matter." Purse located, Bonnie took Sean by the hand and pulled him through the crowd and out the front door. "Walk me to Waco Hall, and don't ask any questions."

"But what's the matter? You can tell me."

"Please, no questions. I'll meet you at the Judge Baylor statue on … the day after tomorrow … at two."

They went quickly and in silence, for she refused to say another word before they crossed Seventh. Even then, it was only a brusque "Good night. And thank you." Bonnie did not go up the Waco Hall steps until the boy was about to head around the corner toward James Avenue.

Sean glanced back, just to make sure she was safe. Then he shook his head and kept on walking. "That is one strange girl," he said aloud. "But cuter than hell."

◆　◆　◆

Lieutenant Billy Fowler was a ruggedly handsome man but already taken. In fact, his marital status was probably the only reason Bonnie ever met him. Billy was one of the very few subordinates in Captain Decker's command whom Jack felt he could trust implicitly when it came to matters of female companionship. Billy and his wife, Melinda, were from Knoxville, Tennessee, and they had a lovely daughter, Peg, who was three years old. Jack gave this unassuming first lieutenant what he considered to be the most important assignment of the war: to look after his girlfriend while he was away in England. Billy accepted the role and took it seriously, right from day one.

"Hello there," he said, cap in hand. "I presume that you're Miss Ploughwright."

Bonnie was standing on a wooden ladder, arranging a display of hanging greenery for the USO's Friday night dance. "Yes. May I help you?"

"On the contrary, let me help you." He reached out his hands and, securing the girl's sides, hoisted her off the ladder. Then he climbed up and used his six-foot-three height to string the imitation palm branches in no time.

Bonnie welcomed his deft proficiency on this, of all days—her head spinning and her stomach still woozy from the confrontation with alcohol. "Thanks," she said. "That would have taken me an hour to do."

The officer stepped to the floor. "Billy Fowler," he told her.

They shook hands. "I'm Bonnie Ploughwright, but it seems you already know that."

"And you fit the description very well. That's a compliment." His accent was melodious, distinctly southern.

"What description?"

"The one Captain Decker gave me."

"Why did he do that?" she asked.

"So I'd be able to recognize you."

"No. I mean why did he want you to find me?"

"Because I'm your guardian angel."

Bonnie laughed nervously, suspecting that this young officer was a tad nutty in the head. "My guardian angel?"

"Not literally, of course, but Jack wants me to watch over you while he's overseas."

"Oh, I see. To shoo the wolves away."

"Partly that, yes. He admits that he's being selfish about it." The lieutenant pulled out his pack of Chesterfields. "Smoke?"

"No, thank you."

"Mostly, though, he just wants me to check on you every once in a while—to be certain you're all right." He flicked his lighter and took a drag.

"That's very kind of him, I'm sure, but what makes Captain Decker assume I can't take care of myself?"

Billy grinned. "He warned me that you might react that way. Yep, he knows you pretty well."

"Did he tell you anything else about me?"

"He said I could bail out whenever I felt like the flak was getting too heavy."

Bonnie had to smile. "That sounds like something he'd say."

"I'll drop in from time to time, if you don't mind."

"Why should I mind? It's a free country." She reached for the ladder. "By the way, lieutenant ..."

"Yes?"

"How do I know you're not on the prowl yourself?"

"I suppose you'll just have to take my word for it—along with Jack's glowing recommendation of me. Besides, I'm married to a terrific gal, and we have the prettiest daughter in all of the forty-eight states." Billy opened his wallet and produced a snapshot of the little girl.

"Aw, she's sweet," Bonnie said. "What's her name?"

"Peggy, but she wants to be called Peg. She's very ladylike for her age."

"How old is she?"

"Three and a half now. That picture was taken about a year ago, I guess."

A patrician woman with silver hair had approached them and was standing nearby. At the first opportunity, she motioned to get Bonnie's attention, but when she spoke, it was directly to the officer. "Pardon me, sir, but Miss Ploughwright has a telephone call. I'm sure it won't take long, if you'd like to have a seat." She pointed toward the reading area.

"Thank you, Mrs. Cagle," Bonnie said. "I'll only be a minute, lieutenant."

"Please ... just Billy."

"Yes, of course." Bonnie nodded to him and walked away.

The telephone call took much longer than expected. For twelve minutes, Billy Fowler sat at a table, smoking cigarettes and thumbing through a copy of *Look* magazine, a recent but already dog-eared issue with Admiral Halsey on the cover.

"I thought maybe you crawled out the back window," the officer told her when she returned.

"No, but you must excuse me, lieutenant. That was—"

"Billy—remember?"

"All right ... Billy. That was my boss on the phone, and he wants me to spruce up the place for tomorrow night. Apparently, they'll be trucking in a bunch of Baylor girls for the occasion, and Mr. Patterson wants the place to look extra nice."

"Need any help? I'm handy with a hammer and saw."

"No. This is mainly just decorations. You know, women's work."

Billy stood up. "Okay, okay, I can take a hint." He laughed, and so did Bonnie.

"Don't take it personally," she said. "It's just that I'll be too busy to keep you properly entertained—like we're supposed to do."

"That's fine by me. I'm not here to be entertained, so don't feel like you're letting down Uncle Sam."

"Still, it was awfully nice of you to come see me, and I appreciate it. Really, I do."

Billy shrugged his shoulders. "Glad to help out a pal." He extinguished his current cigarette in the ashtray. "Has Jack written to you yet?"

"No. You?"

"Nope, me neither. I'll write to him about you late tonight, after I'm off duty."

"Are you on duty now?"

"Not until sixteen hundred hours. That's—"

"I can subtract, thanks."

"Goodbye, Bonnie. It was swell meeting you."

"Same here, Billy. Give my love to Jack, and please tell him to drop me a line. I know for a fact that it won't cost him any postage."

Billy chuckled for a moment but then thought of something. "Oh! Before I go ..." He reached inside his coat. "... I need to give you this." He handed Bonnie a sealed envelope.

Her face became pale. "What is it?" she asked.

"A small token that Jack entrusted to me as he was leaving. Don't open it now. Jack wants you to be alone when you see it."

"Do you know what it is?"

"No. But he seemed to think you'd like it."

Bonnie held the envelope to her chest. "I'll write to Jack soon, to thank him. Will that shortened address really work?"

"Yep—APO 343, New York. It's all you need."

"Now I'm getting curious about what's inside this."

"Don't be. He says to tell you it's nothing much—only a little keepsake, that's all."

"Just the same, I appreciate your kindness, Billy Fowler." She kissed him on the cheek.

He blushed. "Say, I think I'm going to like this job."

Billy turned to leave, placing the cap just so on his head. He waved goodbye, and Bonnie waved back. The USO club was rather deserted this early in the afternoon, but that would change before too long. It always did.

Bonnie's dormitory clock read 8:20 before she finally garnered sufficient courage to open the remembrance from Jack Decker. The tan envelope, Army-issued with USAAF as a return address, measured about four by six inches. What she found inside made her cry. She pulled out a picture of her and Jack. They were standing on the sidewalk of Austin Avenue, smiling, with arms around each other and heads nearly touching. It was the photograph taken by that street cameraman on the day Jack told her he was soon to be going away. With tears in her eyes, Bonnie turned the snapshot over and read, "All my love to the most wonderful girl in the world. May God grant that you are there for me when I return. Jack."

♦   ♦   ♦

Bonnie made her way across Speight Avenue to the Judge Baylor statue at the appointed hour, two o'clock on Thursday afternoon, but Sean Nixon was nowhere to be seen. That was not unusual, she figured. In fact, it would have been extraordinary for a college student, especially a male of that notoriously unreliable species, to show up just as advertised. While waiting for him to arrive, she made use of her spare time by roaming around the area known as Founders Mall. In so doing, she became aware that the granite lampposts, scattered about campus, had small plaques affixed to them, each commemorating a former Baylor student who was killed in the war.

William Silver Edgar, killed in Scotland, April 2, 1942; Marshall Neil Sanders, killed in training, Florida, December 21, 1943; Henry Arthur Myers, killed in action, England, July 26, 1942; Weston L. Moore, lost in action off Tunisia,

March 22, 1942; Robert Houston Daniel, Jr., killed in action, France, October 5, 1944; Tipton Orren Tate, killed in action, Burma, September 15, 1943; Oliver Joseph Goldsmith, killed in training, Florida, September 10, 1942; Robert Woodfin Boggess, Jr., killed in action, Sicily, July 15, 1943.

Most poignant to her were the plaques that honored servicemen who would not lose their lives until after March 12, 1943. From her unique perspective, those were rare glimpses of the future, and she had no right to know of them. It was for this very reason that Bonnie did not allow herself to dwell upon the latter stages of the war, either here or in books at the library. She was convinced that to manipulate events, no matter how minutely, was to alter the course of history. But that did not keep her from speculating whether she could, with great care, make limited, selective changes without causing a progression of ever-widening consequences to occur. Otherwise, why would she have been given this remarkable gift?

"Bonnnn-nnnnie!" came a shout from the direction of Waco Hall. It was Sean Nixon, standing between the Judge Baylor statue and the monument to Reverend William Milton Tryon. Bonnie, who by then was reading the Boggess plaque near Pat Neff Hall, waved to him and began heading toward the rendezvous spot. They met about midway.

"Sorry I'm so late," he told her. "I was dumping some new songs to iTunes and then synching them to my iPod."

His words sounded like gibberish to her. "That's all right. I've been reading the memorials," she said.

"The what?"

"Memorial plaques on the lampposts."

Sean chuckled. "I don't have a clue what you're talking about."

"These." She pointed to the closest plaque, that of Weston L. Moore.

He read it silently. "So? What of it?"

"Doesn't it mean anything at all to you?"

"Nope—just ancient history. I was never any good at it."

They began walking together toward Tenth Street, on which Sean's apartment was situated, not far from Wood Avenue.

"I want to apologize for how I acted on Tuesday night," Bonnie said. "That was totally unlike me, to behave that way."

"What way? I thought you were fun."

"Drinking," she told him. "I mean, I never drink. Never."

He laughed. "How'd you feel yesterday morning?"

"Same as you, probably—only worse. You're more used to that sort of thing than I am."

"It takes practice."

Although Sean's apartment, unlike Ryan's, stood on a single level, there were nearly as many rooms in the floor plan: kitchen, living room, two bedrooms, and one bath. With his roommate away in Brownwood for spring break, Sean and Bonnie had the place to themselves. Until this point in her life, she would never have acceded to such an unseemly arrangement, but her determination to learn the rudiments of future technology— without stirring up intolerable suspicion—granted her little other choice in the matter. Besides, he was kind enough to offer his instruction, free of any ulterior motive, and Baylor boys generally could be trusted to give at least a casual nod to moral integrity.

Sean's computer lay upon a desk in the bedroom. He brought in one of his roommate's chairs for Bonnie to use and reserved the ergonomically designed office chair for himself. The demonstration began with a blank Google page, but soon Sean was nimbly unearthing all manner of facts, jumping from this to that with the click of a button. For being such a powerful research tool, "surfing the internet," as he termed it, certainly did seem mighty diverting as a form of amusement.

"Is *everybody* on there?" his guest asked. She was overwhelmed by the sheer scope of it.

"No, not everybody. My grandparents might not show up in a search—or even my parents, for that matter. But most people under the age of forty have some version of an online footprint, whether they want it or not."

"Are you on the internet?"

"Of course!" he said. Sure enough, when he typed in his name, "Sean Aaron Nixon," there were at least a half-dozen links displayed, including Facebook and Twitter, both of which he described as social networking websites. "In my case, those are just exercises in narcissism, blatant self-promotion, but lots of people use them for legitimate purposes—like getting to know others with similar interests, all around the world."

Bonnie was thinking of something entirely different. "If I were trying to locate a person from way back—decades ago, maybe someone who fought in the war—would that be there, too?"

"Could be," he said. "No promises."

"How would I find him?"

"Hard to say. It would take a long time, that's for sure. You'd probably have to know what unit this person was in or other info of that sort. Maybe what ship he was on or where he fought, who his commanding officers were—things like that. Even then, who knows? Genealogists dig for the tiniest bits of trivia. They become fixated on it."

"But you're not?"

"Like I said, I'm not much into the past. The '80s are prehistoric to me." He stared at her for a moment. "What's your major at SMU?"

"English. I'm a writer—or at least I want to be."

"I thought maybe you were studying history."

"No, but I might like to tie history in with some things I'm hoping to write."

"Like ...?"

"Novels about the war, for instance."

He grinned. "Somehow, I'm not surprised."

"What makes you say that?"

"Well, who else would go around reading those signs on the lamps?"

About 4:45, Sean stood up to stretch his arms and legs. He asked Bonnie whether she would like something to eat, and she told him no. Actually, though, her stomach was beginning to feel empty, and the mere mention of food reminded her that all she had eaten since breakfast was a grilled cheese sandwich at the Varsity Inn on Dutton. Consequently, when he said, "Are you sure?" she was quick to change her mind.

He drove them in his dust-encrusted truck to a delicatessen called Subway, and they brought back two twelve-inch-long wheat loaves that were filled with every conceivable kind of raw vegetable, piled high atop the cold meat of their choice. Sean insisted on paying, which was more than acceptable to Bonnie. She did not relish the notion of buying her dinner in Walking Liberty half dollars, Standing Liberty quarters, Mercury dimes, and Buffalo nickels. The poor attendant might have suspected that she was from another planet. Besides, food prices in this future century were astounding, and she did not carry enough currency with her to cover the bill.

They sat on the living room sofa, trays balanced upon their laps, and Sean told her this was how he always ate these days, now that his roommate waited tables five nights a week at an Italian restaurant whenever school was in session. Sean flicked the television on, and there appeared a quiz show in which a New York City cab driver presented questions to his customers, who could earn magnificent sums of money by giving the correct answers. Bonnie recognized at once that she would have done very poorly, for not only was she incapable of providing answers, but most of the time even the questions made little sense to her. For example: "Luciano Pavarotti, Plácido Domingo, and José Carreras sometimes performed as what singing trio?" It was plain to see that she was out of her element, and Sean fared much better. He must have thought she was a real dimwit.

After their dinner break, the learning atmosphere in Sean's apartment was compromised by a pair of palpable changes. For one thing, the boy's taste in beverages went from Diet Coke to Coors Light. For another, he allowed his hands to take liberties that had seemed out of bounds prior to sunset. Bonnie drank one beer, just to avoid the indignation of being considered a prude, and then she downed a second can to demonstrate her adult status. Already her head was beginning to swirl—being a novice at withstanding alcohol—so, for the time being, she sensibly refused the generous offer of a third.

Sean was back at the controls, as before, but now his internet surfing veered off the historical and into a realm that came as more of a shock to Bonnie than she could ever have imagined. "Look what I stumbled upon," he said in passing.

He typed in three words—"natural," "girl," and "tubes"—which seemed innocuous enough on the surface. But what proceeded from that, on countless pages of search returns, was a smorgasbord of debauchery that was unthinkable to someone from Bonnie's world. Sean clicked on link after link, and within them were hundreds, perhaps thousands, of photographs and movie sequences, which spared the viewer nothing in the way of full frontal depictions of the female form. A great many of the images, of course, also exhibited the male as an eager participant. That Bonnie was so slow in turning away from this seductive eroticism can only be attributable to the alcohol, which stunned her inhibitions into a pleasant state of permissiveness.

The beers had a more predictable effect as well, inducing Bonnie to excuse herself for a visit to the bathroom. During the girl's absence, her host placed another can of brew beside the computer screen, a thoughtful gesture whose significance did not go unnoticed. Declining the offer a second time was futile, and besides, Bonnie was beginning to enjoy the warm, carefree sensation that the drinks instilled. Perhaps *too* carefree, for Sean's exploring hands were becoming incrementally more familiar with her anatomy, both above and below the waist.

Truth be told, Bonnie was quite willing to endure this agreeable experience and not at all inclined to put a stop to what she saw as nothing more than harmless petting. In her deliciously muddled state of mind, she recalled the intimacy between her roommate and Greg Furmin in the movie house. This was how Julia must have felt, except that her indecency went even further, with fully exposed skin and taking place right there in the open, where others could see. Now that Bonnie thought about it, being so daring in public was the ultimate thrill, and suddenly she wished she had been bolder, a touch more inebriated, at Tuesday's party. She should have competed against those three community college girls in their impromptu contest, with all of the male eyes locked upon them. And she knew just what it would have taken to win.

Bonnie's reverie was interrupted when Sean presumed to go a bit too far astray, crossing her newly relaxed limit of propriety when fingers ventured beneath an article of underclothing. Bonnie instinctively put a stop to her clouded indulgence at this juncture of the relationship—but not before she squeezed his hand for a final few seconds, luxuriating in the novel sensation of physical abandon.

The next morning, while lying at leisure in the dormitory room, Bonnie took stock of her actions and had surprisingly few regrets. It was the alcohol at play, she told herself—that and the sexy images. They simply fed upon one another to make her juiced up and receptive to the young man's advances. Her response to the stimuli was perfectly normal and spontaneous. Never in a million years would she behave that way on her own. Or would she? Bonnie had to stop and think. How much might she have permitted, were it not for Sean's gracious consent to refrain from pressing the issue?

She giggled quietly and glanced over at her snoozing roommate. Julia would have been proud.

◆　　◆　　◆

Professor Courtney's English 272 course, "American Prose," was not even remotely what Bonnie foresaw when she registered for it ten days earlier, back on March 8. She assumed that it would present excerpts from popular writings, both fiction and non-fiction, with magazine articles and perhaps a novella or two thrown in for good measure. What the class proved itself to be was a philosophical seminar on nineteenth-century essayists and their published *oeuvre*. Her professor, Luther Weeks Courtney, was sixty-three years old and nearing the end of a long and distinguished career in higher education, but he was not particularly interested in English composition, except insofar as it might relate to government, debate, and Baptist doctrine. Although Bonnie would have been the first to acknowledge that Dr. Courtney was excellent at what he attempted to do, she found the subject matter to be impossibly dull, much too abstruse for her liking.

Immediately after Thursday's class, she went from Pat Neff Hall to Carroll Library and immersed herself in a transcendental treatise by Ralph Waldo Emerson. If the assigned reading seemed tedious to begin with, it was rendered positively indigestible upon further confrontation. Bonnie nearly came to tears over her inability to make heads or tails of such passages as ...

"We lie in the lap of immense intelligence, which makes us receivers of its truth and organs of its activity. When we discern justice, when we discern truth, we do nothing of ourselves, but allow a passage to its beams. If we ask whence this comes, if we seek to pry into the soul that causes, all philosophy is at fault. Its presence or its absence is all we can affirm. Every man discriminates between the voluntary acts of his mind, and his involuntary perceptions, and knows that to his involuntary perceptions a perfect faith is due. He may err in the expression of them, but he knows that these things are so, like day and night, not to be disputed."

That was when her mind wandered, inevitably, to Captain John Tynes Decker. For the moment anyway, she decided to forsake her gallant effort to make sense of Emerson. It was time that she penned a letter to Jack. She had not yet received one from him, but that was immaterial. He was at war, and allowances had to be made for a serviceman's posting overseas. Perhaps her very first missive would inspire regular communication between them, especially if she were to enclose a small photograph of herself, which he could carry with him while he was away. She had a yearbook picture that was not too bad, and a print copy of that pose would have to do for now. Later on, maybe she could come up with something slightly more like a pin-up girl.

Bonnie pulled out her Big Chief tablet and, after a few minutes of thought, began writing.

Dear Jack,

I hope that you had a fine crossing and that you are now settling in to your new responsibility. I miss you more than words can say and wish you could have stayed in Waco. However, I know that the world has much larger concerns these days than the desires of one frivolous girl. The photograph that you find enclosed with this note was taken for use in Baylor University's annual, the "Round Up." I trust that you will not consider it too presumptuous of me to send my picture along, giving you something to remember me by. For all I know, maybe you are trying your best to forget me, and this has just ruined your plans. Too late now!

Baylor's spring term opened a week and a half ago. So far, so good, I guess. My most boring class is one on American prose, which means studying the dry-as-dust philosophies of such thinkers as Thoreau, Emerson, James, Holmes, et al. Personally, I much prefer Twain, Fitzgerald, Tarkington, and Mitchell, but to each his own.

My brother has written home a couple of times in the past month, and my parents report that he is doing fine. Keith is an airplane mechanic, so maybe you'll meet up with him one of these days. Probably not, though— it's a pretty big war. He and his girlfriend have become engaged through the mail, which is a rather novel way to do it. I suppose Keith wrote his proposal while down on one knee.

I still telephone home each week, and of course it is nice to hear what my parents have to say. But now that you're not here, there is very little of substance for me to discuss. You were always my main topic of conversation.

Did your ears use to burn every Sunday afternoon at two o'clock (Texas time)? I wish you could have met Mother and Daddy before you left. I'm sure they would have loved you as much as I do. Well, ALMOST!

Lt. Billy Fowler wants me to assure you that I am being watched over quite well. He is taking splendid care of me and being vigilant in chasing away all of the USO's lounge lizards, of which there are plenty.

How funny the human brain is. I never hear the name "Tchaikovsky" anymore without thinking of you. Nor do I pass by the Purple Cow Sandwich Shop or the Elite Café without seeing you in my mind's eye. It gives me a warm feeling to recall the swell times we had together.

Write to me when you can, and send me a snapshot of yourself in your dress uniform. I will put it next to my bed and kiss it each night before going to sleep. Now, don't you feel special? Thank you for the sweet picture of us on Austin Avenue! Do you want me to send it back, or may I have it?

Well, it is time for me to stop writing and begin studying again. I am in the library, and it is lonely here without you.

All my love, Bonnie

After ineffectually struggling with Emerson's "Self-Reliance" for another hour and a half, Bonnie packed up her materials and returned to Alexander Hall. Just as she was about to go in the main entrance, her roommate was leaving through the same door—with an airman on either arm. Evidently, the soldiers had been relieved of duty at 4:30, for they were relaxed and in no hurry whatsoever. "We're going for a bite to eat," Julia said. She, too, appeared to have not a worry in the world, least of all her schoolwork. "Want to come along? I'll lend one of them to you if you grovel low enough. That would still leave me with two fellas for myself because we're going to pick up their friend on the way."

"No, thanks," Bonnie told her. "I've got a test tomorrow, and I'm dead in the water."

"Sounds like a job for the Navy," one of the men said. He was very nice looking, and he eyed Bonnie from top to bottom. The other airman, younger than Bonnie by a couple of years, grinned at her but chose not to leer.

"Sure you won't join us?" Julia asked. "We shouldn't be gone for more than an hour."

Bonnie knew what her roommate's idea of an hour was—especially when the opposite sex was involved—so she shook her head. "You three have a good time."

"Four!" Julia shouted with a laugh as they walked away.

Bonnie hoped Julia was not tempting fate with these prurient relationships. Venereal disease was all too common around military bases, and, by every account, Julia did not know where to draw the line when things began to heat up with a man in uniform. And yet, if there was a positive facet to her well-earned easy reputation, it was that she usually attracted more than one admirer at a time, and perhaps there was safety in numbers. Unless strong liquor had corrupted his judgment, the typical young man was not apt to become as aggressive when a rival was there to share his interest. Inasmuch as Julia Johnston's *métier* was psychology, it could be that she gravitated toward multiple liaisons for that reason. More likely, she was just an inveterate pleasure seeker.

While Bonnie was unlocking the door to her dormitory room, someone sneaked up behind her in the hallway. "Hello, Bonnie," the girl said. It was Evelyn Branch from the winter term's short-story class. She looked radiant and gleeful.

"Ev?" Bonnie did a double take. "Ev! What brings you here?"

"May I come in? I need to talk with you."

The two girls entered, and Bonnie shut the door behind them. "Please have a seat," she said. "You get a choice between uncomfortable chair and comfortable bed." Evelyn opted for the chair, so Bonnie sat on her bed, staring in awe at the visitor. Her physical transformation was almost incredible: no eyeglasses, a smart dress, and considerably more make-up than before, but tastefully applied.

Bonnie could hold back no longer. "You look lovely, Ev," she said. "Absolutely lovely! What have you done to yourself? We should all try it."

Evelyn blushed. "Just taking a little more pride in myself, some proper hygiene, and a whole new frame of mind."

"My goodness. What brought all this on?"

"Can't you guess?" Now her crooked teeth, once a liability, somehow made her seem even cuter. "I'll give you a hint. His name is Jim."

"Ev! You don't mean ..." Bonnie ran over and grasped her friend's hands. "Are you ...?"

Evelyn nodded, and there were tears of joy in her eyes.

"You're getting married?"

"Yes! I told him yes."

Still holding hands, the young ladies became adolescents again, dancing around in a jubilant circle until both were out of breath. Bonnie fell onto the bed, laughing. "This is marvelous news!" she said. "And I'm so happy for you."

"Thank you. It hasn't quite seeped into my brain yet."

"When is the big day?"

"Soon." Evelyn's face darkened a bit. "It's got to be as quickly as possible."

Bonnie tried to read into her friend's eyes. "But you're not ..."

"No, of course not. It's just that Jim is about to be reassigned and then probably sent overseas, and we want to be married before he has to leave."

Bonnie beamed another smile. "I think that's a swell idea. If you're in love, there is no reason to wait."

Evelyn turned her head away and fought back the tears. "Jim is so wonderful. I can't believe that he has chosen me, of all people. He's learning to be a flight engineer, but in real life he's a songwriter. Isn't that absurd? Teaching a musician to keep bombers in the air?"

"Well ..."

"Oh, don't get me wrong, Bonnie. I'm all for the war effort—a hundred percent—and the bombs do need to fall. I understand that. But I'm ready for this horrible fighting to be over, so Jim and I can start our life together."

"Is he stationed here in Waco?"

"Not anymore. He was when I met him, obviously, but now he's at Las Vegas Army Air Field. That's way out west, in Nevada—the middle of nowhere. When he graduates from flexible gunnery school, he'll probably go to Langley, Virginia, before being posted abroad."

"Does he like what he's doing?"

"I think so. It's interesting work, and he knows how vital it is. He's assigned to B-17s, and Jim has to know how to fix just about everything. He's also what they call a top turret gunner. I think he must be extremely brave to do that."

"Yes, he is. They all are—all of our boys." Bonnie sat upright on the edge of the bed. "What's Jim's last name?"

"Peaks."

"That sounds nice: Evelyn Peaks. Is he from Missouri, too?"

"No. He's been up to Saint Louis several times—as a boy— but his hometown is Lawton, Oklahoma."

Bonnie looked puzzled. "A songwriter from Oklahoma? Will you two be moving to New York at some point?"

"I should say that he writes mostly western tunes. In fact, he's offered some of them to Milton Brown and Ernest Tubb, and even to Spade Cooley out in Los Angeles."

"Do you like that kind of music?"

Evelyn giggled. "Not much, but I'd better learn to enjoy it straightaway."

"You never did tell me when the wedding will be."

"I need to talk to you about the date, and that's one of the reasons why I dropped by."

"Oh?"

"You see, I don't make friends easily, and you're one of the very few Baylor girls whom I was able to talk with and feel like I was not an outsider."

"Now, Ev ..."

"Really. And I appreciate your kindness."

Bonnie could see that her friend was embarrassed, so she lightened the subject. "I remember that train trip to Dallas, when we first met," she said, "and the sack of lemon drops."

Evelyn gave a quick smile but then came right to the point. "Listen, Bonnie. I want you to be my maid of honor at the wedding, if you are able to—and want to."

"Of course! I'll be delighted."

"It will be here in Waco, which is kind of a middle ground between Las Vegas, where Jim is stationed, and Saint Louis, where my parents live. Besides, I need to continue my studies at Baylor, and I can't miss any more days. I'm already close to being placed on probation, as it is."

"I don't remember you missing many days at all. You were nearly always there."

"That was only for Dr. Smith's class, English 206. I love the short story."

"I could see that. Everyone in the class could."

"But my attendance record was not so sterling in other courses, so I'm right on the verge of being expelled."

"Oh, dear."

"Anyway, to answer your question, we're hoping to have the wedding on either April 10 or 17."

"That soon?"

"Jim says it has to be one or the other. The Army is bending over backwards to give him any choice at all."

"Will it be at Seventh and James?"

"No, I don't think it would be proper to have the wedding in a church," Evelyn said, "seeing as how I've been married before. Did I ever tell you that?"

"Uh-huh. You told me it didn't last for very long."

"One month of pure bliss, followed by four months of misery. We were too young, and it was an unmitigated disaster. That pretty well sums it up."

"Then, where are you planning to have the wedding?"

"Jim and I both want to hold the ceremony outdoors—at a picturesque site we love near Lake Waco."

"Gee, I don't know. That's awfully chancy at this time of the year. You could get washed out."

Evelyn's face saddened. "Well, we haven't reserved a hall, which means the only alternative would be the justice of the peace. Neither one of us really wants that."

"No, I don't blame you."

"It seems that we're having to throw ourselves at the mercy of Mother Nature, and I just pray to God that this doesn't turn out to be a bad omen." Evelyn had to bite her lip to keep from crying. "Sorry to be so emotional, but our wedding means the whole world to me."

The dormitory room went quiet, as Bonnie did not respond immediately. She was weighing some exclusive options of her own, and she could feel, slowly but surely, that her steely resolve was beginning to weaken. Then it all became clear. She knew what she had to do.

"Don't decide anything now," Bonnie said. "Give me a couple of days to investigate. Let me speak with some weather folks at Blackland, and I can tell you which of those two days will be better—as near to a certainty as you can get."

Evelyn gazed at her for a long moment, not knowing quite what to think or say. "You would go to all that trouble for me?"

"Sure."

It was as if no one had ever done anything so considerate in her life. "You are a true friend, Bonnie, and I don't know what I have ever done to deserve such kindness."

"Hogwash. I'm glad to do it—and of course to be your maid of honor." Evelyn smiled when Bonnie told her, "Let's just say that I like happy endings."

◆   ◆   ◆

Jones Reference Library was connected to Baylor's Moody Memorial Library by means of a long, enclosed hallway. An otherwise attractive student worker, with a pearl bolted to the middle of her tongue and four thin, silver rings through her left eyebrow, pointed Bonnie to where she needed to go. "You'll thee it right through there," she lisped. "Athk at the front dethk." Bonnie grinned to hide her shock and did as she was told. The poor girl seemed intelligent enough. Did she really think those self-mutilating ornaments enhanced her appearance?

A reference librarian arranged to have Bonnie use what was called a microform reader. This was an ingenious device, enabling the researcher to project strips of miniaturized photographs onto a viewing screen. It was a concept similar to V-mail and spawned for precisely the same principle, that of saving space. Bonnie went to the microfilm shelves and located the *Waco News-Tribune*. Then, within that title, she selected a box containing April through June of 1943—her near future.

Much to Bonnie's relief, the machine was not difficult to master. The metal spindle to her left was easily loaded, and the plastic reel to her right was simple to thread. Buttons directly in front of her advanced or reversed the film, and a cylindrical lens system provided the capability of zooming in or out, as well as a wheel for focusing the enlarged image. The entire process was, as the fly-boys would say, "a piece of cake."

What Bonnie discovered in those Sunday editions was that either one of Evelyn's suggested Saturdays would be quite satisfactory, with pleasant temperatures and no torrential rainfall. Now she could return to the present day and convey her findings with utter confidence. She even caught herself smiling smugly at the foolproof elegance of her scheme. No doubt about it— consulting the next day's climatological review was a whole lot more accurate than depending upon a weather forecast.

But Bonnie was not yet finished with the microform reader. While still seated there, she could not resist the temptation of browsing further through those same issues of the newspaper, to see on which of the two proposed dates Evelyn's wedding actually took place. She viewed the nuptial listings for both April 11 and April 18, from beginning to end. Strange to say, a record of the Peaks-Branch marriage was nowhere to be found.

Thus far, Bonnie's research into the future had done nothing to change the course of history, even in the minutest detail. What she needed to determine, once and for all, was whether it was indeed possible to do so. Could it be that the future was consecrated and would automatically marshal all of its forces to reject any attempt at imposing alterations from without? To answer that mystical question, Bonnie had devised a modest but indisputable experiment, and she felt that now was as good a time as any to conduct the inaugural step. For that, she went back to Moody Memorial Library and proceeded up the stairs to the serials floor.

She wanted to identify a publication whose current holdings—whether complete or interrupted—encompassed, at the very least, some issues from the early 1940s. Magazines that came to mind were *Collier's*, *The Reader's Digest*, and *The Saturday Evening Post*, and she finally settled upon the second of those titles for no reason other than she happened to turn right at the double doors, and it was nearest to her. From among the pre-1943 editions, Bonnie chose one at random, flipped it open, and noted what she saw: page 154. This page and all adjacent pages appeared to be in pristine condition, with no irregularities. She jotted down the precise citation on a slip of scrap paper, which she then tucked into her purse for later reference.

When she made it back to Waco Hall and passed through the time portal to her own present day, Bonnie's hunger reminded her that she had not eaten since noon—and that was only a lettuce salad, topped with cucumber slices and croutons. Alexander dining room would be opening soon, and, at this hour, she figured to beat the main convergence of students.

"Ev told me I would find you here," came a female voice, and Bonnie turned to see Priscilla Downing just inside the room's entrance. The violinist had been sitting at a table but now stood.

"Oh. Hi, Prissy," Bonnie said. She did not know what else to say, having been taken off guard by the girl's unexpected presence.

Priscilla grinned at her friend's reaction. "Sorry to drop in on you like this." Some textbooks were lying in front of her on the table, so she evidently had been studying. "I came by to tell you that I'm entitled to two complimentary tickets for Thursday night's concert, and my roommate wondered if you wanted to go with her."

"Sure, I'd love to. The Waco Symphony?"

"Yes."

Bonnie giggled. "I guess Ev told you what happened at the last concert I went to."

"She said you met Mr. Right."

"Well, I don't know about that. I did meet a wonderful guy who's an officer in the Air Corps. He's stationed overseas now, but we plan to stay in contact by writing to each other."

"Have you heard from him yet?"

"No. So far, it's been a one-sided correspondence, but of course there's a war on, and I understand how busy he must be."

Priscilla smiled her acknowledgment and sat back down. Bonnie took a seat directly across from her, so the violinist offered to keep one eye on the serving line, which was yet to open.

"Ev has changed a lot in the last few weeks," Priscilla said.

"So I noticed. She's really quite pretty. It sounds coldhearted to say, but honestly, I never would have guessed."

"And it's not just her outward self. Something spiritual has happened to her, too. She's even begun reading the Bible each night before she goes to bed."

"I'm sure that's mostly due to her boyfriend—her fiancé," Bonnie said. "You can see in her eyes that she's delirious about him."

"Sergeant Jim Peaks. Have you seen his picture?"

"No."

"He's rather handsome, at least in my opinion. Looks Italian or Greek—very Mediterranean—but I don't think he is."

Bonnie hesitated to divulge that she had agreed to be maid of honor, afraid that might hurt Priscilla's feelings or cause disharmony between the roommates. But the violinist's next words made it clear that such fears were unfounded.

"I may have to miss the wedding," she told Bonnie.

"No! How come?"

"I'm on call for the first three weekends in April, so it's possible that I'll be in Houston, subbing for one of the second violins down there."

"Gee, that's a shame."

"Well, the money helps, and I know my father appreciates it."

"Your father?"

"He's a cellist in the Houston Symphony—loyal to the string section, you know."

Priscilla stood up to leave when she saw that the serving line was forming, and Bonnie hurried over to claim her place.

"It still could work out for me to be at the wedding, but nothing is certain right now," the violinist said. "Anyway, I'll give the concert tickets to Ev whenever Mr. Reiter distributes them to us."

"Thank you."

"It should be a good program—with the Tchaikovsky Piano Concerto and *Boléro*—but I can't promise to deliver you an Army officer again."

Bonnie laughed. "That's all right. I'm satisfied with the one I have."

◆　　◆　　◆

The next time Bonnie went to Carroll Library was a rather frenetic visit, squeezed in between her Monday morning classes. She only had five minutes to spare—just long enough to return a book to circulation—but she made it a point to accomplish another task as well. After sliding her book into the deposit slot, she rushed over to where the periodicals were shelved and found the "R" section.

Soon she was holding the very same issue that she had noted on the slip of paper in her purse. It was *The Reader's Digest* with a cover date of September 1942. Bonnie felt her heartbeat quicken as she turned to page 154. Once there, she proceeded to fold upward a small portion of the bottom corner. All she made was an insignificant crease, not wishing to deface the magazine any more than necessary. It was exciting to think that this simple experiment, when completed, would tell her something that surely no one else in the world could possibly know. She left the library with a scant two minutes remaining before her next class. Good thing she was a fast runner.

In common with most people, Bonnie was prone to impatience whenever she was the bearer of glad tidings, while likely to procrastinate if the news was less than pleasant. That is what made her Monday afternoon so frustrating—the anticipation of sharing her happy secret with the soon-to-be bride. Evelyn Branch was not a member of her one o'clock class, nor would she be on campus later in the day, having acquired a part-time job to help pay for the wedding and her college expenses. By four, Bonnie simply could wait no longer, so she stopped at the front desk to use the dormitory's public telephone.

"Yes, operator," she spoke into the mouthpiece, "thirty-six hundred, please." That was the number for the Goldstein-Migel Company, located downtown near Sixth Street, across Austin Avenue from the Strand Theatre. When the store's telephone attendant answered, Bonnie specified, "Girls' Wear Department, please. Thank you."

There was a considerable delay before somebody finally said, "Yes. May I help you?"

"Ev? This is Bonnie Ploughwright."

"Hello, Bonnie. Listen, I can't talk right now because I'm helping a nice lady and her daughter."

"I need to tell you that either of those Saturdays will be fine for an outdoor wedding. No rain on the tenth and eighty degrees.

And just scattered sprinkles on the morning of the seventeenth, with a grand afternoon of seventy."

The elation in Evelyn's voice was audible. "That's marvelous! You don't know what a relief that is. But—"

"It's guaranteed," Bonnie added with reckless abandon.

"How can you be so sure? That's almost a month from now."

"I have very dependable contacts at Blackland Field," she said. "Jack knew everyone in the Weather Service there."

"Thank you so much! I'll plan accordingly and try not to fret about it anymore. I know I'm probably driving Jim half crazy with all my worrying." Bonnie could hear a woman talking in the background, after which Evelyn whispered, "I've got to go now. 'Madame' is starting to get huffy."

No sooner had Bonnie hung up the telephone—her friend's wedding plans seemingly back on an even keel—than she felt herself drawn by intense curiosity to the mysterious cylinder in Waco Hall. As on her last couple of ventures, she abstained from any preparations. She just went. Her one concession to practicality was to begin utilizing the upper portal, a precaution inspired by the peril of close calls, with unpredictable numbers of people milling about on the "other side," hidden from view until it was too late.

This time, when she came walking down the stairway, there were no people around. Monday had become Sunday, of course, and neither the big auditorium nor the small recital hall were in use. Impulsively, she decided to explore for a few minutes before going to Jones Reference Library. Instead of leaving through the east exit, she went across the carpeted lobby and then down a corridor on the west side. This, she knew, would lead to an unfamiliar wing of the building. A cleaning lady had alluded to it on Bonnie's initial foray into the future, but that was eight weeks ago, so the girl could not remember what this "mirror image" of Waco Hall East was called.

When she came to the end of the corridor and turned right, she encountered some heavy wooden doors that, swung aside, led to a rather characterless lobby. A sign revealed that the adjacent performance venue was named "Roxy Grove Hall." On the opposite side of the lobby from this medium-sized auditorium, within a glass case, was a schedule of musical events. Sunday, March 22, showed two listings, both of which had already occurred: a junior organ recital here in this hall at 2:00 P.M., and a Wind Ensemble performance in Jones Concert Hall, wherever that might be, at 3:00 P.M. Two pianists could be heard playing in Roxy Grove Hall at present, a man and a woman—faculty age—rehearsing music for keyboard duo on a pair of nine-foot Steinways.

The weather was partly cloudy and eighty-one degrees as Bonnie set out across campus for Moody Memorial Library and a resolution of her experiment in time. Soon she might know, beyond any reasonable doubt, the answer to an ancient riddle: was it conceivable to tamper with history, or would inherent safeguards prevent such willful manipulation? She tried to think what this astonishing power of hers must mean. Had she been touched by God? Was it her duty to right a cosmic wrong before it ever happened? The infinite possibilities made her feel wonderfully blessed but also unimaginably small, insignificant, and humble. Who was she to be entrusted with such a gift, unless there was a specific purpose to her mission?

Upon entering the library, Bonnie paused at a group of five computers, just to determine whether she would be able to employ this extraordinary research technology on her own—without the assistance of Michael, Sean, or somebody else to provide basic instruction. What she found came as a discouragement to her independent nature. The screens displayed a message that read, "Press Ctrl-Alt-Del to unlock this computer." But even then, each so-called "libraryguest" required a "username" and "password" to progress past that point. Apparently, only those people currently associated with Baylor University were granted the privilege of using the machines, which left her no option but to ask for help. That would have to wait for another day.

She went out the glass doors and slowed for a moment at the bottom of the stairway, taking a deep, nervous breath. As she would willingly concede, matters of such astronomical magnitude as modifying the future were far in excess of her intellectual capacity. Still, she had no choice but to discover for certain what parameters applied in her unique existence. With that objective in mind, Bonnie advanced up to the second floor, to the "R" section of bound periodicals, to *The Reader's Digest*, to the September 1942 issue, and ultimately to page 154.

A cold chill went up her spine as she witnessed a private miracle. On her original viewing of this page, it lay pristinely flat. Now the page's corner was turned up, just as she had altered it that very morning—more than six and a half decades earlier.

♦   ♦   ♦

The two seats that Priscilla supplied for Thursday night's 8:15 concert by the Waco Symphony Orchestra were thirty-three rows back, slightly right of center in the middle section—perfectly acceptable, if less choice than those that Bonnie and Jack had occupied in late January. While Evelyn Branch did not pretend to be an authority on music, her cogent remarks left little doubt that she was far more knowledgeable than her evening's companion. For example, it was Evelyn who stated categorically that the Tchaikovsky Piano Concerto was really the first of *three* that the great Russian master wrote, the third being just a single movement. Somehow, she also knew that the Brazilian Antônio Carlos Gomes, whose overture to *Il Guarany* opened the program, was regarded as the first operatic composer in the New World to be esteemed, by European critics, as worthy of mention in the same rarefied context as Rossini and Verdi.

Appearing as soloist in the Tchaikovsky concerto was Arnaldo Estrella, who was in the midst of a North American goodwill tour, highlighted by engagements with four of the "Big Five" orchestras. His Waco stay was marred for a couple of days when he complained of digestive problems, prompting an emergency trip to Providence Hospital. Although admitted to a room for observation, the Brazilian pianist ultimately secured his discharge in plenty of time to rehearse properly with the Waco Symphony. Facilitating his collaboration with the orchestra was the fact that Senhor Estrella was fluent in Portuguese, Spanish, and French, the last of which coincided with one of conductor Max Reiter's lingual proficiencies.

In addition to the Tchaikovsky and Gomes compositions, the concert offered a pastoral work called *Bethlehem* by the Memphis Symphony's Burnet Tuthill (son of Carnegie Hall architect William Tuthill), plus the famous "On the Trail" movement from Ferde Grofé's *Grand Canyon Suite* and the *Boléro* of Maurice Ravel. Bonnie particularly enjoyed the flashy opening of the Tchaikovsky and the hypnotic repetition of the Ravel. The Grofé piece made her think of cigarette commercials on such radio shows as "Philip Morris Playhouse" and "Johnny Presents," the latter named for diminutive bellhop Johnny Roventini, who would hawk the product by shouting his signature line, "Call for Philip Mor-rayss! Call for Philip Mor-rayss!"

But more than anything else, the March 25 concert brought back heartwarming memories of an earlier evening in Waco Hall. There was even a "Tchai-KOW-sky" work on the program, and the very thought of it made Bonnie smile. After three weeks of separation, she was beginning to fully sense the depth of her affection for Jack Decker and to realize how fervently she missed him. Her letter of March 18 could not have caught up with the Army captain yet—in England, she assumed—but whenever it did, she was sure to receive a flurry of correspondence in return. That, at least, is what she kept telling herself.

What made the absence of mail all the more dispiriting for Bonnie was the fact that Billy Fowler had already received a letter from Jack. Softening the blow somewhat was the reported nature of the subject matter—mostly about her. Bonnie asked to read this letter, but Billy declined. "Too personal," he said. "Don't want to give away any of his trade secrets." One inkling came on Friday when the lieutenant saw Bonnie in the USO and invited her to have supper with him and his wife the following night. That ploy had Jack's fingerprints all over it, she thought. It was a considerate gesture, though, so she accepted at once, without allowing time for her suspicions to cloud the issue.

The Fowlers lived in a small rental home on Lyle Avenue, and they counted themselves lucky to have it. Many of Billy's fellow officers and their wives were consigned to the married quarters on base, through no fault of their own. The housing scarcity was so acute that entire families, in many cases, were forced to make do with a single room in someone else's residence. Not only did Billy, Melinda, and Peg have a ramshackle place to call their own, but they also had a fenced-in back yard for their pet canine, Doc.

"We have a sausage dog," were little Peg's first words to Bonnie—not more than thirty seconds after she arrived—and, as Melinda later explained to the Baylor coed, this is how the pooch's name originated: it was a dachshund.

"That's a breed that won't be jumping the fence," Bonnie said.

Melinda frowned. "But they're very good at burrowing under. We've learned that the hard way—twice."

If Jack's plan was to expose Bonnie to the bliss of marital life, he could hardly have chosen a more ideal couple as models. Billy and Melinda appeared to be supremely compatible, almost as if they were on an extended honeymoon. They had remained sweethearts since childhood, growing up together along First Creek in Fountain City, just to the north of Knoxville. He was one year older than she, so they shared three terms as students at Central High School.

"Roy Acuff was our most famous alum, but he was mainly a ballplayer back in his school days," Billy said. "I don't know that for sure, but it's what has been accepted into campus lore. He was way before my time."

Bonnie smiled with recognition. "I've heard of Roy Acuff, so he must be pretty famous. I'm not a big fan of western music."

"No, neither are we," Melinda told her, "but we do have a couple of his records—just because he was a Bobcat, I guess."

During the course of the evening, while the three adults were having an after-dinner coffee, Melinda reminded her husband of something that she clearly deemed to be very important. "Honey, have you read that passage to her yet?"

Indeed, Billy had forgotten. "Wait here. I'll find it for you," he said to their guest. Off he went to the other room.

Melinda grinned shyly at Bonnie and whispered, "Our Peggy doesn't know it yet, but she's going to have a baby brother or sister in the fall."

"Gee, that's swell," Bonnie told her. She looked across the cramped living room, to where Peg was playing in the corner with some dominoes. The youngster was having difficulty trying to make them stand on end atop the uneven carpet. "I hope you'll still be here in Waco when the baby comes," Bonnie added.

"I doubt that very much, the way this war is going," Melinda said. "Most of Billy's battalion expect to be shipped out within a couple of months—tops. And if Billy is overseas, I'll be on my own. Wives can't follow their husbands out of the country."

"Where was Peggy born?" Bonnie asked.

"She was a peacetime baby, of course—born at a hospital in Knoxville."

Bonnie blew on the surface of her steaming beverage and took a cautious sip. She was trying to develop a taste for coffee, but all too often she managed to burn her tongue.

"Here we are," Billy said. He was triumphantly waving an envelope overhead as he returned from the bedroom. "Someone had laid a stack of folded laundry on it." He glanced in the general direction of his wife. "Not to mention any names, Lindy."

Melinda rolled her eyes and smiled at Bonnie. "We don't have enough room in this house to lay anything, except on top of something else."

Frustrated by the toppling dominoes, Peg walked over to her mother. "Can I go play with Doc?"

"No, sweetie, it's too late for you to go outside. It's almost bedtime."

"But I wanted to show him to *her*." She pointed at the guest.

"Well, maybe just for a minute," Melinda said. "But then it's into your pajamas, young lady."

"Oh, boy!" Peg snatched Bonnie's hand and pulled her toward the back door. "Do you have a dog?"

"Yes, I do—back home. It's a Yorkshire terrier."

"What's his name?"

"It's not a he. My dog is a girl dog, and we call her Tiffany."

"That's a funny name."

Bonnie chuckled. "Yes, I guess it is. We named her after a jewelry store in New York."

"How come?"

"I don't know. It was my daddy's idea."

Doc was so excited to have unanticipated company that he raced to the fence and back as fast as his short legs would carry him. Then he flipped onto his side and let the child pat his stomach for a moment, prior to repeating the entire routine. By the time he had done it four times, his tongue was hanging out of his mouth, and he was panting to catch his breath, much to the amusement of both spectators. When Doc finally calmed down a bit, Bonnie knelt to pet the "sausage dog" and received a sloppy lick of the hand. That settled it. Yes, she and Jack would have a dog—and a little daughter.

Melinda escorted Peg to her bedroom, but Billy stayed put, standing next to the end table while he removed from its envelope the letter that Captain Decker had sent him from "somewhere in Europe." A coffee pot lay within arm's length on a hot pad.

He began by telling Bonnie what she already knew. "I don't think it's any secret where Jack has been stationed."

"England. I've been aware of that all along, though of course he never came right out and informed me before he left."

"It's an airfield called Polebrook—about eighty miles north of London. Jack's in the 351st Bomber Group (Heavy), which is part of the Eighth Air Force. I won't elaborate, but I do think you deserve to know that much."

"Thank you."

The remainder of Bonnie's cup of coffee was still quite drinkable, so she waved him off when Billy asked, "Care for a warm up?" After refilling his wife's cup, he carried the coffee pot into the kitchen.

Bonnie used these few seconds of solitude to brace herself for what was to come. She put on a brave face, determined to register no emotion when Jack's words from abroad finally reached her. Why was she so jittery? It could be that the message would prove inconsequential, like "How is your weather? Ours is cold and rainy." Surely Jack would not share his innermost thoughts with even the truest of fellow officers.

Billy walked back into the room, sat down in his well-worn easy chair, and tried to break the tension with a joke. "I'll have to be careful what I recite here because some of Jack's sentiment for you gets awfully steamy, and I don't want to fog up the windows."

"Ooh, sounds interesting!" Bonnie said. "So why don't you let me read it to myself? He won't know the difference."

"Sorry, but that is called 'dereliction of duty.' What kind of friend would I be?"

"It'll serve him right for not sending *me* a letter in all this time."

Billy grinned at the girl for a moment, but then he lit a cigarette and became more serious.

Bonnie detected the change and said to him, "All kidding aside, there's nothing embarrassing or mushy in it, is there?"

"No, not really. It's more of an apology for not writing to you, though I guess even that could be interpreted as an expression of love. Ready to hear it?"

She nodded her assent and swallowed the last mouthful of coffee.

Billy picked up the letter and unfolded it. "Actually, there are two parts that I wanted to tell you, so I'll read them both." Clearing his throat, he perused the single sheet of handwritten text—front and back—and stopped at the first relevant paragraph. "Jack says, 'Please assure Bonnie that my inability to write as soon as I would like is no reflection of her place in my heart. I have been unbelievably busy since my arrival here, and the last thing I want to do is toss off a hurriedly scrawled note that undervalues my feelings for her.' And then, farther down ..." Billy turned the sheet of paper over. "... he writes, 'I pray to God that she is there for me when I return from this war. It saddens me to think that we had so very little time together—really not enough to establish a lasting bond, I'm afraid. I certainly will understand if she falls for some other fellow while I'm away. If so, then our relationship simply was not meant to be. But I will never forget my beautiful Bonnie, and I wish for her nothing but the best. Please let her know that I will try to write in the next couple of weeks, when our duties over here become more settled. And give her my love.' That's the gist of it, pretty much." He glanced at Jack's letter once more and then laid it, faceup, on the end table. "There, now—that wasn't so bad, was it?"

"No." Bonnie took a deep breath and sighed. "I think it's sweet of him to say such nice things about me—someone he doesn't know very well."

"You've made a good impression on him."

She gave that some thought. "Maybe so, but I'm sure he's met a lot more worldly girls than me. And he'll probably meet others before I ever see him again."

"Nah, Jack's not a carouser, if that's what you mean."

Bonnie frowned. "It's just that any normal man is susceptible to an attractive young woman, especially with a few drinks and in a foreign country—the excitement of it all, you know. Jack is only human."

"You're worrying too much. I know him fairly well, and from what I've seen, Jack's got a level head on his shoulders. He's sure not one to go chasing after the skirts. And he can hold his liquor well. He gets quiet and thoughtful, not amorous. Sirens aren't used to that, and it throws them off the scent."

"I hope you're right."

Four days later, when Bonnie eventually did receive a letter from Jack Decker, she carried it around during all of her classes, occasionally gazing at the unopened envelope, the handwriting, the return address, and even the APO postmark, quietly savoring the exhilaration they brought. Late that afternoon, she read the letter while sitting on a wooden swing in Burleson Quadrangle—the same swing she shared with Jack the first time they were truly alone together, after church, on the last day of February.

Dearest Bonnie,

I wanted my debut note to you from overseas to be something special, overwhelming in its eloquence, but all I can think of telling you is what is on my mind. Oh, well, it was a grand idea while it lasted.

We arrived at our destination without mishap and set up shop immediately. Two of my fellow BAAF officers made the trip with me, so I already had some familiar faces around. Not my best pals from Waco, but at least we had some common ground to talk about while we went through the inprocessing. Without divulging too much information, I think it is safe to tell you that the boys in my crew would get a superior critique from me. The funny thing is, one of them is from Texas (Dallas, like you), and another is from Indiana (Logansport). Two of them are from New York City and sort of hard for me to understand when they talk—especially Henry Selkirk, who was a chiropractor in civilian life.

The officers' mess is just like back home in the States, which means good food but not too much of it. They certainly do not want to make us fat—that's pretty evident. Still, there are lots of cigarettes to be had, and chocolate candy is much easier to find than I can remember in Texas. No wonder there's a shortage for civvies. We've got it all over here. By the way, one of our DROs is a Jewish teenager from Akron, Ohio. He was at the ballpark in Cleveland a couple of years ago when Keltner made two great plays at third to stop DiMaggio's hitting streak. (Are you a baseball fan? Can't recall.)

Drop me a line as soon as you can. When you do, please also send a photograph of yourself, which I plan to keep at eye-level on the top shelf of my locker. The enclosed snapshot of me is strictly government issue, but I'll try to get you a better one before too long. A handful of the fellows I know have cameras over here, so maybe I can get them to shoot a picture of me at some unidentifiable location. It can't give away much geography, or the censor will confiscate the shot, and you'll never see it. There is not an abundance of leisure time, but occasionally we are permitted to go into town for a couple of hours.

I miss you, Bonnie, and cannot begin to tell you how much I treasure the time we spent together in Waco. I have many pleasant memories of you stored away, and it is nice to call upon them whenever I suddenly feel a little lonely. Usually there are _more_ people around than I would like. That does not include my crew, though, as they are top-notch, and we would go through hell to save each others' lives, just like brothers. I hope that you will not forget all about me by the time I return home from this war.

But where is home? Veedersburg? Waco? Anywhere I happen to be with you.

Love, Jack

As Bonnie was gently refolding the letter and placing it back in its envelope, she heard the rumbling sound of an airplane. Off in the distance, just above the treetops to the northeast, was the silhouette of a cargo transport, similar to the C-47 in which she and Jack flew from Houston to Waco. She could see that there were two engines. Maybe it was the very same plane, only this time departing toward the south from WAAF. She stood up and watched the aircraft for as long as possible—until visibility was obscured by the weather-beaten, dilapidated houses across Fifth Street. Even then, straining to hear, she did not lose touch for another minute or more.

◆　　◆　　◆

Bonnie's primitive experiment with a 1942 issue of *The Reader's Digest*, while admittedly unscientific, nonetheless demonstrated to her that she possessed the power to reshape a tiny piece of the future without necessarily upsetting the course of history. Thus convinced, she was ready to set her plan into action, and for that she would require a much deeper mastery of computers than her cursory sessions with Michael and Sean could impart. Most of all, she needed a username and password.

It was the first Tuesday in April, and Bonnie was seeking the help of Ryan Andriessen, that Baylor student who gave her a tour of the campus and later introduced her to television and frozen pizza. He seemed quite fond of her, and she hoped that he might volunteer his technical services.

But all of the apartments in Ryan's housing complex appeared to be pretty much alike, especially after the passage of nearly two months. Bewildered by the array of choices, Bonnie twice walked through the parking lot from end to end, trying to recall the precise location. She felt certain that this was the correct building, but the individual units were maddeningly identical from the outside. Any of a half-dozen of them might be his.

Bonnie took another look from afar, scanning the entire breadth of the property, and yet some doubts remained. Purely at random, she came closer and knocked on one of the doors. A male student answered.

"Excuse me," she said, "but do you know where Ryan Andriessen lives?"

"Nope—sorry. I just moved here, though, so I'm probably not the best person to ask." The boy smiled politely at her, but even before the door shut, he had resumed conversing with someone else on a wireless telephone. When Bonnie knocked at the adjoining apartment to the left, another young man answered, but with similarly futile results. And the ensuing door was even less productive, for no one seemed to be at home.

The obvious solution to her dilemma was to locate a telephone booth and give Ryan a call, but Bonnie was unable to find his number. She never expected to see him again, so she did not treat his contact information with adequate care. Now she was annoyed at herself for being so shortsighted. Honestly, she brooded, how much space would that minuscule slip of paper have taken up in her purse?

As Bonnie systematically proceeded to the next unit, she happened to notice a red car coming from the street into the paved lot. Crouching low, she scurried behind the nearest parked vehicle. From this hiding spot, she watched as a boy and a girl got out of the car and, holding hands, approached the building. The boy unlocked one of the apartments, and they both went inside. It was Michael Tinsley and Nicole Hulen. Bonnie made a mental note of the numeral that was nailed to the door—12—but she left without knocking. She had no desire to renew acquaintances with Michael's fiancée, and she was fairly certain that the feelings were mutual.

Stymied, Bonnie considered going over to Sean Nixon's apartment on Tenth Street. He knew computers rather well and would be willing to give her some basic instruction. *More* than willing, she thought, which is why she now rejected the notion of seeing him again. It was Sean who exposed her to the pitfalls of alcohol and explicit images, perhaps in the interest of rendering her vulnerable to sexual advance. And yet, maybe he was slightly tipsy at the time and not in complete control of his faculties. The least she could do was grant him that much latitude. Still, Bonnie was a little afraid of what he might try to do to her—and that she might not try very hard to resist.

Then inspiration struck. She could find Ryan at the weight room, where, by his own admission, he made use of the barbells and exercise machines almost every day. Although Bonnie could not remember the name of the gymnasium or where it was situated, the very first person she met along Bagby Avenue was able to give her some helpful directions. "That's what we call the Slick," the girl said. "Turn left at the traffic light, and you'll see it. A humongous, red-brick building."

As promised, there indeed stood the Student Life Center, and an imposing structure it was. Bonnie went in through the front entrance and immediately came upon a muscular young man, whom she presumed to be a student assistant or trainer of some sort. "Where would a friend of mine go to lift weights?" she asked him.

"Does this friend of yours have a name?" The youth's manner was amiable and easygoing.

"Ryan Andriessen."

"Ryan? Yeah, he's one of our regulars."

"Is he here today?"

"Yes, he is. Go around there—first room on the right. Once you're inside, take the ramp down to the third level. We'll sign you in as a visitor." He watched with an appreciative gaze as Bonnie passed by and continued toward the weight room. Not many girls wore dresses these days, and hers was very becoming.

Bonnie was surprised to discover that literally dozens of people—mostly students, but also several who appeared to be faculty or staff—were exercising on the various stationary machines. Some had positioned themselves strategically, so as to allay their physical discomfort by viewing television screens as they worked up a sweat. The ramp in question was all the way across the room, and she followed it to the left until it descended no further. This took her to the free weights, an entire level filled with barbells, dumbbells, and padded benches. She did not notice her friend at once because he was reclining on a bench, wiping perspiration from his face with a towel. A few seconds later, it was Ryan who observed her, and he could hardly believe his eyes. "Bonnie?" he asked.

She turned to him and smiled. "Hello, Ryan."

The boy sat up straight, sporting a befuddled grin. "What brings you here?" He felt flattered that she had traveled all the way from California to see him.

"My father is in Waco on a business trip, so I thought I would tag along and take another look at Baylor."

"What about your classes?"

"I have a good attendance record, so it won't hurt me to miss a couple of them, here and there."

"How long can you stay?"

"Just a few more days—whenever my father has to go back to Los Angeles."

Ryan stood up and walked closer, seemingly at a loss for words. He took both of her hands in his own but stopped short of kissing or hugging her.

Bonnie, too, was self-conscious, not fully sensing how much familiarity to show. "Do you need to finish your weightlifting? I can come back later," she said. That, at least, would give him a graceful way out of their meeting.

But Ryan chose otherwise. "No. I'm nearly done. All I have left are some squats, and one of my knees is bothering me anyway, so it might be a good idea to skip that set." Then, something he remembered made him laugh. "Did you take the train again?"

Bonnie blushed, caught in her own deception. "No. We flew to Dallas, and my father rented a car to drive us down to Waco." She had learned a thing or two since the last time they spoke, and she trusted that it made her sound more convincing than before.

"How did you know I'd be here at the Slick?" Ryan asked.

"I knew you came here quite often—being the athletic type." She glanced at his sculpted arms and torso.

"Yep, that's me." As it happened, he was admiring her upper body, too. "Where are you staying?"

This took Bonnie by surprise. "Oh ... in the tall hotel downtown."

"The Hilton?"

"Maybe so."

"On University Parks Drive, near the suspension bridge?"

"Yes, that's it."

Ryan draped his towel over a shoulder and led Bonnie toward the exit. "Want something to eat, or is it too early?" he asked.

"Actually, I was hoping you'd do me a favor."

"Anything you say. Just name it."

"Teach me how to use a computer."

"Absolutely—glad to."

Outside the exercise room, they walked past a huge, man-made rock, fifty-two feet tall, upon the sides of which five or six people clung, in their attempt to scale the wall to its summit.

Ryan turned to Bonnie. "As I recall, you're from a very ... traditional family."

"Yes, my family are strictly twentieth century—if not the nineteenth. Sorry to be so backwards."

"Don't apologize. I think it's fine."

"Unless, of course, I'm trying to use modern technology."

"Well, I certainly don't mind giving you some pointers." He did his best to hold back a smile. "In fact, I think I'd kind of enjoy it."

Ryan swung the exit door open for her, and Bonnie expressed her thanks. But when he appeared to be heading south instead of north, she said, "If it's all the same to you, could we do this in the library?"

"Sure. Any particular reason?"

"Michael and Nicole are at the apartment. I saw them go inside a while ago."

"And you don't want to pop in on them, unannounced."

"No."

"I did that once," Ryan said with a laugh. "They were in the center of the living room, and she was sitting straight up on his ... well, you know. I felt like I had wandered into a skin flick."

"A skin ...?

"A dirty movie."

Her eyes widened, and she swallowed hard. "They were completely naked?"

"In the buff! She's got a nice build, though, so I'm not complaining."

Bonnie chuckled for an instant but then became serious. "Actually, Nicole's attitude is the real reason why I don't want to go to your apartment. I get the feeling that she doesn't like me very much."

"Aw, that's just the way she is—always thinking that someone is trying to steal her Mickey away. You should see how she acts toward his ex-girlfriend."

"Heather?"

"Heather Whaley, yeah." He looked surprised. "That's right—I guess you know her, don't you?"

"We've met."

Bonnie and Ryan went to Jones Reference Library and sat together in front of one of the available computers. "Show me how familiar you are with the internet," he said, "so I can figure out where to start."

"I really don't know anything at all, except how to type in 'libraryguest.' It doesn't let me go any further."

"Okay, there's your snag. Don't mess with entering as a guest. That won't get you anywhere but the library catalogue. For the full-blown internet, you'll need a username and password, and you can borrow mine whenever you want them. I trust you."

"Gosh, thanks."

"First, type in 'Ryan ... underscore ... Andriessen'." She did as he said. "Then, 'Larsen56' with a capital 'L' for the password."

"How come?"

"That's just what I picked—for Don Larsen's perfect game in 1956." He spotted a misspelling. "But it's Larsen with an 'e.' A password has to be exact, or the computer will reject it."

She corrected the password, and the computer admitted her into the system. Ryan taught her how to open what he called a "search engine."

"Have you ever done a search before?" he asked.

"Not personally, no, but I've watched other people—Michael and someone else."

Ryan smiled. "And now it's your turn. Ready?"

"I guess so. What'll I search for?"

"For practice, try to find out how many home runs Ted Williams had in 1949. You might want to type in 'williams 1949 home runs.' Then hit return." He waited while she did so. "Lots of options come up, and you just explore those that seem the most promising. I would probably click on that one there— Baseball Almanac. I use it all the time."

"Baseball Almanac, huh?"

"Well, that's just an example. Look, Williams hit forty-three homers that year. See how it works?"

Within a half-hour, Bonnie had learned enough searching techniques to become somewhat proficient, and Ryan was pleased by how rapidly she absorbed the concepts. "You're not going to have any trouble at all. I'm impressed."

"Thank you." She smiled and kissed him on the cheek.

Startled, he asked her, "What was that for?"

"Just for being nice—for taking me under your wing, so to speak."

"Hey, no problem. I think you could already solo," he said. "You're a natural."

The word brought a mischievous twinkle to Bonnie's eyes. "Someone was telling me that you can type 'natural,' 'girl,' and 'tubes,' and it will give you all sorts of nasty stuff. Is that true?"

Ryan grinned. "I wouldn't be surprised. Anything even remotely off-color will turn up tons of porn."

"What's porn?"

"Pornography—graphic images and movie clips. You know, obscenity."

"Oh." She giggled and glanced around the room. "Shall we try it?"

"Don't bother. It won't work in here."

The girl seemed disappointed. "Why not?"

"Baylor's system has a filter that blocks the pornographic sites from appearing."

"So, you've tried?"

"By sheer accident, yes." He was amused by her naughtiness. This girl was a lot different than her first impression had led him to believe. "Of course, if you're really interested, there's always my computer—sometime when Nicole is not at the apartment."

"You've had 'accidents' there, too, huh?"

Ryan laughed aloud. "Occasionally. I'm just a red-blooded American male." He stood up and playfully swatted her on the back with his towel. "I've got to go take a shower."

"Watch out for Nicole. She might want to join you."

"Fine with me, but I don't think Michael would approve."

◆   ◆   ◆

The very next day, when Bonnie should have had pen in hand, tackling a difficult "compare and contrast" project for her American Prose class, instead she was in 2009 again, poised before a computer within Jones Reference Library. Seeing her at work, an observer from the early twenty-first century might have assumed that her major in college was history rather than English, for she was combing through service records of the US 8th Air Force in Britain during World War II. Of particular interest to her was the 351st Bomber Group (Heavy), stationed at a former RAF base near the Northamptonshire village of Polebrook.

Wing personnel, officer rosters, casualty lists, reunions, memoirs, reenactment groups, memorabilia, vintage photos, maps of airfields, and a profusion of other sources were at her disposal. And yet, nothing helped. With a single tantalizing exception, it was almost as if John Tynes Decker never existed. The name did appear on one early roster, but that was from November of 1942, identifying him as a flight instructor at Blackland Army Air Field in Waco, Texas. Historical research was an imperfect science, Bonnie conceded, but it stood to reason that she should have been able to uncover a trail of some sort, even if it only led to scattered, isolated snippets of data. Maybe she was not up to the task. While soloing might gratify the self-worth, it was no substitute for expertise.

She decided to give computer searching another couple of days—Thursday and Friday afternoons—and hope that Ryan Andriessen showed up to provide some insight. Above everything else, Bonnie did not want to be regarded by him as a pest, so she fought off any inducement to revisit the Slick, disrupt his weight training, and beg for assistance.

What she could not know was that Ryan was starting to become enamored of her. Something about this peculiar young lady from California had captured his deepest feelings and would not let him go. Maybe it was her generally sunny disposition. Or her winsome face and figure. Or the outmoded sweater-skirt combinations she invariably wore, which made her look like the girl next door of every virtuous man's fantasies. Then, too, there was her evident interest in sensuality, suggesting that this traditional lass was not so puritanical after all.

The next time they encountered one another was at 4:40 on Thursday afternoon. Bonnie was about to depart from the library after an unavailing session on the internet when Ryan entered the room and hurried over to the computer she was using. "You've got to see what I just found," he told her. He sounded excited, as if his discovery was something she would value quite highly. He pulled up a chair and sat alongside her, typing in a website address without even taking the trouble to inquire whether she was in the midst of a search. "It must be an ancestor of yours," he added. "Look!"

The screen displayed an obituary from the *Dallas Morning News*, dated May 5, 1976. When Bonnie viewed it, she could scarcely breathe, and her heart was beating so fiercely that she wondered if others in the room could hear it. The deceased woman had succumbed to an unspecified ailment at a relatively young age.

FAYETTEVILLE, N.C.—Bonnie Elaine (Ploughwright) Mills, 54, a former Dallas resident, died here Tuesday morning following a brief illness. Mrs. Mills was employed for twenty-three years as a civilian secretary at Fort Bragg military reservation and for the past three years at Pope

Air Force Base. She was born on August 14, 1921, in Corsicana, Texas, attended Baylor University, and moved with her husband, Sergeant Harvey Mills, to Fayetteville in 1950. Sgt. Mills was killed in a training accident the following year, and Mrs. Mills never re-married. She is survived by her mother and one brother. Memorials should be addressed to the American Lung Association.

Bonnie's face turned pallid, but she quickly regained her equanimity. "No, it can't be a direct relative," she managed to say. "This woman and her husband didn't seem to have children, so where would that leave me?"

"Oops. Yeah, you're right. That didn't even cross my mind," Ryan said. "I just saw her name and birthplace."

"It's probably a great-grandaunt on my father's side. Now that I think about it, there was someone else in the family who had my name." Bonnie felt uncomfortable lying to her friend, but she could hardly tell him the truth.

"What's your middle name?" he asked.

"Elaine." There was no denying the fact.

That validated Ryan's theory and gave him the bravado to discredit any lingering doubts. "She had to be related to you somehow—with a last name like 'Ploughwright,' being from Dallas, and going to Baylor. That's just too many similarities to be a fluke."

Bonnie nodded her head, staggered by the implications. She had heard many people say that it was a blessing to be unaware of what the future held for yourself, and now she knew for certain that they were right.

"I can print off a hard copy for your files," Ryan told her. "Do you want to have one?"

"What's a hard copy?"

"This same obituary ... but printed on a piece of paper."

"A piece of paper is hard?"

He smiled. "Well, in the sense that it's tangible. You can hold it in your hand. A print-out is harder than binary data on a computer screen."

Bonnie watched as Ryan pressed three or four buttons, a nimble series of actions that triggered a machine across the room to bring forth two exact copies of the obituary on white sheets of typing paper. He handed Bonnie one of them.

"By the way, if you want a change of scenery," he said, "feel free to try out my computer tomorrow. I think you'll find that it's quite a bit faster than these. Don't feel like you have to, but come if you can."

"Won't Michael be there with his girlfriend?"

"Nope. They'll be going to her parents' home in Longview after lunch and won't be back until late Saturday night." Ryan shook his head in disgust. "Nicole's father is a big-shot lawyer in east Texas, with more money than he could possibly spend. I figure that's got to be one reason why she's such a spoiled brat."

Bonnie closed the notebook and slipped it and the obituary into her purse. "When are Nicole and Michael getting married?"

"In the middle of July—the eighteenth, I think, if that's a Saturday."

"Do you really expect them to make it that long?"

Ryan looked baffled. "Sure they will. Why wouldn't they?"

"Well, I only saw them together that one time, and they didn't appear to be very compatible."

"That's because you were there to gum up the works. Nicole can smell blood when her Mickey's eyes are wandering."

"Poor Michael," Bonnie said. "He's going to have a rough time of it, putting up with his wife's jealousy for the rest of his life."

"Not necessarily. That wedding band will identify him as her property, and then she'll be fine. Nicole wants to get an extra wide set of rings, so people can see them from a mile away."

Bonnie frowned. "How sad—to have so little trust in your mate."

The longer Ryan stared at her, the wider his smile grew. "Jeez, you really are an old-fashioned girl," he said. "You should have lived in the '20s or '30s."

Stung by the remark, Bonnie eyed him with suspicion. "Why do you say that?"

"Oh, I meant it as a compliment—believe me!"

◆   ◆   ◆

When Bonnie awoke on April 10, it was a Saturday for her but a Friday for Ryan Andriessen. She kept having to remind herself of that anomaly—something people pursuing normal lives had no need to consider. If she traveled to his apartment on a weekday morning, he would probably still be in class. In view of that, she decided to get up relatively early, put in three intensive hours of studying, and then help other volunteers with the scrap drive at church. She would eat lunch in the present, to save money, and pass over to the future for her computer research. By that time, Michael and Nicole would be out of town. It was the best of both worlds, or so she thought.

Bonnie arrived at Columbus Avenue Baptist Church about a half-hour before noon and went to the administrative offices, where she asked the youth minister how she could be of service. He consulted a sheet of paper on his clipboard and told her, "Ride along with Kenny, and help him load up the next shipment. You'll be going to the Sanger Heights, Brookview, and Dean Highlands neighborhoods, and all the metal ought to be out by the street. Frances and Wade can go with you."

She and her fellow volunteers followed Kenny to his truck. Wade hopped into the flatbed, and the two girls joined their driver in the cab. "Here," Kenny said. "You'll need these." He tossed each of the female passengers a pair of work gloves to protect from tetanus. Kenny Mackey was a man in his early forties who walked with a pronounced limp. He appeared to be on very familiar terms with Frances, causing Bonnie to wonder whether they were husband and wife. They exchanged few words but invariably perceived what the other was thinking.

When the quartet arrived at their predetermined pick-up points, Bonnie and Frances handled the small items such as frying pans, hubcaps, and egg beaters, while Kenny and Wade hoisted larger or heavier discards like bed springs, automobile fenders, and lawnmower blades. In due course, Bonnie's curiosity prevailed upon her to speak up and ask Frances whether she was the driver's wife.

The woman appeared to be rather tickled by this comment. "How could you tell?" she said.

"I don't know. I just could."

"We've been married for nineteen years now. We're both from Waco, but we met on a mission trip to El Paso. Kenny always teases me that I was playing hard to get—going all the way to west Texas to elude him."

Wade Taggert was much younger than the Mackeys, only eighteen and a student at Waco High School. It was clear from the outset that he was carrying a torch for the attractive Baylor girl. Seldom did Bonnie glance his way when the teenager was not peering wistfully at her. He had it bad but was too bashful to say a word. Feeling sorry for the boy, she figured that some playful badinage would not be amiss. "Do you go to Baylor University?" she asked him.

Wade's ego was bolstered by the assumption, which made him break into a grin. "No, ma'am. I'm still in high school."

"Then you must be a senior."

"Yes, ma'am. I graduate at the end of next month."

"What then?"

"I'll be joining up. The Marines, if I have a choice."

"I'll bet a handsome boy like you has lots of girlfriends, huh?"

"No, ma'am." He looked away. "Well, I'm pretty sure Frieda Cowell kind of likes me. She's in my home room."

"Do you like her, too?"

"Sure. She's a peach. Everyone thinks so."

"Have you ever dated?"

He laughed. "Only in my dreams. She's already spoken for—by an end on the football team."

"Oh, dear. Well, don't give up. Everything works out for the best if it's meant to be."

Wade threw an armload of assorted metal into the flatbed, and Bonnie stood by, watching him. Suddenly, after mustering all of his courage, the boy said to her, "How old are you?"

"Me? I'm twenty-one."

His spirits sank. "Gosh, I have a sister your age. She's already married and has a baby."

"I guess I'm not a very fast worker."

"Do you have a boyfriend?"

"Yes, I do. He's in the Air Corps."

"Are you engaged?"

Bonnie blushed, but even hearing the question made her feel nice. "No, not yet, but I hope to be someday—presuming that he'll have me."

"He will," Wade told her. He seemed a lot more certain about it than she did.

Within three hours and nine stops, the volunteers had stockpiled a whole truck full of scrap metal, which naturally meant that Wade could no longer ride in the flatbed. Up front he went, pressed tightly between the Baylor coed and a protruding door handle that poked him in the ribs. He was pleased to lean imperceptibly to the left, where he could feel her breath dancing upon the hairs of his forearm.

Kenny Mackey and his crew deposited their accumulated mass of salvage—destined for rebirth as war matériel—at an East Waco collection site, festooned with a red, white, and blue banner that proclaimed, "MAKE ADOLF WHIMPER!" It was a job well done, said an elderly custodian who received the shipment, and his praise made the pain in their muscles disappear without a trace. Like countless others across the nation, they felt the pride of doing their bit for a patriotic ideal, citizen soldiers on the home front.

After she rode the streetcar back to Baylor University, Bonnie showered and dressed, only to discover that the dormitory cafeteria had already closed. A member of the dining staff was kind enough to sell her two leftover sandwiches and a bottle of Pepsi-Cola for twenty cents. And then, by 2:30, Bonnie was passing through the lobby of Waco Hall and into the future. The temperature abruptly dropped from seventy-eight degrees to a pleasantly cool sixty-nine.

Unless she missed her guess, Ryan had already finished his exercise regimen by now, so she headed straight toward Daughtrey Avenue instead of the Student Life Center. The walk gave her an opportunity to mull over a comment that had been troubling her since the last time they spoke: "You should have lived in the '20s or '30s." Was this simply an offhand remark, or a telltale sign that inconsistencies were subverting her airtight story?

To Bonnie's surprise, sound was coming from behind the door of the apartment. It was Ryan's television, playing loudly, so he must have already returned from the workout session. She knocked, but there was no answer, even after allowing a couple more minutes to pass. Maybe he was upstairs and could not hear that somebody was at the door. Again she knocked, now with more insistence. Still no response. Stepping back, she glanced up at the second-floor window, just in time to see the curtains part slightly. Ryan spotted her from above and held up an index finger to show that he would be right down.

"Sorry," he said, upon opening the door. "I was drying off after my shower." His hair looked wet, and he was wearing only a pair of basketball shorts. "Come on in."

As Bonnie entered his living room, she noticed that Ryan peeked at the parking lot before shutting and locking the door. "Are you waiting for someone?" she asked.

"A girl from my math class said she might drop by to pick up her study notes. That's who I thought was here when I heard you knock."

Bonnie could not resist fishing for a compliment. "I hope I didn't disappoint you too much."

And Ryan took the bait. "No way! It's awsome to see you." She half expected a kiss from him, but he was too sensible to hazard such a chancy move. Bonnie stole a moment to admire the boy's bare chest—hairlessly smooth and with muscles solid enough for striking a match. Only in the interest of maintaining proper decorum did she turn away so quickly.

The television continued to carry a sports report—discursive analysis concerning the first week of the Major League Baseball season—and part of Ryan's attention was naturally drawn there. "The Tigers killed the Rangers in Detroit today," he said. "Something ugly, like fifteen to two. Are you a Rangers fan or Astros?"

Having heard of neither of those teams, Bonnie chose the easy way out. "I usually root for the New York Yankees."

Ryan's head jerked toward her. "Say it ain't so, Joe!" he said in mock horror. But then he laughed. "I'll try to pretend I never heard that. At least your Dodgers grabbed Torre away from them."

She laughed, too, relieved not to have blundered with yet another entangling anachronism. (Why, though, did he think Brooklyn was "her" team? She never said as much.) Things were going well so far, but she reminded herself to stay watchful, cautious, on her toes. Ryan already seemed excessively intrigued by her, and one more miniscule flub might convince him that this Bonnie Ploughwright was not who she claimed to be. He used the battery-powered remote control to switch off the screen and motioned for her to follow behind him.

Unlike Michael's computer, which sat upon a table in the corner of the living room, Ryan's was situated in his bedroom, upstairs. Two chairs were already in front of it, causing Bonnie to wonder whether he expected her to drop in today or if he had positioned them like that for the girl in his mathematics class. Either way, it was a very cozy arrangement, with the chairs placed so close together that they nearly touched. By now, Ryan had put on a T-shirt—sky blue, with "Mavericks" in white across the chest—and it did not coordinate very nicely with his bright yellow shorts. Unconcerned by aesthetics, he sat down next to Bonnie and spread his fingers over the keyboard.

"What's your relative's name again?" he asked.

Bonnie looked confused. "Which relative?"

"The soldier."

"That would be John Tynes Decker. But he wasn't related to me—I mean, biologically."

Ryan tapped out the letters very efficiently, almost as if he were a professional typist. "Is that T-Y-N-E-S?"

She smiled at him. "Yes. How did you know?"

"Just lucky, I guess." He squinted at the screen. "How else could you spell it?"

As Bonnie had discovered two days earlier, this particular Army captain was not well represented on the "web." Ryan, too, ran into setbacks aplenty, with no clear indication that such an individual ever drew a breath. But there was an important difference between the two searches: Ryan kept a wildcard up his sleeve. It so happened that his aunt in Utah had a passionate interest in the science of genealogy. She was the younger of his father's two sisters, and anything she did not know about the Andriessen family could be safely dismissed as negligible.

Using Gladys Maynard's active contacts with genealogical societies, gradually the blanks in Jack Decker's life story began to be filled by certifiable facts. Many were joyous for Bonnie to learn, but others were disconcerting or even tragic. At one point, she gasped, "Dear God," and Ryan was startled by her inordinate emotional connection to someone who was, after all, little more than an in-law, twice if not thrice removed from the nuclear family. She scribbled in her notebook everything they found, and, when compiled, the data amounted to a rather sketchy but passable biography of the late Captain Decker. According to contradictory records, he either was killed in action during a daylight raid over Kassel, Germany, on July 30, 1943, when seven B-17s were lost, or on a non-combat mission in Cheshire, England, shortly thereafter. Whichever the case, Jack's death occurred less than five months after his deployment to the European Theater of Operations.

By the end of their research session, which lasted two and a half hours, Bonnie appeared rather shaken by what she had learned. Ryan sensed that she was not at all herself, and he became worried about the abnormal way she was acting. One moment she would be chipper and positively effervescent, and the next she would descend into a profound anguish that compelled her to choke back the tears. How odd it seemed to be so personally attached to events that were by now relegated to the annals of history, nearly two thirds of a century in the past.

Ryan offered to accompany Bonnie to where the girl's father was to meet her, but she respectfully declined. When he came right out and insisted, she was every bit as adamant in her refusal. But she did thank him wholeheartedly for his "detective work," as she called it, and kissed him on the cheek. "Sorry to be so sentimental," she said, "but I can't help how I am. I feel close to people who were important in my life." Almost as an afterthought, she hastened to add, "Or in the lives of my parents and grandparents."

"Will I see you tomorrow?" he asked.

"Yes, I suppose so. My father has decided to stay for another day, at least."

"Great. What time works for you?"

She shrugged her shoulders. "It doesn't matter. Anytime after church."

"Tomorrow's Saturday," Ryan told her.

"Oh, of course," she said. "Then, how about three o'clock?" It would be Sunday for her, and missing the weekly telephone call to her parents would be cause for their alarm.

Alone with her thoughts, Bonnie tearfully returned to Waco Hall—cursed, she felt, with a vision of what was to come. Jack would perish in service to his country, they would never meet again, and she, too, would die prematurely, her writing career forsaken and unfulfilled. Could this really be all that the future held?

♦　　♦　　♦

Julia Johnston was not much of a churchgoer, but she did make rare appearances whenever the situation demanded. One such instance took place just two days after Sammy DeRosa, in the course of a casual chat at chapel, let it slip that he went to Columbus Avenue Baptist Church. "So do I," she told him, "and my roommate does too. Where do you usually sit?"

That explained why Bonnie's coterie of Sunday coeds had an extra disciple with them on the morning of April 11. Moreover, Julia announced with a wink that she would probably not need a ride back to campus if all went as planned. She attired herself very properly, with a modest, high-neck dress that buttoned all the way up the front and flowed down to just above the ankles. There was no belt to accentuate her eye-catching waistline, and white gloves and pert hat contributed an aura of refinement.

Seated next to her in the church's center section, Sammy DeRosa wore a costly, dark blue, three-piece suit with narrow pinstripes. And the Bible on his lap had a black leather cover that complemented his ensemble perfectly, in a masculine sort of no-nonsense way. Little did Sammy's inveigling companion suspect that he was as guileless in his approach to worship as she was contrived. He actually followed along with the scripture readings and sang aloud rather than just moving his lips. Never had Julia seen anything like this righteous display of piety, not that she had been exposed to the most devout practitioners of the Christian faith. He must be a Bible major at Baylor, she surmised—or maybe a preacher's kid—and going to church with him turned out to be not much fun at all. Sammy paid almost no attention to her, even after her top three buttons came undone while he was busy filling out a check for the offertory.

A couple of sections over, on the piano side of the sanctuary, the other girls from Alexander Hall were seated together in their customary pew, and it was apparent to most of them that something was bothering Bonnie. "Can I help in any way?" Annie Teakel asked after the opening choral anthem. She always had the best of intentions, and Bonnie liked her very much indeed, but occasionally Annie's intrusions into private concerns overstepped the bounds of acceptable meddling.

"I don't know what you mean," Bonnie whispered.

"You seem awfully blue today, and that's just not like you. Is there anything I can do to help?"

Bonnie smiled at Annie and patted her hand. "I'm all right, really. But thanks."

"Even so, I'm going to add you to my prayer list. You know, I've got a fellow in the Army, too."

How well Bonnie knew! Seldom did more than two minutes go by without Annie mentioning her precious Christopher to anyone within earshot. This was an endearing and undoubtedly selfless quality, but it could rankle the patience upon repeated hearings. Christopher Lowrey was stationed in the Aleutian Islands, and his battalion had earned a Meritorious Unit Commendation for its part in constructing the Alcan Highway. That was all positively grand, of course, but he had not quite yet single-handedly won the war.

When Bonnie turned away from her compassionate friend, she caught a glimpse of Julia's profile. She and her "chapel date" were now sitting like total strangers, with the girl's purse lying on its side between them and plenty of room to spare. No longer was she flashing coquettish eyes in the direction of his Roman features. As for Sammy, he seemed content to do nothing more than listen to the sermon, thumb through the Broadman Hymnal, and locate passages of the Biblical text in a timely fashion. How inconsiderate of him to be so self-centered.

Thus it was that, in the absence of lively flirtation, Julia had nowhere to look but the guest preacher for making her trip worthwhile. It was the first day of a two-week revival, leading up to Easter Sunday, and in the pulpit was James W. "Big Jim" Kramer, an independent evangelist from Denver, Colorado. His sermon

RICHARD VEIT

topic was "If I Had a Million." Although undeniably a powerful message, one that inspired no fewer than eleven receptive souls to come forward at the time of invitation, somehow it failed to touch Julia in a meaningful way. Unrevived, she bid farewell forever to Sammy DeRosa and sulkily rode back to campus just as she had come—between her roommate and Eleanor Moss in the back seat of Wanda Litchfield's Packard sedan.

♦   ♦   ♦

Whenever Michael Tinsley and his fiancée traveled away for the weekend, their normal mode of operation was to return sometime after eight o'clock on Sunday evening. No matter if both he and Nicole had early classes the next morning, they would come rolling into town well past sunset and watch a couple of DVD movies before saying goodbye to one another for the night. But Saturday, April 11, 2009, became, by choice, the end of an abbreviated, thirty-hour trip for the pair. The next day would be Easter, which meant the annual Hulen family reunion in Longview. This was a stodgy affair that Nicole, conditioned by past experience, was every bit as anxious as Michael to avoid. With that in mind, they planned to convey their regrets and be on the road back to Waco by Saturday night at seven.

And yet, even with Michael away for only the first half of the weekend, Ryan estimated that he would have a minimum of five hours alone with Bonnie, and a good deal of research could be accomplished in such an extended period of time. They went upstairs, each with a tin can of soda pop in hand, and got straight to work. He sat in front of the screen and operated the "mouse" and keyboard, while she sat alongside—offering her suggestions, for whatever they were worth.

Unfinished business took precedence. Further genealogical probing substantiated one harrowing incident that, until then, was still very much open to question. John Tynes Decker definitely was not killed in combat over Kassel on July 30, when one hundred nineteen B-17s bombed the Fieseler aircraft plant in the Bettenhausen district. Initial reports stated that seven aircraft were lost, but that was later amended to six. At the controls of the missing plane was Captain Decker, who was able to coax his flak-riddled Flying Fortress to England on three engines, making an emergency landing at Horsham St. Faith in Norfolk. This was conclusive evidence that might well lead to additional discoveries somewhere down the line.

Around six o'clock, Bonnie and Ryan took a dinner break at a seafood restaurant called Long John Silver's, named for the antagonist in Robert Louis Stevenson's *Treasure Island*. Ryan picked up the tab, which was just fine with Bonnie. Prices in the twenty-first century were beyond her means, for she certainly had not come prepared to sacrifice the equivalent of two days' wages on a single meal. Bonnie was amazed by how many eating establishments had sprouted up so near the Baylor campus— probably more than a dozen just within that single four-block expanse of commercial real estate.

The final two hours of their day together were not as productive as those that preceded them, and Bonnie felt that she was chiefly to blame. Upon returning to their "loft," as Ryan characterized it, Bonnie wasted no time in removing her white sweater to reveal a charming, light-blue blouse underneath. She did so modestly and without any hint of seductive intent. The room's temperature had grown too warm for wearing the outer garment, despite a five-bladed electronic ceiling fan that stirred up the air rather well. For the sake of propriety, Bonnie made a creditable effort to ask the boy, "Do you mind?" and he nodded his acceptance, hardly giving a second glance at the lovely top.

That Ryan misinterpreted her wardrobe adjustment soon became evident, but only with the benefit of hindsight. Not ten minutes thereafter, he, too, complained of feeling a bit uncomfortable. He walked over to the air-conditioning vent and reported that the apartment's cooling system appeared to be functioning normally. "What the heck," he said with a shrug, not the least bit self-conscious. He tossed his shirt onto the bed and, stripped to the waist, sat in front of the computer screen, wearing nothing but his pair of royal blue athletic shorts with a white stripe down each side. Bonnie watched his shoulder muscles ripple whenever he typed information on the keyboard.

Without warning, Ryan's portable telephone began emitting a raucous tune. He answered it and, smiling with familiarity, went down the stairs to converse with whoever called. That left Bonnie alone with the computer, and she was sorely tempted by her curiosity. Sensing that Ryan would be away for quite a while, she hesitantly typed in the words "natural," "girl," and "tubes," something Sean Nixon had done in her presence about a month ago. Within mere seconds, there came forth page after page of links to click, a fair portion of which took her to unimaginable collections of nudity and even the sex act itself. Bonnie wondered how many thousands of girls had posed for such photographs and movies. Were they all paid to undress for the camera, or did they do so just for the excitement of exhibiting themselves to others? It seemed to her that half of the young female population must have disrobed on the worldwide web.

Twenty-five minutes later, the sound of footsteps alerted Bonnie to her friend's impending return, so she hurriedly clicked the mouse on an "X" in the top-left corner of the computer picture, a useful trick that Sean had shown her how to do. And it worked, too, for Ryan was none the wiser. Unfortunately, their ensuing research led him to a shortcut called "History," which, to Bonnie's mortification, displayed every single webpage that she had viewed during his absence from the room.

"And what do we have here?" Ryan asked. He grinned, first at the screen and then at Bonnie herself. "Your focus appears to have drifted away from the war."

Embarrassed beyond words, she could not think of anything to say. Her face turned crimson, and she grimaced, eyes covered with hands and mumbling something incomprehensible.

"It's all right," Ryan said. "Everyone has explored the unsavory sites at one time or another. They're just sitting there for the choosing."

Bonnie finally found her voice. "I know, but I'm a girl," she told him. "I'm not supposed to be as lecherous as some gigolo in a saloon."

"Not lecherous. Just less than perfect, like the rest of us."

Intrigued, she asked him, "Have you ever looked at pages like those—when it wasn't by accident?"

"More than a few times," he said. "But I sure don't go overboard with it, unlike lots of people."

Bonnie took a deep breath and sighed. "I'm awfully sorry for behaving like that. Shall we go back to why we're here?"

"Why *are* we here?" Ryan asked. He twisted an imaginary handlebar mustache.

Again Bonnie blushed, but this time she did not turn away from the boy. "To research, I assumed."

"That can mean a lot of different things."

She continued to stare at him. "Yes, it can," she whispered. There was the merest hint of a smile.

Ryan studied Bonnie's face for a moment, hunting for a clue. Then, as if in slow motion, he reached over and unfastened the top button of her blouse. She did not resist. Bonnie was staring at his sinewy chest and thought he resembled a professional athlete—like the newspaper photo of some shirtless ballplayer during a World Series celebration in the victors' locker room. Beguiled by the manly physique, she ran the fingers of her right hand across his pectoral muscles. When their eyes met, she giggled slightly.

"You're strong," she told him, genuinely impressed.

Ryan's gaze settled upon the alluring fullness of her blouse. "So are you."

Very methodically, he unfastened all of the other buttons to open the garment wide, pulling upward until it was no longer tucked into her skirt. Bonnie alone wriggled herself free of the arm holes, allowing the downy-soft blouse to spill over the back of the chair. Her eyes closed involuntarily as

Ryan leaned forward and skimmed kisses along the base of her neck. Almost as a reflex action, she reached back to unclasp the hooks of her brassiere.

But at that moment, unaccountably, the girl experienced a change of heart, and her body stiffened. "We need to stop," Bonnie said. She was breathing rapidly.

In disbelief, overcome with fleshly desire, Ryan kissed her once above each breast and then extended both of his arms around her, fumbling in search of the tiny hooks.

"Please, Ryan. Michael might walk in at any second," Bonnie said.

"No, he won't. Not for another hour or so." Ryan sounded positive enough, but clearly this was only wishful thinking on his part.

Bonnie used both of her elbows to gently guide his arms apart and away from the undergarment. "I want you to know that this is nothing against you." She glanced down to retrieve her blouse and, in no particular hurry, slipped it on and began the process of rebuttoning.

"Well, then ... why?" He looked sad and frustrated, and Bonnie felt sorry for him, responsible for coming across as a tease.

"I don't really know. I'm just not like that, I suppose. It's not how I was brought up."

"So ... maybe sometime later, after we get to know each other better?"

She gave him a sympathetic smile but did not answer. Then she watched in silence as he stood up and gloomily reached for his shirt on the bed. They spent the next minute or two dressing themselves, no doubt striving to grasp the uncertain significance of what had happened between them.

By the time they arrived downstairs, their spirits were somewhat lifted through friendship, and Ryan offered to escort her back to campus. She said no, as he knew she would. Bonnie was awfully secretive about her father and their occasional trips halfway across the country, and it made Ryan wonder what she was trying to hide. More than that, he was concerned for her well-being. Darkness was beginning to set in, and this was a far cry from being the city's safest neighborhood. He even considered trailing after her—less as a prying snoop than as a protector from assault—but he would have to do so on the sly, for he was afraid to risk losing her trust.

"When will I see you again?" he asked. They stopped and were now facing each other, just a couple of feet outside his front door.

"Daddy needs to come to Waco for at least one more sales call," Bonnie said. "How about next Saturday afternoon at half past three? We'll need to drive down here from Dallas."

"Your father sells on weekends?"

"Yes. In his line of business, he can."

"He must be kind of wealthy, to afford all that flying."

"Oh, the company pays." She hoped what she said made sense.

Ryan nodded his head. "And he's probably getting a lot of frequent flyer points, on top of a hefty *per diem*."

Bonnie chose to turn a deaf ear rather than further demonstrate her ignorance of modern life. Ryan did not seem to notice, for other things were occupying his mind at the moment—recalling the sight and softness of her smooth skin. "See you in a week," he said, and they shared a warm kiss. Its passion suggested physical undertones that, for the time being, would have to be suppressed. The girl's mind, too, was racing—with memories of Ryan's muscular build and hard masculinity.

While she was walking away, Bonnie heard him shout to her, "Saturday at 3:30," which she acknowledged with a wave of the hand. In a matter of minutes, her weekend would advance twenty-four hours—minus sixty-six years, of course—and soon it would be time to return to class. Now it was she who became sad and frustrated, regretting a missed opportunity to experience her first true sexual encounter. As much as the new century seemed alien to her in most other respects, there was no denying the attraction of its casual permissiveness—something that was unthinkable in her own era, except for wanton whores who chose to throw their lives away in the pursuit of ill-gotten gain.

Still in a daze, Bonnie entered the Waco Hall lobby and went directly up the stairs to her mysterious point of departure.

Kneeling motionless in the distant shadows of the balcony, Ryan was mesmerized by what he saw. After a few seconds, he ventured forward, but the girl was nowhere to be found.

◆　　◆　　◆

My Dearest Bonnie,

As you might suspect, things are extremely busy over here. I am "somewhere in Europe," which is what the censor likes for us to say.

I hope all is well with you and your higher education at good old Baylor on the Brazos. In honor of you, I would become a Bear football fan—if only they had a team! Maybe they will again someday, after we whip the Krauts and Japs.

I think I told you before that two fellow officers from Blackland are in my unit. I see one of them pretty frequently, and our chats always remind me of Waco—and you. But BAAF is long behind us now, and we have a very different job to tackle these days. At least it calls for flying instead of showing instructional films on a projector.

One of my new pals is Artie Polk from Cincinnati, and we spend a lot of time together in the office (i.e., cockpit). Also at pubs, whenever we're granted a couple of hours in the village. I'm not much of a drinker, you know, but it's the only choice for socializing around here because I avoid dances like the plague.

Enclosed is a photograph of most of our crew, snapped by the flight engineer, Olan Collins, when we went to an undisclosed location on a forty-eight-hour pass. In case you think we spent our leave in Berlin, no, that is a fake mustache under Artie's lip. He really doesn't look that much like Herr Adolf. Next time I write, I hope to have a better photo of myself to send. By the way, I would love to receive another snapshot of you, as the Baylor picture is the same one that anybody can see in the college yearbook, and I want something a little more personal—preferably with a lipstick kiss on the back.

My Uncle Foyle tells me that the Ford is running great, and he is giving Aunt Kathleen driving lessons— something I never thought would happen. He is teaching her in their own car, so she won't tear up my gears in the process. After she learns, I guess Foyle will use mine, and she'll drive the Buick. I'm just glad my Ford will get some road mileage while I'm gone. Otherwise, the car would be in dismal shape whenever I see it again.

That's all I have time to write—briefing for an op. I miss you very much and think of you often.

All my love, Jack

Bonnie read the letter in the privacy of the USO workroom while waiting for her Tuesday shift to begin. A touch of panic gripped her, hammering home the certainty that Jack would meet his death in less than four months' time unless she could subtly alter history to the extent of saving him and his crew from their fate. But even with her marvelous gift, how was it conceivable for a civilian girl—halfway around the world— to influence the mighty United States Army Air Forces? She prayed silently for wisdom and what she called a "miracle." For a time, she did feel a sense of comfort wash over her, but it was short-lived, swiftly replaced by the anguish of gnawing doubt.

Despite the fact that Easter Sunday of 1943 was nearly two weeks away, Bonnie's supervisor, elderly Roberta Boggs, was already anxious to make preparations for her "soldier boys." This year's observance would be on April 25, the latest date possible in the Gregorian Calendar—a rarity that had not occurred since 1886, back when Mrs. Boggs was an eighteen-year-old newlywed.

The USO had a haphazard assortment of decorations for Easter, ranging from secular baskets, eggs, and bunnies to sacred crosses and paintings of the Crucifixion and Resurrection. Bonnie's assignment was to arrange them in a tasteful and artistic manner throughout the first floor, wherever they might be appreciated by the servicemen. Then, time permitting, she would design a seasonal bulletin board to replace the winter motif, which had long since outstayed its welcome.

Her co-worker, a high school junior named Janice Stoneham, was involved in showing a gangly PFC how to use the voice-recording machine, so it was Mrs. Boggs who notified Bonnie that a soldier had arrived, wishing to speak with her.

"Do you know who it is?" Bonnie asked.

"He didn't say," the old woman told her, "except that he's a friend of a friend."

Bonnie's first thought was that the visiting soldier must be Lieutenant Fowler, but Mrs. Boggs knew Billy by name and would have said as much.

"Have you ever seen him in here before?"

"No, I don't think so—not that I can recall."

"Thank you, Mrs. Boggs." Bonnie laid down the package of Easter egg dye, furtively glancing at herself in the mirror as she made her way up front.

"Are you Bonnie?" the soldier said. He was cordial enough but also quite serious.

"Yes."

"I'm Jim."

When Bonnie did not respond, he elaborated. "Ev's Jim ... Jim Peaks."

She broke into a smile. "Sergeant Peaks, how nice to meet you. I didn't expect you to be here for another couple of days."

"Neither did I. But there's been a change of plans, and Ev told me to come see you pronto."

"Gee, nothing bad, I hope."

"Let me put it like this—we won't be needing a maid of honor on Saturday."

Bonnie's face darkened. "The wedding is off?"

"No, not by a long shot." Suddenly, Jim appeared to be enjoying a guessing game, and his placid attitude took her by surprise.

"Postponed?" she asked.

"Well, you're right about one thing. Our wedding date has been changed."

"I give up," Bonnie said. She did not know whether to joke or commiserate.

That was when Jim began to laugh. "Honey?"

Bonnie could hear soft footsteps, and she noticed that Jim was now looking behind her. She turned around, and there stood her fellow coed, wearing a playful grin. "Ev! What gives?" The girl did not reply.

Confused, Bonnie stared back at Jim, who finally explained. "Please say hello to Mrs. James Peaks."

"What?"

"We're married," Evelyn said. She scampered over to take her husband's hand.

Bonnie's mouth was agape. "Married!"

"I'll be leaving for Virginia in the morning," Jim told her. "The Army couldn't wait until the seventeenth, so we had to tie the knot right away."

"Justice of the peace?"

"Yep, Wayne Lee at the courthouse," the sergeant said. "His wife, LaZalle, was one of the witnesses. She just happened to be there, and they could see that we were in a bind. We already had the marriage license."

"When did all of this take place?"

Evelyn blushed. "This morning. We knew you'd be in class, so we couldn't invite you to be there. Dr. Armstrong was very understanding about it. He gave me an excused absence."

Bonnie could hardly fathom that her good friend was already married. She smiled at the giddy couple and said,

"Congratulations—both of you." Then, leaning forward, she kissed Evelyn on the cheek. "So, what comes next?"

"We spend our wedding night together, natch!" Jim said.

Bonnie laughed. "No, I mean after that."

"Jim takes a train to Langley," Evelyn told her, "and I'll follow him there at the beginning of June."

"Will you have a place to stay?"

"Married NCO housing. Jim says it's not too bad."

"What about your degree?" Bonnie was speaking to Evelyn, but it was Jim who answered.

"She'll come back to Baylor whenever I've shipped out. I made her promise to do that."

"Yes, he did," Evelyn said. Clearly, she was delighted to have her husband's support.

"And I also made her promise to keep writing. I want her to finish at least two novels before this war is over."

Evelyn shook her head. "Personally, I hope he's home so fast that I can't even get halfway into the first one." She squeezed his arm. "What a selfish author I turned out to be!"

That night, as Bonnie lay in bed, her mind persisted in mulling over the day's events. She recalled that hasty letter from Jack and how difficult it must be to find enough time to write from a war zone. She thought about Evelyn's extemporaneous marriage ceremony and the joy that enlivened the couple's eyes. And she found herself imagining what it would feel like to have Jack's strong arms around her on their own wedding night.

The alarm clock registered one thirty, and then some, before she finally drifted off to sleep.

♦   ♦   ♦

Like anything else in life, even traveling through time can become almost routine if done often enough and on a fairly regular basis. But that did not prepare Bonnie for what happened when she returned to AD 2009 on the afternoon of Saturday, April 18. Emerging from her upper-floor portal at 3:24 P.M., she stepped forward and heard a familiar voice say, "Hello ... Miss Ploughwright." Her heart pounded.

Sitting cross-legged in front of her, less than fifteen feet away, was Ryan Andriessen. He seemed perfectly calm, all things considered, and took a sip of liquid from a transparent, plastic bottle with the word "Ozarka" on it. Astonished at seeing him there, Bonnie could not speak. She stood still for what seemed an eternity—perhaps ten seconds—struggling to decide how to react to this shocking apparition. "Ryan, is that really you?"

"I should be asking you that question," he said. "You're the one who just materialized from thin air."

"That's how it looked to you?"

"Yes, and I also saw you disappear a week ago—from this same spot."

She sighed. "So that's it."

Setting the bottle aside, Ryan climbed to his feet. "What gives? Why are you able to do this?"

Bonnie tried her best to smile. "You tell me. I honestly have no idea. All of a sudden, I just could."

"Are you real?"

"Sure, I am. Feel, if you don't believe me."

Ryan went toward her and, with both hands, touched her on the shoulders. "But where do you go?"

"Home."

"To ..."

"1943."

He took a deep breath, studying her face. "And that's why you seem so old-fashioned. What did we call it?"

"Traditional. I come from a very traditional family."

"Traditional, yeah." Ryan walked around her, as if he were a scientist observing some interstellar visitor. "Are you human?"

"Of course I'm human, silly. I'm every bit as human as you are."

"Oh, really! I can't travel through time."

"Neither could I, until recently. Believe me, I'm totally normal."

"Except for that one tiny, insignificant quirk."

"Yes."

Again he paced around her, staring all the while. "So, you're ... what ... eighty or ninety years old? Is that what you're telling me?"

"No. I'm twenty-one." And she repeated, "Do you want to feel?"

Ryan grinned, and so did she.

"Can I step through that invisible door and go back, too?" he asked.

"I don't know. Try it."

He laughed. "You'd be surprised if I could, wouldn't you?"

"Not as much as you."

Understandably hesitant, Ryan stood there, rubbing his chin. "Okay, here goes. What happens if I make it through?"

"Just come right back."

He scanned the vicinity. "And where exactly is this mythical time machine of yours?"

"About there." She pointed.

Ryan stepped forward to the indicated spot, but nothing unusual happened. He walked all around and through the area, to no discernible effect. "I guess I'm stuck with the present," he said.

"That's too bad because I wish I could take you back with me sometime. You'd like it there."

"Where is it, in Waco?"

"Sure. The second floor of Waco Hall, to begin with—but sixty-six years ago."

He let that sink in, bending down to take another sip of water. Then, as he was screwing the cap onto his bottle, he said, "What do you think of 2009?"

"It's very strange, of course, but I do like the televisions and computers—especially the computers."

"What about the people?"

"I like you."

"I like you, too—always have, right from the start. Even before I knew you were a space alien from the planet Xenon."

Bonnie giggled. "I must say, you're taking this awfully well. Most people would be running around, screaming that the Martians have landed."

"You don't look like a Martian to me."

"Why, thank you. What a charming thing to say!"

He stepped back and allowed himself to assess her beauty. "Are all California girls as pretty as you?"

"I don't know anything about California. I've never even been there."

Ryan shook his head, mystified by that announcement.

"It's true," she told him. "I only said I was from the West Coast to throw you off the track. Actually, I'm a Baylor gal through and through—a junior, Class of 1944."

"So, your father doesn't sell for a Los Angeles company."

"No. He has a dental practice in Dallas."

Ryan's face brightened. "Does that mean you'll be staying in town?"

"That should be rather obvious, at this point."

"What do you mean?"

"Well, I sure can't wander too far away from Waco Hall—at least for very long."

"I hadn't thought of that."

"I'd be stranded in the twenty-first century."

Swallowing nervously, he looked directly into her eyes. "Would that be so horrible?"

Bonnie smiled. "Ryan, you're a swell guy, but I don't belong here. I have a boyfriend in the war."

"Do you love him?"

"I do."

"Is he the one who ...?"

"Yes—Jack Decker."

"I'm sorry I found that. It must be a terrible thing to learn."

"I was very depressed at first, but now I'm more optimistic," she said. "Because of your researching ability."

Ryan motioned toward the stairs. "Shall we?" he asked. "Or do you prefer to beam yourself by teleportation?"

"I'll just walk, thanks."

The weather was seventy-four degrees and drizzly, which explained why Ryan had brought his umbrella along with him. He deployed it to share with Bonnie as they headed toward Third Street, adding a touch of romance to their fifteen-minute stroll. Here and there, puddles of standing water dotted the route, so it must have rained considerably harder that morning or early afternoon.

The first thing Bonnie noticed when they neared Ryan's apartment complex was a red sports car in the parking lot. "It looks like Michael is here," she said.

"Yeah, he is ... and Nicole, too," Ryan told the girl. "But don't worry. We'll go upstairs and leave the downstairs to them."

The television set was on, playing at such a high volume that its sound was fully audible through the closed door. Rather than unlocking, Ryan winked at Bonnie and knocked. "That'll break up whatever is going on inside." No one answered, so he inserted his key and entered.

Nicole was sitting at one end of the sofa. Her fiancé was stretched out in a supine position with the side of his head lying in her lap, watching a war picture called *Flying Tigers*. Neither of them bothered to move. "Sorry," Michael said, "but there's a John Wayne flick on TCM."

Ryan sighed, as if used to such treatment. "You remember Nicole, don't you, Bonnie?"

"Yes, of course. Hello again."

"Hello," Nicole said. There was a distinct lack of enthusiasm.

Michael sat up and smiled. "Are you a Baylor student now or just visiting?"

"Only here for the weekend."

Ryan walked directly to the stairway, not even waiting for Bonnie. "We're going to be doing some internet work for her term paper," he said over his shoulder.

"UCLA?" Michael asked the girl.

"Yes, that's right," Bonnie said. With a polite nod, she hurried to catch up with Ryan.

By the time Bonnie reached the top of the stairs, her friend had already activated the computer. "Well, we made it past them unscathed," he told her.

"That was a little rude of us, though, don't you think?"

"I really don't have much use for that Barbie doll of his." He scooted a chair over for the girl. "We had a falling out last week, and she'll hardly speak to me anymore."

Bonnie opened her notebook and waited for Ryan to turn on the search engine. He seemed to have an idea in mind, and it was not a happy one. "I'm afraid there's a problem concerning Waco Hall," he said. "I remember reading about it a month or so ago, but now it's taken on a whole new meaning."

Her eyes widened with fear.

Ryan typed in "waco hall renovation 2009," and Google brought up a press release from Baylor University's Facility, Planning, and Construction Services. The brief news item read, "Waco Hall will close May 10 for renovations. This work will include a minor renovation to the pre-function areas (foyer and hallways) outside the main theater. The building is scheduled to re-open the first full week of August."

"Oh, dear!" Bonnie stood up and re-read the passage out loud.

Ryan listened patiently and said, "I guess that means I won't be able to see you for three months."

"It's much worse than that. In fact, it's catastrophic. All the renovation might destroy my time passage, and I may never be able to come back again."

"Could it do that?"

"Who knows? But I sure can't take a chance. If I happen to be here when May tenth arrives, I'm sunk."

Ryan grinned. "You'll be one of us. Care to be my new roommate?"

"Well, it may be funny to you, but not to me." She sat down, benumbed by the cruel revelation. "What day of the week is that?"

Ryan clicked on something called "Dashboard," and a calculator, weather forecast, clock, and calendar suddenly appeared on the screen. One more click, and he had the answer. "It's a Sunday—three weeks from tomorrow."

Aghast, Bonnie began wringing her hands. "So, I have three weeks to save my entire world from crashing down."

"What do you have in mind?"

"Please, Ryan. You've got to help me."

He looked bewildered. "Hey, I've tried everything. I don't have any more rabbits to chase—no leads."

By now, Bonnie was panic-stricken, nearly hyperventilating. "Dear God!" she said. "What can I do?"

"Anything new?" Ryan asked. "Any clues? Think!"

"I got a letter from Jack."

"Did you bring it with you?"

"No, but—" Frantically, she flipped through the pages in her notebook. "He has a good friend named ... Artie Polk."

"Who is he?"

"It could be his co-pilot, but I'm not sure. He said they spend time together in the cockpit."

A half-hour later, through divergent Army Air Forces sites and genealogical sources, Ryan found someone who seemed to match. "Here's an Arthur Polk, from Ohio, about the right age."

"Artie's from Cincinnati."

"He was a captain and a pilot, stationed in England at Polebrook."

"That's him."

Ryan was able to discover that Arthur Polk was killed on August 11, 1943, when his aircraft went down, with the loss of all ten aboard, on a post-repair shakedown flight east of Manchester. The Flying Fortress was too low for parachuting to safety. This crash, attributed to "undetermined mechanical failure," occurred in the countryside near the village of Tintwistle. The USAAF report concluded, and Ryan read the passage aloud, "Preliminary investigation suggests that Captain Decker performed valiantly and did everything possible to save the craft and her crew."

Bonnie gulped when she heard Jack's name. "August eleventh," she whispered to herself.

"There's still time," Ryan said. "We can't give up yet."

When Bonnie presented her friend with another name from the letter, that of flight engineer Olan Collins, Ryan seemed confident that further information would surface, but that proved not to be the case. Neither did the names Foyle Decker and Kathleen Creel Decker provide any useful details—except insofar as they might be advantageous to family historians.

It was Ryan's idea to pursue the doomed mission further, and he was very good at digging deeply into the most tenuous of leads. His painstaking search turned up a brief article in the *Manchester Guardian* of August 12, 1943: "An American bomber plunged to the earth and burnt near Tintwistle yesterday forenoon, killing at least ten crew members. Lookers-on said the aeroplane, a B-17F called 'Scarlett Woman', had one engine aflame before the crash occurred, and the pilot endeavoured to steer away from three farmhouses in the vicinity."

Moisture filled Bonnie's eyes at the sight of the aircraft's name. She was sure that Jack had christened the bomber in her honor, if only indirectly, knowing of her veneration for Margaret Mitchell, *Gone With the Wind*, and the novel's spirited heroine.

She asked Ryan, "Do pilots name their own airplanes?"

"I suppose so. I don't know who else would do it. Consensus of the crew maybe."

"Do you think the airplane had a picture of Vivien Leigh painted on it?"

"Could be," he told her. "In fact, I'd say that's very likely."

Bonnie smiled through her tears until Ryan thoughtlessly added, "Of course, they could have gone the other direction with that term and showed a prostitute instead. Some nose art is pretty risqué, from what I've seen."

She frowned at his ill-advised humor. "But it's written with two 't's, and that can't be pure happenstance. They wouldn't have spelled it that way from carelessness."

"No, I'm sure you're right," he said, less out of conviction than trying to comfort her.

By now, Bonnie was not even listening. With a determined look on her face, she made a solemn vow. "I don't care if I have to swim all the way to England—I'm going to save Jack Decker."

◆   ◆   ◆

The main gates to Blackland Army Air Field opened at 6:15 on the morning of April 25, permitting limited access to thousands of Wacoans for Easter observances. The sun made its scheduled appearance at 6:49, and the worship service commenced eleven minutes later, at seven o'clock sharp, with the singing of "All Hail the Power of Jesus's Name."

Bonnie rode to the base with Lieutenant Billy Fowler, his wife, Melinda, and their daughter, Peg. The weather was ideal for the occasion, with a temperature of sixty-four degrees and no rain in the forecast. Although the thermometer would peak at ninety degrees by late that afternoon, conditions at daybreak were pleasantly cool.

Forming the centerpiece of the annual sunrise service was a fifteen-foot-tall white cross, behind which stood a panoramic backdrop depicting Golgotha. The choir of 150 voices, under the direction of Baylor's Robert "Pop" Hopkins, was drawn from thirteen Waco churches. Arrayed in a semi-circle around the choristers were various squadrons of soldiers from Blackland, and, further removed in another concentric multitude, were the civilians, including the families of servicemen. Speakers were Pastor Thomas Gallaher of First Presbyterian Church, who recited the Resurrection story from the Gospel of Luke, Professor Benjamin Oscar Herring of Baylor's Bible Department, who offered a prayer for the nation, and BAAF Chaplain Leslie Rogers, who delivered the benediction. Contributing musically, in addition to the massed choral forces, were a vocal quartet of soldiers and a large detachment of instrumentalists from the 339th Army Air Forces Band. It was an exalting, Spirit-filled hour.

Later that morning, by the time the Fowlers and their Baylor guest pulled into the driveway at home, Peg was fast asleep on the rear seat, and her mother carried the little girl straight off to bed. Bonnie, truth to tell, felt much the same and appreciated the adult stimulant of black coffee for rousing her back to full consciousness. She needed to speak privately with the lieutenant and found an opportunity to do so when Melinda went to the kitchen to prepare breakfast. Moreover, Billy's wife chose to have the radio on—KGKO's "Do You Remember?"—to keep herself company as she cooked, so the others' conversation in the living room remained discreet.

Billy lit a cigarette and relaxed in his favorite chair. "What did you want to tell me? It sounded important."

"It is." Bonnie looked away, embarrassed. "You're going to think I'm crazy."

"Maybe not." He chuckled to put her at ease.

"I need for you to send a message to Jack—whenever you write to him again."

"Glad to," he said, "but why don't you do it yourself?"

She squirmed in her seat on the sofa. "It's not quite that simple. This is a ... an unusual matter that requires someone ... in a position of authority to say it."

"And that's me?"

"Well, yes. Someone in uniform like you—not just a civilian girl. In other words, Jack would consider my message to be much more credible if it came from you."

Billy took a full drag on his cigarette and exhaled slowly, blowing tobacco smoke toward the ceiling. "Maybe you should come right out and say what's bothering you."

Afflicted with rampant nerves, Bonnie stood and paced the floor. Then, turning around toward Billy, she blurted out her secret, point-blank. "I've had a premonition—of sorts. Something dreadful is going to happen to Jack, and I want to warn him before it does."

The officer smiled warmly, a grown man humoring a toddler in some childish folly. "Was this a nightmare, or did you go to a fortune teller?"

"Neither. I can view the future." She appeared to be serious.

"Listen, there's probably not a serviceman's wife or girlfriend in the whole world who hasn't feared for her loved one's safety at some time or another, imagining all kinds of horrendous things. It's only natural during a war."

"I'm not *imagining* anything," Bonnie said. Her face was flushed with anger. "I'm positive this is going to happen—and I can even tell you when."

Billy sighed, flicking the ashes off his cigarette. "Bonnie, I think you're swell, and I'd very much like to help you, but put yourself in my place. I'm an officer, a professional soldier, and I can't be spreading ... delusions ... around the fighting men."

"Don't call them delusions!" she shouted. The kitchen became quiet, as if Melinda had laid down her implements and started listening. "They're not delusions," Bonnie said, now in a whisper. "And I can prove it to you."

Billy was not trying to be difficult, but neither was he willing to place his career in jeopardy for the sake of some irrational foreboding that had lodged itself in the brain of this sweet girl. "I'll do a lot for Jack," he told her, "and I promised to watch over you while he's gone. But I have to draw the line at telling him your bad dreams."

Bonnie's eyes flooded with tears, so hurt was she by the lieutenant's bluntness of speech. "You're not my guardian angel at all," she said. "You're just watching out for your own hide."

"No. You've got me wrong. I'll do anything reasonable to go to bat for you and Jack, but that does not include blindly accepting your fears as the gospel truth." The instant he stood up for emphasis, she sat back down on the sofa, defeated for the moment. "Where would we be if our top brass started doing that?" he asked. "We can't run a war on tea leaves or crystal balls. That would be national suicide. This is not a game we're playing."

Crying softly, Bonnie stared at the folded hands in her lap. "Then it's finished," she said. "Jack will be killed, and so will his crew. He and I will never see each other again."

Billy took a few steps toward her and stopped. "Now, don't get all upset over nothing. There's absolutely—"

Melinda came into the living room, under the pretense of bringing a glass of orange juice to the guest. "Is everything all right?" she asked. Seeing Bonnie's tears, she sat alongside the girl and placed a comforting hand atop hers. With a stern look, she turned to her husband. "What's going on? What happened?"

Billy cleared his throat. "I ... I guess I've made her cry. I've been an officer instead of a human being, and I should have learned by now that you can be both at once." Bonnie glanced up, hopefully. "And I think I've just volunteered for duty," the officer added. He returned to his chair.

Gazing from one to the other, Melinda managed a confused smile and walked back toward the kitchen. "Breakfast will be ready in about five minutes," she said. "I'll bet the two of you are starving by now."

When KGKO's "The Chuck Wagon Gang" began playing at a considerable volume on the kitchen radio, Billy felt safe in resuming his discussion with Bonnie. "You said you could prove something to me. What did you mean by that?"

"I can see into the future."

He sniggered. "You're sure not making this very easy for me. How far do your headlights shine—a thousand years from now?"

"That's not the point. What's important is that I have the ability to see far enough to save Jack's life." She took a drink of juice and thought for a moment. "I believe that I've been presented with this gift for the sole purpose of rescuing Jack Decker from disaster—to 'fine tune' history, so to speak."

Billy was less persuaded than ever. "And who offered you this remarkable power, some genie from a bottle?"

"Being a Christian, I have no choice but to assume that it came from God."

"Well, it's Easter, so maybe that's why He picked today to grant you a vision."

Bonnie glared. "Hardly. This has been going on for quite some time—three months, to be exact. And I would thank you to kindly stop belittling my plea for help. I'm trying to be honest with you."

The lieutenant nodded his head, giving her the benefit of the doubt. "All right, I'm sorry. But you do have to admit that this is a little hard to swallow. Can't you see that?"

"I suppose so. I really can't blame you for being skeptical, but please don't turn it into a joke. I'm deadly serious about this, and you are my only hope."

"Your guardian angel?"

"Yes."

Billy emitted a loud sigh. "I told Lindy that I volunteered, so I can't back out now. Just tell me what you want me to write to him. I'll try to make it as plausible as I can."

"No, not yet. First I want to show you some proof, so your heart will be in this. Name any date, and I'll give you the newspaper headlines beforehand. Will that convince you?"

Billy shrugged his shoulders. "How about next Saturday?"

"Saturday it is," she said. "In the meantime, I'll be working at the USO on Wednesday night. Can you drop by then for a sneak preview of the future?"

"You're pretty sure of yourself, aren't you?"

"I've got to be. It's a matter of life and death."

"Okay, I'll be there." He flashed a sarcastic smile. "Actually, I'm kind of curious to know what the top stories will be on May first."

Bonnie held her tongue. Imagining herself in his position, she could not condemn him for playing the role of a doubting Thomas.

"Breakfast!" Melinda Fowler shouted from the kitchen. She knew that Peg was a sound sleeper and would not be disturbed.

◆　　◆　　◆

Bonnie went to Jones Reference Library two days later, which of course was a Monday on the 2009 calendar. By now, she was becoming rather adept at using the microform reader, so she had her answers within a matter of just a few minutes. After switching off the machine, she had to smile. Time traveling was great fun—or would be, if so much were not hanging in the balance. Bonnie departed with a most valuable possession: her handwritten headlines from the May 1, 1943, edition of the *Waco News-Tribune*. This unpretentious scrap of paper could very well mean a reprieve from death for ten brave servicemen.

Her first thought upon leaving the library was to walk to the nearby Student Life Center, for she felt certain that Ryan Andriessen would be there, exerting his muscles against the self-imposed resistance of exercise contraptions. How surprised the boy would be when she suddenly appeared, unannounced, on a weekday afternoon. Anxious to see him again, Bonnie took a shortcut, the footbridge over Waco Creek. Halfway across, she gazed down and watched five fresh-water turtles paddle to the surface for air. Then, almost like synchronized swimmers, they disappeared from view, descending into their natural habitat of the depths.

Once she convinced two officious attendants to give her permission to enter the SLC as a visitor, Bonnie proceeded straight to the free weights, only to discover that Ryan was not present among the barbells and sweaty benches. She wandered through much of the room before finally locating him. He sat with his back to a complex machine, eyes closed, channeling his will to pull a column of heavy-looking metal plates into the air by the sheer strength of his legs. Soon the weights were moving up and down in a steady rhythm of athletic prowess.

When he opened his eyes momentarily, Ryan was startled to see her standing there, just a few feet away. "Bonnie!" he said with a wide grin. "What brings you to the twenty-first century?" He felt safe in making such an outlandish remark because no one could possibly guess how much truth was hidden therein. And his leg extensions continued without missing a beat.

"Research at the library, of course," she told him. "What else is there?"

"Oh, I'm sure we can think of something."

Bonnie smirked at the impish comment but chose not to counter with one of her own. In due course, she sat through the young man's entire workout routine, chatting on occasion but mostly just enjoying the sight of his powerful limbs triumphantly vanquishing the force of gravity. Ryan explained to her that he wielded different groups of muscles on alternate days, in order to allow them a decent period of rest and recuperation before being pressed into action again. When Bonnie kidded that her only forms of exercise these days were typing term papers and turning the pages of overweight textbooks, he insisted that her figure seemed perfectly fine to him.

Judging from past experience, Bonnie suspected that Ryan would invite her back to his apartment, and he did not disappoint. She, however, declined the offer, instead agreeing to meet him early on Saturday morning, which they both knew could well prove to be their last day together before renovation endangered the cylinder's existence. He drove her across campus to Waco Hall, but she preferred that he not accompany her upstairs. A perfunctory kiss and wave were all that marked their parting.

◆　　◆　　◆

It was 7:30 on Wednesday evening when Lieutenant Billy Fowler arrived at the USO club. Bonnie had been waiting for the officer, so she walked straight over to him before he was five feet inside the Washington Avenue doorway.

"I'm here for the unveiling," Billy said. But his wisecrack and smile were forced. He realized that this was no joking matter.

"Here" was Bonnie's sole word of greeting as she handed him a folded piece of paper.

The lieutenant nodded his thanks, unfolded the sheet, and began reading to himself:

GENERAL COAL STRIKE BEGUN; ARMY SEIZURE SEEN

STALIN SAYS AIR ASSAULTS LEADING TO SECOND FRONT

JAPANESE LAUNCH SUB CAMPAIGN IN AUSTRALIA WATERS

McLENNAN TOTAL ON BONDS TO PASS 8 MILLIONS MARK

VISITORS URGED TO BRING LUNCH TO WAFS PARTY

"You must think I'm ready for the funny farm," Bonnie said.

"I don't know what to think," he told her. "All I can say is Saturday's newspaper should be very illuminating."

"I promise you, this is exactly what you'll see—verbatim. Then will you believe me?"

"Let's cross that minefield when we come to it." Billy refolded the headlines and slid them inside his shirt pocket.

"Will you be able to meet with me again on Saturday morning?" Bonnie asked. "We need to talk, and we're running out of chances."

He thought for a moment. "Here at the club?"

"No—too many people around. Can you come to Baylor?"

"I guess so. What time?"

"Please pick me up at eight sharp in front of my dorm—Alexander Hall on Seventh Street."

He nodded his head. "I'll be there, with my Waco newspaper."

"Good. So, the next time I see you, you'll know for sure—one way or the other."

Saturday dawned fair and dry, and Bonnie was standing outside the entrance of her dormitory at precisely eight o'clock. She watched and waited. Ten minutes went by with no sign of the officer, and she thought how unlike Billy it was to be late. As another quarter-hour slipped past without his appearance, she was about to go back inside and give the Fowler residence a telephone call. But then a moving vehicle captured her eye.

Bonnie had ridden in Billy's automobile before, to the Easter sunrise service, so she was fairly certain that he was driving when a dark green 1937 Chevrolet business coupe pulled up to the curb and stopped. The man who got out of this car was Lieutenant Fowler all right, and he had a grim expression on his face. He approached Alexander Hall without so much as glancing up at Bonnie until he was about twenty feet away.

"Sorry I'm late," he said, "but it's been a wild morning." They walked to the automobile in silence, neither of them feeling the need to speak.

Once inside the Chevy, Billy looked at his passenger. "Have you eaten yet?"

"Enough—but I wouldn't say no to a cup of coffee."

"I thought you weren't overly fond of coffee."

"I'm starting to like it. Another vice to blame on the war."

Billy turned the car left at Speight Avenue and then left again onto Fifth Street. Bonnie noticed that a newspaper was lying between them on the seat, face down and folded in half. "Is that today's paper?" she asked in all innocence.

Scowling, the officer ignored her question and, in fact, remained quiet until they pulled up to the PDQ Coffee Shop at Second and Franklin. "The place looks pretty crowded," he said, mostly to himself, "but I guess we'll give it a try." He opened his car door, tucking the newspaper under one arm, and waited for the girl to catch up to him on the sidewalk.

Sure enough, the PDQ's interior was noisy and bustling at this popular hour on a Saturday morning—probably not the best choice for such a momentous session as theirs figured to be. Billy directed his friend to the most isolated table he could find and waved away the waitress's offer of menus. "Just two coffees, thanks." He stirred milk and saccharine into his own cup, but Bonnie was cultivating a taste for drinking her coffee black.

"So, how did you do it?" Billy asked, unsmiling. He tossed his newspaper onto the table.

"I told you. I can see into the future."

"Look, if you want me to help you, I'm going to need the truth."

"That is the truth—honest to God."

"And you had the Saturday newspaper delivered to your dorm room on Wednesday. Is that what you want me to believe?"

"Of course not."

"Well? Then how?"

"I can't tell you," she said. "I'm not free to speak about it."

"Fine. In that case, I'm afraid I can't help you."

Bonnie's eyes flared red. "Then you're condemning Jack Decker to death."

"How could you possibly know that?"

She sighed with exasperation. "I showed you these headlines almost two whole days before the events happened. What will it take to convince you?"

"I admit that was an impressive trick, however you did it. But I've never believed in magic or astrology, and I'm not going to start now—not with a war to be fought."

Bonnie was appalled. "You actually think I concocted these headlines by reading my horoscope?"

"No, but I think that's why you're scared of one particular day in Jack's future." He glanced at his wristwatch. "Another cup?"

"Sure—however long it takes. You're my only hope."

"Warm these up, will you?" he said to the waitress. Then, for the umpteenth time, Billy scanned the front page of the May 1

Waco News-Tribune. "You know, there's some real dough to be made with that psychic act of yours. Can you pick horses at the racetrack, too? Who's going to win today's game between the Brownies and the White Sox?"

Bonnie saw that their discussion was getting nowhere, and her trepidation mounted when she heard what the lieutenant had to say next.

"Listen, Bonnie," he told her, "I'll be shipping out soon, so it wouldn't do any good for me to write to Jack anyway. I might be overseas before the mail even gets there, and he couldn't reply."

She was stunned by the news. "How long will you be here?"

"Just until Wednesday or Thursday. Lindy's already packing, which is why I was so late."

"Where will she and Peggy go?"

"They'll live with Lindy's parents for the duration."

"In Knoxville?"

"Yep. And I suppose that's where the baby will be born." He stirred his fresh cup of coffee. "Anyhow, this is what I wanted to tell you about. You'll be on your own, from here on out—no big brother to save you from the clutches of the USO wolves."

Suddenly, it became clear to Bonnie what she had to do, and there was no time to lose. "Take me back to Baylor," she said.

"What?"

"Please take me back."

Billy seemed hurt by her change in attitude. "Did I say something wrong? I'm sorry to be such a cynic, but I have to think of—"

"No, it isn't that," she said. "I need for you to come with me to Waco Hall—now."

"What's there?"

"Jack's future.... His crew's future.... Mine."

❖　　❖　　❖

Billy risked driving fifty miles per hour across South Waco and parked his Chevrolet at the curb on Seventh Street, near James Avenue. Bonnie got out of the car the instant it came to a halt, and she motioned for him to follow. Through the side entrance they went, then to the left, and up the carpeted stairway. When they reached the far end of the balcony, she stared at him for a few seconds, as if trying to determine what should come next.

"Watch carefully." She turned away, took a couple of steps forward, and dimmed into nothingness.

"Bonnie?" With a gasp, the lieutenant walked toward where she had been. He looked around, suspecting a prank. "Okay, I give up. How'd you do it?" No one was there to hear. "Bonnie?"

Just as quickly as she disappeared, she was again standing in front of him.

Billy beamed with delight. "You really are a magician!" he said. "Amazing!"

And yet, the girl remained strangely blasé about the trick and how it was achieved.

"What did you do?" He was wide-eyed, an excited child at the circus.

"I saw the future," she told him.

"How?"

"By traveling to the future."

Billy's grin slowly faded, to be replaced by a look of curiosity, wariness, and then something akin to fear. "You traveled to the future?"

"I was in the twenty-first century."

"Just now?"

"Just now. The year 2009, to be more precise."

The officer laughed aloud, but it was a nervous laugh and of short duration. "Are you willing to prove that?"

"Certainly," she said.

He reached into his trousers pocket and pulled out a quarter. "Bring me change from the future."

Bonnie looked at the coin. "I can't," she told him. "That won't work."

"You don't say!" Billy gloated for a moment. "Losing our confidence, are we?"

"Nope. Standing Liberty quarters stopped in 1930, so they've probably never seen one. Do you have any Washingtons?"

Back into his pocket he dipped, and he handed Bonnie a twenty-five-cent piece with George Washington's likeness on it. "Better?"

"Much." She gave him a broad smile. "This may take a while. No telling what I'll find."

"I can wait."

The girl promptly repeated her vanishing act, and Lieutenant Billy Fowler, with a skeptical shake of the head, made himself comfortable by sitting against the wall.

Bonnie emerged from the staircase on a Friday morning between classes, so she immediately encountered a lobby filled with scores of students walking this way and that. Among the masses, she noticed a sorority-looking girl with bleached blonde hair. The coed was seated on a bench with her legs crossed, viewing a portable computer—something Sean Nixon had referred to as a "laptop."

"Excuse me," Bonnie said to her. "Do you happen to have two dimes and a nickel for a quarter?"

"I don't know. Maybe." The coed opened her purse, retrieved a small pouch of some sort, and fished out some silverish coins. "How about three nickels and a dime?"

"Close enough," Bonnie said, and the exchange was made. She peered at the laptop. "Are you on the internet?"

"Yes."

"Would you mind looking something up for me?"

"No problem."

"Go to Baseball Almanac."

A few minutes later, the twenty-first-century coed watched with keen interest as this odd stranger walked away. Her garb was rather bizarre, the sorority girl mused—kind of, like, retro. But then the blonde's mobile telephone began playing a tune, and she gave the matter no further thought.

Billy stood up when Bonnie returned to the visible world. "Well?" he said to her. There was defiance in his voice, for the lieutenant still harbored some healthy doubt.

Bonnie extended her closed fist, teasing him by hiding the coins from view. Finally, she allowed the metal disks to drop, with a familiar clinking sound, into Billy's hand. He took a deep breath and studied the coins. Two of the nickels appeared to be quite normal—that is, until Billy saw that the dates read 1998 and 1984. He glanced at Bonnie but said nothing. The other Jefferson nickel's obverse had a peculiar, three-dimensional profile of the third President. Furthermore, the buffalo on its reverse was facing the wrong way. The date, Billy noted, was 2005.

Most startling of all was the dime, dated 2001. The winged head of Liberty (commonly misidentified as Mercury) had been replaced by ...

"Is this FDR?" the officer asked.

"Yes."

Billy was dumbstruck, astonished by the immensity of what he had seen. "Did he ... outlive the war?"

"I can't tell you."

"But you do know?"

"Yes."

"Don't you think your country should share in that knowledge?"

"I can't divulge anything else," she said. "I don't dare to tamper with the course of history."

"Saving Jack Decker isn't tampering?"

Bonnie bit her lower lip, formulating an answer. "I feel that I've been entrusted with correcting that one flaw in the progression of time," she told him.

"Entrusted by God?"

"Apparently so."

"But God is omniscient. How can He have made a mistake?"

"Maybe He's testing me. All I know is that I am able to travel ahead by sixty-six years. There's no denying that."

Billy swallowed hard and stared at her, as if she were from outer space. "Jeez, what can I say? I believe you—unless I'm going loony, too."

"No. We're both perfectly sane." Bonnie asked for the futuristic coins back, and the lieutenant gave them to her. Then she posed the most important question of all: "Will you help me?"

He gave a slight nod of the head. "I'll do everything I can. I promise."

"One thing, though," Bonnie said. "You mustn't tell anyone about this."

"Not even Jack?"

"Sorry, but not a soul. I've had months to think this over. Saving Jack's life and his crew's—that's as far as we can go. Leaking information could lead to terrible consequences down the line. Any fiddling with history might cause an unpredictable series of reactions. We can't take the chance."

"Except for trifling things, I suppose."

"Huh?"

"Bringing twenty-first-century coins into the present."

Bonnie grinned. "I think that's relatively harmless, as long as I don't let them out of my sight—and eventually return them to where they belong."

This caused Billy to ask, "When are you going back again?"

"Tomorrow." The girl felt some relief at no longer having to be so secretive. "And it may be the last time I can ever do it."

"Why is that?"

"Renovation of Waco Hall starts in about a week, from their perspective."

"So what?"

"So, it could close off my passage to the future—that's what. Who can say for sure?"

"Do you have all the information you need?"

"I think so, but I'm still going to make one final search tomorrow."

"What if you happen to get stuck there?"

She shrugged her shoulders. "What could I do? I'd have to start a whole new life ... and do my best to blend in with that society. I suppose my 1940s self would become an unsolvable case for the Bureau of Missing Persons."

"And what about Jack?"

Bonnie grew glum. "Jack would never even know about it. If I'm not able to come back and tell you everything I know, he'll die in exactly three months and ten days."

"Don't you think you should give me all the details now, just to be safe?"

"Not until I authenticate everything that we've found so far. Even one slight inaccuracy could be disastrous."

Billy started to smile. "You said, 'everything that *we've* found.' Do you have a boyfriend in that other life of yours?"

"I guess you could call him that," Bonnie said.

"What's his name? Or don't people in the next century have names?"

"Sure they do. It's Ryan, and he's a Baylor student."

That intrigued Billy, and he gave it some thought. "If Baylor survived the war, then that means the Allies must have won."

"Obviously. You saw the United States coins, didn't you?"

"How many years will it take?"

"I deliberately try to learn as little as possible—except for that one area where I feel entitled to roam freely and gather facts."

"Jack Decker."

She nodded her head. "But some information just falls into my lap. It's unavoidable."

"Like?"

Her eyes twinkled with mischief. "Like the White Sox will beat the Browns today, five to four, at Comiskey Park."

Billy could only stare in amazement.

"Well, you did ask about that game," she said.

"I've got to introduce you to a good bookie!"

"Sorry, but I don't gamble."

Billy grinned, jingling the coins in his pocket. "By the way, don't forget that you owe me two bits."

◆   ◆   ◆

If this was to be her last excursion to the future, Bonnie wanted to ensure that the clock would not constrain it. She telephoned her parents on Saturday evening and informed them that she would be away on a research project for most of the following day. She did the same with Annie Teakel, who would let the other girls in their church contingent know the reason for her absence. Bonnie suffered no sense of shame in telling them this story, inasmuch as she would indeed be occupying most of her time in front of a computer, double-checking details about the 351st Bomber Group's daylight raids in July/August and particularly the fate of *Scarlett Woman* and her crew. Seeing as how Ryan had offered to lend his expertise again, their ultimate session promised to be a worthwhile endeavor, and Bonnie felt that she needed every conceivably pertinent shred of evidence. In delving into historical minutiae, there was no margin for error.

It was just after 7:30 in the morning when Bonnie knocked on door number twelve in her friend's apartment complex. To her surprise, Ryan answered the door at once, and he did not seem to have been rudely awakened from a night's sleep. Much commotion was evident for such an early hour, as Michael Tinsley and his fiancée flitted about, gathering together canned drinks, snacks, and towels for the day ahead.

When Nicole went upstairs to retrieve something, Ryan gave Bonnie a quick kiss. "They're going to the beach, and they want us to come with them," he said. "Well ... Michael does, anyway."

Hearing this, Michael winked a greeting to her. Then he tactfully excused himself to join Nicole, allowing his roommate and the "California" girl an opportunity to talk in private.

Bonnie was shocked at the very suggestion of such an outing, and she confronted Ryan in no uncertain terms. "What are you thinking?" she asked. "We can't go playing at the beach.

We have to verify all of our findings for 1943. The lives of ten servicemen are at stake—including someone I love very much."

"Not to worry," he told her. "I spent most of this week examining every single fragment that we've uncovered, and I even came up with some entirely new material. Did you know that Jack's flight engineer, Olan Collins, came from Richfield Springs, New York? Between his junior and senior years of high school, he and his dad attended the first induction ceremonies for baseball's Hall of Fame—Cobb, Ruth, Wagner, Johnson, and the others."

Bonnie had a disgruntled look. "That was very thrilling for him, I'm sure, but what exactly does it have to do with the war?"

"Nothing. I thought it was interesting, that's all."

Her face softened. "It does sound like you've been busy."

"I double- and triple-checked every scrap of information that we have. There's nothing more to be done, believe me."

"I still don't feel right about gallivanting to the beach when I should be paying attention to something a lot more important. We need to keep on digging."

"We've already found it all," Ryan said. "Come on. It'll do you some good to unwind for a while."

"Well ..." She seemed to be wavering.

"And this isn't the actual beach—only a big lake somewhere—so it's not all the way down to the Gulf."

Bonnie giggled. "But Ryan, I'm wearing a dress!"

"You can use one of Nicole's swimsuits. She won't mind."

◆　　◆　　◆

The trip in Michael's Nissan GT-R only took about seventy minutes, for he drove at a breakneck clip, and their destination turned out to be not anywhere near the ocean but a public park along the shore of Lake Travis in northwest Austin. After paying the entrance fee of ten dollars, plus a two-dollar surcharge, Michael parked the car in a nicely paved lot. He and Nicole had been there on several previous occasions, so they invested no time in discussing what to do next. They assembled their gear and started toward a clearing in the trees and brush.

Bonnie was confused. "Where's the dressing room, or is there one?" she asked Ryan.

"Beats me." He, too, looked around in vain.

Michael overheard their words and pointed to a nondescript cement structure that evidently served as a rest room. "We'll wait for you here," he told them. Michael and Nicole must have had swimsuits underneath their shirts and shorts because they felt no need to change. Both seemed anxious to be at the shoreline and miffed by the delay.

Ryan entered the MEN side of the facility, with his towel and spandex swimming briefs in hand. Bonnie carried a plastic sack containing three pairs of swimsuits from which to choose—all furnished by Michael's fiancée, who appeared to be amused by the girl's fussiness over summer apparel. No one else was in the WOMEN section of the rest room, so Bonnie planned to try the suits on in front of its mirror. Upon opening the sack, however, she nearly cried. She had seen two-piece swimwear before, but nothing like these. If all three of the sets were combined, there would not have been enough fabric to make a single proper suit.

One "bikini" (as she heard Nicole call them) was a lovely turquoise in color, but its top covered barely a two-inch swath, and its bottom would have required meticulous trimming in the name of decency. The yellow set was more modest in front, both top and bottom, but its rear consisted of a solitary string that settled annoyingly within the crack between her buttocks. The third set, of a bright purple hue, had a skimpy bottom that left little to the imagination, and its top failed to provide any support for her breasts, causing them to jiggle without restraint whenever she moved.

By the time she came out of the rest room in her own clothes—having no choice but to disdain all three swimsuits— her companions, Ryan included, had grown visibly impatient at the perceived dawdling. Nicole, in particular, was not on civil speaking terms after suffering such a slight. Beyond wasting a perfectly good twenty minutes of her life, this Bonnie had been nervy enough to reject every one of her favorite bikinis. When the girl handed them back to her, Nicole indignantly stuffed the sack into her tote bag.

"Weren't they fancy enough for you?" she asked.

Bonnie glared at her. "The tops were too small."

As the four young people slowly made their way down the winding path, Bonnie resolved to stay on dry land while the others swam. At least she could relax, soak up some healthful rays, and spend an enjoyable final day in company with Ryan. Nothing about this park seemed the least bit unusual until they neared the water, light reflecting off its surface through the rustling leaves. Coming toward them and passing on the narrow trail were a pair of college-age boys who wore nothing but leather moccasins. The youths were lithe and bronzed by the sun, and their manhood swayed back and forth as they walked.

Bonnie could hardly believe her eyes, and Ryan, too, was a bit surprised at the sight of such eccentricity.

She whispered to him, "Did you just see what I saw?"

"I guess that's Austin for you," he said.

Shortly thereafter, the lakeview panorama opened to them, with a jagged bank of rocks overlooking shimmering waters. Several swimmers' heads could be seen bobbing up and down above the peaceful surface, and the entire scene was utterly quiet. Dozens of sunbathers were stretched out on their blankets, hugging the shoreline at roughly regular intervals for as far as the eye could see. When Bonnie looked more closely at them, she noticed that a vast majority of these tanned hedonists were totally nude. There were people of all ages and shapes—male and female alike—some standing, some lying face downward, and some reclining on their backs, attired in nothing but dark glasses to shield their vision from direct sunlight.

Ryan smiled shamefacedly at Bonnie, as if disclaiming any part in the selection of this recreational site. Nicole and Michael, though, were oblivious to any impropriety and proceeded to spread two beach blankets atop a relatively flat slab of stone, appropriating one spacious rectangle for themselves and leaving the other for their guests. All four seated themselves in their assigned places, but not for long. Within a minute, Nicole was on her feet, kicking off her sandals and slipping out of her pink shorts. Her gray athletic shirt came next, leaving her clad in nothing but a red brassiere and matching panties. Michael, too, stood up and purposefully stripped to his underpants. Bonnie glanced at the slight bulge therein but pretended to be viewing the natural vistas beyond.

"Bonnie, I ..." Ryan said. He could not finish the sentence, offering instead a miserably apologetic shake of the head.

"I know. I don't blame you. It wasn't your idea."

Bonnie turned again toward Michael, who was contemplating the gallery of nude bodies that surrounded him. When his eyes finally settled upon her and Ryan, he grinned at them and asked, "Aren't you two going to join us?" He did so not in a crude manner but as if the shedding of clothes in public were the most intuitive instinct of mankind. Although Bonnie smiled back, she did not respond in either word or deed. Meanwhile, Ryan silently simmered, resentful of his roommate's perceived attempt to see Bonnie Ploughwright undressed.

Soon Nicole and Michael were sitting down again, only now they were more demonstrative in their mutual affection. They gave each other a long, lingering, perhaps lustful kiss, and he reached over and unfastened the clasp of her brassiere. The garment fell aside, exposing her resplendent breasts for everyone to see. In turn, both of her hands wandered down to his underpants, the waistband of which she calmly slid the full length of his legs. Bonnie, observing from an enticingly close vantage point, found this show of exhibitionism to be of considerable interest—too fascinating to disregard for such an acquired reflex as modesty.

Michael was only vaguely aroused, confirming what Bonnie had been told by her roommate, psychology major Julia Johnston: experienced naturists do not characterize their chosen way of living as being overtly sexual. Even when Michael saw that Bonnie was peeking at him, his body did not display any perceptible loss of composure. He smiled, bringing instant embarrassment to her, and yet she willed herself not to look away—a small victory for her newfound sense of freedom.

Still seated and sensing that Michael's attention was divided, Nicole took it upon herself to remove the frilly red panties, unabashedly revealing her most private parts. She spread her legs just enough to optimize the effect without appearing too dissolute. Then she secured a tube of ointment, known as "sunscreen," and started smoothing it over her arms and shoulders. "Mickey, dear, please help," she said. He was only too willing to pitch in, cupping his hands around her breasts and gently massaging the lotion into the already browned skin. In minutes, virtually her whole body was covered by a thin layer of the medicinal cream.

That agreeable task accomplished, Michael began to apply sunscreen to his own body. He glanced at Bonnie, seated about five feet to his right, but did not ask her for assistance. Of this she was glad, fearing that she did not have the self-control to firmly refuse. A wave of ecstasy swept over her, a tingling sensation too pleasurable to name. Bonnie now knew, beyond question, that she wanted to give herself entirely to these seductive delights. But something was standing in the way, separating her from the euphoric feeling of total surrender.

Lying alongside her on the blanket was Ryan, who had leaned back on his elbows to view the erotic drama unfolding to his left. He savored Nicole's exquisite form and studied Bonnie's demure reaction to the open show of nudity around her. By contrast, he felt contempt toward his roommate, who seemed to be taking unfair advantage of the situation. And yet, to be absolutely impartial about it, Ryan could hardly indict Michael for trying to lure Bonnie out of her clothing when he also would love nothing more than to set eyes upon her unclad body. To Ryan's credit, however, he wanted her to disrobe because she truly wished to do so, not as a response to peer pressure or sense of occasion. Whimsically, he wondered what would happen if he followed his friends' lead in sunbathing *au naturel*. Would Bonnie be disgusted by his depravity, or would she be emboldened to play along, indulging in the sheer enjoyment of letting her inhibitions run free for a short while? It was risky business, he thought, but worth a try.

"Well, when in Rome ..." Ryan said. He reached up to grasp the collar of his shirt and pull it overhead.

Much to his relief, Bonnie seemed amused by the comment and not at all displeased to gaze upon his bare chest once again. She did not remove the boy's athletic shorts for him, but neither did she strenuously object when he proceeded to slide them down his legs. From the telling contour of his swimming briefs underneath, it was clear that he was not an experienced naturist.

Ryan slipped his fingertips under the swimsuit's waistband and issued a jaunty dare. "If I do it, will you? Both at once!"

Bonnie was eager to join in the sexy romp but could not. "I'm sorry, Ryan, but that would be much too embarrassing."

Stoically, he nodded his head. Although disappointed, as any man honest with himself would be, Ryan was respectful enough of the girl's beliefs to accept her refusal without ridicule.

Bonnie remained as cheerful as possible in the circumstances, ludicrously sitting in her long dress while only a few feet away from the cool waters of an inviting lake. Her legs were bare—stockings being a luxurious rarity in wartime—and she had removed her shoes and socks. It felt nice to wiggle her toes in the summer breeze.

Ryan smiled at Bonnie with more tenderness than ever before. "I apologize for everything that's happened here."

"That's all right. It's not your fault."

A few seconds later, he reached down again and pulled his athletic shorts over the swimsuit. "Now you won't feel so alone."

"Thank you, but I don't mind—really."

"At least rub some sunscreen on yourself," he said. "Your face and arms will get awfully burned if you don't."

He offered her the tube, but she just stared, as if it were a loaded revolver. "Doesn't that stuff sting?"

"Not unless you get some in your eyes."

Oddly enough, the concept of protective lotion was new to Bonnie. All her life, she had been told that lying in the sun was good for you, that it incited the healthy production of vitamin D. And now, here was Ryan, repudiating the whole theory by contending that prolonged exposure to ultraviolet radiation can lead to variegated strains of skin cancer. "Please put some on," he told her. "Do it for me."

She agreed, but only after he volunteered to do the spreading. "How magnanimous of you," she said with a grin. He applied cream to her face and arms, and then, with the girl's acquiescence, to her ankles and feet as well.

"Too bad one of Nicole's bathing suits didn't fit," Ryan said. Bonnie was not sure if he was kidding.

The lake itself seemed to be populated by a disproportionate number of water-treading males, but that gender disparity did not deter Nicole. After lying onshore for two hours, wearing only a pair of sunglasses, she was more than ready to plunge in for a refreshing dip. She took off the glasses, rose to her feet, turned around as if posing, and then languorously stretched, with shoulders back and both arms skyward. Even her subsequent entrance into the water was handled with aplomb, standing motionless for a dramatic moment before jumping in, toes pointed, with nary a splash. Michael consented to accompany her on the swim, though he had been quite comfortable on their blanket—sandwiched between two lovely young women—and was in no particular hurry to leave.

♦   ♦   ♦

Not until early evening, when the four of them were dressed and walking through the parking lot, did Bonnie first hear mention of the place's name. "It's called Hippie Hollow," Michael told her. "Nicole and I come down here every once in a while."

He glanced at his fiancée. "Whenever we're feeling especially horny, I guess."

"Like today," Nicole said, and she meant it. She was the last to put her clothes back on and surely would have ridden home in the nude, were it not for the slim chance that a state trooper might pull them over for speeding. "Mickey and I will probably stay up all night at my apartment, getting kinky and wild. How about you two joining us?" She looked at Bonnie with unexpected warmth, almost friendliness, and the "California" girl smiled in return. "Please say you will," Nicole added. "Our outdoor pool has a hot tub." Michael nodded his encouragement.

"Bonnie needs to meet her father by 10:30," Ryan told them, "and they'll be driving up to Dallas for a morning flight."

"Oh, that's a shame!" Nicole said. "It would have been fun." Michael contributed nothing more to the discussion, but his forlorn, pining gaze spoke volumes.

During their homeward trek up Interstate 35, the red Nissan would occasionally veer a few inches out of its lane—never when other cars were around—and the two backseat passengers whispered to each other about what unseen diversion was taking place. Other than that single brief conversation, however, Ryan was uncharacteristically quiet, and it was not difficult to speculate why that might be. He grasped his friend's hand, squeezing it while taking a deep breath and dejectedly exhaling through his nose. The boy's face, Bonnie noticed, was etched with emotion, but he scarcely said a word.

There was little reason to doubt that Michael and his fiancée did indeed plan to cohabit the night away at her apartment—despite the fact that Nicole's roommate would be present as well. This female third party was probably used to such an arrangement because Nicole made no secret of her penchant for improvisatory sex. For all Bonnie knew, the roommate was invited to participate in their carnal behavior, but that seemed unlikely. Although self-gratification ranked high on the list of personality traits for both Michael and Nicole, there was no denying that this engaged couple were far from unscrupulous libertines. They had been dating each other exclusively for more than six months, ever since his October break-up with Heather Whaley.

When Michael dropped Ryan and Bonnie off at apartment number twelve, Nicole told the guest, "We hope to see you again, sometime soon."

Bonnie frowned, sad at their parting and still baffled by this girl's inexplicable change of attitude. Maybe Nicole had initially judged her to be a sanctimonious prude, a rash assumption that was shown to be untrue by her sufferance of their steamy antics at the lakeside retreat.

"No, I'm afraid that you won't," Bonnie said, mindful to stay in character. "I'll be in California until long after you two are married, and I don't know if I'll ever be able to come back."

"But you might be transferring to Baylor," Michael told the girl. "I thought that was the whole reason for your visit." He glanced hopefully at his roommate.

"That's beginning to seem less and less likely," Ryan said. "I'd guess the odds are very much against it."

With affection far beyond what Bonnie would have considered possible only a few hours earlier, she wished these new friends happiness in their coming years as husband and wife, and then Michael Tinsley and Nicole Hulen regrettably passed out of her life forever. Bonnie waved to them as the red sports car drove away.

Time was now running short for her to beat the stringently enforced curfew at Alexander Hall. Ryan walked her to campus, offering some comfort with an arm around her shoulders.

"I've been dreading this moment," Bonnie said. "I wonder if you know how special you've become to me." Tearfully, she looked up at him. "I can't thank you enough for your kindness and help."

Ryan gave a deep sigh, and he, too, felt his eyes beginning to moisten. "Having you go away is like a nightmare," he told her. "Worse than a nightmare ... because I'll never wake up from it."

Bonnie pulled an envelope from her purse. "I have something for you—a note that I wrote this morning before I came to your apartment—but you can't read it until September fifteenth at the earliest. The timing is very important."

She handed the sealed envelope to him, and he paused along the sidewalk, shining his iPhone's built-in flashlight to illuminate the inscription: "To Ryan. DO NOT OPEN until September 15th!!!" He carefully tucked the envelope into the back pocket of his shorts.

Bonnie and her friend resumed their walk in silence, holding hands. Quite soon, on whosever initiative, their fingers became intertwined. But what should have been a romantic stroll was no longer possible. Waco Hall loomed ahead, only two blocks away.

Suddenly, Ryan stopped again, his face brightening. "I know what! You can come back one more time next week. Construction won't even start until the tenth—you saw the dates—so there's no reason why you couldn't."

Bonnie wanted desperately to agree, but instead she shook her head. "Something would happen between us—something physical—and that's not supposed to be. It *must* not be."

"But I think I'm falling in love with you," Ryan said. His voice trailed off, shaky from nervousness. "I guess there's no harm in telling you now—nothing to lose."

Bonnie kissed him on the cheek. "It still makes me feel nice to hear you say. You're a wonderful boy, and I'm very fond of you— even more than I probably realize."

Ryan took the girl's hand again and accompanied her into the lobby. The place had become dreary and forbidding, and the two young people trudged its length and then up the west staircase as if going to meet their executioner. When they neared the balcony's invisible portal, Bonnie threw her arms around him, saying not a word, and they squeezed tightly to one another in a long embrace.

Finally, though, she relaxed her hold on him and raised herself tall, trying to remain brave. "Goodbye, Ryan," she whispered. "You'll be in my thoughts and prayers."

"Goodbye ... sweet Bonnie."

She turned away from him, took three small steps, and was gone.

◆　　◆　　◆

Bonnie saw that she had just ten minutes to spare before the dormitory's curfew would arrive. Consequently, there was no chance to console herself with the therapeutic properties of a good cry—in private, alone with her grief. She was emotionally drained, shattered by the loss. Against all probability, what began that morning as a supplemental research junket had blossomed into a relationship so meaningful that she was unable to grasp its true significance until after the moment had slipped away.

She left Waco Hall at once, hoping not to encounter anyone she knew. Her eyes were puffy, she felt certain, and what little cosmetics she applied at dawn surely had been smudged by the application of sun lotion and the flowing of tears. To regain her poise en route, she did everything in her power to avoid any thought whatsoever of Ryan. However, the anguished goodbyes had taken their toll, and her efforts were largely in vain.

Mrs. Tanner, a friendly but meddlesome lady who handled Alexander Hall's front desk duties on Sunday nights, must have detected something odd in Bonnie's appearance when the girl hurried past because she made it a point to call out to her.

"Yoo-hoo, Miss Ploughwright."

Bonnie pivoted around. "Ma'am?"

"A note came for you today while you were out." But rather than retrieving the correspondence, Mrs. Tanner proceeded to engage in her usual small talk. It seemed obvious to Bonnie that the woman's real intent was simply to satisfy her own curiosity.

"Are you all right?" Mrs. Tanner asked. She was studying the coed's face. "You look like you've been crying."

"Yes, thanks, I'm just fine," Bonnie told her. "I've been reading a very sad novel for class—and it brought a few tears to my eyes, that's all."

"Are you an English major, then?"

"Yes, ma'am." Bonnie gestured toward the mail slots. "You mentioned a note?"

"A what?"

"You said somebody left a note for me today."

"Oh, yes, the note." Mrs. Tanner located a folded slip of paper and handed it to Bonnie. "It's from an Army officer—a very courteous young man, and quite good looking. He came around five o'clock and sat in the drawing room, waiting for you. He was here for about half an hour, but then he couldn't wait any longer, so he wrote the note."

"Oh, dear."

"I gather that he was here this morning, too. Mrs. Flynn was at the desk, so it had to be before noon."

"Thank you, Mrs. Tanner." Bonnie carried the note to a chair in the entry room. The handwriting was somewhat difficult to read, having apparently been scribbled in great haste:

Bonnie—
Ship out at 1900 hours today instead of at mid-week. Imperative you write me, c/o APO 343, New York. Won't be simple matter at my end. Seems we're in different outfits, hundreds of miles apart. Give me details or we're done for.
—Billy Fowler

Absorbing this distressing news made her shudder from guilt. Bonnie's selfish toying with sensuality had caused her to miss seeing the only person on earth who could save the life of Jack Decker. Not once, but twice, she had been granted opportunities to meet with the lieutenant, and yet she was far off at a pleasure spa, frittering away her precious time in blissful ignorance.

"Well, where have you been?" Julia asked when Bonnie opened the door to the room they shared. "Some officer has been looking all over the place for you."

"So I understand," Bonnie said. "Mrs. Tanner described the entire scene for me."

"I explained that you were away on a research project, but I'm not sure he believed me."

"You talked to him?"

"This morning—yes. Mrs. Flynn let me know that Billy was at the desk, so I went down there and told him what little I knew."

"Billy, is it! So you're already on a first-name basis."

Julia smiled. "No sense in being formal about these things," she said.

"What things are those?" Bonnie was in no mood for her roommate's games.

"Men, of course. But it turns out that this one is married, with a daughter named Peggy and another baby on the way."

"Sounds like you two had a nice, chummy conference."

"I enjoyed it—and I'm pretty sure he did, too."

"And what makes you think that?"

"Oh, just how he was staring at me. I can always tell." Julia began to squint, as if analyzing her roommate. "God! You look like hell."

"Thank you very much."

"Have you been in a dogfight or something?"

"Not recently."

"Well, whatever happened, it's a good thing your officer got here too early to see you like this."

Bonnie's eyes flared. "Lieutenant Fowler is not my officer—as you well know."

"But yours is serving abroad, and that's as good as past tense. Time to go to the bullpen, I say."

"Who asked you for advice? I haven't noticed an engagement ring on your finger."

"You can have sex without being married."

"No fooling? I hadn't heard," Bonnie said. "That suddenly changes my whole life."

Julia giggled. "Every once in a while, you should take my free advice. Do you realize how much a psychologist would charge?"

♦   ♦   ♦

During the ensuing weeks, Bonnie immersed herself in schoolwork. She had fallen behind in her studies, having devoted so much time and effort lately to investigating what the future held for Jack Decker and the crew of *Scarlett Woman*. The last class session for the spring quarter would be on Monday, May 24, and then would come four rounds of final examinations, in the first three of which she would take part. Bonnie had to perform at her customary high standard or be prepared to suffer the consequences: a stern talk from her parents and, worse yet, the provoking of unwanted suspicion.

The more she concentrated upon academics and concerns of the present, the more dreamlike her recollection of that "other" world became. For instance, her day at the clothing-optional park seemed unbelievable in the extreme. Had she really indulged in the viewing of casual nudity? Had she passed within an arm's length of naturists along the footpaths? Had she and the libidinous Nicole become sympathetic friends? Had she shared tender words with a swell boy named Ryan Andriessen, whom she probably would never be able to see again? And had she failed to convey even the most fundamental instructions to Billy Fowler—in effect, sentencing ten valiant servicemen to die in a fiery crash?

On May 18, eight days after the renovation of Waco Hall was due to begin—sixty-six years hence—Bonnie decided to test the time portal and determine whether her odysseys into the future had come to an end. Her American Prose class, English 272, was not meeting that afternoon, so she had a free hour to evaluate the cylinder's condition. She knew, from something Ryan had said, that Baylor would not be in session during this interim period, between the spring and summer terms of 2009. He called them "semesters," which Bonnie supposed were roughly equivalent to administrative quarters.

Going upstairs to the balcony's lobby had become her routine precaution, so as not to attract attention from startled observers. On this particular trip, it behooved her to be especially wary of what she might find at the other end, for a construction site did not figure to be hospitable to the ill-prepared visitor. Then again, there was every likelihood that no time traveling would occur at all, that her door to the future had been irrevocably disturbed and closed forever. Fearing the unknown, she stepped forward with a sturdy literature book clutched overhead, to protect her from the potential dangers of falling debris.

Bonnie did pass into an alternate existence, but so otherworldly was it that she became disoriented at once, stupefied by the unfamiliar mats and drapings that were strewn everywhere. She could hear distant voices and the discordant sounds of physical destruction below. Down a littered stairway she crept, not knowing what might be awaiting her at the bottom. When she reached the main floor and allowed her eyes to take in the ghastly spectacle, Bonnie concluded that something had gone terribly wrong. She was viewing the remnants of a desolate outpost on another planet. Through the blowing dust, she could discern men in white spacesuits, walking about, unleashing their scrapers and crowbars and hammers and vacuums on the structure's disfigured walls and ceilings. They wore goggles, gas masks, and gloves, and their shoes were amorphous footwear of the grimmest utilitarian sort. Out of self-preservation, not a single inch of these spacemen's skin was exposed to the harmful effects of the planet's toxic atmosphere.

Three of the beings came closer but did not spot her in the chaos. Apparently, their vision was impaired by the translucent goggles and dust-laden air, so Bonnie was able to retreat into the alcove and evade detection. To her astonishment, it sounded like these men were speaking a language closely related to Spanish, and their frequent laughter belied the notion that they were gruesome, unearthly fiends.

When the three men finally began walking the other direction, Bonnie worked up enough courage to explore her options. She could see that the building was indeed Waco Hall, but its interior demolition was so pervasive as to render it almost unrecognizable without recourse to a blueprint. Edging her way through the cluttered corridor leading to Waco Hall East, she noticed that the exit doors were taped securely shut, with warning signs prominently posted. This was a chilling sight, for it denoted the closure of her temporal mobility. Even if she managed to force her way outside, her freedom to wander could amount to nothing more than a one-way trip. She would be marooned in the twenty-first century. That being the case, Bonnie had no choice but to abandon all hope of using the portal again until at least the middle of August, when renovation would be complete. By then, of course, the fate of Jack Decker and the others would already be sealed. And so, reluctantly, she returned to the present, feeling disappointed, fearful, and more than a little helpless.

On Thursday, May 20, Bonnie finally wrote to Lieutenant Fowler, convinced that enough time would have elapsed for him to reach England and settle in to his new assignment. Someone had told her that mail going in either direction—not just from a soldier to home—was subject to censorship, so her wording was deliberately circumspect with regard to Jack.

> Hello, Billy.
>
> This is just to let you know that I am thinking of you here in Texas. Melinda sent me a postcard a few days ago, saying all is well in Knoxville and that Peggy is having fun being treated like royalty by her grandparents.
>
> I am finishing my spring quarter at Baylor University, with just two more days of classes remaining—and then comprehensive exams. No summer school for me this year, so I'll be heading back to Dallas after my last final on the 27th. How odd it will seem to be living with my parents again. They receive letters from my brother, Keith,

about once a month, and he is doing fine, considering that he has been away for a year and a half now, with no furloughs. His girlfriend (and former fiancée) sent him a terse note on the last day of March, informing him they were through. I was never very fond of her anyway, so good riddance.

Maybe I should tell you what I have heard about Uncle Jack, who will be embarking on a long voyage July 30. No doubt this will inflict serious damage on that old jalopy of his. We'll let him do it, but he must not be allowed to go again on August 11, under any circumstances, even though that trip will be much shorter. At all costs, he must be talked out of it, until a good team of mechanics can re-check everything on his vehicle. It will not be roadworthy, and even going for a test drive would mean disaster.

I miss seeing you at the USO club, where I continue to volunteer about a dozen hours per week. After leaving there for the summer months, I'll probably resume my USO work in September, as this fits quite nicely into my school schedule. By helping the boys in uniform, I feel that I'm contributing in some small way to the war effort, though of course I would rather be employed in one of the heavy industries, like my mother.

That's all for now. Please write soon to let me know that you received this.

Best wishes,
Bonnie

On the envelope, she carefully printed her home address, knowing that Dallas was where any communication from Billy should be directed for the next seventeen weeks. Classes for Baylor University's fall quarter would not start until September 15.

◆　　◆　　◆

A wet tongue licked across her nose and mouth, jolting Bonnie awake on the day after final examinations concluded. "Tiff!" she shouted with glee. Lying in her own bed now, not the dormitory's, she sat up to play with the hyperactive Yorkshire terrier, which romped about, exhibiting boundless energy—like some wind-up toy with an inexhaustible spring.

"Sorry," her mother said. She stood, arms folded, in the open doorway to the girl's bedroom. "I couldn't keep her out any longer. Tiffany was so excited to have you home again."

"That's all right, Mother. I thought I wore her out last night, but obviously I was mistaken." She glanced at the alarm clock on her nightstand. It was 8:10. "Is Daddy already at work?"

"Oh, yes, he left a half-hour ago. But I don't have to report until four."

"Swing shift?"

"Uh-huh. And then I have a day shift, so just enough time to catch some sleep in between."

"Do you like it there—at North American?"

"You bet. I wouldn't ever tell your father this, but I enjoy going to work each day, rather than staying around the house."

Doreen Webb Ploughwright was a devoted housewife and mother of two, but occasionally she became restless and wanted more out of life. The war brought adventure and a sense of doing her bit to aid the nation's armed forces.

"Is the job interesting?" Bonnie asked.

"Usually it is, yes. Very much so." Doreen lit a cigarette, blowing the smoke away from her daughter. "There's quite a lot of stress, though, when the foreman is trying to meet his quotas."

Bonnie glared her disapproval. "Since when did you take that up again?"

"What?"

Bonnie nodded toward the cigarette. "You remember what Doctor Ellard said."

"That was before I was a working woman. I'm sure he'd understand now. He smokes a pack a day himself, you know."

Sensing the futility of argument, Bonnie changed the subject. "Are there any openings at your plant?"

"My goodness, no. Not for part-timers anyway. They're looking for people to handle shift work, and they get full-time applications every day."

"What about temporary full-timers?"

"I don't think so." Bonnie's mother smiled with amusement. "No summer jobs for building P-51s, if that's what you mean."

"I want to do something useful with my time off. Something in a war industry."

"Well, what about the USO? They can always use another pretty face."

"That's small potatoes, Mother. I might as well be a cocktail waitress, for all the good I do."

"Now, that's just not true, and you know it." Doreen snapped her fingers, and Tiffany obediently leaped off the bed and sat down by her feet. "Did you hear that Becky has started working at the USO club? About a month ago."

"Keith's Becky? Well, used to be ..."

"I still think of her as Keith's. She'll come back to him."

"I hope not—that bitch!" The word slipped out before Bonnie could stop.

"I .... beg .... your .... pardon, young lady!" Doreen snarled. She was red-faced with anger. "Is that how they teach you to talk at Baylor?"

Bonnie could not recall ever seeing her mother quite this furious. Indeed, she was much more outraged at the clumsy vulgarism than she was at Rebecca Duke, who had jilted poor Keith when he was away, fighting for his country. All Bonnie did was tell the truth, and that did not seem fair.

"I'm sorry, ma'am. No, they don't talk like that at Baylor, at least not the girls." Still unforgiven, Bonnie resorted to invoking a convenient excuse that absolved every lapse in appropriate behavior: "But there's a war on." Doreen sighed, accepting that logic without further comment, and the matter was dropped.

Before the next week was out, Bonnie had secured summer employment to help pay for her Baylor tuition. On Friday, June 4, she became the proud operator of a typewriter at the *Dallas Morning News*. It was a job she got because her father had a patient whose sister's husband worked there as a circulation assistant. The position was not exactly war work, but it did allow Bonnie to stay apprised of community efforts on the home front, and her boss, Roy Shanks, seemed willing to accept the fact that she would be leaving for college even before the arrival of autumn. Most of all, it gave her the opportunity to write—for hours on end and with a sense of urgency. This was good training for someone with aspirations of becoming an author.

The *Dallas Morning News*, one of the nation's largest newspapers, was housed in a building at the corner of Young and Houston Streets. Dr. Ploughwright insisted upon driving his daughter to work for the first several days, but then, when Bonnie felt confident enough, he relented and allowed her to ride the streetcar instead. In time, she became close friends with a young woman named Susan Blount, whose father was a radio announcer at KGKO, a station that, like the newspaper, was owned by the A. H. Belo Corporation. Susan and Bonnie were in the same typing pool—classified as secretarial jobs—and they had identical schedules, too, from eight to five on weekdays. Only on weekends did their office duties diverge, with irregular assignments on Saturdays and Sundays, sometimes during the daylight hours and sometimes late into the evenings.

"Have you noticed the way that old man over there is sizing you up?" Bonnie asked her friend one day in the lunch room.

"Who?" Susan turned to see an attractive gentleman with graying hair. She whispered, "He's not so old."

"About fifty, I'd say."

"Nah. No more than forty."

"Even so ..."

"What's wrong with that? Aren't men permitted to admire ravishing beauty when they see it?"

Bonnie giggled. "You wouldn't think someone that age would be ogling college girls."

"I'm not a college girl."

"Just the same—you're college age."

Susan glanced at him again. "I think he's very distinguished looking."

"This war is making you easy to please."

"No, it's not. Actually, I'm quite selective." Yet again she gazed at him. "Anyway, there's no charge for window shopping."

"He's wearing a ring on his left hand. Surely you're not that much of a bohemian."

Susan scrutinized him more closely and grinned. "No, I draw the line there. I'm not a home wrecker." At that, she turned back to her food and gave the man no further thought. "But, you know, my boyfriend did give me permission to date as much as I want while he's away."

"He must trust you a great deal."

"Not really. It's just that we only knew each other for two weeks before his number came up. We didn't have time to get very serious."

"Some people get serious overnight," Bonnie said. "Signed, sealed, and delivered, all in the span of a single twenty-four-hour pass. Stranger things have happened, you know."

"Well, yes, but not to me. I'm overly cautious when it comes to men." Susan reached into her purse and pulled out a photograph. "This is Randall." She offered it to her friend. "He's the one on the left."

Bonnie studied the photo with great interest. "He's rather handsome, isn't he?"

"I think so, but of course I'm biased."

"No, he really is quite dapper in his Army uniform. Who's the man with him?"

"A good pal of his from when they were both stationed in Mississippi."

Bonnie turned the snapshot over and read the inscription. Her face became ashen. The photograph fell from her fingers and onto the table.

"What's the matter?" Susan asked. She stared with alarm, genuinely concerned for her friend's health.

"Oh, nothing. I'm fine." Hastily, Bonnie picked up the picture and returned it to Susan. "How often do you hear from Randall?"

"About once every couple of weeks, on average. He's very matter-of-fact in his letters—not romantic at all. Honestly, I might as well be reading the telephone book."

Bonnie smiled, trying to mask her anxiety. The scrawled words on the back of the photo read, "Here I am in Biloxi with my buddy, Harvey Mills."

◆　　◆　　◆

The summer months sped by in a whirl of activity, a common phenomenon when workdays are as repetitious as Bonnie's proved to be. Her livelihood as a glorified typist was not as personally fulfilling as she had wished, but at least it honed some writing skills while drawing a modest paycheck in the bargain. Among other tasks, her daily routine included anonymously revising outdated stories, composing original articles for no by-line credit, and transcribing scribbled notes from the newspaper's lionized cadre of senior reporters.

Susan and Bonnie served under the same supervisor, Roy Shanks, so their paths crossed quite often through the course of a typical day. Whenever a surplus moment presented itself, the girls would share spicy tidbits of office gossip, including the scandalous relationship of the newsroom's Claudia Sandowski and Richard Hocking, both of whom were married but not to each other. Also high on the friends' agenda were any pieces of correspondence that came from abroad—Bonnie from Captain

Jack Decker and Susan from Sergeant Randall Hunt. They did not recount them in their entirety, of course, but only those salient excerpts that were not too intimate.

Their first such exchange took place in early July, when the girls received messages from their boyfriends only two days apart. They read selected portions aloud while waiting for Mr. Shanks to locate a half-dozen wire stories for rewriting.

"Haven't been getting much sleep lately," Bonnie recited from Jack's words, "but can't complain because the Krauts haven't been, either. Two new guys joined our outfit last week, and one of them is from Gatesville, Texas, not far from Waco. We hear the 'Lux Radio Theatre' every so often, by shortwave, and I always think of you whenever it's on because I know that is your favorite radio show. Last Saturday I had a lengthy visit (over a few pints) with Billy Fowler, who had a forty-eight-hour pass at the same time as I did. We met at the only pub in a town about halfway between our two posts. Never expected to bump into him way over here. My aunt in Houston wrote to me—the first time I've heard from her—and she says Uncle Foyle and my Ford are both doing swell."

Susan seemed a little envious of what she heard. "He writes a fine letter, doesn't he? I wish Randall would put an ounce of effort into his."

"Some people just don't like to write," Bonnie said. "It's really not their fault. They're not very communicative, that's all."

"I suppose you're right, but it's still maddening. I go to a lot of trouble with what I send."

"But you're a good writer, and it comes naturally to you." Bonnie set her eyes upon the envelope her friend was holding. "Aren't you going to tell me what's inside?"

Susan sighed loudly, rather embarrassed. "Just don't laugh. He writes like a fourth grader."

"Okay, but I'm sure his heart is in the right place."

"And I have to explain that he calls me 'Chick.' It's his pet name for me."

"That's cute," Bonnie said with a grin.

After clearing her throat, Susan began. "Hi, Chick. Good to hear from you again, after so long. I shouldn't talk because you write lots more than me. It's hot and windy here today. There's plenty of cigarettes and candy for us now, now that the shipment came in. It was just like Christmas. My buddy Calvin stole a pouch of coffee from a shop in town—just stuck it under his shirt and walked out. It was better than our cook makes for morning chow. A jeep fell off a lift the other day and broke someone's arm. He'll be out of action for six weeks, they say. My other buddy Harvey beat all of us at darts on Sunday—threw a bull's-eye to win it by ten. Well, Chick, I've got to go now. Me and Harv have guard duty, and the war can't go on without us."

Bonnie looked down at the floor and smiled. "He sounds very nice."

"He is nice," Susan told her. "Just not very educated."

"How did you two meet?"

"At a county fair—more like a carnival really. Randall was eating an ice cream cone, and it dripped onto my coat. He was mortified at first, but then he said that was the best nickel he ever spent."

"Is he from Dallas?"

"Sulphur Springs—off to the east. He was in Dallas to visit his brother, who works here."

"At the newspaper?"

Susan laughed. "No, not right here at the newspaper. I just meant somewhere in Dallas—doing residential roofing, I think."

"Well, he sounds like a nice boy."

"Want to know a secret?"

"Sure." Bonnie leaned forward, for the sake of privacy.

"You can't tell a soul," Susan whispered.

"I promise."

"Randall's pal, Harvey Mills, has written to me a couple of times."

Bonnie swallowed hard. "My goodness! He has?"

Susan noticed that her friend appeared to be shocked by the statement, and she appreciated the empathy that Bonnie felt.

"I'm not proud of it—going behind Randall's back like that," Susan said. "But the letters were perfectly innocent."

Bonnie glanced around the workroom, idly inserting a sheet of paper into her typewriter. "Did you write him back?"

"Yes. It would be impolite not to, don't you think?"

"I guess so. How did this Harvey become interested in you? Did you send your boyfriend a snapshot?"

"Yes, but I never dreamed that Randall would pass it around to his pals."

"Do you think anything will come of it?"

Susan grinned. "You never know. Harvey is very handsome, as you could see from his picture. He was standing next to Randall."

"Is he from Sulphur Springs, too?"

"Oh, no. He's a Yankee—from Ohio, I think, or maybe it was Iowa."

"Is he better educated than Randall?"

"Two years of college, he says. Then he enlisted."

Bonnie rubbed her chin nervously, and again Susan was impressed by how attentive this friend was to her boy dilemma.

"He says he might even come to see me after the war," Susan whispered. "That is, if it's all right with Randall or we're on the skids by then."

◆   ◆   ◆

When Bonnie's alarm clock awoke her at 6:15 on the morning of July 30, her first thought, like millions of American laborers, was that this would be the end of another work week. But as the cobwebs of sleep waned, a much more solemn realization dawned upon her: Jack Decker, after completion of his bombing run that day, would be flying through a living hell before landing his crippled B-17 at a provisional airstrip in Britain. Silently, Bonnie said a prayer in behalf of the pilot and his crew. She also prayed that her well-intentioned tampering with history had not led to tragic repercussions in the skies over Germany.

Ten days later, in the afternoon mail, Bonnie received a chatty missive from Billy Fowler. Much of it amounted to little more than textual camouflage, shallow ramblings whose purpose, she suspected, was to conceal the letter's essence from the diligent inspection of a military censor. The noteworthy paragraph read, "Saw Jack for a couple of hours in a country bar yesterday. Explained the situation to him—warning him to be careful on the eleventh. Better yet, avoid that day altogether and go over the old buggy with a fine-tooth comb. Impressed upon him the urgency of this action, but he seemed doubtful. Finally said it was his only hope of ever seeing you again, and that may have done the trick. Think he is convinced, but am unable to tell you for sure. As boss of his office, he has complete authority, so can deny its usage until cleared."

When the fateful day of August 11 arrived, Bonnie Ploughwright was a useless employee of the *Dallas Morning News*. She concentrated on deeds far loftier than typing—to gaze with tearful eyes at Jack's snapshot, to remember his touch and the way he spoke, and to recall passages from his recent letters. Susan sensed the girl's distraction and tried her best to make allowances, even covering for her when a stack of rewrites was plopped into the job basket. After all, sometimes she, too, became lost in thought. It was an occupational hazard for any working girl whose sweetheart was a serviceman at war.

On the nightstand in Bonnie's bedroom lay a calendar, the same one that she had consulted so often in the college dormitory. Circumscribing its second week of August was a boldly drawn oval, applied by her with a fountain pen to indicate when the Waco Hall renovation project was due to be finished. Having now been separated for nearly three months from her miraculous conduit to the future, she was sorely tempted to use her next day off, August 14, for traveling to Baylor and testing whether the portal continued to function or had been eradicated by construction workers. If the passage was indeed operational, she could sit down at any Jones Reference Library computer and ascertain at a glance the destiny of *Scarlett Woman*, not to mention that of an ill-fated lady named Bonnie Mills. But what would such prescience really accomplish? She could no longer exert any influence upon the first eventuality, which had already occurred, even in her own time. And the second was controllable, in theory at least, by staying away from Susan's boyfriend and his pal in a postwar world, while also shunning the perilous habit of tobacco. She resolved to maintain her lonely vigil in Dallas.

Each day thereafter, Bonnie ran home from the streetcar stop and breathlessly flipped through the mail. Sometimes her mother was already there and unwittingly relieved the suspense with a downcast look in her eyes. Usually, though, the house was empty, and Bonnie was obliged to witness for herself the stark truth that nothing had come. Why did he not write? What, if anything, did his silence portend? Waiting for definite word was almost unendurable, so much so that Bonnie actually found herself wishing she had not been cursed with foreknowledge of the future. Such a thankless thought was patently absurd, of course, for it spurned the very blessing that represented her only hope that Jack might survive the war.

On the seventeenth of the month, when a communication finally did arrive, it appeared not as a letter but in the dreaded form of a telegram. Bonnie was at work, and her mother left a telephone message with Adrienne Potter, who served as part-time, lunch-hour receptionist at the *Dallas Morning News*. Mrs. Potter, in turn, placed a handwritten memo on the appropriate employee's office desk. At five minutes past one o'clock, Bonnie viewed the alarming note: "Your mom called to say that a wire was delivered." Bonnie started to cry, closing her eyes as if to make the terrible message cease to exist.

When Susan saw her, she feared the worst. "What's happened?"

Bonnie was speechless. With eyes still tightly shut, she shook her head and pointed in the general direction of the receptionist's memo. Her friend read it and laid the slip of paper back on the desktop. Then she put a soothing hand on Bonnie's shoulder. "It might not be anything bad. Not all telegrams are bad, I'm sure."

Through her sorrow, Bonnie managed to say, "Have you ever received a wire?"

"Of course I have—several of them."

"During the war?"

"Well, no," Susan said. "But just before it started."

"That's not the same. Everything has changed now."

"Yes, I suppose so."

Bonnie reached up to pat her friend's compassionate hand. "I apologize for going to pieces like this, but there's more to it than you could possibly imagine."

"Tell me."

"I can't. I'm not at liberty to say." Bonnie took a deep breath to steady her nerves, but when she spoke, it was in a quivering voice. "There's every reason to believe that my Jack has been killed."

Susan forced a smile. "Just because a telegram came? Western Union delivers hundreds of them every day—probably thousands. Besides, you're not married to Jack, so the War Department wouldn't be notifying you directly."

"I know that, but something tells me this one's not just any telegram. The timing of it scares the daylights out of me." Bonnie glanced down at the offending piece of paper.

"I'll be happy to come home with you when we get off," her friend said.

"Oh, Susan, would you? My mother's working late today, and my father never gets home until 6:30. I can't bear to be there alone."

"I don't have a thing in the world to do," Susan told her. That was a fib, but she wanted to sound encouraging.

The girls talked with ease, almost flippantly, on the streetcar—until it screeched to a halt near Bonnie's house. "This is my stop," she said. The pair of them stepped off and walked without speaking, staring straight ahead. It was a typically hot summer afternoon, hitting ninety-three degrees at five o'clock, but that was a pleasant change from the previous day's scorching 107. Bonnie unlocked the door, slowly opened it, and escorted her friend a few feet inside. She could see the mail from where she stood, and there on top was a Western Union envelope. A current of air caused the door to slam shut behind them.

As they approached the wooden entry table, Susan noticed that a letter opener was lying next to the small stack of mail. She turned to Bonnie and asked, "Do you want me to ...?" The girl's eyes were shut, perhaps in prayer, so Susan said no more. When Bonnie finally looked toward the table again, she nodded her head.

Susan picked up the letter opener and sliced across the envelope's crease. Then, unflinching and without delay, she removed the telegram, unfolded it, and began reading to herself. By now, Bonnie's eyes were closed again, and tears streamed down her cheeks. Hours seemed to pass before she heard Susan say, "Well, it's not bad news—about Jack or anyone else."

That was all Bonnie needed to know. She opened her eyes and confirmed that Susan was indeed grinning. Now Bonnie's tears were from relief instead of dread. "Let me see!" she said. But Susan made her giggle by holding the paper just out of reach. The telegram, Bonnie was soon to discover, came from a most unexpected source.

WILL BE STOPPING IN DALLAS ON WAY TO VISIT BROTHER IN HOUSTON. JACK ASKED ME TO SEE YOU. SATURDAY TRAIN FROM FORT WAYNE, IND.
  REGARDS,
  HOLLIS DECKER

Bonnie read the message again and again until the reality of it finally sank into her frazzled brain. She would be meeting Jack's sole surviving parent. This was a good sign that the Army officer was serious about their relationship. She kissed her typing colleague on the cheek and then walked her back to the streetcar stop. Susan Blount was a wonderful friend, and Bonnie would like to repay the kindness someday—preferably in less stressful circumstances.

◆　　　◆　　　◆

Having never met Hollis Decker or even seen his picture, Bonnie had no idea how she might identify him whenever he detrained among a swarm of other travelers at Union Station. She telephoned the passenger depot and learned that most likely he would be arriving on a Missouri Pacific train, the Texas Eagle, at 11:30 A.M. The agent reckoned that Mr. Decker would then be departing for Houston aboard Sunbeam No. 14, a train belonging to the Texas and New Orleans Railroad (a subsidiary of Southern Pacific), at 1:05 P.M. This anticipated layover of ninety-five minutes figured to give her more than ample time to track him down and have a leisurely visit. Her best bet, Bonnie decided, would be to search for someone who resembled Jack's Uncle Foyle.

The overhead clock read 11:47 A.M. when the Texas Eagle finally pulled into the station, more than a quarter-hour behind the timetable. It was a long train, with multitudinous Pullmans being hauled by a steam locomotive. Bonnie tried to tally how many cars there were but lost count when a toddler ran by, coming precariously close to the moving train before his mother caught up, snatched him away from danger, and administered a solid spank on the posterior.

Aware that there would be little chance of guessing the right railcar from so many, Bonnie decided to stay put in the waiting area and hope that Mr. Decker would pass her on his way to the T&NO window. But instead of Bonnie spotting him, it came about that Hollis Decker walked straight up to her and extended a greeting. "Miss Ploughwright, I presume." He removed his hat and bowed at the waist.

"Yes, sir. Are you Jack Decker's father?"

"Right you are, young lady. I'm proud to say that I am." He seemed quite nice—less serious than his son and every bit as friendly.

"How did you find me?" Bonnie asked. "There must be a dozen women here who fit my description."

"Jack told me to look for the prettiest girl in Union Station, so here I am."

Bonnie laughed. "Really, though, how did you pick me out as Jack's ... uh ..." She stopped, embarrassed.

"Sweetheart?"

"All right. I can accept that," Bonnie said with a smile.

"Well, miss, I just asked myself what sort of lass my son would like to find—in his wildest dreams—and you were the winner."

"Thank you."

"Actually, I cheated ..."

"Oh?"

"... by using this." He showed her a two-by-three snapshot. "Jack sent it to me when he found out I'd be changing trains in Dallas sometime this month. I wasn't sure when." Hollis handed it to her. "He wants you to post it to him in your next letter."

Bonnie tucked the photograph into her purse. It was the first of four pictures she had sent to Jack, an old high school yearbook pose that made her look like a pre-adolescent. She had half a mind not to return it to him, now that he was in possession of three more mature snapshots, one of them tastefully suggestive. "When did Jack write to you?" Bonnie asked. Nervously, she slid her sweating palms down the surface of her skirt.

"Most recently?"

"Yes."

Hollis sat on his upright suitcase and opened the overnight bag. "I brought it with me, right here in my grip." He rummaged under some toiletry products and spotted the letter, lying flat on the bottom. "It's postmarked August fifteenth."

"But when was the letter written? It's very important."

He unfolded the paper inside. "The date is ... August fourth. It took quite a while to get here."

Bonnie looked disappointed. "Still, you would have heard by now—if anything happened."

"How do you mean?" Hollis asked. A troubled expression overtook him.

"Nothing. I'm just a worry wart, that's all," she told him. "Call me superstitious."

He grinned. "Personally, I don't believe in such tommyrot. Nothing bad happened on Friday, the thirteenth, of all days—no black cats or broken mirrors—so it looks like we're home free."

Bonnie chuckled at his reasoning, and the pair of them walked over to the passenger depot's restaurant. "Hungry?" Hollis asked.

"No, sir."

"I'm starving. That train food leaves much to be desired. Care to keep me company?"

"I would enjoy that very much." She smiled at him and tried to imagine what it would be like to have him for a father-in-law. "Are you older or younger than Foyle? I can't recall."

"What do you think?"

"Younger, of course," came her quick reply.

"Excellent answer—right or wrong."

"Well?"

"He's three years older than I am."

Hollis ordered a full meal, but Bonnie settled for a chilled Coca-Cola with no ice.

"I'll have you know, that telegram of yours gave me quite a fright," she said.

"Did it? I'm sorry. I didn't want to take a chance on the mail getting to you too late to do any good, so I sent the wire. What did you think it was?"

Bonnie peered down at the table. "I'd rather not say." Her eyes were moistening again, just thinking about it.

"You're a delightful young lady, Miss Bonnie. I can see why Jack is hooked on you."

She blushed. "Is he? He never told me that."

"No, he wouldn't," Hollis said. "But I can. I'm his father."

She was on cloud nine from that moment forward, and she hated to see Mr. Decker leave. Something about him made her feel good, and it was not just because he was Jack Decker's father, either. Maybe it was his optimistic spirit or the way he grinned at her when he thought she was not looking. One thing she did not allow herself to ponder was how devastated this kind soul would be, if her efforts in his son's behalf fell short of her ardent prayers.

All too quickly, it was time for his departure. As he stood on the steps of the Sunbeam, turning to say goodbye, Hollis Decker thanked Bonnie for being so willing to meet him at the station and also for being such a charming companion during his layover between trains.

"My pleasure," she said. "Be sure to say hello to Foyle and Kathleen for me."

"I'll do that."

"How long is the trip to Houston?"

Hollis knew that by heart. "This is one of those Streamliner mile-a-minute trains, so it'll take exactly 265 minutes. That means I'll get there at 5:30. Foyle says he'll pick me up in Jack's Ford."

Bonnie smiled at how appropriate that would be, how meaningful as a symbolic reunion of father and son. "Where does he want to live, following the war?" she asked.

"Jack? I really can't say. I don't believe he's letting himself think that far ahead."

"That's understandable."

"One thing I can tell you," he said. "He'll probably settle for Texas if you don't want to go north." Hollis winked and made his way inside to a window seat. It was 1:05 when the train began to move. The Dallas-to-Houston Sunbeam was right on schedule.

"Goodbye, Mr. Decker!" Bonnie shouted. She jogged alongside the train for a few seconds.

"Goodbye, sweetie," he called back from the open window. "It was swell meeting you, and I think Jack is an awfully lucky man!"

♦   ♦   ♦

The final week of Bonnie's hiatus from school arrived, and with it came a heartening communiqué from Billy Fowler in England. The single-page letter revealed that Billy had spoken with Jack Decker in a pub again—on August 19! That was eight days after *Scarlett Woman* had been destined to plummet into a Cheshire field, which meant that Jack and his men did indeed escape death, at least for the time being. Bonnie was so elated that she could hardly sleep. She disliked insomnia as much as anyone, but she was more than happy to tolerate it for the sake of such a joyous piece of military intelligence.

That Tuesday morning, at her newspaper job, she reminded supervisor Roy Shanks that Baylor University's registration would be the following Monday, September 13, with classes starting two days later. Inasmuch as she was not slated to work on Sunday anyway, Saturday would be her last day on the staff of the *Dallas Morning News*. This disclosure seemed to take Mr. Shanks by complete surprise, though Bonnie had mentioned the fact to him on at least three separate occasions during her summer employment. Glowering, he jotted something down on his clipboard. "All right, then. I guess that's what we get for hiring temporary secretaries." The way he said it made her feel like she was letting the whole company down and creating insurmountable problems for personnel. He walked away without so much as a word of appreciation for the young woman's three and a half months of reliable service.

On a more positive note for Bonnie, it was good to see Susan Blount again after their four days apart. Miss Blount had been ill on Friday. Then she worked on Saturday while Bonnie was off and had Sunday off while Bonnie worked. Being a full-time departmental clerk, with more seniority than the other typists, Susan qualified for enjoying Labor Day away from the office.

Now it was Tuesday, September 7, and the two friends climbed aboard the "up" elevator at virtually the same moment.

"Well, hello again!" Bonnie said to her. "Feeling better?"

"What do you mean?"

"Friday. You called in sick."

"Oh, yes." Susan covered her mouth and whispered, "Female complaint."

"I know the feeling."

"I wish Mr. Shanks was a woman. Then he'd be a little more sympathetic."

"I doubt it."

The elevator door opened, and the girls—plus six or seven others—rushed to their various time clocks.

"I heard from Randall over the weekend," Susan said after they punched in for duty. "He asked me whether I know anybody who'd be interested in going out with his buddy, Harvey Mills, if they ever get a furlough together. You're going to kill me, but I gave him your name."

Bonnie's jaw dropped. "You did *what?*"

"I told Randall about you."

"And who authorized you to do that?"

"What's so terrible about it? You're not engaged or anything, are you? Besides, Harvey will probably never come within five hundred miles of Texas. The duration is a long time, you know. For what it's worth, I also suggested Lorna Shannon."

"Gee, thanks a lot," Bonnie said. "Grouping me with that slut."

"Don't you see? It's just a big joke, really."

"Well, I don't see the humor in it. Look, Susan, I cannot run the risk of ever meeting Harvey Mills."

"What is he, a werewolf or something?"

"Not that I'm aware of, but I can't take any chances."

"You won't have to, I'm sure. It's me who wants to meet Harvey someday, and this is the only way—without hurting Randall's feelings. I can't very well suggest myself as the interested party."

"No, that's true."

"I think Harvey Mills and I might have a lot in common, much more than Randall and I do."

"Why didn't you just make up a couple of names?"

"That would be dishonest."

"And this isn't?" Bonnie asked. "Making your boyfriend act as a go-between?"

"It's only some harmless fun. I'm hoping that his pal might drop me a note, that's all."

A frightening thought struck Bonnie. "You've never given Randall my address, have you?"

"Of course not. This little ploy is nothing but a conversation starter, and I hope Harvey shows enough initiative to write me."

Bonnie tried to be philosophical about her friend's long-distance parlor game. She still had her misgivings, but the damage, if any, was already done. Besides, her own mailing address remained a private affair, and that is what mattered most. If Susan had a desire to flirt with multiple soldiers, more power to her. Bonnie had credible evidence—though no personal recollection yet—that Harvey was a very nice fellow, nice enough to marry.

"I hope you'll be working here again next summer," Susan told her on Friday, in parting. Then she laughed. "Hey, if the war's over by then, maybe we can double date."

Bonnie smiled in response but offered no commitment. As fond as she was of Susan Blount, the *Dallas Morning News* was the last place on earth she would consider seeking a job again. It was much too close for comfort.

♦　　♦　　♦

On Sunday afternoon, Bonnie disembarked from a Texas Electric train in Waco and then rode a streetcar south, to the intersection of Fifth and Speight. From there, she lugged her heavy suitcase to Catherine Alexander Hall and laid it inside the room that she continued to share with Julia Johnston.

Fortunately for Bonnie, her roommate had remained on the Baylor campus for two elective courses in the summer quarter, and that is why the girls were able to secure the room through May, June, July, and August, rather than vacating the premises and placing everything in storage. Julia did not happen to be there at the moment, but her belongings were much in evidence—including four pairs of coveted nylon stockings, which appeared to be in impeccable condition and no doubt were favors from a GI or two.

Bonnie left the dormitory and walked directly to the big auditorium, hoping against all odds that her ability to travel through time had sustained itself through the ravages of the 2009 construction project. If that did prove to be the case, she wanted to verify, by means of internet sources, that her efforts to alter history had achieved their limited objectives. But when her thoughts inevitably strayed to an impending reunion with Ryan Andriessen, there arose within her a nervous excitement, a titillating promise that something physical would happen between the two of them in the seclusion of his bedroom. Instantly, she forced herself to think of something else, for such imaginings served no purpose and seemed very disloyal to Jack.

The lobby of Waco Hall was empty when she arrived, so Bonnie deemed it safe to utilize the downstairs portal, from which she would emerge on a Saturday. She approached the exact point where she knew her passage to exist—but every step confirmed that the conduit was no more. In growing despair, she ascended to the upper floor. Once there, she paced back and forth, by now only dimly expecting to be transported to another world. Nothing of the sort occurred. Just as she feared, her gate to the future was closed for good, irreparably dismantled by the advance of progress.

For what felt like hours, she sat cross-legged on the upstairs landing and quietly wept, with both hands covering her face. She experienced a dreadful emptiness inside, a sense of loss, something—and someone—taken from her that she would never find again. When the paroxysm of tears finally subsided, she left Waco Hall, walked down Speight Avenue to the corner of Fifth Street, and went in the front entrance of Carroll Library. There was a sense of calling about her as she marched up the stairs to the Serials Department. Bonnie had promised Ryan that she would be in contact again, and she was not about to renege on what she valued as a hallowed covenant.

Sunday, September 12th, 1943

My dear Ryan,

I miss you very much, and it pains my heart to know that we'll never see each other again. I shall treasure the memories of our hours together—and no, I don't only mean those special moments you're thinking of, either! Even our strolls around the campus were pleasant and romantic. I guess you could say that I just enjoyed your company. Please do not feel bad about my leaving. You will find a beautiful Baylor girl soon, I'm sure, and become a perfect husband and father.

Perhaps apologies are in order for the way I acted in front of you and your friends. When I said I came from a traditional family, that was my excuse for knowing nothing of the technology involved with 21st-century living, and I am grateful for your tact and patience in accepting me as an equal. You must try to understand that I am the product of a much less permissive society than yours, so I suppose I must have seemed kind of prudish at times. I will not forget you, and I trust that you feel the same way about me. But I'm sure you can appreciate that I had to return to my own world, for I was an alien in yours.

As you know, my only hope and prayer was that I could help to rescue Jack Decker and his men, and it appears that we were successful. According to a letter from Lieutenant Fowler, their airplane did not crash in England on the appointed date and now has been properly repaired to fly on bombing operations again.

That said, there are still more dangers to come because this war is a long way from over.

I am convinced that the time cylinder was put there for a purpose and that I was led to it for a specific reason. I also think that you came into my life for a purpose, and if Jack does survive this terrible struggle, it will be in no small part a result of your willingness to help. I thank God daily for Ryan Andriessen because I could not have done this without you.

Love always,

Bonnie

By referring to a citation that she had jotted down for herself months earlier, Bonnie was able to pull from the shelf a carefully selected magazine and then leaf through it to a predetermined point. This was where Ryan might go to find her letter to the future. The chosen magazine was a back issue of a rather obscure title—one of minimal popularity but which stood a fair chance of being retained indefinitely among the library's holdings.

Before leaving the serials area, Bonnie read her words once more. All in all, she was satisfied with the finished product of her writing efforts. She folded the two sheets of paper in half and inserted them between the designated pages.

What a pity it was, in many ways, that Ryan Andriessen would never see what Bonnie wrote.

◆   ◆   ◆

Michael Tinsley and Nicole Hulen were married on a Saturday afternoon, July 18, in Longview. It was a splendid affair, as befitted the opulent financial portfolio of the bride's father, who had practiced law in east Texas for more than twenty-four years. The happy couple flew to Athens and spent their days of honeymoon heaven on a Mediterranean cruise.

For Ryan, his roommate's departure transformed the late summer of 2009 into a period of adjustment. A business major named Gary Robbins moved into the apartment, and he brought with him a large-screen plasma television with surround sound. That made the transition much easier.

Ryan thought of Bonnie quite often. In fact, for several days since their final parting, the young man's vivid remembrance of her filled most of his waking hours. He still held out a stubborn hope that this twenty-one-year-old coed might return to him one day, despite the fact that she herself had expressed strong doubts about that prospect. Everything depended upon whether Baylor's extensive renovation project had irreversibly disabled the cylindrical passage. The earliest that she could reappear in the "present" was August 10, when construction crews were to vacate their work zone in the frontal chambers of Waco Hall.

But that day came and went—as did a succession of four others—and Bonnie did not knock on his apartment door. Nor did she surprise him at the Student Life Center or call him on his mobile telephone. Either the portal was terminated or she had decided to remain home in Dallas straight through, right up until the fall quarter started.

Even his internet searches reflected Ryan's fondness for the girl, though he did not bother to probe too deeply until after the watershed date of August 11—Jack Decker's appointment with destiny—had elapsed in Bonnie's world. This chronological line of demarcation represented the actual point in time when her subtle influence upon history might begin to take effect. Ryan patiently waited for an extra week to pass, just to be sure, and then he consulted a pair of pivotal websites that he had bookmarked long ago, back in early April.

What he saw in the *Dallas Morning News* issue of May 5, 1976, caused his throat to tighten with emotion. Bonnie's newspaper obituary, announcing her premature death at the age of fifty-four, was not to be found. With tearful eyes, Ryan pumped his fist in the air and whispered quite loudly, "Yes!" This drew some startled looks from nearby students in Jones

Reference Library, but so overjoyed was Ryan at his friend's deliverance that he could not have cared less.

And only a few minutes later, he was able to verify that the August 12, 1943, edition of the *Manchester Guardian* carried no account of an American bomber crash near the village of Tintwistle. The disaster never happened, so an entirely different article occupied that column inch. Ryan gazed upon the screen, marveling at the fact that Bonnie's decisive action had saved the lives of nine crewmen and their pilot, Captain John Tynes Decker.

Lying on the computer table in Ryan's bedroom, next to his Texas Rangers MLB mouse pad, was a small envelope bearing the words "To Ryan. DO NOT OPEN until September 15th!!!" Bonnie had given this to him when they saw one another for the last time, before she departed for her return to the past. Since then—over a span of four and a half months—Ryan had cast his eyes upon it every day, more often than not wondering what she had written to him on the slip of paper that was hidden inside.

When the middle day of September came, and she still had not appeared, Ryan carried the envelope with him to campus, planning to read its contents immediately following his eleven o'clock class. The time was 12:35 when he reached the Bill Daniel Student Center, and—having arrived at the peak of lunch hour—he had to wait another ten minutes, Dr Pepper in hand, before a table finally became available. Then Ryan sat down and laid his knapsack in front of him. He unzipped it, pulled out the sealed envelope, and carefully sliced it open with his pocket knife. Soon he was holding a handwritten note, in Bonnie's own distinctive, decidedly feminine penmanship.

Dear Ryan,

    The fact that you are now reading this can be regarded as conclusive proof that the cylinder no longer functions—assuming, of course, that you obeyed my instructions and waited until the 15th. Had I been able to travel to your century again, I would have told you so in person on September 13th or 14th and retrieved the envelope from you, unopened.

   If I am fated never to see you again, the very least I can do is wish you a proper good-bye and pass along some thoughts from my world of the 1940s to yours of the 2000s. It goes without saying that I can no longer communicate with you directly, but my experimentation in tinkering with history has given me an idea that might work. Go to the Serials Department in Moody Library and find the September 1930 edition of The Rotarian, page 48. With any luck, you'll be hearing from me again.

   Your friend,
   Bonnie

Ever since their concluding moments with one another in early May, Ryan had steeled himself for the receipt of bad news about the portal—to such an extent that the finality of it, while agonizing enough, did not come as an outright shock. Bonnie had repeatedly cautioned him that the construction project in Waco Hall could very well subvert her access to the future, and this merely served as written confirmation.

   Perhaps what surprised him the most was that her wording seemed so reserved and aloof, as if she thought of him more as a brother than a possible love interest. And closing with an impersonal "Your friend" did not help matters any. But Ryan's heart skipped a beat when he remembered that Bonnie penned this note *prior* to their warm familiarity at the lake, not to mention the lingering farewell. He assured himself that there had been far more to their relationship than currently met the eye.

◆　　◆　　◆

Opening day of the fall quarter—September 15, 1943—was darkened by a shattering message, which affected Bonnie profoundly and caused her to dread the sound of any and all radio reports about the war. Around a quarter to three, Julia Johnston interrupted her roommate's studies to say that somebody was waiting downstairs to see her. Normally, Julia would tease about such things, intimating that it must be a soldier wanting to snatch her away, but this time she was totally serious.

Bonnie closed her textbook and hurried to the lobby area, having no idea what to expect. A student worker was assigned to the front desk, and, upon spotting Bonnie, she pointed toward the drawing room without uttering a word. Bonnie turned to see Priscilla Downing, her violinist friend who played with the Waco Symphony Orchestra. There were tears in Priscilla's eyes, and she could hardly speak.

"Hello, Prissy," Bonnie said. She led the coed musician to the sofa, where they each took a seat. Three other girls were in the room, too, but they were considerate enough not to stare.

"What is it?" Bonnie asked. "What's the matter?"

"It's Ev," Priscilla said between sobs.

Bonnie swallowed hard but said nothing, waiting for her friend to continue. Priscilla could not, so Bonnie spoke up again. "What about Ev? Has something happened to her?"

Priscilla nodded her head and sniffled. Finally, she found her voice. "It's her husband, Jim. He's been killed."

"Dear God! Are you sure?" Bonnie's finger tips came together over her mouth.

"She received the cable this morning. He died eleven days ago, I think it said."

Eyes still wide in shock, Bonnie slowly lowered her hands. "Where is Ev now?"

"She's at home. You know, she's living with me again—ever since Jim went overseas."

"Yes, I thought she was."

"She asked about you. I think it might do her some good if you were to talk to her."

"Certainly," Bonnie said. "Do you want me to come right away?"

"Would you?"

Priscilla and Evelyn lived in a rental property on Ninth Street. The plan had been for Mrs. Peaks to reside there until graduation. Then she would wait out the war at her parents' home in Weldon Spring, Missouri, before moving with Jim into a house of their own. Now everything was changed.

Bonnie prepared herself to be startled by Evelyn's appearance, but she need not have worried. Considering these most grievous straits, the young woman was holding up remarkably well. "I've cried all morning long," Evelyn told her fellow English major. "I guess I don't have any more tears to shed." She was sitting at the nearer end of the sofa, and the visitor seated herself in an overstuffed chair at its front corner.

"I'm terribly sorry," Bonnie said. "Jim seemed like such a swell fellow—so friendly and honest."

"Thank you."

"I could tell that just from the few minutes I talked to him."

"On our wedding day." Evelyn gave a brave smile, her eyes glistening.

"Yes."

"It means a lot to me—to hear you say that."

Priscilla had been standing all the while, simply listening. But now she reached for her violin case. "Is there anything you need, Ev?" she asked. "I've got to go practice, but I'll be happy to run an errand or two, if you want me to."

"No, thanks, Prissy. I appreciate your kindness. The Lord has blessed me with some wonderful friends." Evelyn looked from one to the other.

Embarrassed, Priscilla backed out of the room and headed toward the Music School's basement. There she could practice her Paganini *Caprices* in isolation and, for a couple of hours anyway, remove herself from the horrors of the real world.

"I pray to God all the time now," Evelyn told Bonnie. "That is one thing that Jim will always leave me—my belief in Jesus Christ." She looked down at her folded hands, as if they belonged to someone else. "You know, Prissy said a funny thing to me earlier today, not long after the wire came."

Bonnie's eyes darted to the coffee table, on which lay an envelope from Western Union.

"She told me ..." Evelyn paused for a moment before she could continue. "She told me that she was afraid I would fall apart now and revert to my old, cynical past."

Bonnie looked at her in surprise. "My goodness. She told you that?"

"Not in those words, but that's what she meant."

"And what did you say?"

"I explained to her that I was not the same person I was before—and that no trial or tribulation could possibly knock the knees out from under me."

Bonnie studied her friend's face. "Do you think this is a trial?"

"Certainly," Evelyn said. "All life is a trial."

"From God?"

"No. Jim died while fighting evil in the world. The Nazis killed him, not God."

Bonnie nodded her head, trying to comprehend.

Evelyn picked up the envelope and cradled it to her chest. "But I do think God brought Jim into my life. In fact, I'm positive that He did, and no one will ever convince me otherwise. You might say that Jim was my guardian angel."

The words sent a chill down Bonnie's spine, and she wondered whether it was pure coincidence that Evelyn used them. She thought of Billy Fowler, and a truth descended upon her. Were it not for what she could only regard as a miracle, very likely she, too, would have been the addressee of a telegram—not directly from the War Department, but from Jack's father in Indiana or his uncle in Houston.

"What will you do now?" Bonnie asked.

"I'll finish my senior year at Baylor, just as I promised him," Evelyn said. "And I'll continue to write. I'm working on two novels."

"Two at the same time?" Bonnie was dumbfounded, mightily awestruck by such formidable ambition.

"Well, one is comedic, and the other is dramatic, so there's not much chance of getting them mixed up. Jim wanted me to write, so I'll honor his memory by doing exactly that."

Bonnie took leave of Evelyn Branch Peaks with a renewed appreciation for the young widow's strength of character. Had the tables been turned, had Jack Decker been killed in action, how would she herself have responded? Was she as firmly rooted in her faith as Mrs. James Peaks? She searched her own heart and found it wanting.

Acutely shaken by this tragic turn of events, Bonnie's fortitude deserted her mere seconds after she departed from the rental house. She buried her face in her hands and began weeping—so uncontrollably, in fact, that out of consideration for her friend, she felt compelled to hurry away, across the stepping stones, in order that Evelyn would not hear. It was a quarter-hour later before Bonnie finally managed to recover enough of her composure to again concentrate on what she must do next.

An odd realization came to her as she walked north on Seventh Street, a concept that was patently true but which she had never seen in quite this way before. By virtue of Bonnie's unique perspective of time, it seemed only natural to think of her parallel worlds as existing simultaneously. Traveling from one to the other in the blink of an eye created that illusion, though of course she was well aware that more than six and a half decades would actually transpire between the two.

For her, it was Wednesday, September 15, the first day of the fall quarter in 1943, but she presumed that Ryan—on Tuesday, September 15, 2009—had read her sealed note by "now." She could even guess when he might have done so: following his last morning class and prior to lunch. She knew him to be extremely regimented, seldom deviating from his personal schedule.

But as for the much longer letter, the one that she concealed in a magazine, Bonnie was unsure whether he had seen it yet or, indeed, if he ever would. That correspondence was not clashing with a time barrier, and so—in a peculiar twist of natural law—she could alter its content over and over, or even substitute an entirely new text at will, and the only version he would ever encounter was the most recent. She could perform rewrites for as long as she desired because he would not be observing the letter in its final form until nearly a decade into the next century.

◆   ◆   ◆

After Ryan read Bonnie's brief, dispassionate note, almost another whole week of his life went by before he nervously retrieved the full-length letter that she had left for him. The date was Monday afternoon, September 21, 2009, and he had finished his daily workout at the Student Life Center. Although a stickler for cleanliness, he did not take the trouble to shower. Instead, he toweled off the perspiration as best he could and went straight to the Serials Department on the second floor of Moody Memorial Library. There he located the September 1930 edition of *The Rotarian*, in a bound volume marked July to December 1930. When he began flipping through it, the magazine fell open to a couple of neatly folded pieces of white paper, which had been inserted between pages 48 and 49. By all appearances, the flattened sheets had been undisturbed from then until now.

Perhaps a bit more deeply smitten than even he might have suspected, Ryan felt a surge of affection as he reverently placed the precious papers inside his knapsack and walked from the library. Something was drawing him to the upstairs lobby of Waco Hall. He sensed a pull, a yearning to be where Bonnie had been—or was still, if only in spirit. Maybe she was thinking of him at that very moment, testing the area where, not so long ago, an inconceivable passage to the future existed. It occurred to Ryan that this would be a most fitting place to lay eyes upon her closing words to him.

He had not viewed the auditorium's lobby since its remodeling, for he was a senior and thus no longer required to attend chapel sessions. The new touches looked wonderful: tan-painted walls, floral-patterned carpet in forest green, elegant art deco lighting fixtures to complement the building's 1930 provenance, and, with a practical bow to modernity, two large-screen video monitors to promote upcoming events.

A few people were ambling through the vestibule, probably headed for lunch or to their next classes, so he stayed put, web browsing on his iPhone. The moment he saw that the pathway was clear, he went up the east staircase and stopped on the balcony landing, about where Bonnie had demonstrated her amazing ability to pass from one era to another. Sitting with his back to the wall—just as he had done when Bonnie was so astonished to discover him there—Ryan opened his knapsack and took out the sheets of paper, still folded in half, one enclosing the other.

It was a long letter with tiny but clearly defined penmanship, as if the author had so much to convey that she felt a need to conserve space and make use of every square inch of the writing surface. Ryan smiled upon recognizing Bonnie's familiar, stylized script, so refined and evocative of the period in which her words were composed. Before reading, he shut his eyes for a few seconds and took a deep breath. Now he was ready. "Dearest Ryan," the message began, and already he could feel a gentle balm settling over him. He pursed his lips and wiped away a tear. Thankfully, there was no one around to notice.

Dearest Ryan,

    I am writing to you on October 23rd, 1948, just after the Baylor Bears' 20-14 victory over the Texas A&M Aggies at Municipal Stadium. Jack and I are in Waco for homecoming—mine, not his, as he is a graduate of DePauw University in Greencastle, Indiana. We were married on June 14th of last year in Terre Haute, where we now live and Jack owns an automobile dealership—mostly used, but gradually branching into the new-car market as well. He is quite a talented businessman.

Our daughter, Mary, was born on April 22nd, and we have just learned that number two is expected to arrive about three weeks before the date of our second anniversary. Mary is accompanying us now, and she journeys like a champ, a very good baby who seems to share our wanderlust.

Jack was discharged from the Army as a major, after completing twenty-five missions over Germany and German-held territories during the war. He had some narrow escapes but rarely talks about his flying days. I have never dared to ask him about the month following that July 30th raid, when "Scarlett Woman" was so badly damaged—and neither has Billy Fowler, who was sworn to secrecy by me. Speaking of Billy, his airplane was shot down over Germany. He was a prisoner of war for nearly a year, but he came through it reasonably well and was liberated before he had to endure the adversity of a second winter. Now he is fine and residing with his wife, daughter, and son in their hometown of Fountain City, Tennessee. I think Melinda is also pregnant again. It must be contagious!

Mother continues to work for North American Aviation, one of only five thousand employees to stay on the company payroll after the war. Aircraft designs are more experimental these days than during the war, when production goals were so intense. Daddy is doing well, too, with his dental practice growing larger than he can handle. He is looking forward to retirement. My brother, Keith, is attending Texas Christian University on the G.I. Bill but eventually hopes for a vocation in law enforcement.

As for me, the writing career has taken a back seat to motherhood, I'm proud to say, but I do find time to pen some fiction on the side, despite the busy responsibilities of a housewife. I have one completed novel to my name and another one in progress. The first is rather mammoth in scope, causing literary agents to shy away, but I love it like a first-born child. That story deals with the war years on the home front, and I put my whole heart and soul into it. I remain hopeful that someday soon it will interest a publisher. The second novel is a romantic fantasy that explores the scientific possibility of ... well, that should be fairly easy to deduce!

And now, last but certainly not least, to you. I cherish the memory of our lovely days together, Ryan, and appreciate your patience and understanding with me—someone who was technologically backwards and from an old-fashioned family. You did not make fun of me and were always there to help. Of course, I shall remember one thing above all else: without you, very likely Jack Decker would have met his death in an air crash, and my life would have been far less than the happy experience it has proven to be. I never heard what became of the man I was once destined to wed, Harvey Mills, nor do I wish to know. Maybe, God willing, he wound up marrying a Dallas friend of mine, Susan Blount, and left the USAF before his untimely death.

I presume that you will be graduating from Baylor University in May of 2010. That is sixty-one and a half years from now, and I hate to think how old I will be at that time—a doddering great-grandmother of nearly ninety, I suppose—but if Jack and I are healthy enough to travel, please be aware that an elderly couple from Indiana may account for two of the anonymous faces in the crowd. In any case, I will not step forward to introduce myself after the ceremony. I much prefer that you remember me as I was: a silly girl of twenty-one who spent some wondrous time with a swell 21st-century boy—learning about technology, life in the future, and herself.

My love forever,
Bonnie